Red Viper

The Kingdoms of Blood, Volume 1

Des M. Astor

Published by Des M. Astor, 2020.

This is a work of fiction. Similarities to real people, places, or events are entirely coincidental.

RED VIPER

First edition. December 7, 2020.

Copyright © 2020 Des M. Astor.

Written by Des M. Astor.

For all of my friends and family who supported me and stuck with it through this journey. This is my first book, and it's an honor to be pushed ahead by encouragement.

CONTENT WARNING: Some parts contain heavy gore. There is an explicit sex scene.

Part 1: Through the Eyes of the Serpent

Seek not to tame this dragon, for it bites back. Hard.

Sambuca's Perspective

Chapter 1

July 20, 2019

I do hope you believe in monsters, because if you're not careful, we'll strike when you least expect it. And we sure as hell believe in you. Take it from me.

It was the dead of night when the smell of blood hit my nose; right away I knew that my prey was near. My grin widened as I slipped into the shadows, intent on ending him.

What's that you say? Me, a vampire, a leech? Hah. Far from it, actually. What gave you that impression?

I had no weapons, for I didn't need them. Other hunters had plenty, be it stakes or knives. I was satisfied with venom. Often criticized by my fellow vampire hunters, I learned to distance myself from everyone else. It was hard being an outcast among my own people, but I learned to deal with it a long, long time ago.

Covered from head to toe in black, my face hidden under a thick scarf aside from my eyes and mouth, I knew I was ready to hunt.

Slipping from shadow to shadow, I spotted him crouched over an innocent girl. Disgusting. He was drinking her dry, eating her alive. Vampires were just as bad as those damn shapeshifters, except a vampire's murder was a lot less grisly.

After a pause, I determined that it was the right moment to strike—I leaped from hiding and sliced cleanly into the vampire's back with my claw-like nails. That might sound strange, but it was my typical way of killing for a peculiar reason. The vampire whirled, his mouth twisting into a scowl. Yet I was nowhere to be seen. Time to watch and wait.

He looked very confused, and suddenly held his head. His bloody, blonde hair fell into his eyes that were suddenly glowing with pain. He gasped and fell to the ground, and I knew this was my chance. I emerged from the shadows with a grim smile, my fingers spread and fixed like battle-claws. The vampire stared up at me, obviously growing weaker.

"How...?" he whispered. I yawned, pretending to put a finger on my lip in thought. Not having shown my teeth before, I decided to display them now. They were unnaturally sharp, each one having been ground to pin-points. This struck fear even into the bloodsucker's heart; I had the satisfaction of seeing his pupils dilate to a large degree.

"R-Red...Viper.." he gasped. I gave a thumbs up and slowly bent down over him.

"My fellow hunters are so unoriginal in their killings. I love to weaken my prey, then end them slowly..." I whispered. I drew my needle-sharp nail down his cheek, watching blood well up in the wound. The vampire was growing weaker by the second.

"But...you're only human... How is this possible?" he hissed. His nostrils flared and his jaw dropped as if he'd realized something. "Wait..."

I had no time for games.

So, I smiled and gave the most simple response, paying no mind to whatever revelation had struck him. "Venom." With that, I swiftly bit down onto his neck, chuckling as he screamed with pain. My venom made the entire death experience extremely uncomfortable, which is exactly how I loved it. I was gone long before his screams died down.

Now, I suppose I should explain myself. No average woman could possibly have venom naturally, the mutation would be too strong. Which was true, my venom wasn't my own—rather, it belonged to a couple of the most toxic snakes in the world, who were housed right at my tiny hut for a home. So. How didn't I die from my own snakes' venom?

While I wasn't able to produce my own(come on now, that would be ridiculous), I was unique in my immunity. Somehow I was immune to every bit of snake venom that entered my blood... interestingly enough, I was also immune to vampire venom.

I'll teach you a bit about that. Vampire venom is designed to do one of two things—weaken/paralyze, or provide excruciating pain. In rare cases, there were other types that I didn't care to know about because it wasn't important. I'd found out the sickening concept of pain in blood. Apparently, the more painful the bite, the more delicious the blood, so I'd heard.

Disgusting.

My venom worked differently. When I struck, it acted immediately to weaken my victim. If I decided to let the vampire survive, the weakness would fade in a few days. My bite was just as deadly as a snake's because it provided a very painful, but short, death. The mix of venom I used specifically targeted the nerves and heart. If I wanted to be really nasty, I could use my store of hemotoxins, which basically would cause my victim to bleed out of every pore and opening of their body. No worries, I *rarely* ever used that particular venom.

So, how did I get it in my nails and teeth? I had specialized hollow nails, somehow I was born with that as well. I had a large supply of toxins in them since just a small amount would suffice to kill; this meant that I rarely needed to refill. As for my teeth, well, they were the same way. Both grew back if one broke off in combat, which is strangely similar to how vampires' worked too.

But I definitely was a human. I had to be. There wasn't anything in this world but vampires, shifters, and humans... Right?

Otherwise I'd be a freak or something.

That's what I kept telling myself over and over and over again, anyway. These oddities had to be just mutations. I was just a woman with long red hair that shined like fire, skin pale like ivory, sharp teeth, and snake-like eyes.

Perfectly normal!

Anyway. Now you know how I do it. But the real question is *why*.

I'd go into detail with a convoluted backstory, but no one wants to hear a full life story in Chapter 1 of any tale.

The important thing to know is that I was a vampire's blood slave for a time before coming upon a Boomslang snake, likely obtained from the exotic pet trade, finding out that it couldn't kill me, and realizing I could use its venom to my advantage. Made friends with the snake in one second, saw a vampire kill it in the next. Killed the vampires through sheer dumb luck, ran off, you get the point.

Whatever, back to reality.

I bent down and carefully drew a snake about to strike with my nail, ripping into skin to form a design. Specifically, I drew it on his neck. Any vampire knew that it was a challenging mark. I grinned, my sharp teeth flashing.

What a satisfying night it had been. I was ready to go home and relax. Perhaps I would kill even more vampires tomorrow, for those gangs were getting awfully rowdy lately. More and more humans were vanishing, and it was up to me to control them. Rarely did I let vampires go, but when I did, I was confident they warned others about me. Truly a prideful and stupid mistake on my part that I didn't care about at the time.

The other hunters didn't seem as intimidating, oddly. I didn't know if maybe the 'Hunter Association' in this city was the issue or what. But I was the only one around here getting rid of the vampires that captured and killed tons of people.

Normally you'd expect to see fellow hunters around at night somewhere, especially in a big city like this. Were they being lazy? Busy elsewhere? Ah well. It was time to make my exit, there wasn't time to dwell on such notions. I was tired and needed my rest.

Well, I would have made my leave, hadn't I heard chuckle behind me. I whirled, coming face-to-face with blood red eyes. A male vampire stared me down, his dark shaggy hair partially covering his eyes. He wore all black, like me, and had on a masquerade mask. I wasn't impressed. Instinctively, I leaped away and managed to place my back against the wall.

The vampire advanced on me, seeming simply curious. I could see the question in his eyes...*who was this huntress? Why was she so afraid?* I would prove the second question to be quite the contrary, and would find out the first one he knew the answer to already. Regardless, cornering a snake was a terrible, terrible idea, one that he would soon learn. I narrowed my eyes in wait.

Making a decision, the vampire lunged forward and grabbed my arm. His red eyes met mine as I peeled back my lips and let out an angered hiss. He tilted his head, trying to distinguish some features and finding none since most of my face was covered with a thick black scarf. His nostrils flared as he took in my scent.

I had enough of this, no more playing games. I'd tolerated his existence up to this point.

With a snarl, I hissed, "Wrong move."

Chapter 2

A simple tactic, really. He'd fallen for the 'broken tail' method, as most always did. The vampire blinked, seemingly confused for a second. It was as if he knew something about me that even I didn't.

So suddenly did he lunge forward and bite into my hand that I had no time to move away. A pained gasp came from my mouth, and I wrenched it from his grasp. Boy did the bite hurt, but luckily it wasn't my neck that had been chomped into. My eyes lit up in fury. I'd not been bitten for a decade, so how this one managed to do so was beyond me. I needed to get my act together, that was for sure.

Now he would die like the rest! My mouth twisted into a snake-like grin as I brought my other set of claws out and quickly sliced into his arm. Instinctively, the vampire backed off with a cry of surprise. He stumbled, hitting the wall then sinking to the ground. Wincing as I stalked closer, he gasped, "Wait! I wasn't planning on harming you further. I wanted to see if the rumors were true..."

But a snake doesn't wait. I lunged for his neck and sank my teeth in, quite like how vampires feed on their prey. Karma's a bitch. I leaned away and wiped my mouth of his blood(gross), staring into his eyes.

My own were glowing a bright green as I observed the vampire. Making a decision, I drew my bloody snake on him with a silver-edged nail as he was dying. Silver slowed their healing, after all, meaning the wound wouldn't fade in his final moments. I preferred venom over silver, but venom wasn't used for this process here. My little mark of death was to prove my point loud and clear. I didn't feel like waiting for him to die this time, for I was impatient.

His eyes closed as he cringed, convulsing, so I thought, from the venom. I wasn't alarmed so much by his talk of 'rumors'. I knew that most vampires here were aware of my venom immunity, which was why they tended not to try and bite me during battles; they just went right to hardcore attack. Even though this guy happened to be different, he would just perish.

The vampire's breathing grew ragged. It was my time to leave. I turned away, slipping into the night. I figured I'd never see that vampire again other than the obituary.

If only I knew how wrong I was.

Perhaps I should have unmasked him before running off.

FROM THE SHADOWS...

You see, this one was an excellent actor. As the huntress got up and turned to leave, his red eyes opened once again, and a small smile formed on his face.

"See you later, then, Sam Viper," he whispered to himself. What an interesting one she was. He knew now that it would be futile to kill her off like the rest. He had no desire to, honestly, and cared little for the orders of his father. She was very strong, though; maybe she could be the key to his opposition to the hunter corruption. No doubt she'd prove to be a problem in the uprising.

Regardless, the first step was getting to know her.

THROUGH THE EYES OF Sam Viper

Joy, oh joy. After a tiring night of killing those bloodsuckers, I could finally sit back at home and relax.

I was just closing my eyes when I felt a smooth, scaly body slither over my hand. Opening them, I spotted a long green snake with huge eyes staring right at me. The snake opened its mouth wide, leaning towards me. He had two rear fangs that glistened with saliva. What did I do? Why, I gave a smile back of course.

"Boomey!" I giggled, playfully poking the Boomslang on the nose. As it happened, Boomey was the son of the snake friend that helped me escape the slavers. I took him in when I found him outside in the cold winter snow.

In my eyes, Boomey's kind was beautiful and not a danger at all. Sure, they were one of the most toxic snakes on earth. But...well, they were just so cute!

Anyway, Boomey stopped smiling and slithered up my arm and onto my shoulder. "*How was hunting?*" I heard him hiss into my mind. Snakes couldn't speak aloud, they only connected with the 'chosen ones' via telepathy. One of them happened to be me, apparently. I didn't get into snake history much; I just knew that most were my only friends. The snakes had never really explained to me how I could communicate with them. I was pretty sure they had no idea as well.

"It went rather well. Killed two...well, three if you count a vampire who tried to catch me on my very last kill," I added. Before I arrived home, I had wrapped a bandage around my hand. The mark would fade over the next few days. The vampire's bite had been very minor compared to what they usually did. It was best to hide any marks from the snakes, since they tended to be, well, protective.

Boomey gave a satisfied nod. He hated vampires too since they'd killed his father and neglected him terribly when he was kept as practically a display piece by them.

Not many knew, but even snakes found family extremely important. Most humans just think that they grow up and leave, but I knew in reality they stayed connected their entire lives, often making visits. I was happy to be a part of his family now. "Where's Copper?" I asked curiously. Copper was my other resident snake. She happened to be a copperhead...shocker, huh?

"*Hunting. She told me a few hours ago that she was worried about you...*" Boomey began. He peered into my eyes, pupils in slits. The snake's tongue flickered in and out of his mouth, gently touching my nose as he stared. "*Something is amiss. Someone is watching you now, hunting you even. We began sensing it a few hours ago*," his voice chimed.

I frowned. A few hours ago I had killed my last vampire, the one who'd grabbed my arm and bitten my hand. No one had been around. I'd have sensed them. I'd been paying more attention since that surprise from that final vampire. So what could it be?

"Perhaps you are thinking too much into it. We need some rest, maybe we can work it out tomorrow. Listen, I need to shop tomorrow ok?" I sighed. Boomey hissed in disapproval.

"Dangerous. Sam, you know how we hate you going out. A snake should never show itself," he snarled in disapproval. I shrugged, grinning to reveal my pointed teeth.

"I know, I know. But we're out of frozen mice for you guys. I know how you like to hunt, but I also love spoiling you. Plus summer's over and soon you won't be able to anymore. Too cold. Let me do this for once, ok? For god's snakes, your venom has made my life possible. It's the least I can do," I started. After a stern look from the Boomslang, I continued. "And, I'm out of food for myself. I just want to pick up some dinners to cook on the stove."

The snake sighed, but it sounded more like a hiss of defeat. *"Fine. Be safe, Sammy. You know how much we care about you,"* the snake seemed to mutter. I smiled and hugged him gently(well as much as one could hug a snake, that is).

"I promise you I will," I replied. I stood up and yawned, making my way to my bed. Copper came in some time later. I gave a wave of hello, but was much too tired to strike up a conversation. Before drifting off to sleep, I glanced over to both the snakes staring at me with clear concern.

"For god's snakes, I'll be fine!" I chuckled. Copper and Boomey just slithered to me and coil-cuddled as I fell to sleep. I'll admit, I did sense some hidden danger. Acknowledging it would bring fear, and as soon as I radiated fear, Boomey and Copper would put me on curfew. Yeah, snakes could sense strong emotions.

Yes, yes I know that sounds ridiculous. Snakes making the rules? They were the ones who led me to the hunters, actually. They sensed something about me that I still could not figure out for myself. They also taught me how to survive like a snake, and they pretty much took me in as their own. Yes, I was older than Boomey, but he was wiser somehow. So while I could leave at any time, I really *couldn't*. They were my family, and consequently, the leaders of the household.

Some people didn't believe snakes cared. I, on the contrary, thought that sometimes they cared too much. Be safe, blah blah. There were leeches to kill, goddammit.

With that thought in mind, I ignored the growing uncertainty and began to drift off to sleep. None of us heard the door creak as it opened. None of us sensed the vibration of the footsteps—he was treading too softly. None of us knew he stared for a while, red eyes gleaming, until suddenly he left, after whispering, "So...this is his target, hmm."...nope. None of us knew what exactly I'd gotten myself into by 'killing' the vampire that night.

But...we were all about to find out.

I AWOKE WITH A YAWN, glancing about to find my friends missing. Meh...probably out hunting. I stretched and sat up, leaping from my bed and quickly getting dressed. With a glance out my window, I determined that it was sunset. In other words, a perfect time to go shopping! I entered my tiny living room and stopped. Both Boomey and Copper looked up at me, eyes more concerned than ever.

"...What?" I asked, confused. What could I have possibly done while I was sleeping? For god's snakes, the glares they were giving me made me feel like some mass murderer(erm...well that term is relative, heh).

"We don't want you hunting tonight. Shopping is fine, but hunting is certainly not. It is too dangerous," I heard the Copper's feminine voice say in my mind. I proceeded to frown. What was she, my mom? Well, she was more of one to me than my biological mother, which was sorta sad.

"But it's my job to make sure others don't end up like me!" I hissed angrily. The snakes warily shook their heads; there was no changing their minds. "Fine," I grumbled. "But I *will* go out tomorrow. Got that?"

The snakes paused and gave a solemn nod. *"That's fine. But not tonight. I sense...something...unknown,"* Copper whispered into my mind. Boomey gave a silent nod of agreement.

"I'll hurry up then," I muttered. Without another word, I angrily grabbed my stuff and hurried out of the door. No use letting them worry even though they had virtually grounded me. Grounded by snakes...hah. It was almost funny how that had happened, but I was used to it.

Bolting through the forest, I jumped from shadow to shadow until I reached the outskirts of town. I just needed groceries, that was all. Anxiously waiting at the bus stop, I entered and paid my fee. All was well until *he* sat next to me.

He looked to be around my age and was wearing a fancy black suit paired with a red undershirt. His hands had white gloves, and his dark shaggy hair fell over his fathomless green eyes. He had a tophat that tilted slightly over his face, adding a shadowy effect. At first, I paid no attention. But then he turned to me and said, "Hello there. You must be new here! Haven't seen you around much." His voice was like silk. It reminded me of Boomey's calm, calculating hiss.

I blinked and gave a slight nod. "I don't get out much..." was all I said.

The guy cleared his throat. "Well. Want me to show you around, then?" he asked smoothly. His voice was familiar, but it was unlikely I'd met him anytime recently. I stuck to myself mostly, and anyone besides the snakes I struck up conversation with normally ended up dead. No, not humans silly! Vampires loved to small talk, and sometimes I played along until I got bored.

This man was most certainly not a vampire, anyway. Natural born vampires, which were alive and a biological species just like humans, had pointed ears and jagged fangs lining their mouths. Their eyes were a blood red, and they had claws instead of nails. Even humans turned into vampires (yes, natural-born vampires *could* turn others into their species, but it was a concept I didn't really understand quite well) had the jagged fangs and claws, missing only the pointed ears. None of those qualities displayed on the man before me, so hell knew *who* he actually was and why I recognized his voice. Probably in passing.

Instinctively, I shook my head to his question. "Nah, that's fine. I'm just picking up groceries for my parents," I replied, shifting in my seat.

The guy blinked, as if surprised. "What a coincidence. I'm heading that way as well," he chuckled.

Chapter 3

I scowled, wondering why exactly this guy was talking to me. OK, yeah, maybe it was nice to be social, but for god's snakes, I really didn't like interacting with people.

Perhaps this once, I should be nice. After all, I only rarely went out in public. It wasn't like my face was showing during hunts anyways. The rule was never to show your identity, for it could be the death of you.

Half of my face, at the moment, was covered in a thick, black scarf. My long red hair was tucked into my shirt, and my bangs fell partially into my face. Really, all this guy could see were my cold, venom-green eyes. I had nothing to lose by acting nice.

"Interesting," I commented, giving the guy a sideways glance.

"Yeah. Maybe I can show you around there, since you seem so shy as to not even introduce yourself, dear," he joked with a small laugh. I stared at him, not having much experience with guys in general. He had an odd way of speaking, so smooth and formal that I was caught off guard.

"Uh... my name is Sam," I replied with a questioning gaze. Perhaps I was being too shut out to the world. Normally my coldness would ward off others. This guy was persistent, but I sensed nothing hostile about him. Perhaps he was just overly polite to the 'new' people in town.

The city was big, but many knew one another here since the forests that surrounded it cut it off from most other civilization. Small town vibes, you know, but for a city. People rarely moved, and generally looked average in clothing and stature. I knew I always stuck out, perhaps that was why this guy thought I was a newcomer. The fact that I rarely wandered out of the shadows didn't help.

He dipped his head and gave a stunning smile. "Well, nice meeting you, darling. My name's Goliath. I'll be happy to accompany you, if you'll let me. Admittedly I'm rather new as well, and you seemed a bit more friendly than others here. I confess finding my way around with company is much better than being alone," he admitted hopefully. Huh, that was new, me seeming friendly?

I sighed, thinking for a moment before finally giving in. Maybe he was flirting. Why, I'd no idea. Like I said, I was covered from head to toe in black. Some would say I looked very intimidating. Not all people were afraid of snakes, I supposed. "Alright. I guess I can show you around. I'm not new here, even if you are," I muttered, grumbling under my breath about wanting to be alone.

He ignored my mumble and flashed another bright smile. "Great! You sure you want to just go to the store, though? I mean, there's a ton of stuff to do besides shop, and it's a Friday! You can't have much to do if you never go out," he added with a frown.

I blinked, remembering the snakes' strict warning. As secluded as I was, the aspect of just hanging around with someone was tempting. Especially someone with an aura similar to my own. I'd never really had a friend that was my own kind. Since no one ever talked to me, not even other hunters, I got rather lonely. So while I didn't like interacting with others, a friend would be really nice. Contradicting, I know, but sometimes my mindset was scattered. Perhaps lightening up a bit would be a nice change. "I can hang around for like an hour. But then I need to go home. My parents put me on...curfew," I replied, though it wasn't really a lie.

Goliath chuckled again, always seeming amused. "For what? Staying out a second too late? You look to be in your early twenties, and you have curfew?" he asked in an amused voice.

I rolled my eyes in response. "No, They're just worried about me, and yes, I do," I growled. Goliath shook his head, grin never seeming to fade.

"Whatever you say, princess of the guarded castle," he laughed, crossing his arms. I had no idea what this guy found that was so funny!

Well. Now I needed to think of a witty response. I opened my mouth to reply but was cut off by the roar of a bus coming to the stop. I stood up, glancing at Goliath and watching it dawn on him that we arrived where I needed to be.

"This looks like our stop, let's go," I muttered. He nodded, taking a deep breath and looking about with vague curiosity. Goodness, he seemed so relaxed and emanated joy, as if he hadn't a care in the world. I read him deeper, though. His outward happiness was masking something cold and calculating. He was something like me. He hid it well. Way better than I possibly could. Maybe, just maybe, he was a vampire hunter too.

There wasn't only the emotionless cold within his eyes. There was something more, something I really couldn't sense. That frustrated me. Normally I could read people like a book when it came to emotions.

Hesitantly, I took his hand and let him lead me off of the bus and into the store. I took out my list and studied it for a moment, ignoring Goliath as he read over my shoulder. Did he not know the meaning of manners? "Milk...eggs...salmon...frozen mice?" he read, staring at me as if I'd grown three heads.

I had to laugh; that's the exact reaction I'd expect from virtually anyone. "Ah, yes; They are for my...pet...snakes," I replied. I choked on the word 'pet', because Boomey and Copper were no more my pets than I was their amusement. We were a family, regardless of what outsiders thought of us.

Goliath stared, clearly intrigued. "Oh? What kind of snakes?" he asked as we walked along the aisles. I paused, wondering if I should tell him the truth.

"Just corn snakes, really," I finally said. The guy nodded, appearing to be deep in thought. I took a deep breath, deciding that it was way too hot in here. Grabbing my scarf, I put it into my small bag. Only humans were here, so it didn't matter, right?

Goliath stopped and stared into my eyes. I blinked, irritated. What was he doing, exactly? "Uh..." I started, taking a step back.

"I'm sorry Sam, just haven't seen you without the scarf or up close, and was taken aback by how..." he started, but then cut himself off while blushing. "Anyway. I know where we could hang out for an hour after shopping. Wanna join me at the park? That's one place I know about here. It was the first area I stopped by," he added.

Raising a brow, I merely shrugged off his reaction to my face. Odd phrasing, but perhaps he was stammering. As for the park idea, I gave a nod. Parks always helped me relax and appreciate nature. It had been a while since I was able to visit one. "I'd love to," I replied with a smile.

We took a while shopping, mainly because we both talked. I learned that Goliath worked part-time at a fancy restaurant as a host, having just moved up here from down south. I told him that I stayed at home, and mostly just worked on investigations on criminals. Which, for the most part, wasn't a lie. Goliath seemed very curious about that, but when I told him it was top-secret, he didn't press for information.

After getting everything on the list, I slung the grocery bag over my shoulder and promptly nodded to my new friend. "All set. I have about a half hour now to spare. We took a while in there," I pointed out, checking the time from the little clock that hung over the entrance of the store. Goliath gave a nod. He was excited, I could tell, to bring me to this place.

When we arrived at the park, the sun was still dipping under the horizon. Nevertheless, the darkness was closing in. Unlike most, I felt comfort in the dark. There were more places to hide and more places to plan. We sat on a bench, talking for a little while longer.

"So, you're living with your parents right? Is that why I haven't seen you around in my first few days here? Are you in college, or something?" he asked. I shrugged, looking to my feet.

Once upon a time I had considered taking classes of some sort. The thought had been shoved away quickly, as I realized my duty was in the city. I got money from the hunter association, just barely enough to live off of. But my past memories prevented me from pursuing anything else. Since my parents gave me up, I had the mindset that I belonged nowhere. Nowadays, I was content with the thought. Interaction with Goliath, though, made me realize how lonely I really was.

"Well, I was home-schooled. Never considered higher education. Like I said, I don't get around much," I only replied with a slight sigh, regretfully having to lie once again. I mean, I read and wrote often when not hunting to keep my mind sharp. I had a rocky past with school in general. Completed it, yes, easily, no.

Goliath was watching me carefully. He saw my expression change to sadness and gave me a sympathetic look. For some reason, I hated when people did that. But I didn't want to be rude, so I didn't say anything. "Gosh. You must be lonely. Well, we could hang out some more if you want," he suggested.

I looked at him, my head tilted slightly. Making a decision, I nodded. "Sure. When I'm not working, I'd love to come around and hang out," I said, giving a genuine smile. It was time to break out of my shell and step out of my comfort zone for once. Boomey and Copper wouldn't be very happy about it, but I was old enough now to handle things on my own. It was about time I had a real friend. This guy, unlike those who just avoided me, was really polite; I could tell we would have interesting conversations if we kept on talking.

Goliath smiled back and dipped his head. "I'll be seeing you around, dear," he grinned. His green eyes flashed for a second, making me wonder why he was suddenly in a hurry. "I'm a bit hungry, so I'm going to go off and get a bite to eat. Hope I didn't keep you out too late! Want to meet here tomorrow at sunset?" he asked in a hushed tone.

And now, *I* was in a hurry. I just remembered my curfew! I got to my feet quickly and gave a nod. "Yeah, sure; ugh hope I'm not late! See you around!" I replied. I darted away quickly, praying that I wasn't too late. Yikes, I hadn't realized the time!

Hopping on the bus, I quickly asked the time and gave a sigh of relief. I had about five minutes, just enough time to get back before an hour was up. Any longer and I knew that I'd be questioned.

I rode in silence before getting off at my stop. Three minutes now. I took off running into the woods, panting hard when I arrived home. Silent as a snake, I opened the door and sat on the couch, wondering if the overbearing reptiles were home yet. When the light clicked on, I knew they were, and right away I sensed their anger.

Copper glared at me, her tongue flicking in and out rapidly. "*You took a while. An hour might not seem like a lot, but we were worried,*" she hissed into my mind. "*I don't think it takes that long to shop!*"

Boomey took a place next to her, coiling and turning his stare to me. "*You were watched by danger tonight. I can sense it—we are worried more than ever. You cannot go out at all tomorrow,*" he added.

I stared in disbelief. No way I was going to follow that! They'd promised that I'd be allowed to hunt then! Not only that, but I had made plans. I figured I could do the dirty work and meet Goliath after that. Well, there was only one solution. Without a word, I stood up, entered my room, and slammed the door. OK yeah, I was old enough to handle things, just not old enough to refrain from a tantrum. I had a rather short temper, you see.

Ah, here's an idea. Tomorrow I'd sneak out. That was a foolproof plan, I'd do it while the snakes were hunting and be back before too many hours passed. They normally took around four to catch and eat enough, so that's when I'd leave. Why not, right? Too bad they were smarter than me when it came to my well-being.

Chapter 4

The next night, I awoke with a sigh. I really wanted to see that guy, Goliath, again. He seemed so much like me, yet so different as well. Luckily it was a hunt night for the snakes. Boomey and Copper left together after warning me to stay home. The consequences would be huge, they said. Did I really care? Nope!

I took a deep breath and entered the forest. The air was cold and crisp against my skin as I wandered along, careful to listen for any sounds of slithering. If I was caught now, I'd be shut in my room for weeks. Arriving at the park, I took a seat at the bench and waited. It seemed like a few minutes had passed when I heard the crunch of a leaf behind me.

I'd been about to turn when two hands came from behind and blocked my eyes. I tensed like a snake ready to attack, preparing to rip away and face my enemy. A voice stopped me. "Guess who?" came a smooth male voice, one belonging to none other than Goliath. I held in a hiss as I gritted my teeth.

"Don't surprise me like that. I'm sorta quick to attack," I gasped. Truthfully, one more second and he'd be poisoned by my nails. I heard a laugh and all of a sudden the guy was sitting next to me, staring down with laughter in his eyes. Today he wore a black T-shirt with a fancy, warm looking overcoat and a chain necklace, with black jeans and combat boots. Hmm...he looked familiar. Not because I'd seen him last night, but I knew I'd seen him before somewhere. His eyes put me off, though, because I'd never seen that venom green on anyone but myself.

"Good morning, erm, I mean evening, dear. Sorry, I take night classes so sunset begins my typical day," he said smoothly. I shrugged and gave a smile. Couldn't be any worse than 'homeschool' I supposed.

"Ah same here. I usually work at night. More shadows to hide in," I replied. Goliath smiled back, silent for a moment. His eyes seemed surprised.

"Your teeth...are they...?" he asked. I was confused for a second before a realization dawned on me. Crap. I usually hid my teeth while I talked, but this time I hadn't been paying attention. So many slip-ups lately, perhaps I needed a break!

"Yeah, uh, the dentist made them like that so I can eat more easily. I need more meat in my diet due to a condition," I lied. In reality, I did eat a lot of meat, but my teeth weren't sharp because of that.

Goliath stared for a moment, curiosity clear on his face. "Interesting. I've never heard of such a procedure. Well. We can walk around the park if you want," he offered. Goliath stood and offered his hand, flashing another smile. I obliged, giving a nod and accepting the gesture.

We walked for a while, talking while it got colder and colder. I began to shiver, which gained the notice of my new friend. He took off his jacket and offered it to me. "Here you go. Wouldn't want you catching a cold," he muttered. I stared for a moment, confused.

"Wait, won't you be cold?" I asked. Obviously, I wasn't used to interacting with guys. Goliath just laughed and helped me get it on. It was cozy, and I daresay I appreciated it.

I'd love to say all was well, and that we had a wonderful night. And sure, we did, up to a point in which a woman's laugh sounded out behind me and caused me to freeze. Goliath heard it too and whirled, only to be thrown into a tree before he could react. Vampires using their powers in public?! They were supposed to remain hidden. What was going on? This one probably was trying to end the both of us.

I stared at a woman with long white hair and red eyes. She was smirking, showing off jagged fangs, and I could tell by her pointed ears that she was a natural vampire. Her stare lingered at my neck. Unfortunately, I recognized her as a royal vampire from a nearby kingdom. "Princess Anivia. Fancy seeing you here..." I growled. Figures I would be caught unprepared.

The vampire let out a loud hiss. "My father's assassins haven't vanquished you yet, Viper....you killed all but one," she chuckled.

First of all, how did she know I was the Viper? I never showed my face to anyone at all during my hunts, like I always emphasize. Second of all, why were royals sending assassins to me, and who was the survivor? Was my past catching up finally?

I suddenly remembered Goliath, and turned to look only to see that he was gone. Well, maybe he ran for it out of fear. I hoped so, since I honestly didn't want him to get hurt. It would be rather inconvenient if he went for help, though. The police were not that understanding, they didn't know, like much of the rest of the world, that vampires existed. They'd also take one look at me and haul me into custody due to my odd nails and sharp teeth for being *crazy*.

I wasted no time to strike. Leaping forward, my claws sliced into Princess Anivia's arm. The vampire was too fast; she dodged at the last second and darted behind me. I whirled, only to be slammed down by her shove. It wasn't over yet. I went limp to form the assumption that I was hurt or in shock. Playing dead or feigning a wound was a nice tactic that usually worked. I was right about this time, too; the vampire princess bought it, and she lunged down toward me right as I decided to slice upwards with my nails. I felt them go through soft flesh. Oh, that would be a very painful wound.

She screamed and held her bleeding eyes, staggering back. "How's your brother?" I taunted, wanting to make her angry. It worked, but I didn't expect one thing. The princess drew a knife and pounced on me, sinking it into my shoulder.

I cried out and grabbed the handle to pull it gently from my flesh, but I took too much time. Lady Anivia, despite getting weaker, had me pinned down with my arms behind held by hers. "He's not doing so well in Hell, thanks to you," she hissed smoothly. Her blood dripped into my face, much to my disgust. Even a blind vampire could be a deadly one. "But now of course I can avenge him, slave."

The vampire lunged down and sank her fangs into my neck. The painful poison didn't affect me, but the jagged fangs did. The vampire's bite from a couple nights ago didn't hurt so much since it was a very fast strike.

A prolonged vampire bite, however, was horrible for me. My mouth was open in a silent scream as she slowly began draining me. I heard a chuckle, though just barely.

"Y'know, it's not nice to randomly attack one's new friend, princess," came a male's smooth voice. Was that...Goliath? I gasped as the princess tensed. Suddenly, she pulled away and her expression became horrified. Her hand flew toward her chest, I saw it wrap around what appeared to be a silver stake. I was too weak to even stand, but I rolled away from the dying vampire. She had taken a *lot* of blood in a very short period of time. Damn, these royals really wanted to see me dead.

Goliath bent over me, gently checking my pulse. With my eyes narrowed weakly, I probably didn't look like much of a threat. I gave a warning hiss and raised my arm. "Stay back," I muttered, not trusting him. Something was...off.

The guy stared down at me, amused. "Well, love... Frankly, I'm the only one you really can't kill," he responded. With that he brushed away some cover from his arm to reveal five long gashes. Then, he lifted his head to show me his neck. He had a huge bite and the symbol of a striking viper. Shit, that was *my* symbol.

I stared, horrified, as Goliath's eyes slowly shifted to red. His ears changed into being pointed and elongated. As the illusion continued to fade, I noticed all of his teeth *sharpen* to points, with the canines of his upper and lower jaw displaying the longest fangs.

Blood loss made me dizzy, but I could still think and talk. "How...is...that...possible?" I gasped. The vampire gave a soft smile. Ah great, I was in for it now.

"As it turns out, you're not the only one who is immune to venom. Very few of us are. You happened to stumble upon someone who can't be killed by your methods, hunter," he murmured. He bent down and took me into his arms, never taking his gaze from my eyes. I cringed and tensed, knowing I was in *huge* trouble.

"Why not kill me when I tried to kill you?" I asked in a small voice. Goliath's eyes sparked in thought.

"I...don't know, really. Your blood drew me to you. You see, I can sense unique blood from a mile away. Very few can, but since I have some myself, it was easy to find you. I didn't kill you because you're like me in a sense, dear," he responded. There was something in his voice that told me this explanation wasn't the entire gist of it.

I hissed at him, my eyes lighting up in fury. "I'll never be like a leech like you!" I spat. Goliath looked hurt, but his gaze never thinned.

"Maybe not. But, Sam, there's something about me that you don't know. I'm like you in that I'm a hunter myself. Not of vampires, but of vampire hunters. Anyone who kills the truly innocent deserves to die," he hissed.

I blinked, thinking for a moment. "So you're saying I kill the innocent every time I hunt?" I asked in bewilderment.

Goliath shook his head, frowning. "As a matter of fact, no. You target the true parasites of the streets that grab innocent humans off the road. You're an independent hunter, but most aren't. Most will kill any vampire on sight, including children," he replied.

I tensed, just wanting to get away from him. "So you've been hunting me? Otherwise, how would you know this?" I asked in disbelief. Now that, in my opinion, was creepy. Sure, I killed street urchins, but I'd never before tracked a particular vampire down to kill.

A vampire actually hunting specified targets, though, was probably a lot more specialized and dangerous. *Especially* a royal vampire. I didn't underestimate their power, no, I just never thought I would be a target. Hopefully I wasn't in the arms of one right now.

Goliath shook his head, focused. "Not at all. I wanted to find out more about you, Sam," he responded with a smile. "You're so alone, like I am. I originally thought all vampire hunters were savages, until I met you. You kill with venom rather than stakes. Most importantly, you target the truly bad rather than the innocent. I saw you spare that child, love."

Oh wow; he'd even been watching me a few months ago? I remembered that I'd been on a hunt, and had found a child with a literal bag of blood sitting in an alleyway. She had no home, and obviously was a vampire.

I had approached and debated whether or not to kill her... but really, the decision was easy. I merely told her that a safe-haven house for children like her was a couple of blocks down. Yes, I knew the location of a vampire orphanage, though I'd never gone there. I grew big-girl pants and took her there, too. The people there accepted the child and thanked me, but I didn't stick around long enough to learn more.

And yes, vampires could have children. Like I said before, born vampires were a natural species just like humans or shapeshifters. They were also apex predators with a diet specialized specifically for human blood. Most myths coined them as undead, but nothing was farther from the truth. Plus, since they had no need of any type of food other than blood, the 'two fangs' and *just* that with human teeth was a myth likely founded on the fact that their canines were longer than their other *sharp teeth*. Their dentition was very similar to that of felines.

"Alright then, so what are you going to do now?" I asked with a sigh. Goliath stared at me for a moment as if debating the next thing he was going to say.

"I was thinking we could work together," he replied simply.

Chapter 5

I stared at him in disbelief. "Work with you...? Are you crazy? Me, work with a vampire who hunts exactly the people who I work for?" I growled. The vampire looked sullen at my lack of positive response. I struggled in his arms to no avail. For gods' snakes, I just wanted to get away! Never had I been in a situation like this before, not even as a slave, where I was unable to run.

"I could help you weed out the evil vampires, and you could help me destroy the hunters who ruin innocent lives," he proposed, looking deeply into my eyes.

"Forget it," I said flatly. "Kill me now, or next time we cross paths I will slaughter you!" I spat. Yes, I was angry. How could I let myself be tricked so easily? And of course he could take me up on my suggestion, though obviously I hoped he didn't.

Goliath seemed disappointed. "Well. I won't kill you now, but I'm not giving up. I initially *was* sent to kill you, but that plan was vanquished weeks ago. I'll simply find you again when you least expect it. You'll come around, Sam," he chuckled. Figures, I *knew* there was more to the story than just blatant curiosity! But like that, he was gone.

I was laying flat on my back, utterly confused as to what just went down. Well, I knew one thing, It was time to tweak my methods. I needed to get to the association pronto! After wrapping my dark scarf around my neck to hide my wound, I was off at a brisk pace.

It took me all but ten minutes to find the base. I sneaked into the back-entrance and entered the lobby. Ignoring several withering glances that were shot in my direction, I headed to the weapon room. A 'guard' stood there and stared me down.

Robert Smoke. He was one of the bigwigs here, and took his position seriously. I knew how greedy he really was, though, and had little trust for him or those who worked with him. To most, he looked intimidating with his slicked-back shaggy snow-white hair, cold blue eyes, a muscular form, and sharp jawline. He had several golden-ringed eyebrow piercings and some chained necklaces of the same material, one of which had a spider on it. Not only that, but upon the ivory flesh of his arm was the tattoo of a knife piercing a bat.

"Red Viper. What are you doing here? You never use weapons," he growled. I shrugged, my eyes dark. Luckily I had covered the bite marks on my neck on the way here.

"I figured it was time for a small change. I need a simple weapon that melds with my methods, not a stake nor a gun, but something different," I hissed. Robert stared at me, and after a moment's hesitation, he grabbed the handle and let me through.

Several weapon racks lined the wall, from swords to bows. I examined them thoroughly but couldn't find any that suited me, until a flash of silver caught my eye. I grabbed what seemed like five blades with straps attaching them together. With a gasp I realized that it was a hand weapon: claws meant for easy melee combat. I slipped the glove-like weapon on my right hand. It fit easily, and looked like a biker glove with five long blades jutting out of the knuckles. I knew it was perfect, and gave the guard a genuine smile. He returned it with a frown of disgust.

"Your teeth are like theirs, all of them sharp as a snake's. Fitting, I suppose. But unnerving," he observed. I just chuckled and exited. No one stopped me or tried to say hello. I was the outcast of the outcasts, and not even my own kind accepted me. Which was perfectly fine.

Something did indeed catch my attention. The worried whispers of my 'fellow' hunters caught my ears. *"They're growing in number...they say the war will come sooner than we think... If they take over, there will be no hope..."*

Well. That was news to me; I had no idea that there was a war brewing. I knew exactly who *they* were. And I knew now exactly what I had to do. I needed to find out what the vampires were planning and put a stop to it in any way I could. I know how futile it would be if I went alone, but I had no choice. No one trusted me, and the feeling was mutual.

I returned home and slipped inside, glancing around for any signs of my family. Giving a sigh of relief, I began walking to my bed, when a light clicked on. Cringing, I turned to see both Boomey and Copper staring me down. "OK OK, I know, I disobeyed you, but I found out something tonight that I need to stop!" I tried. Leaving Goliath out of the conversation was probably the best idea.

Boomey stared at me with pure anger. The snake was wrapped around my neck in a flash. No, not constricting. He'd never do that, but his eyes were mere inches from mine. "*Sambuca. Why...on...earth....*" he began. I gulped, because oh crap, he was angry. "*I can't even find words to tell you how worried we were. There's something coming, Sambuca, and I NEED you to listen. Copper and I don't want to lose you!*" he hissed into my mind.

I winced as I saw a realization dawn on him. He opened his mouth and clamped down onto my scarf, ripping it off. From there, both he and Copper stared at my bite mark in pure silence. I felt Copper slither over and spy the small bandage on my hand. Like Boomey, she lunged forward and ripped it off. Now both were staring at *me.* "I...can explain...I got rid of the attacker and got a new weapon, don't worry," I tried.

Copper was in my face and hissing like she was insane. "*You got BITTEN?! We told you to stay here, and you got bitten for the first time in a decade. That's it. You can no longer leave this hut until we deem that it is safe,*" she hissed.

I gasped angrily. No, hunting was my duty. I needed to fulfill that task! "But they are planning something!" I yelled out. "I need to stop it, I can't let others fall to the same fate as I! I'm not some dumb child anymore!"

Boomey's glare softened. "*Sam... I know you're a strong woman. You don't see how much we care, little Sam,*" he hissed softly. I gently took him off of my neck and pulled both snakes in for a hug.

"I know I need to be more careful. Let me go out this once, tomorrow night. I won't ask again. Just grant me this, and I will stay and obey for however long you want me to," came my sigh.

After a long pause, both snakes gave a hesitant nod. One night couldn't kill me, right? No, but it sure could change my life.

AND SO, I WAS OUT AS soon as the sun began to set. I wandered through the forest, my eyes flashing darkly. My hand-weapon was equipped, and I had refreshed my poisons in prep for tonight. I would track down a leech and get information from him or her.

From experience, I knew that many hung out in alleyways. But those were the out-of-society vampires, ones that were mongrels that fed off of whoever they saw. No, this time I was going for the extremely dangerous royals, the very vampires that haunted me today. I hadn't revealed nearly any of my past to anyone, yet.

Anyway. It was time to track one down. I'd always known where to locate a royal, but cornering them would be another thing. They were often surrounded by guards that wouldn't hesitate to slaughter me. I'd need to catch one alone.

And I knew just where to do that. One of the princesses resided here in the city. She appeared innocent, like a blooming flower that couldn't do anyone any harm. But I knew the truth. The other hunters explained that she secretly ran an underground slave trade. Most vampires only did so in their filthy kingdoms, but she was bold living in the human city and had to keep things quiet.

Sure enough, as I walked down the street a mansion came into view. I sighted the dark spires rising up from the roof and knew already it was a vampire's residence. By the gods, it seemed like they always loved to be creepy and old fashioned. Sure, I hated vampires, but maybe they'd be accepted by the public if they were a little less, I don't know, aggressive or evil. And, you know, if they weren't so adamant on hiding from humans in general for whatever reason.

The house was a blood red with a completely black roof. Dark roses decorated the sides; it was the princess's mark. She was basically a rose that looked and smelled sweet, but had thorns of all sorts. "So freakin old fashioned," I muttered, rolling my eyes. What was this obsession with the old ways? They had been the ones in power in the medieval ages, yes, but would never again become so again if they refused to adapt to the real world. So I thought.

Now, I know, I sounded odd, being a vampire hunter and talking about their acceptance and all. But I'd honestly accept a truce if both sides agreed to peace. Goliath had offered me one, yes, but *that one* I couldn't take. I truly feared him, because no one ever before had been immune to my venom. That was my own flaw and fear that I didn't feel like working on just yet.

Approaching the mansion, I gave a pause. The feeling of being watched was frightening, but I dismissed it and moved on. Yeah, sometimes I really needed to trust my instincts more. I darted to the window and peered in, seeing nothing of interest except darkness. Well, I'd have to go inside if I wanted to accomplish anything.

I lock-picked the window easily and entered the room, careful not to make any noise. The snake venom neutralized my scent from most vampires, *again* so I thought, anyway.

I wandered through the house until a light caught my eyes. Sighting what appeared to be a dining room, I stuck to the shadows and peeked in. What I saw almost made my heart stop.

Several vampires sat around the table with the rose princess at the head. I narrowed my eyes. Each was very important. But one vampire in particular caught my eye. It was no other than Goliath, wearing his fancy suit and tophat. His long dark black hair hid part of one of his eyes, which glowed a deep red at the moment.

I held my breath, feeling a little light headed. Ever since he vanished, I couldn't forget his words. *I'll simply find you again when you least expect it.* They echoed in my head over and over. Wait, why did I care? I *should* feel no fear. Fear was a weakness. Fear was my flaw. I couldn't get rid of it, much as I tried. But by the gods, I wanted to. Refocusing, I listened in on their conversation.

"So...You failed to destroy the Viper, Goliath. I'm disappointed," the princess frowned, staring the vampire assassin down. Goliath flashed a fully-fanged smile and shrugged.

"I've never failed before, dear. What makes you think I've given up?" he chuckled smoothly. I had to control my heart-rate with extreme focus. Unlike many humans, I could slow it to almost null, which, in this situation, was nearly impossible.

The princess scoffed. "Whatever. Get it done before she attempts to stop our plans. Many hunters have tried and failed. Her immunity to our venom makes her a threat to everyone," she growled. "Luckily she hasn't allied with those other vermin yet."

I saw Goliath's eyes flash for half a second. He frowned, seeming bothered by her words. The vampire said nothing, just looked down at his untouched steak. "I'll take care of it," he muttered in a cold voice.

The Princess ignored his hesitation and continued. "Now. I want you all to prepare for the assault on the base tomorrow. From there we'll take over the city. Then, the world. All kingdoms are striking at once. The human armies will not see any of it coming, and have no proper means to stop us," she chuckled coldly. My eyes widened. Did...did they know where the hunter base was?! And what was that about taking out *human armies*?

Alright, I had to stop this mess somehow. The first thing I needed to do was get out of here and warn the hunters. I crouched and quietly walked forward toward the way I came. Come on...come on. The window was in my sight. I quickened my pace, almost making it, until—

I held in a scream as I felt a strong hand wrap around my chest to restrain me. A soft chuckle sounded in my ear, making my blood freeze. "Now now. Where do you think you're going, darling?" Goliath's smooth voice chimed in my ear.

Chapter 6

Immediately I tensed. Like a viper about to strike, I virtually coiled when I drew my arms close to my chest. As an automatic reaction, I tried to get him to release me by biting down onto his arm. Unfortunately, that only got me a slight chuckle from him.

"Y'know, if you keep biting me, I'll need to bite back," he muttered. I let out an inhuman, metallic hiss and released his arm. I had to calm down and control myself, it would be the only way I'd be able to survive.

Taking a deep breath, I growled, "Some heroic vampire you are, 'killing those that murder the innocent'. You're planning on taking over a city for god's snakes." I felt Goliath tense.

"It's for the better, Sam. We're tired of hiding, tired of being hated and having to scavenge for the littlest things. Humans no longer have a place being the dominant species. We're not going to slaughter the city, no, we'll just defend ourselves when the need arises," he answered with a sigh. I thrashed in his arms to no avail, for his arm was like steel.

"Gonna kill me now, then?" I asked, no fear in my voice. That didn't mean I wasn't terrified. On the contrary. Just, I knew how to hide it well. I felt myself being turned around to face him. Goliath's hands stayed on my shoulders, holding me and preventing my escape. His dark red eyes looked almost hurt.

He inhaled slowly and shook his head. "You heard everything, didn't you. It's not like that. I might've promised to be rid of you, but I can't. They know not of you being here. I could just barely scent your unique blood over the venom on your skin," he told me. Really, he could find me even through my scent-masking methods? Next time I wouldn't use venom. I needed to find better ways of utilizing stealth.

I narrowed my eyes, giving up on my attempts to pull away. "If you were ordered to destroy me, then why haven't you yet?" I hissed, irritated. I'd at least fight back as much as I could, but he was honestly confusing me.

Goliath shrugged, never tearing his gaze from mine. "I told you before, Sam. But now I'm not letting you go. You know too much," he hissed. Suddenly, we were outside, and I was in his arms. I didn't approve, so I let out a loud snarl and thrashed to no avail. "I'll take this!" Goliath said in an amused voice as he slipped off my hand weapon. "Wouldn't want to get hurt now would we?" he chuckled. I just hissed loudly and tried to slice at his chest with my claw-like nails. Despite my shredding his tux, he seemed fine.

"You ruined my good suit, love. I'd stop fighting, you'll tire yourself out," the vampire smirked. Some gentleman he was. I bared my sharp teeth, causing him to flash his fangs at me. "Listen, I might let you go when we're finished with the conquest, alright? You'll be fine. Like I said, I'm not planning on killing you," Goliath said smoothly, as usual.

I didn't approve of him capturing me, obviously. Sure I was spying, but it was vital for me to find out what the vampires were planning. Too bad Goliath somehow found me wherever I went. I struggled again to no avail, and let out yet another frustrated hiss. Soon enough we arrived at a small house in the outskirts of town. Goliath entered and walked through the dark halls to a room. It had a small bed and no windows, and a door which I assumed led to a bathroom.

"Sorry your accommodations aren't the best, but I honestly had no idea that you'd try to spy on the meeting tonight, love," he sighed. He placed me on the ground and moved to block the door, as if expecting me to make a break for it.

I narrowed my eyes at him and paced, trying to figure out a way to get past him. "Why are you keeping me here?" I muttered angrily.

The vampire raised his eyebrows, dark hair still hiding one of his eyes. "Because you'll get yourself killed if I don't," he muttered, staring at me.

I took a few steps back, crossing my arms. "I still have no idea why the hell you care," I mumbled. Goliath laughed and took a step towards me, causing me to tense once again. I was weaponless, my venom didn't work, and I was trapped. Yeah, in no way was I a happy camper.

"Because, Sam. You're a lot like me," he answered with a smile. I shook my head, scowling.

"I'll never be like a leech!" I yelled, repeating what I had said to begin with. He flinched, his smile turning into a frown. The vampire's eyes flashed a dangerous red for a moment.

"Why do you hate us so much, Sam?" he asked in a wary tone. I blinked, not expecting that question. Well. I refused to answer at the moment and just turned away from him.

"None of your business," I responded quietly. I mean, he was a strange vampire who had captured me and was planning on keeping me here. I fully expected him to bite or kill me still, too, despite his words. However, I only heard Goliath sigh.

"I'll be back tomorrow with food. I need to hunt now," he growled creepily. I just walked over and sat on the bed, hanging my head. It depressed me that I'd been caught, but I wouldn't give up so easily. I heard the door close and lock. My eyes flew to the smooth handle. It had no lock in here, only outside. It was completely human proof, no windows, no way of escape.

Nonetheless, I was determined to get away. I flew at the door and clawed it, making deep gouge marks in the wood. If I kept it up, I would eventually grind away my nails, and that would do me no good.

Why did Goliath bring me here?! Like hell did he care if I died. I tried wracking my brain for the answer, but none came. I cursed and paced several times, unable to figure it out. I only knew now that I needed to get away as soon as possible.

With a drawn out sigh, I fell deep into thought. There was nothing here to pry the door loose, and since it was locked from the other side, I couldn't pick it. I couldn't hide and escape when he tried looking in the room for me. Despite my best efforts, he could scent me wherever I was. Great. Trapped in a house with a vampire who literally hunted my people. Perhaps he was planning on torturing me.

My pupils turned to slits as I thought. It was a strange thing that happened, leading me to think that I really *wasn't* all that human. What else

I could be, I had no idea, but it was interesting to try to figure out. Sometimes I ignored my delusions of normalcy and thought it through. Whatever, I had people to protect. No one deserved to end up like I did, so I needed to get out at all costs!

Time to try a new approach. My eyes widened as a plan came to mind. I opened the bathroom door and came to something I suspected. A simple bathroom, with a shower, toilet, and mirror. My eyes focused on the mirror. Perfect. I darted to it and slammed my fist into the cold glass, shattering it easily. Ignoring the blood that welled up in my knuckles, I grabbed a shard and exited the bathroom. I wedged the shard into the part of the door handle that was up against the wood itself.

Then, I took care to pry loose my side of the handle. Just...a...little...more... I focused and managed to wiggle it just enough to come off. From there, I could examine the contents of the lock. A cog seemed to be keeping it locked; using my nails, I turned it just enough to unlock it. All I needed to do now was open it. I assumed the rod that had been attached to the handle would do the trick. Replacing the door handle, I jiggled it just enough to make it open. I cheered silently and slipped out.

No time to waste. I hastily opened a window and got out of that cursed house for good! Except... I had no weapon now. Sure, I had venom, but what if Goliath found me again? With a reluctant growl, I turned back to the place and entered through the window again. I looked around the house and spotted a glint of silver. I lunged at it and pulled out a silver stake. Wait, what?

This wasn't what I was looking for, and it wasn't what I expected to find. I put my fingers on the cold surface and stared at my reflection in it, surprised.

"What...what is this?" I muttered. I honestly half expected a voice to answer behind me. None came, so I resumed my search. In hindsight, keeping the stake would have been a wise decision. I never claimed to have a gigantic amount of common sense, though. Remember, I was a street huntress, not an expert assassin for snake's sake.

I walked around to what appeared to be a kitchen. My eyes fell on the fridge, and I cringed, knowing what was inside. But my curiosity got the best of me. I opened it to see vial upon vial of red liquid. I scoffed, not surprised in the least. But a glint of metal caught my eyes. There, on the bottom shelf, was my weapon. So. He assumed that I would be too afraid to look in the fridge just in case I escaped? Psh. Underestimation to the max!

Smirking and closing the fridge, I equipped my weapon. Good, now onto plan 'save the city'. Darting away, I went outside and examined my surroundings. Not many houses were around, and those that were appeared very run down.

I ran down the tattered street and stuck to the shadows. Something wasn't right. Once I got to town, it seemed like everyone was in a panic. People ran left and right, screaming about monsters invading the town. I knew it meant only one thing. My eyes widened as I saw people cloaked in shadows lunge at humans and sink fangs into their necks.

Screams filled the night as I snarled. Goliath was a liar! People were *being slaughtered*! Already did corpses litter the streets, bathed in pools of blood. Some limbs were strewn left and right, and I even passed a dying man that had intestines spilling out of his lower body. Some vampires weren't bothering to feed at all, and just lunged to *kill.*

I turned the corners and got to the center of town, and saw what I didn't expect yet again. A guy was surrounded by a bunch of vampires. Upon closer look, the vampires were from dinner last night. I spotted the princess step forward and circle him. He was in a suit and top hat, and his hair covered his eyes. Definitely a vampire. Wait.

"Goliath?!" I whispered in surprise. I stayed hidden behind the corner of a brick building and watched. Focusing, I could now make out his words.

"You lied, princess," hissed Goliath. The vampire threw back her head in a laugh.

"Did you really think we'd take the city by civil means? Don't be silly, brother! We are meant to rule over these filthy humans now. I don't know what's turned you soft, you used to be more of a tyrant than Ash, but I will end you myself for being *weak,*" she snarled. I raised my eyebrows. So the snake-like vampire was a prince. A *royal vampire* with a ridiculous amount of power. Somehow I wasn't surprised.

Goliath let out a metallic hiss and lunged. Chaos broke loose, and I could see him lash out at his attackers. He dissolved into shadows and ripped several of them limb from limb, but the princess fought in a similar fashion, following her brother in her own mist of darkness. I knew for a fact there were too many, and though he was a powerful royal, his sister likely matched his strength since royal blood ran through her veins too. I winced and got my claw weapon ready. No, I don't know why I did it. But for some reason, I couldn't let him die.

With a snarl and a hiss, I launched out of the shadows. My eyes locked with Goliath's, and with a sharp-toothed grin, I began my *own* slaughter.

Chapter 7

There was no hesitation. I very simply dove into the fray, slicing at any bit of vampire flesh I laid eyes on. I lunged like a snake in a frenzy. My teeth sank into several vampires' arms before I felt myself being restrained. I thrashed and kicked, giving an inhuman hiss. I was covered in vampire blood, and my venom green eyes beheld only slits for pupils. Something changed in me at that moment. I wasn't normal. I never had been. But now I knew that I was something far more deadly than I could've imagined.

Exactly what, I didn't know. The comments of the snakes always hinted that I was an abnormal being. Goliath's words on my unique blood also were odd. Eventually I would learn exactly what I was. And it would be a surprise to me, that was for damn sure. But the time hadn't come quite yet.

I ignored the person who held my arms behind my back for just a moment. My gaze swept over the bodies. All were dead, including the princess. Well, all but Goliath were dead. I didn't need to turn to know it was he who was holding me back now.

"Release me," I commanded in a low, dangerous voice. I felt the vampire sigh, then squirmed to no avail. I tried again, this time my voice was even lower and more of a hiss than actual words. "Let. Go."

Goliath slowly withdrew his hands and stepped away. I whirled and faced him, my own venom green eyes meeting his blood red. "So, vampire prince," I spat. He winced, taking another step back. Despite the battle, his new suit was barely ripped, though it was stained red with blood. He bent down and returned the top hat to his head, a grim look in his eyes. "You kill those who deserve it, huh. You kill murderers. Well look around. Look what you've done!" my voice was loud now.

Goliath blinked, and suddenly I was on the ground beneath him. His eyes were red with pure fury as he bared his fangs in my face. "This wasn't my doing, Sam," he began in a snarl. "My sister betrayed me. My only *last remaining* sister lied to me for years, apparently. Yes, plenty are dead now because of me. But under no circumstance did I wish for this to happen," he finished. Whoa, I had not expected him to get so angry. Nonetheless I bared my teeth and let out a hiss.

I was angry, and though he was fully capable of ripping me limb from limb, I didn't care. My eyes were unwavering as I stared at him straight on. "Well it did," I hissed bitterly. With that, I managed to shove him off of me and get to my feet. He clearly wasn't putting much effort into keeping me there.

I turned away and slowly began walking. I heard Goliath collapse behind me and halted. Turning, my eyes caught him as he was on his knees. I had the horror of seeing tears blossom in his eyes as he looked from the bodies, to me, to the chaos on the streets. What the hell? It struck me...I'd never seen an adult vampire legitimately cry before.

"Why are you crying?" I asked softly, no trace of the previous venom in my voice. I was genuinely surprised. Goliath looked up at me as if surprised I hadn't left yet.

"It's because of me that so many are dying," he gasped in a broken voice. "I didn't want to murder the undeserving again. I thought I had put that behind me, but now I've doomed everyone. I actually *tried* this time. I'm so *used to killing... it comes so easily* that when I actually made an attempt to change, I failed." He wiped away the tears that spilled over his pale cheeks, yet was unable to stop the stream of sadness.

I scoffed so suddenly that he looked up at me, hurt. Lost. "Well I wouldn't cry about it," I started with a smirk. "Indeed, it is your fault. You doomed a lot of people, though you clearly regret it. Well. Only one thing to do now," I growled. I took a step towards him, drawing my hand weapon. I wasn't unprepared this time, and he'd made a mistake by releasing me from his tackle.

The only time *I'd* been the one to kill a royal vampire was when the stroke of luck had hit me as a teenager. Goliath had finished off both of the other princesses, his sisters, including the one tonight while I'd been distracting her guards. Killing royal vampires was highly difficult, and *he* was immune to my venom. Come to think of it, why was he specifically immune while the others weren't? Bah. I couldn't dwell on that. If I didn't strike now, I wouldn't have a chance again. He wasn't immune to silver, which slowed his healing and if used enough, poisoned him.

He was still weak from the other vampires, yet that wouldn't last for very long at all. The window of time was open now and only now.

I didn't take it.

Rather, I smirked and pointed the glistening silver claws at him. "You can always fix it, Goliath. Giving up doesn't cut it, eh? See ya 'round. Oh yeah, and I don't like being captured. You'll die if you do it again," I hissed. I turned away and vanished into the shadows, leaving behind a very confused vampire.

The experience had shaken me to the core, though. Vampires, in my eyes, were only killers. Yeah, I had spared that child, but I had no idea why. In fact, I still don't know why I didn't just kill Goliath right then and there, while he was vulnerable. I inherently knew it would be the wrong thing to do, so was able to keep my 'goodness' by not killing without reason. It left a very sour taste in my mouth when I thought about going after vampires *not* on the streets. I heard some hunters went after entire families for just being vampires. While my hatred ran pretty deep, I would not ever go that far. I continued walking, my inner voice swarming in my head either telling me off or congratulating me. Ugh, I needed a break still, though I wasn't going to get one anytime soon.

Ah, now for my favorite part of the night. My eyes caught sight of some vampires on the streets, now fighting among themselves. While I didn't go after families of vampires, I now had a reason to slaughter whatever I saw in my way. They were on *my* turf, and there was no excuse for killing off such a large number of the people that I had promised to protect from death or a fate like mine.

However, I gasped, coming to a realization. Some vampires were fighting the aggressive ones, snapping about lies and how they were being too cruel. Well then. Maybe not all the leeches here were my enemies. While many were bad, not all here were murders. There were two sides to every story, and sadly I could not just destroy whoever was in my way. I guess just like how not all hunters were dignified, as Goliath had pointed out, not all vampires were evil.

In fact, I realized that some members of a vampiric *gang* I had no recognition of were defending small groups of humans, who were standing there in shock, watching them fight. A strong male voice with a city accent rang out. "Yah, you royal vampires are bad fucking news, and I ain' gonna let you enslave these widdle humans I'm here to protect. Bastards. I don' care about any sort of uprising, this city is *mine* and the humans aren' your livestock!" I couldn't see where it was coming from, though, and the rest of his shouting was drowned out by the battle. Shit, well, that confirmed my realization even further. Even the *gangs* had nuance.

With that new thought in mind, I leaped out at two vampires arguing violently. One, a man with light blond hair and a sharp jaw, was hissing about taking the city one human at a time. The other, a girl with long fiery red hair and beautiful hazel eyes, argued the opposite, saying that there were ways to make a peaceful negotiation. You can guess who I chose to attack.

The man cried out as my blades plunged through him. I bit into his arm for good measure, causing him to bleed out and fall to the ground. My gaze fell on the woman, who was cowering before me. Obviously she wasn't a fighter. The poor vampire had no weapon and was looking at a full on vampire hunter with long claws and silver blades. I was the one who now felt like a monster.

She turned to run, but I stopped her by placing a hand on her shoulder. The vampire yelped and quivered. "Hey hey hey! I'm on your side, don't worry!" I reassured, giving a snake-like smile. She turned, took one look at my teeth, and screamed. I blinked, my venom-green eyes surprised. Vampires being afraid of me was sorta different. Well. They appeared to be a lot more like humans now, that was for sure. "No I promise! I'm here to help," I tried again.

Slowly the vampire woman relaxed. "Y-you are? I'm so scared. I thought they were going t-to talk to them, t-to try and make peace," she started. When she burst into tears, I sighed. Too much crying for my liking tonight, thank you. "They started k-killing everyone..."

I smirked. "Well. I'll make sure to stop that!" I reassured. Like always, I left abruptly and darted away from the woman. Targeting vampires that were gorging on humans, I downed a few before ending up surrounded. I gave a smirk and chuckled, "Well well. Looks like I've gotten myself into a bit of trouble. Though, you all have as well!" I shrieked.

I lunged like a snake, first making a gash with a venomous claws then slicing them with my weapons. It worked for many, but I couldn't overcome an entire army. I was knocked down and pinned to the ground finally by a very angry looking guy. His red eyes pierced into my soul as he slowly smirked.

"Well well, Viper. Time to see what a snake tastes like," he snarled, licking his lips. I hissed angrily as he ripped off my hood and scarf, revealing my neck. My eyes went into slits as he bent to my skin, his breath warm on my skin. It would be painful to be drained slowly, unable to escape. All alone, I would die here.

Of course, he just had to intervene with everything, even my death. So I can honestly say I wasn't surprised when a smooth voice rang through the night. "Caught in the coils of another I see. Well, I won't let you get bitten. Not this time," Goliath chuckled.

Chapter 8

I felt the weight of the enemy vampire being lifted from me. My venom green eyes narrowed as I watched Goliath reach into a hidden bag and withdraw a long silver knife. Before the other vampire could turn and lunge at him, he was stabbed in the back. More of them leaped at Goliath, but the vampire was too fast.

He must have recovered rather quickly, for now Goliath was the one on a rampage. His knife was brandished with such grace; it sliced through skin with such ease that I couldn't stop staring. Blood of the enemy vampires was spilled everywhere, and Goliath didn't stop until all were more still than stone.

I laid my head down on the hard ground, groaning in pain and exhaustion. Really, I just wanted to go home. There was a town I needed to save, though. His voice filled my ears, so close that I hissed in surprise. "Well well, love. Looks like you were able to escape my wonderful home," Goliath purred while looming over me. He was in pretty bad shape as well, but I was worse off now. Great, *now* he remembered that I had made a grand escape. Despite my actions to save him, he probably was gonna hold that against me.

"Leave. Me. ALONE!" I yelled, taking a deep breath. As if that would scare him away, of course. Goliath didn't even flinch.

"I have to say, you *did* save my life. And that means that I need to do the same," he responded. With that, he took me in his arms for the second time tonight. That idea mortified me; vampires might recover really fast, but I would need a night now to rest. At the moment my life was in either his hands... or his fangs.

"I just want to be left alone..." I sighed, too tired to fight back. The chaos around this particular spot had reduced, but the rest of the city was bathed in the blood of battle.

"Unfortunately you get into too much trouble for me to leave you alone," Goliath chuckled. He stared into my eyes with his own blood red. I frowned, letting out a sigh.

"My parents will be expecting me," I tried. Yeah, I know it was a pathetic excuse, but I was desperate.

That made him laugh. "That's your own fault for sneaking out," he muttered. The sun was peeking over the horizon, and he gave a yawn. "Listen. I'm not forcing you to stay this time. But hear me out and at least let me help you," he pleaded. I wasn't the only tired one here, at least.

My eyes narrowed in distrust. I couldn't stand *this* vampire, but I knew that if I refused, I'd probably die from a *different* vampire seeking revenge. I was too weak to fight back even with venom. "Fine. But then I want you to leave me alone forever," I snapped.

Solemnly, Goliath nodded. "If that's what you wish." He began walking down the street. We passed by many dark buildings, oddly there was no police or ambulance anywhere in sight. I cleared my throat and looked up to Goliath with confusion.

"Where are the authorities? They are normally fast to respond," I asked, knowing that something was off. The vampire frowned, letting out a drawn out sigh that did worry me somewhat.

"Well, the vampiric royalty took care to control that before launching this attack. They were either dead... or have been purely made up of vampires for a while. I'm not into the details, I can just hope it is the latter," he told me. Lovely; how long had the association known about this, I wondered?

Soon we were walking towards the house I was in before. I gave a hiss of disapproval, squirming in an attempt to break free of the vampire's arms. No surprise, it was to no avail. Goliath chuckled, glancing down to me. "No worries. I'm not planning on trapping you there," he promised. Sure he wasn't; I already had an escape plan in mind.

When we arrived, my eyes were half closed. The vampire gently placed me on the couch and seemed to disappear into the kitchen. Coming out,

Goliath had two cups; one full of red liquid, and one full of water. He handed the water to me and took a sip from his other glass. Seeing my scowl of distaste, he smirked. "Blood drives work to keep us alive," he explained very sarcastically. He turned away, obviously deep in thought. "But fresh blood is the best, in my opinion. Unlike many think, vampires can hunt without killing. Venom regulation is the key; I'm sure you're aware of that process," he muttered, turning to fix me in a red stare.

I blinked, unsure of how to respond. "Uh...yeah, venom output is a controlled factor, at least in snakes," I said slowly. My muscles relaxed even more despite the tension of me being in a vampire's household. I was very, very tired...

Goliath slowly walked up to the couch, licking his lips. "As you know, I can control whether I kill you with a bite, right?" he whispered, now by my ear. A realization dawned on me. I cried out and moved to sit up, but he easily pushed me down with a strong hand. My weapon...was disarmed. He'd taken it off when he put me on the couch.

"Please...no!" I gasped in horror, holding in tears. He leaned toward my neck...and burst out laughing. Tears came from his eyes as he chuckled, staring at me as if I was the funniest thing in the world.

"Well, looks like you're terrified of either me or me biting you—when you've bitten and killed countless others. Do not fear. I have no intention of going through with my threat. I just wanted to see your reaction, oh fearless serpent of the night," Goliath joked.

I was seething—he'd hit a nerve. My venom green eyes flashed with hatred as I looked straight at him. "I had no idea you were a heartless jerk, Goliath," I hissed in a broken voice. He had no idea *why* I was so afraid. Immediately the laughter faded from his eyes. It was replaced by worry, but I didn't care. I turned so that my back was facing him, and my face was towards the couch.

What he did brought up memories of being trapped as a slave; I shuddered as I remembered the first time fangs sunk into my neck. Yeah, the now deceased princess had bitten me too, which had been just as horrible. Every single new bite made me more afraid, since it was not only painful, but afterward I was vulnerable to anything.

"Oh...I'm sorry, love..." he whispered, now seeing that he messed up big time. I let out an inhuman growl, finding that at the moment I was not so forgiving.

"It's too late for that, vampire. And stop calling me 'love', goddamnit—I don't love you and never will!" I yelled. My voice was very loud now. However, silence stretched in the room, and I forced my eyes to close. Now, I was very uneasy being here. There was nothing I could do about it, though.

I tensed when I heard a soft sigh of regret. "Hey, love...I mean, Sam. I truly am sorry—I just found it, well, sorta ironic. I didn't mean to hurt you. I say 'love' because I care. You're different from the rest, Sam.... and as much as you hate it, I feel obligated to help you," he muttered. Oh really, he felt obligated to help when he actually was ordered to destroy me in the first place? I wondered why I was a specific target, though. There had to be more to it, just being a hunter didn't call for assassination. If that was true, the targets should be the higher-ups. I was just a street killer.

Thinking about his words, I scoffed. "Is that so? Well, vampire, I can help myself," I snapped. I felt him shake his head and stand up. Biting my lip, I decided to ask one thing. "Why do you own silver stakes?" I asked, my voice unwavering. My eyes opened and fixed on him; I wanted to find out exactly what he was up to.

I felt the vampire's eyes piercing me. "I don't only hunt unjust vampire hunters, Sam. I hunt vampires who do evil as well. Call me a murderer if you want...but I like to think of myself as a missionary," he replied.

My response was a surprise to him. "Humph. Well I respect you for that, vampire," I said quietly. My whole outlook on him had changed right then and there. Then I said something that surprised both of us. "And, Goliath, thanks for caring. Not many others in this world do...even to have a previous enemy care means a lot."

Goliath chuckled softly. "We were never enemies." With that he turned and left me to drown in my own thoughts. Luckily it didn't take long for me to fall into a deep slumber.

Chapter 9

I awoke as the sunlight began to fade from the day. Wait a second, I'd been asleep the entire time?! I sat up quickly and took in my surroundings. Memories of last night came flooding back, and I blinked. Where was Goliath?

As if on cue, the vampire emerged from the kitchen. He looked tired but happy to see me awake. "Hey there Sam, glad to see you're well," he muttered. I noticed he was now refraining from using 'love'. His effort to silence a passive label made me frown somewhat. Perhaps I'd been a bit harsh last night.

Clearing my throat, I forced a smile. "Thanks for helping me last night. I really do appreciate it," I sighed. Goliath's eyes lit up. At the moment, they were a striking venom green like mine. Very atypical for a vampire, and something that wasn't a permanent state for him apparently.

In fact, his eyes reminded me of a snake's...oh crap. My eyes widened in realization. "Gah! My family is expecting me home! Oh no. I'm in so much trouble," I snarled. I stood up and began to pace. Goliath looked at me with concern.

"I could help you get home, lo—," he began, cutting himself off with a look to the ground. I let out a sigh.

"It's fine, Goliath," I said, knowing he would get what I meant. I mean, if he naturally called someone that, why should I stop him? I bit my lip. "My family doesn't really, ah, like your kind," I mumbled. Goliath smirked, coming to sit beside me now.

"Not many humans do," he replied, staring at me. I choked in a laugh at a realization. He didn't know I spoke about snakes. I wondered how he would react when I told him otherwise. He gave me a confused look, and I decided it was time to explain.

"I'm not a normal human or hunter, you see. I don't connect with people as well. I do for certain animals, though. Those animals happen to be serpents; in summary, my guardians are venomous snakes," I summed up, waiting now for the vampire's reaction.

Rather than laugh, Goliath raised his eyebrows. "Interesting. Snakes. Why am I not surprised?" he smiled. "Well. We'd better get you back then...love. By the way, have you thought about my deal?" he added. I frowned slightly, recalling it.

"You mean regarding working together? Yes, I've given it some thought. But like I said, I don't work against humans," I responded. Goliath's eyes flashed darkly and looked distant.

"If only you knew that the hunters are just as cruel as the vampires they slay. I want to show you something," he said suddenly. He vanished into the kitchen, leaving me mildly confused.

"Uh," I muttered, wondering exactly what he was going to bring out. The vampire walked in and sat next to me. In his hand was a newspaper.

"Read this," he told me, staring intently now at my expression. After a pause, I took the newspaper from him and read the headline. What I saw horrified me so much I had to wince.

Vampire Capture a Success. Intense Testing Commences.

The town raid of the demonic leeches has led to surprisingly satisfying results. Young and old vampires have been taken into custody for important testing of weapons and practice. This will further advance our knowledge of the best way to kill them.

There were images of vampires being sliced with silver. Molten silver was being poured on one, and on another there were silver nails being driven into the flesh. Most pictures showed adult vampires, but a few displayed the torture of children. "This is no joke, Sam. I've been investigating this for years now, and know exactly where to find whole cities of hunters. This newspaper is an issue from last week that I stole from Huntsmaster City," Goliath growled.

I felt tears spring into my eyes. How could they? During my limited time in the hunter association, I was taught mercy and dignity. Was it all some lie? "There's a reason, of course. It's always the same. Money. The more hunters they hire, the more vampires they kill. Where does the vampiric money go to, love?" he asked softly.

I put a hand on my forehead, suddenly dizzy. "It...needs...to...be...stopped..." I whispered.

"That's why we've been hiding for so long, love. If we emerge from the shadows, we'll be killed without prejudice," he finished, then paused. "Granted, many kingdoms have decided to stop hiding, but that isn't the point right now." I numbly stared into his eyes, knowing now why he hated 'my kind'.

"There's only one thing to do, then. We need to stop this and find equality for all. But vampires aren't angels, Goliath. We need to free the blood slaves too," I explained. The vampire gave a fierce nod.

"Of course, love. And I won't stop until that injustice is halted as well. But I do need your help. I'm a single royal vampire, and can't do anything without allies," he added. Giving a nod, I smiled.

"Count me in," I said firmly. Goliath gave a wide, charming smile and took a sip from his glass. I spotted his eyes again and my own widened. "Crap! My family!" I exclaimed. I shot up and darted to the window.

"Well, you could always use the front door, dear. Mind if I come meet them?" he asked hopefully. Letting out a sigh, I shrugged.

"They won't like you, but sure. Anyway, I need to assure them that I've been with you and safe. Let's go," I finished, now clearly in a hurry, as if it would make a difference. I walked toward the door and blinked, surprised when it opened up in front of me. Turning my head, I caught sight of Goliath's hand on the knob. He was leaning over me with a charming smile.

"Allow me, love," he said, pushing the door open with the palm of his hand. I narrowed my eyes and let out a huff.

"God dammit you're fast. But thanks, I guess," I replied, stepping out. Goliath seemed amused at my awkward response and chuckled. He grabbed his top hat from a hook nearby, still smirking when he returned to the door. I ignored him and walked along, finally recognizing where I was.

"Wait. I've walked these woods for years. Your house, I always thought it was abandoned," I gasped. Goliath shook his head, serious now.

"That illusion is in place because I'm wanted by so many hunters. I need to be able to hide efficiently. Apparently my ploy worked, Red Viper," he chuckled. I bared my teeth, annoyed at his boasting. Ok, so maybe I wasn't the most attentive of hunters. I wasn't a specialized assassin. I aimed to get the filth off of the streets as fast as possible.

"Congrats," I said sarcastically. I moved along with haste, knowing that the snakes would be worried sick. A small house appeared in the distance, causing a smile to form on my face. Home. It had only been a couple days, but it felt like weeks. It was good to finally be back.

"Now they might, er, strike upon seeing you, but that won't matter. Snake venom doesn't affect you, so there are no worries," I explained. Goliath gave a nod, his eyes getting rather serious now. Taking a deep breath, I approached the door and opened it quietly. I tiptoed in and motioned for Goliath to do the same.

All was quiet until I heard a hiss from the shadows. I whirled to see Boomey and Copper launch at Goliath. Their fangs sank into his arm rather deeply, causing the vampire to wince somewhat. Kind of ironic, considering that sensation of being bitten was exactly what a vampire bite felt like. "Guys! It's fine, he's with me!" I gasped. I darted over and pulled the snakes away. Luckily, they let go of his arm. Unluckily, they fixed their angry gazes on me.

"Sambuca! How dare you lie like you did! We were panicking, we thought you were dead! Copper even traveled to town to see it in chaos!" came Boomey's angry hiss into my mind. With a glance to Goliath, I sighed.

"I got sidetracked. I completed my objective. The princess has been slain. She's the one who started the mess," I stated, not really getting into the whole story. "But a new problem has come up. The hunters aren't who they seem, and Goliath has opened my eyes up to the reality of the world," I finished. From there, I explained to my guardians exactly what I had learned.

Copper stared at me for a moment, tongue flickering in and out as she seemed deep in thought. *"So you say that this vampire isn't a villain, huh. What's with the bite marks on your neck, then?"* came her question. My eyes widened as I whirled to Goliath. The memory came back quickly, though. Copper had seen those from a few days ago. There were no new ones. I narrowed my eyes at her little trick.

"Not from him. Trust me. I'm old enough now to know what I'm doing," I hissed. Goliath cleared his throat, and once again I turned to him with my eyebrows raised.

"Sorry for interrupting, but I'd like to say that Sam here has saved my life on occasion. I do wish to aid her in finding these reported blood slaves, and in turn she stated she'll help me with ending this torture. Mark my words, not all vampires are evil. We emerged from the shadows in the city today as an attempt to be free once again. Once the aggressive vampires were eradicated, some humans and vampires there made a temporary peace. The world is changing whether we like it or not. I wish to do what I can to ensure humans aren't, well, I don't need to elaborate on the implication," the vampire finished. The two snakes stared at him, and I could tell they were having a telepathic conversation with one another.

Finally, Boomey let out a sigh. "*I trust that you will protect our little serpent, vampire. I don't know why I do. But you are one with the serpents as well. You can understand what we are saying, even telepathically, which is a gift,*" he said. My eyebrows raised in surprise. Goliath had been following the conversation the entire time. I just assumed he heard my argument along with a series of hisses.

Goliath gave a joyous smile. "Looks like we have a team then, love!" he exclaimed, looking over to me. I rolled my eyes and gave just a small smile. Copper slithered over and draped over his neck, staring at him as if trying to learn more about this strange vampire.

"Fine, it looks like we do. In fact, we should probably get to planning right away," I gasped. Goliath gave a serious nod, his smile vanishing.

We were about to sit down when a crash sounded around the front door. Both snakes let out loud hisses, but it was too late. The power was cut, and I heard yelling from the outside. Something metallic broke through the window, and I realized too late that it was a smoke bomb.

I choked and clawed through the fog. Yelling and laughter filled my ears, and I could see almost nothing. However, a green tint caught my eyes. I reached out and grabbed the tail of Boomey. He turned and almost lunged, but upon seeing my eyes, he refrained and let me pick him up.

The smoke cleared as fast as it had come, and I gasped to find Goliath and Copper missing. Eyes wide, I let out a cry.

"What happened?!" I shrieked. Goliath, while he was somewhat of a nuisance, had saved my life a couple of times. He was a friend now, as much as I hated to admit it. Boomey had a grave look, and turned to me. His tongue flicked in and out of his mouth quickly.

"They have taken him and Copper. Sambuca. They are alive, but won't be in about two days. Copper is telling me the mutterings of the hunters, they must've spied on your little alliance," he hissed. I narrowed my eyes as my pupils practically went into slits.

"Well then. We need to save them. If it means killing the very people who trained me long ago... so be it!" I snarled.

Chapter 10

It was the dead of night now. No sound could be gleaned from anyone or anything. Neither my nor Boomey's breathing was heard as I practically slithered through the forest. All of my training came down to this moment. I needed to defeat the very people who had betrayed me. I had an idea. I was a traitorous being, a snake that turned on its allies in the flash of a scale. *Or so it could be assumed.* No one wanted to be around me nor my snakes. They didn't know me, so perhaps that bit could help.

"Boomey. I want you to be as convincing as possible. You need to tell Copper to come to our side once we arrive. This is critical. We are going to be betraying Goliath," I whispered. Boomey let out an angered hiss. I could tell he was horrified. So I continued. "We need to first explain how idiotic it was for the hunter association to ruin my plans. I'd been trying to trick information out of the prince, they had to come in and ruin it. I was going to use that information to lead entire masses of vampires to their destruction."

Now, Boomey was more flabbergasted than usual. His glowing eyes met mine as he stared me down, simply lost. Slowly, I smiled. "Then, I need to propose a new plan. Torment. In order to torment him, I'll need Copper back. So they'd need to release her... thereby revealing any sort of key they hold to the cell. That's when we make our move, Boomey. Kill as many hunters as you can while I rescue Goliath," I finished.

Boomey was quiet for a moment, just processing what I'd said. Suddenly, his eyes lit up in realization. "*You tricky little serpent. You had me for a moment there, Sambuca...*" he hissed into my mind. I smirked.

"Be as convincing as I just was, and we're golden. Act like a trained snake and arc up upon seeing the vampire. Pretend to despise him like you did. Tell Copper to do the same upon seeing us," I added. Copper probably wouldn't be aggressive at Goliath while I wasn't there. She had no idea about my plans yet. However, if she did so when I arrived, it would appear as if my presence caused aggression in the snakes specifically towards vampires. Her passive mood while I wasn't there could be explained by her strict training by myself to conserve venom and energy.

And so, we kept going. I knew the route I wanted to take, just didn't know how to approach it. When we emerged from the woods, my eyes widened upon staring at the headquarters. The great building loomed over me as if it was going to engulf me and swallow us whole. The walls were black and green, to blend into the forest behind the place.

I could see no guards yet, but I knew they were always watching. I glanced at Boomey. "Time to put your game-face on, snake," I muttered. I casually walked toward the building, keeping my posture tense and my eyes angry. Suddenly, I felt a hand clamp over my mouth and a whisper in my ear.

"Well well. if it isn't the traitor. I always knew you truly were a snake," came the voice of a familiar hunter. He was the guard I'd met with just a few days when I'd picked up my weapon.

Boomey reacted fast—he lunged and sunk his fangs into the guard's hand. A dry bite, not lethal. Yet. The guard let go for a second, leaving me time to whirl, shove him to the ground, and pin him down. Boomey had his fangs bared in his face. I cleared my throat. "Robert Smoke. Fancy seeing you on guard yet again," I chuckled. Then, I tilted my head. "Why the hell did your posse ruin my plans? You idiots caused me to lose a lot of information that I otherwise could have used for the effort," I growled.

Robert blinked, once, then twice. He narrowed his eyes. "What are you playing at? What plan? I only know that you were conspiring with the enemy, Sambuca," he snapped.

"I'll say it again. You're all idiots. All a part of the plan. I had to get the leech to trust me, didn't I? Do you really think a former blood slave would even want to be around his kind? No, of course not. But I did it in order to gain knowledge to use against the vampires. You hunters had to screw it up, didn't you?" I hissed. I stood up, letting Robert catch his breath.

He brushed himself off and fixed me in a glare. "The boss won't be happy about this. Planning without us?" Smoke asked, looking at me as if I'd gone insane. Boomey shifted around my neck, staring right along with me at the other hunter.

"Yeah, because the hunters always mess it up. You have no idea how deep trickery can run, but I happen to. I've been in isolation and planning my entire life. I don't train with others, I study them. I know how vampires work more than you ever will. I work alone, I didn't need you to interfere," I replied. OK so I was bullshitting, but hey, whatever worked.

Robert was at a loss for words. He broke the stare and turned toward the building. "We have the vampire captive. He hasn't spoken since. Perhaps you can get some information out of him." With that, he started toward the headquarters. I hastily followed, unable to help feeling worried about Goliath. I hoped he wasn't being tortured within those walls, he was my partner now. That's all he'd ever be, of course, but still, I felt horrid.

We entered the building through a creaky door and traveled down the long hallway. Robert turned to me and nodded his head toward a certain door.

"The vampire is within. We will be watching. I need to go tell the master exactly what happened just now," Robert told me. He then continued down the halls while I put my hand on the handle. Taking a deep breath, I entered to see a glass cell. The person within was locked to a chair, his head was bent with his black bangs hanging down. Around his neck was a snake, who lifted her head when she sensed me entering. Upon my entrance, Goliath slowly looked up and into my eyes.

Surprise came onto his face as he saw me safe, with clear access to the room. Realization dawned on him. Already he thought I was a traitor just for being able to walk into this room untouched. I grinned, for the plan was working out just fine so far.

"Well well, vampire. These idiots ruined my plan to trick you. Now I'll need to take other measures to get information," I laughed. Copper reared up suddenly and sank her fangs into Goliath's shoulder. The vampire winced in pain from the bite even though the venom wouldn't harm him.

I couldn't tell Copper to let him know of our plan, for his look of relief for the slightest second would be a giveaway. Smoke was watching like a hawk.

"Sambuca, you planned this out? You were tricking me this entire time?" he cried. His red eyes lit up in fury and sadness. He was betrayed, clearly, and his reaction jerked at my heart.

"That's right, leech. And one way or another, I'm going to get it," I laughed. Boomey opened his jaws in an evil grin, followed by Copper doing the same. Goliath stared, dumbfounded. Behind me, I felt the door open. I didn't have to turn to see who it was.

"Exactly *how* are you going to get it, Sambuca?" came Robert's voice from behind me. I smirked, not bothering to face him.

"Torment. This vampire happens to be very sensitive to venom. I know because I had originally captured him and befriended him after he begged me to spare his life. Too much pain to endure, he said. I had found out he was the prince before, so I took that offer and allowed him to save me a few times to feel comfortable. Pity how easily he fell for it. Now my mercy turns to bloodlust," I giggled.

Confusion crossed over Goliath's features. He knew as well as me how immune he was to any sort of venom. I shot him a glance, hoping he'd get the message. The vampire just bent his head, confused along with angered. His rage blinded him of reason, I saw it in his eyes. No matter how nonsensical I was to give a hint, he'd likely attack when freed. Which was fine, as long as he got out. I couldn't let Copper tell him yet still because slowly catching on was much different from being struck with relief.

"I'm going to need to have my snake in order to formulate the proper venom," I explained. Robert rolled his eyes. From within his pocket he withdrew a key-chain. There were two keys. One for the glass prison, one for the chair constraints. He approached the door, glancing at me with distrust.

"I'll get it then," he growled. I smirked and glanced to Boomey.

"You know what to do," I whispered. The snake suddenly shot off of my shoulders and latched onto the back of Robert's neck. He thrashed for a moment but quickly fell, seizing from the venom. I smiled, this was too perfect! I had to act quickly.

I rushed to the glass door and opened it. Goliath still hadn't moved. I approached slowly, cautiously. "Hey, what I said before was a trick. We need to move now!" I growled. He didn't respond, merely glared through his hair with red eyes. Whatever, angry vampire or not, he was not gonna get away while restrained. I was fully confident I could handle him.

I darted over and unlocked his silver cuffs. Then, I jumped away to watch him rub his wrists. His glare fixed on me. "You're a dead snake now," he snarled.

I found myself literally pinned down a second after his threat. I'd had no time to react, there were no warnings. I let out a strangled cry as he leaned closer to my neck. "Goliath, that was part of the plan! Please listen!" I yelled.

Copper and Boomey slithered in front of my neck, now staring up at him. *"We were a part of it too. We just wanted to get you out!"* they yelled telepathically. Finally, Goliath came to. He warily let me go, got off, and stepped back.

"I'm sorry, Sam. My anger overcame me, I admit. But being hungered as I am, well, I'm more prone to confusion and anger," he explained. "By this point I should have eaten an hour ago." I shuddered but gave a soft smile. Vampires needed to feed quite often to upkeep their metabolism, and could lash out at people unintentionally if hungry.

"That's fine. Let's get out of here," I sighed. I turned, only to see the glass cell sealed shut. My eyes widened in realization.

Outside of the cell was someone I thought had fallen. Robert Smoke took off a thick looking brace that had been disguised before. As it turns out, Boomey's bite hadn't really gotten to him in the first place. Ah, neither of us were paying attention and Smoke had been able to take advantage of that. Curse him.

"I figured you'd run this sort of trickery, Red Viper. That's why I planned ahead," Smoke purred. He held up a set of keys. "As in, another set of locks you don't have access to! Oh but don't worry, your friend will survive in the weeks to come if he keeps you alive. You'll get food and water. But he won't!" he added. "Oh yes, and I was promoted recently. There is no other boss, as I am the only one now. That means I can do whatever I want with you and your leech there! This will be interesting to watch."

My eyes widened as I glanced to Goliath, horrified. His red eyes were hungered, more so than I'd ever seen before. Now I knew what Smoke meant. I was going to be tormented for betraying the hunters by the one who I'd betrayed them for. I took a step back right as Goliath stepped toward me.

"I can't restrain myself...love... I'm sorry..." he gasped, his voice laced with agony. I had no time to move away from his lunge.

Chapter 11

Tired, weak, and unable to move, I groaned, feeling my muscles twitch in an effort to actually send signals to my brain. My fatigue was so thick that I couldn't, at the moment, open my eyes. There was a dull ache to my muscles and head. I could hear my own heartbeat pounding in my ears. *Lub-dub...Lub-dub...Lub-dub...* It was fast, as if trying to compensate for something.

But the pain I noticed the most was the sharp sting on my neck. I could feel the wound, it was worse than the first time I'd been bitten. There was no painful venom, but apparently I was especially sensitive to the bite itself, as it signified a certain kind of weakness only prey had. The pain screamed to my entire being, it almost had a mind of its own. *Danger... you're going to die... danger, you've been made prey... you need to run... but you cannot...*it shouted at me. The panic was so sharp I almost began to laugh, I never imagined it to be so miserable.

Finally, I was able to just barely open my eyes. I saw the thin pupils of one of the snakes, I couldn't think right now to determine exactly who. "*Can you hear me? Sambuca, reply!*" yelled the voice of Boomey in my mind. I replied by letting out a wary warning hiss. I didn't want to be bothered right now. Then, *his* voice rang in my ears. Right now I wasn't all that excited to hear it.

"Is her breathing normal? Gods, I feel horrible," Goliath gasped. I could hear his voice tainted with regret and sadness. He saw it as all his fault, and he couldn't control himself. At the moment, I was angry and afraid of him, but I knew deep down that nothing could have been done. It had been the monster beyond the glass that'd driven him to do so.

I felt Boomey slither off, then felt myself being lifted onto Goliath's lap. Now, my hiss grew louder. I wanted to be left alone. "I'm sorry, love, but I want to make sure you're alright, I know you probably don't want to be near me, but you need some warmth," Goliath warned in my ear. It was true to some extent. I felt myself begin to shiver violently as I realized how ice-cold I was. My eyes still barely open though, I tried to focus on his face.

Goliath's hair messily fell into his crimson eyes. They weren't the hungry red like before, but vibrant and more full of life than I'd ever seen them. I saw a red stain on the bottom of his lip. It was distorted, as if he'd tried his hardest to wipe it away. But it was still there. The stain of my blood. He'd done something that he'd never be able to take back, something I'd never forgive or forget(well, so I claimed). But right now he was trying to fix what he could.

"Leave...me...be..." I barely managed to whisper. Goliath gave me a wounded look, as if I had struck him. Some prince of the night he was. But he didn't leave me be, in fact, he pulled me closer. I tensed and yet again let out a hiss. Then, a voice from beyond the glass. There was no one I could possibly hate more right now.

"Aw, the love fest between the King Cobra and the viper. Fancy to see that the cobra devours the viper, hm? Along with the rest of her pretty snakes, they will fall to the cobra when he gives into his hunger," Robert Smoke mused. I could hear him walk back and forth outside of the cell. I had no voice at the moment to retaliate, but Goliath did.

"Ah, hunter. I remember seeing you somewhere. Smoke, is it? You've been able to avoid me for quite a while," came Goliath's smooth tone. I could hear the smile in his voice, as if this were some sort of game. He was trying to hide his worry from the enemy, a tactic I had yet to master. "Hm well. It's a shame that you assume I have feelings for my prey, I can assure you that I do not. Let's just say you provided me a gift. I'd been planning on tricking this piece of livestock and keeping her in my clutches as a blood slave, but it looks like you set it up for me. You plan on providing her with food for weeks, and nourishing me through her? Perfect. I will only grow stronger while she grows weaker. You *know* as soon as I breach one bit of this prison, I will kill you all and take her. Really, sacrificing her for your studies might help you a little, but it will help me more," he chuckled.

I tensed. He couldn't mean it, could he? My shivering increased, but I felt Goliath's grip tighten. I then heard Robert Smoke snort. "Oh please. I can see you ran to her rescue soon after she awoke, leech," he remarked.

Goliath just laughed again. "All a part of the act. You know, you'll be paid handsomely for this opportunity. You study my blood needs, and get research as well as gold when I am released," Goliath hummed.

"I do this to rid the world of leeches like you. I don't do it for the gold. By learning the length of time a vampire needs in specific conditions, I can time my huntings just right," Robert Smoke snapped, a clear lie.

"Hm interesting. But you can't imagine I haven't done my research, Smoke. I'm fully aware of your being a mercenary. I'll let you research and keep up the act. I'll even fake a death, but I'll pay you handsomely when you allow me to leave with my new blood slave. You ruined my act to draw her in, but you secured her as mine. What will it be, Smoke?" Goliath questioned in a low voice.

I heard Robert pause, as if he was thinking about it. Slowly, he chuckled. "Alright vampire. You think you have more gold than the hunters who make millions every day off of the slaughter of your kind?" That made my heart clench, but right now I was focused on Goliath's seemingly huge betrayal.

"Ah hunter. I *know* I have more than a thousand times that amount. And you know it, too. Think about it, will you?" Goliath said softly. I heard Robert chuckle, followed by the sound of footsteps exiting.

There was a silence that fell upon the room. I heard a voice in my head, one that I was dreading. "*I cannot speak aloud I'm afraid, love. They are watching us from the cameras,*" came Goliath's worried voice. I writhed in his grasp only to be pinned down by him. My eyes were still shut tight, but I felt him lean to my ear.

"Don't struggle anymore, slave, or you'll find yourself in a lot more pain and missing a hell of a lot more blood," Goliath said, just loud enough for such a camera to hear. I felt tears slide down my cheek.

"*Listen to me, Sam. I need you to listen. What I said was a lie. If I'd wanted to take you as a blood slave, I'd have done it the first night I saw you. There were several occasions where I could have, hell, I even captured you at one point. If I really had wanted to prevent your escape, I would have taken a lot of blood to weaken you. But I did not. Sam, listen. These hunters think that my kind places complicated plots into everything. We have that reputation. That is why I set it up to seem like my want for you being a blood slave is some elaborate plan. Those words are a plan into a deeper plan. Please, continue to struggle, then give up, then I will finish explaining. We need to pass this act on."*

I felt myself being shoved into the wall. Then, I felt Goliath lean closer to my neck. I let out a whimper and opened my eyes, fixing them on him. Goliath's red eyes were pleading, but he had an evil smile that frightened me. "If you give up now, slave, I will spare you for a bit tonight. I have taken enough blood already, but that doesn't mean I won't take more if you continue to fight," he growled. I was too weak to fight back anyway, so I let my muscles just relax. I heard Goliath's cruel laughter as he stood up and walked to a chair that had somehow appeared in this odd cell. His eyes fell on me, watching my every move.

"Now. I can continue, just please lay there like you've given up. Robert Smoke is the leader of your organization. He cares little of who he sacrifices in order to do his 'research'. He's one of the leading torturers of vampires. Now, he is led by greed. He works for Huntsmaster city, but gold is always on his mind. He betrays his own kind for money, yet he keeps up his noble act. If I pretend to be on the malignant side of the vampires, he will fall for it and accept the money. He'll let us go, after I make a treaty and agree to betray my own kind to work with him. Sam, the sole reason he murders vampires is to get their money. If he can do it without killing them, he will, because he can make even more money off of live ones. I have built my reputation to be a dark one among hunters, but my castle is one of lies. You'll hear things about me that are horrible, some that are untrue and some that are *true.*

But that isn't important now. You need to act this out with me, pretend to be defenseless and afraid. Unfortunately I might need to bite you a couple more times, but I need to ask if you'll be able to handle it. By playing this off, we can escape not only with our lives, but vital information on the corrupt hunters," Goliath finished. My head swirled with confusion.

So, Goliath was a liar to society and himself? His reputation was a very deadly one, huh. That was news to me, but I supposed I didn't get out much. I had never known about how corrupt Robert Smoke was, but I should have seen it. There were too many hunters vanishing in battle for me to be alright with, though I never brought it up because I figured the matters did not concern me. This problem was very real now, however. It was staring me right in the face. All I knew was turned over. And to be honest, I didn't know who to trust.

Goliath, despite what he'd done, seemed to be my best bet. I reasoned with myself that he was right, why would he go through some elaborate plan to capture me as a slave here if he could have easily done it in the first place? Smoke did not know how often we'd met. He could assume we'd just met once or twice, and were going to make final moves to kill each other soon enough. He didn't know how many times Goliath could have taken me, or how many times I could have killed the vampire. He knew nothing, just what Goliath had told him. If I played my part right, Goliath would be proven right. And as much as it scared me, I planned to.

"*I will, prince,*" I hissed in snake-tongue. Goliath understood. His eyes hardened.

"*You will see me as you have not before. I will be terrifying, you will be convinced that I am a monster. Remember Sam. This is all part of the act. And I won't be reminding you by mind, it takes away from any fear you might show. Just keep your wits, this will be hard,*" he sighed in my mind. I just twitched my head in a nod-like motion, something not suspicious but that would be understood.

Boomey and Copper sat beside me. They'd been following the conversation uninterrupted until this point. "*We will strike back as your guardians when he attacks you, Sam. We'll be here for you, but do not spoil the plan when he harms us too,*" came Boomey's voice. I exhaled sharply.

"*I will not severely harm them. I don't want to have to do this, but it's all a part of the game, all a part of the act. We need to show Smoke how scum I am, and he will be convinced that I will work with him no matter what because I am despicable. He will think that I'll give him gold if he betrays his own. I will ask for more blood slaves for money, in the meantime getting information from each exchange. But in order to convince him, again, I need to be a monster,*" Goliath finished.

"*Do your worst, vampire. I'll play along,*" I sent back. The game was about to start, and if we won, we'd be released. But I knew that it would not stop there. I would need to keep this act up a while after we were free, until we could strike Robert Smoke where he was the most weak. I was prepared for it, though. By appearing weak, I would be stronger than all.

Chapter 12

Yet again I awoke with a groan. My head still hurt, probably from last night. I looked around, noting how Goliath slept in a bed across the room. Things just seemed to appear here, I assumed it was helpful magic of some sort. My eyes turned to the glass, spotting nothing but a blank wall. I glanced to the ground, noticing the plate of food having somehow gotten here as well. I narrowed my eyes, letting out a slight hiss.

Boomey and Copper slithered beside me, trying to catch my eyes. "*Are you alright?*" came the hiss of both into my head. I gave a shrug, slowly crawling over to eat the food.

It was pretty much very rare meat, of what I had no idea. It practically dripped with blood, which was quite ironic. Yet, it was what I normally ate, and Smoke knew it. He wanted me to stay strong, perhaps to see how much of a challenge I was to Goliath. I sank my teeth into the meat, devouring it quite easily. My sharpened teeth made ripping into flesh rather easy, yet other foods harder to devour. Still, it was worth it since I needed the extra protein for speed and agility. Plus, I would learn later that I required a more meat-based diet naturally.

I tilted my head, noticing how Goliath's soft breathing was quieted. That meant he was awake, and that I needed to move quickly. My hands still a bit bloody, I darted to the side right as I heard a frustrated hiss sound by my ear. Goliath had tried to lunge, but luckily I'd leaped out of the way just in time. I turned to face him, kneeling and ready to leap aside again. The vampire smirked, causing me to grow worried.

"Well Viper, it looks as if Smoke will allow me to leave with you as mine. Time to break you, to make you obey. This will be very painful if you don't submit, human," he mused softly. I bared my teeth and responded with a growl. Goliath lunged again, and this time it was slightly easier to dodge.

I skipped to the side, whirling out of the way of another attempted grab. I had no weapons in here, and my venom did not work. I was out of options, and could only run. Smoke knew this was what I feared, I had no idea why he wanted to torment me like this. Perhaps Goliath was completely right, that he was only in it for the money. But I had to wonder if there was a reason for him targeting me specifically.

"Stay back, Goliath, you backstabbing leech. I'll rip your heart out and eat it myself when I have the chance to!" I yelled quite loudly. I didn't mean it as long as Goliath didn't mean what *he* said. I saw a glint in the vampire's eyes, indicating that he knew exactly that. Good thing we both were acting quite well. That didn't mean I'd let him bite me again if I had a choice.

Goliath began to move, circling me, coming closer and closer each time around. I smoothly turned along with him, keeping my venom green eyes on him at all times. Oddly, he was still in his suit. The only thing he was missing was his hat. It probably looked quite odd that he was stalking me in his fancy garb while I sat here in my raggedy combat clothes, all black as usual to blend into the night.

Then, he struck. I swiftly dodged another grab only to be thrown across the room as Goliath switched direction and shoved me to the side. I twisted and landed on my hands. Desperately I used them to propel me forward, now trying to get to my feet. It was too late; Goliath caught hold of my leg as I tried to rush forward. I had no time to stand. I felt myself being dragged toward him, comically letting my sharp nails scrape along the ground as he pulled. I let out an angered hiss as he gave a final tug and brought me against his chest. To restrain me, he put one arm across my stomach. I bucked and struggled now to no avail.

"Bad decision to run, Viper," he whispered into my ear. I felt him lean to my neck again, this time tensing all of my muscles. As the warm air of his breath hit my neck, I lifted my head and sank my teeth into his arm. Goliath, caught by surprise, loosened his grip just enough. I put all of my weight against his arm and broke free, taking advantage of his hesitation. I was sent tumbling across the cell, out of control but able to right myself just as Goliath realized what happened.

He gave an enraged growl, now playing the game seriously. Acting or not, it was horrifying. He soon revealed a power I had not quite known he had. The room was growing darker as mist and shadows gathered. Goliath gave a smile as the darkness consumed both him and me. I couldn't see anything, and there wasn't any noise to his movements. I closed my eyes, feeling Boomey and Copper encircle my arms. "*You know where he is, Sambuca. Feel it... you can feel it...*" Copper's reassuring hiss stated.

I took a deep breath and focused. *Lubdub...Lubdub...Lubdub...* Goliath's heartbeat was close, and was getting closer. No matter how faint and fast a vampire's heartbeat was, I could feel it. The very minor vibrations of his footsteps reached me as well. The problem was, he almost seemed to be gliding. One second he was one one side of the room, the next he was on the other. He was everywhere at once, which was very confusing. As he got closer, I moved swiftly, feeling along the wall. He was behind me... no, in front of me...shit, I had no idea. The only thing I knew was that he was growing closer.

I gritted my teeth, now sensing him just a few feet away. I changed direction, but now he was right there in front of me.

Nope, false.

My eyes flew open as I felt myself being grabbed from behind. Once again I was restrained, once again I struggled. I let out a desperate cry, feeling the snakes slither off my arms and onto him. Goliath just chuckled as I sensed the snakes bite into him. I gasped as he threw me against the wall. Then, I sank to the ground, wincing as my leg got the brunt of the fall. I watched as he grabbed both Copper and Boomey in one hand, then threw them across the room. They landed together in a heap, both hissing in pain.

Now, Goliath turned toward me. I tried to stand, only to sink down as my leg failed me. It wasn't broken, just strained to the point of being useless now. I frantically tried to crawl with my arms away from him. The vampire just walked toward me, in no hurry.

He approached, slowly laughing as I scrambled along. This was fun to him, my attempt to get away. My head swam with pure fear. Because of my damn past, I was terrified of what was to come. The fact that venom didn't affect me did not matter one bit. Since I was not looking forward to the bite, it made the problem no less painful. The more blood I lost, the weaker I became, which was something that frightened me to the core. I didn't want to be a slave again. And this time I knew *exactly* what was coming, unlike the last few times, when I was caught by surprise. I saw Goliath's fancy shoes stop right in front of my face.

Slowly, I turned my green eyes to look up at him. His red eyes were amused, as if he was a cat playing with a mouse. He bent down and offered me a hand. I didn't take it, just stared. "Ah, love, it's a shame we can't play this game of chase anymore. You're hurt, and hey, I'm hungry. Looks like both of us are in a bit of an uncomfortable situation. Well, not me, not for long," he hummed. With that, he grabbed my arm and held me close. I struggled again, lashing out with my claws to no avail.

The only response I got was yet another laugh. He waited no longer. I felt fangs sink into my neck again and screamed. The vampire drank hungrily, gulping down mouthfuls of blood, enough now so that I was too fatigued to even move. He sat on the ground with me limp there on his lap. He ran his fingers through my hair, humming like this was just typical and normal. I felt tears crawl down my cheeks again, this time I was too weakened to wipe them away.

"Just a little while longer, Sam, I promise," came his concerned voice into my head. I just looked away, my rage and fear growing within. My eyes closed, but I could hear someone speak on the other side of the glass.

"You really aren't working with her, are you, vampire. Your method of torment is interesting... might I ask why you didn't just go for the kill?" Smoke's voice sounded out. Goliath laughed again, I could tell he was giving the amused 'I have all the time in the world' vibe.

"Adrenaline, the buildup of fear, makes the blood more empowering. Also improves the taste, I suppose. Though, my kind likes toying with their victims. It comes naturally," the vampire responded. I heard the scratching of a pen on paper as Robert apparently wrote something down. "So about our deal, Smoke," Goliath began, expecting a response.

I heard Smoke let out a sigh. "You realize if I let you go, I will be betraying my entire race?" he questioned. Goliath just responded with a snort.

"When has that ever been a problem?" he asked softly. I shifted slightly, letting out a moan of pain. Goliath just let out another chuckle. I could sense his gesture toward me.

"Mhmm. That one's been a problem to me anyways. Getting rid of the vampires that target those who waste the town's resources. Sometimes we need population control. She seems to not get that point. The people taken by the street leeches provide no revenue. I'd care a bit more if she targeted the real problems, the vampires that go after the association itself," he replied. I almost felt sick at those words. "But, anyway. The association makes money, that's all. I already know it is more worth it to let you go, but I have a feeling you won't keep your part of the deal, prince. I'll keep your slave here while you fetch your money, and you can trade it for her," Smoke promised.

Goliath paused, as if thinking for a moment. "That's fine, hunter. I promise you'll get your money, Robert Smoke. Do not let her free, then. I've weakened her enough." Goliath stood up; I felt myself being placed on the bed, then listened as his soft footsteps approached the glass. I had no idea how he'd get out, but I was still too weakened to lift my head to see.

"*I'll be back, Sam. We've gathered so much important information about how corrupt these people are based on their leader. Listen, I won't hurt you anymore; I am going to go get the gold, then come back to save you. We won't be able to attack right away, he's got several hidden traps and such within this place that even a royal like me should think twice about. We'll need to plan out where to strike—but in the meantime, stay strong. I won't leave you here, I promise,*" he whispered into my mind. I couldn't care less whether or not he kept his promise.

I knew what he did was necessary, to show just how despicable he was, but I had a hard time trusting him still. Smoke would only have believed him if he betrayed me and seemed to want me as a slave. He put his money on me being important to Goliath, and the vampire did prove that by 'playing with his food'.

I hated this game, though, and still had no idea why Smoke would be so traitorous. I put my money on it that it wasn't only him, but the entire society benefiting from this. They were greedy, money-hungry assholes, and they put on the act to the rest of the world that they were 'just' only to make *more* money. Discovering this was painful. Literally.

Chapter 13

When I woke up, my dizziness was almost too much to handle. How long had it been at this point? A few weeks?

I was flat on my stomach, uncomfortably sprawled on what appeared to be a bed. I rolled to my back and yelped as a hiss sounded right by my ear. Boomey slithered out from behind my neck; I must've ran over the snake when I moved. "*Sorry,*" I hissed quietly. It was hard to talk, and my mouth was very dry. I sat up with significant effort and spotted a glass of water beside my bed. Desperately I grabbed for it, chugging it down so fast I choked on the last few swallows. After a coughing spree, I lifted my head enough to see through the glass.

Smoke sat there, watching me with a look of, was it, pity or sadness? I didn't know nor did I care. My eyes narrowed as they met his. I bared my teeth and spoke through them. "Why, Smoke? I was taken into the hunters as an outsider, I was trained, I was different, but I was accepted for the most part. Only to be betrayed here and now. Is this just you? Why do you despise me so?" I said, just barely loud enough to be heard.

The hunter tilted his head, focusing on me. A strand of snow-white hair fell into one of his eyes, to which he didn't bother moving away. He just sat, deep in thought. Finally, he spoke. "It's not that simple, Sambuca. Times have changed. With the wars and crisis going on in the human world, corruption is bound to happen. In this case, I'll admit the hunters are indeed corrupted, and I'm one of the bigwigs within the issue. I'm looking out for my own community, a community of people who can be assured they are safe, and that have plenty of *resources*. Sambuca, why do you think we target specific vampires?

Kingdoms have wars, and we are mercenaries. We have the illusion up that yeah, we hunt *all* vampires. This isn't true. We strike deals with the most powerful among them. They agree to provide protection in exchange for us doing their dirty work and providing them with blood. Yes, we do offer non-hunters to them, that's why roadside leeches are important. I have no qualms with sacrificing an outsider to save ourselves. Anyway, with you, a rogue hunter going around slaughtering freely, it's angering the kingdoms we ally with. Even if you target roadside scum, some of those vampires could be associated with a particular kingdom and stop in. The vampires are pissed. By offering you to the prince of the nearest kingdom, the vampires will continue working with us."

I was appalled. Even if this was all acting on Goliath's part, it still hurt. I had been doing what I'd trained for all my life, and that was killing vampires. I spared plenty of them, I killed those who deserved it the most. Yet, this is what it had come to. Because it was 'inconvenient' that I wasn't killing specific vampires, I was being given as a blood slave. The hunters seemed not to even bat an eye. Well, I had no idea if anyone else knew aside from Smoke. I'm sure if they did, they wouldn't care regardless.

My hand flew to my neck. I felt the bite marks and shuddered. I'd been bitten again and again, so my trust for Goliath was vanishing. I was aware of the acting bit, but I couldn't get the feeling out of my head that I just needed to escape, to run. *Too much time had passed.*

That would be my plan, then. Escape at all costs. I needed to make sure Smoke wouldn't stop me. "*Boomey... Copper... Please, I want you to find the area where the door opens to allow food and such within this cell. Once you do, figure out a way to get through and find the keys. I'll take it from there,*" I hissed quietly. Smoke took no notice to my hissing, in fact I think he assumed I was doing it in pain.

The snakes gave slight nods. I now knew that it was time to act a little more. I swooned and fell flat on my back, sighing. I went limp and closed my eyes, pretending to be passed out. Hopefully Smoke would take the bait. I laid like that for five minutes before I heard Smoke get up from his seat. As soon as he exited, the snakes were on the move. I turned my head slightly and half opened my eyes to watch. They slithered on the side of the wall, feeling for any cracks or holes. After several long moments passed, I was beginning to fear they weren't going to find anything. Just on the point of giving up, I heard a hiss of hope.

"Here, here! I feel a slight indent in the wall. It goes deeper as I press into it," came Copper's hiss in my head. A pause, then another happy hiss. "*This is odd, it is a section of the glass that bends like rubber to an intense bit of pressure. But it is very small, as I press my head against it, only a small area moves. This bit of odd glass, probably tampered with by magic, is probably used to bring in food and water. Other larger stuff might be transported by magic or by opening a hidden door,"* the snake finished. Interesting, I wouldn't have ever thought of pressing up against the glass hard enough to feel for something like that.

The snakes worked together to move through. It was like watching them burst through a bubble when they got out the other side, and the 'glass' just reformed again. They got to the search for keys straightaway. My heartbeat increased as my hope sank. They couldn't find a key, no matter how hard they looked. It probably was time to take it up a notch.

"*The keys are probably held by Smoke,"* I hissed with a sigh. Boomey lifted his head, letting his tongue flick in and out. His huge eyes fell on me, and a look of sadness sparked in his eyes.

"Then we will need to get them from him. I'm tired of seeing you hurt, Sam. We will do everything in our power to help you," the snake promised. I gave a hopeful smile and told myself to just stay strong. I watched them slither off, and felt more alone than I ever had before.

The silence stretched. I couldn't tell if hours passed or just minutes. I heard footsteps approaching, and voices. "That was rather fast," said Smoke. The footsteps got closer, I sucked in a breath as the next voice hit my ear. It was smooth and soothing as ever.

"Ah yes, I'm looking forward to having her as mine forever, hunter. The payment is in the briefcase, surely enough and more to cover for the cost. Do not fear. My Kingdom will continue to support your community as promised," Goliath hummed. Both entered the room now. I snapped my eyes shut, yet could still feel both of their eyes falling onto me. Where were the snakes? I'd unfortunately get my answer soon enough.

"Oh Red Viper? I have your pets caged up here, you're lucky your master is allowing you to take them along. Quickly now, awaken so we can finish the transaction," Smoke chuckled. I don't think I could hate anyone else on the planet more than I hated him right now. I heard thrashing against glass, and knew that the snakes were restrained in a tank.

"Ironic," Smoke commented, "that she is caged up now like the snake she is." I heard the jingle of keys, then the sound of a wall moving against another. The cage was open, and now I could attempt my escape. Maybe not how I originally planned, so now I was just winging it. I rolled off the bed and lunged.

My eyes fell directly on the cage, and Smoke was taken by surprise as I bolted at him and shoved it out of his hands. The tank fell and shattered, sending shards of glass everywhere. Several pieces landed in my arms and legs, but I ignored the pain. I reached down and grabbed the snakes, swiftly dodging Goliath's attempt for my arm. I turned my head up to him and let out a hiss.

Then, I ran forward, opening the door to this room and slamming it behind me. I heard a frustrated growl as it hit my pursuer, that being Goliath. "You didn't secure her?!" yelled the vampire to Smoke.

I didn't stick around to hear the hunter's reply. I darted around the corners, this way and that, unsure of where to find the exit. I passed by several other hunters, who glanced my way but continued on to what they were doing when I didn't stop. What, were they used to this sort of thing?

I found a window that streamed in the sunset and knew I'd reached my escape. I opened it quickly and landed on the ground, swiftly darting forward as fast as I could. I could outrun a vampire, even with their intense speed, but right now I was very weak. I needed to hide out.

Not looking back, I ran for my life. I had no care if Goliath meant me no harm. I was on the run, I was being hunted. The fear was still there, and I just wanted to get away, from both Smoke and him. Soon enough my leg gave way, however. I fell so suddenly that my impact to the ground almost crushed the snakes. They slithered out of the way just fast enough and crawled in front of my face.

"We need to continue on! He's almost here," Copper hissed into my mind, sounding extremely worried. I just relaxed, seeing no point in continuing. No longer able to run or hide, this was it. I'd tried my hardest, but here and now, too weak and in pain to continue, I hadn't done enough.

"I can't any longer, guys. I'm sorry, you just go. I don't want you to be hurt because of me anymore," I whispered. The snakes just hissed at me, angered I'd suggest such a thing. "Please go? Go find help, I don't know?"

"We aren't leaving you," replied Boomey. They coiled in front of me, trying to reassure me within my mind. My eyes shut as I heard a twig snap beside me. I knew my chances had run out.

"Nice escape attempt, love. I paid Smoke, now we'll be heading to my home. Smoke isn't around, I'm not going to hurt you. I promise. Just relax," Goliath's voice sounded from above. I tensed as he lifted me. I felt the snakes crawl onto my arms, and tried so hard not to pass out this time. The blood loss from the glass had weakened me too much, my fatigue from Goliath's feedings had not faded away either. Back there, I'd run on adrenaline. Now, there was nothing left, just pain and exhaustion. I closed my eyes and let everything fade, but not before I heard what sounded like laughter. *Evil* laughter.

Chapter 14

H*issss.... Hssss....* That hissing, was it me? I realized that the drawling growls and hisses were coming from my mouth as my body vibrated along with every noise I made. Now, I writhed and thrashed like a trapped snake, unsure and confused as to exactly why I did so. My eyes flew open, and I could only see heat. My eyes were that of a snake's and I was unsure why. What?

I slithered along, wait, slithered? *What? Am I a snake?* I wondered to myself. To my utter surprise, I got a reply.

"No, Sambuca. You are seeing through my eyes. I cannot detect noise like you as well, as you know I have no outer ear drum. But I'm assuming you can read the lips of humanoids and process it correctly," came Coppers voice in my head. I was so confused, and I couldn't blink. So how the hell had I opened my eyes from the start? "*You went right into my mind, Sambuca. I had no idea you could do this, but I can hear your thoughts and I know you're there. You can also control my actions to a degree. This is odd, but I was on my way to view your captor. I trust you won't give us away,"* finished Copper. So we were both crowded up in her mind, huh? I had to wonder how I got here.

"Alright Copper. Sorry about this. I'm not meaning to do it, uuh... my bad," I tried, smiling guiltily. This caused Copper to do so, which was awkward since she slightly opened her mouth in a crooked position. I heard a hiss of laughter coming from me/Copper.

"No worries. Just watch, just feel." I felt myself slither along the ground and saw the lights dim as we went into the shadows. I tensed as a huge figure came toward us, made up of a mass of reds and yellows. Ah, a humanoid. There was a registered recognition within Copper's mind that communi-

cated with mine. Both of us at the same time realized Goliath was there walking with, well, someone else.

"Vampire," Copper thought. I twitched my/her tail in confusion. How did she know? *"I've been in this body my entire life, Sam. I can recognize things through my eyes that you cannot. It's good that you're here, as I continue not to understand lip-reading. Watch."*

My eyes turned up to watch the lips of Goliath move. Heat surrounded them more than the other parts of his face, probably due to more blood flow in that area. Made sense. I focused on what he was saying to this supposed other vampire. Finally, I was able to fully understand, not by hearing, but by seeing.

"....I had to, brother. I care not if she was my target. You very well know I was due to slaughter her months ago. I'd been tracking her carefully, but she's different."

Then, the lips of the other person began to move. I turned my head to watch, focusing carefully as they formed words.

"Regardless. You're going to ruin our entire plan. You cannot spare one hunter, not with it being so easy to destroy them! She'll warn them of our deception. The kingdoms have worked with that scum for so long, they trust us! They even give us their own as a blood slave! You cannot work with her, Goliath. You need to lock her away until we take back what is ours."

I held in a hiss. What plan? Goliath had never informed me of this. I turned my head as he began to speak as well.

"My thoughts on taking back what's ours have changed, you know that. I saw the light when I saw her. I know I've killed more than any of you. I've silenced more hunters than I can count anymore. Don't you think I want their terror on us to end? But we don't need to do so by killing them all and enslaving the innocent humans. You saw in the city, there was a truce. We can work together."

So, Goliath was a killer, more so than I'd ever imagined? Great. I knew now I needed to get away, and fast. The other person, still unknown to me, began to speak once more.

"I'm telling you right now. The humans will turn around and kill us, like they did once before. Do you not recall? Once there was peace between us, then the hunters began the slaughter for no reason. Not to mention, the other king-

doms are not nearly as merciful, and would scoff at our mercy. It's time we become the dominant species again, and like hell am I going to have our kingdom fall behind. Goliath, if you don't either kill her or lock her away, I will. And you know the consequence of going against me."

I saw Goliath hang his head, and became horrified at his response.

"I refuse to kill her. But I will restrain her long enough for us to silence the hunters. Brother, you must promise me this. The humans that mean us no harm, we can't enslave them like we originally planned. Please... that is all I ask."

I saw the other figure shrug and turn away. I could not see his reply, but I saw Goliath's final words to him.

"So be it. I'll lock them away as well until we are ready to set them free with a proper system I set up. I'll go get Red Viper straightaway, she can't remain active while our forces grow. I'm well aware they want her dead as well. I'm going to do all in my power to prevent that."

Copper turned so suddenly that I hissed in surprise. "*Hush! I could see what they were saying in my mind because of your translating. We need to get back to the room, quick! You need to wake up!*" she yelled in my mind.

All went dark as I closed my eyes again. They'd been open? I felt my pupils return to normal, now I knew they'd shifted to snake-eyes while I'd been in Copper's mind. I sensed her approaching the door of the room I was in, hastily I tried to open it for her only to discover it was locked. Joy!

Boomey was wrapped around my arm, seeming to be focusing on something. After a moment, his eyes turned up to me. "*Copper told me everything you saw. We need to get out of here NOW!*" he hissed.

"*You think I don't know that?!*" I replied in my own hiss, just as I heard footsteps approaching. My eyes narrowed as I heard a surprised voice outside my door. A voice that, at the moment, made my heart clench.

"Copper? What are you doing out here?" Goliath asked softly. I closed my eyes rather quickly again, slowing my heartbeat and breathing. I was pretending to still be asleep. Hopefully he'd fall for it. I'd tricked several vampires into thinking I was unconscious this way, and when they least expected it, when they went to feed, I'd lunged. In this case, any lunge would be ineffective. I'd need to wait it out.

I heard Copper's hiss as Goliath picked her up. "I'll need to put you in a tank. I'm sorry Copper, but for now it's necessary. Same with Boomey." He entered the room and circled the bed. I heard his footsteps stop right in front of me as he gently grabbed Boomey. Both snakes hissed furiously, both yelled in my mind to just stay put.

"He's not going to harm us. You need to get away, to get some trusted hunters to help. We know what the vampires are up to now, regardless if Goliath means no harm, the others won't be so merciful. You need to save them, Sam. Please, just leave us!" yelled Copper into my mind. She made damn sure the link was only to me and that Goliath could not listen in like last time. I was so reluctant to do so, I couldn't leave them behind. But then, Boomey added something that I couldn't ignore.

"We love you Sam, and it would torment us to see you caged up again. Save us later, I promise we will be ok. Don't let us down, don't come back until you know you can win!" he finished. I knew then that I wouldn't be seeing my snakes for a long while. I'd need to save myself and them by making proper decisions.

I heard the steps fade as Goliath took them away. For several long moments, I heard nothing. Suddenly, though, the sound of more footsteps hit my ears. I sucked in my breath and told myself to calm down. *Stay asleep... stay asleep...* I told myself, trying desperately not to have a reaction. The scary part was, this person wasn't Goliath.

A smooth male voice, a bit lower than Goliath's but with a tone like that of a snake-charmer wove through the air. "Hmmm. I don't understand why my brother wants to spare you. I know he's tasted your blood before," he chuckled. Suddenly, my chin was being held by a very strong hand. It took literally everything not to thrash or struggle.

"You're too weak even to wake up now, when you're in danger the most. If I were him, I'd lock you away forever, taking just enough blood each time to make you pass out. Then, repeat. I'd never run out. Pity, too bad Goliath is merciful now. He was never merciful before," the vampire whispered into my ear. I felt him let go and move away. He was walking toward the door now. This was my only chance.

My eyes flew open, and I knew he wouldn't expect this at all. The vampire whirled, but I was already past him. I bolted down the hallway, running for my life. I heard that laugh, it was the *evil* one from before I'd passed out. "You clever little hunter! Goliath can't stop me from having one bite or two now, since you've doomed yourself!" he cackled. I didn't turn, didn't stop. I just ran like I never had before.

That is, until I almost ran head first into a certain someone. I came screeching to a stop as I met the eyes of Goliath. The vampire furrowed his brow, clearly confused. "How did you recover so quickly?" he asked quietly. I lunged away from him right as he grabbed for my arm.

Unable to go past him, I whirled and saw the *brother* coming right for me. He looked sorta like Goliath, but his hair was shorter and spiked. He was a lot darker in style via a leather jacket and with spikes sort of like a biker; his skin was pale, like Goliath's. His red eyes were crazy, insane like he wanted nothing but chaos. It was a far-cry from the gentleness of Goliath's eyes, though right now I wanted to be away from *especially* Goliath.

There was a door right closest to me. I'd have to go toward Goliath's brother though, something I was reluctant to do. I needed to act fast, however, so I threw the door open and rushed inside. From there I slammed it shut, right in the vampires' faces. Luckily there was a classic lock there, of which I hastily clicked into place. Of course I knew they could rip it from its hinges—that's why I needed to act.

The room itself wasn't horrifying, but there wasn't a window in sight. In fact, it was a giant library, with thousands of books. I was in awe for a half of a second before I heard the banging of the door, and Goliath's voice. "Let me in love, I promise not to harm you. Please, don't run, it'll make things all the harder," he yelled.

His brother chimed in a reply. "There's nowhere to hide. You might be a snake but we're the cobras just waiting to devour you," he laughed. This was all some joke to him, apparently. Well, I was not coming out. I heard Goliath hiss at his brother.

"Please, you promised to leave her alone. You can aid me in catching her, just don't harm her!" he snapped. His brother sighed and probably nodded, I didn't care. I was too focused on hiding.

I darted around the bookcases, all while listening to the wood bend and groan to the force of the vampires. It would not hold much longer. I leaped into a spot where there were not many books, essentially an empty spot in the bookcase. I then did something disgusting but necessary. I grabbed the dust from the books and rubbed it all over me, trying hard to disguise my scent as fast as possible.

I put a stack of books in front of me, good thing this section of the wall-shelf was deep enough to fit both me and the stack. Luckily I was just in time. The door burst open in a series of splinters. Now, I was being hunted. I stayed completely still as the vampires stalked around the bookcases. Goliath's brother chuckled to himself, while Goliath just hissed lowly.

I steadied my rapid breathing and lied in wait. They were getting closer and closer. I saw Goliath walking toward me, not yet seeing me, until of course his eyes fell on my hiding spot. He didn't look away, either.

Chapter 15

I resisted shrieking as Goliath strolled over and reached for me, only to grab a book. He let out a sigh, obviously irritated. Thank gods my scent was disguised enough that he hadn't detected me quite yet. That was a matter of time, though. Opening the book, he scanned it before saying, "She's probably gotten out by now. We took quite a while breaking down the door."

His brother just laughed, I could hear he was near as well. "The only way out is the back of the library. We would've seen her by now," was his response.

Huh.

So that's where I could make my escape.

Goliath shook his head and put the book back. He turned away and began walking toward some bookshelves a few ways down. If he got far enough, I'd be able to make a run for it. The vampire approached his brother, looking around with narrowed eyes. He let out a low hiss.

"I can't scent her either. She's a clever one," he grumbled. The other vampire raised his eyebrows, now rolling his eyes.

"Why do you even wanna spare her, Goliath? She's just a hunter. You've killed so many. Why not her?" the brother asked curiously. Goliath's eyes glinted for a moment in alarm. It was almost as if he was worried about this vampire finding out about, well, whatever he was hiding. Actually the question was a good one. Why *did* he care?

"Uh... She could be used for later. For information and such," Goliath replied. I detected the lie in his voice, and wanted to know more, but realized the vampires were enough of a distance away from me for me to make my move. I shoved the books, ignoring the clamoring noise they made as they crashed to the ground. By the time they'd both turned, I was halfway across the library. I zigzagged down the aisles, knowing they'd be on my tail soon. Vampires were fast, but after training all my life I could outrun a vampire for about five minutes before collapsing of exhaustion. Which is why I needed to escape and hide as soon as possible.

The shadows reached out to me as I finally got to the end of the library. I looked around wildly, frustrated as I ran back and forth, looking for a window or door. What in hell? There was no such exit, and that's when it dawned on me.

"Tsk tsk, love. I might not have been able to find you, but I figured you'd fall for his trap," came Goliath's voice in my ear. A powerful arm crossed over my chest as Goliath's face lowered to mine. I turned my head slightly, showing no fear as I tensed and let out a low hiss. "Now now, I know you're aware of what's happening. This planning runs deeper than I originally told you. I'm not betraying you, merely protecting you. You'll understand soon enough, Sam."

"Let me go, leech!" I spat, venom in my voice. Goliath's eyes hardened, clearly he was offended by my insult. I meant it, too; my old term for vampires held heavy meaning for me after Goliath's betrayal. I spotted his brother walk in front of us, grinning as usual.

"Aren't you a feisty one. Still don't understand why my brother doesn't just lock you away and take a good, long drink," he chuckled, leaning into my face. I snapped my sharp teeth when he got too close, causing him to blink in surprise. "Alright brother. Where exactly are you planning on shutting her away?"

"The black cell. I'm sorry love, but you're too crafty for me to risk anything," Goliath sighed. I let out a screech at the mention of the black cell. Having learned about the true vampire castle, I knew of its most notorious dungeon. I'd thought it was just a myth. In truth, the black cell was a dark room, with no light or sound. It was a padded cell, one of those they used in insane asylums. I heard horror stories of hunters being kept in the vampiric castle, shut away until they turned insane. I had no intention of ending up like them.

"Why Goliath? Why are you doing this to me, I thought we were working together?" I whimpered. I felt Goliath turn me around, but he kept a firm hold on my arms. He looked into my eyes, looking both guilty and sad. He couldn't keep his stare, and after a moment his red eyes turned to the ground.

"Sam... you'd be opposed to the true intention of the royal family. My views have changed, but theirs have not. I need to work with them and stop certain horrors from unfolding. Let's just say their idea is to finally end the age of humanity and reclaim the world for their own. Both you and I know that would result in a lot of death, something I need to prevent in this kingdom at least. With you running free, I know you'll just end up getting yourself killed. I'm doing this for your own good," he explained.

I bared my teeth, now thrashing in his hold. "I don't need your help. Goliath, I *will* get away. I *will* destroy you for this, one way or another. Any deal we had before?! It's off," I snapped.

The vampire shrugged. "So be it. You'll see eye to eye with me soon enough, love," he sighed.

"Or your eyes to my neck, leech!" I growled. Goliath seemed surprised at my accusation, but he honestly shouldn't be. He betrayed all of my trust, now it was time for me to escape and save the innocents from *his* plans.

Nothing more was said, not by me, Goliath's brother, nor Goliath himself. I was dragged against my will through the place, which was much larger than I originally thought. So. I was in the kingdom itself. The Elapid Kingdom, where most vampires in this area lived, held most of its royalty. The castle was of the vampire king, a cruel man really that had no care for humans. Fancy that Goliath was a direct son, then. His brother walked alongside me, glancing every so often toward me with curiosity. I didn't struggle. Not yet.

"Hm, little snake, what is your name?" asked Goliath's brother. Goliath glared but said nothing, just continued to carry me along.

"None of your business," I snarled in response. The vampire chuckled and looked ahead, pausing for a moment before replying.

"Well. My name is Prince Ash. Your kind is very interesting. How you struggle even with no hope at all is admirable, but of course it will be put down soon enough," he added. That made me writhe in Goliath's grasp.

"Brother. Enough. She's upset enough already," he hissed.

"Some prince you are, Goliath. Will you betray your people like you betrayed me?" I taunted. Goliath winced, but didn't respond to my question.

"Interesting question. Goliath *will* inherit the throne once the old king passes. His time is coming, you see. He's been drinking blood for thousands of years now," Ash commented. I knew that contrary to belief, vampires were not immortal. They lived for millennia, however did eventually die of old age. If they lived that long without being slain, that is.

We were getting closer to the fabled dark cell, so I would need to act soon. I was desperate, ready for any chance of escape. I had no idea where to run, I just knew I needed to get out before it was too late.

So suddenly I went limp that Goliath let go of my arms. I dropped to the ground, much to the vampire's surprise. From there I rolled away and got to my feet, already on the run. Goliath's angered growl hit my ears, and he wasn't that far behind. "Well played, love. I didn't expect you to just relax like that. I'll have to have a harder grip on you next time," he muttered.

"There won't be a next time!" I replied. I heard Ash laugh, he was running with Goliath now. I turned the corner, knowing instinctively that they would catch up very soon. I was already tired from sprinting this fast, and slowing in any way would allow them to catch me. I turned one corner, than another, listening to the hungered hisses that came behind me.

"If I catch her, Goliath, I'm personally punishing her," I heard Ash say.

"If you catch her, Ash, I'm going to rip your throat out myself. She's mine," Goliath replied.

"Touche," Ash chuckled.

I narrowed my eyes. *His?!* No way in hell. That inspired me to continue on, faster than before. There were several doors I passed by, and I didn't enter them, as I wasn't planning on becoming trapped again. I turned a corner and came upon a spiraling staircase. My eyes widened at how far down it went. I delayed for not even for a second, and rather than running down the stairs, which would take way too long, I leaped onto the railing and slid. Kinda like surfing but a lot more dangerous. Good thing I was trained in balance.

I heard Goliath's surprised gasp as he saw me disappearing in the twisting turns of the structure. The vampire's red eyes met mine, and I gave him a smirk. I saluted him and leaned forward, causing me to go faster. I figured their agility, though commendable, wouldn't be as in depth as my own. Not many would be able to follow what I was doing without falling straight down into the black abyss.

They followed via stairs, which would delay them from me. I would have a chance to hide and outsmart them, then. When I reached the bottom, I could barely see. Torches lit the dark stone walls. I was in the dungeon. This was the place where they'd been taking me, but they hadn't locked me away yet. I knew how to play hide-and-seek. It was time to get the game started.

I darted behind a stone column right as I heard the vampires reach the bottom. Yet again, I grabbed some dust and granite to rub all over myself. Not a moment too soon, as I heard Goliath curse and say, "She's managed to hide her scent again. I almost picked up on it to track her. Now everything down here pretty much smells the same."

Ash's chuckle rang out yet again. "Having an issue finding your prey, brother? It shouldn't be *that* hard to catch a hunter you've been tracking for months now."

That bit made me shudder. I heard them continue to argue as they passed by. My eyes turned back to the stairs where we came. They assumed I'd ran off deeper into the dungeon. The column I was hiding behind wasn't exactly the best hiding place. I'd had to flatten myself against the wall and hold my breath as they passed. Like in so many occasions in a game of hide-and-seek, they'd failed to notice me as they passed. They had been too focused on what was ahead, so now they'd not catch me.

When their voices faded down the dungeon, I crept away and toward the stairs. Slowly, one step by one, I seemed to glide up the stairs. Slow and steady, making no sound. I was sacrificing time for efficiency. At this point I couldn't outrun them up the stairs if they heard me. I was probably three-fourths of the way up when I heard a very loud exclamation below.

"Dusty footprints lead up the stairs, damn it. How could we not have noticed her?!" came Goliath's furious voice. My time had run out. I quickened my pace, though now I'd outdistanced them enough to feel somewhat safe. If I found a window, I'd be golden. My footsteps echoed as I ran panting and out of breath. I returned to the twisting halls, making one turn, then another. Perhaps they'd make a wrong turn when tracking me and buy me time. I couldn't hope for such a miracle, though, because time right now was of the essence.

Finally, I found a window large enough to allow exit. It was partially hidden by dark shades, I had to double-take to actually see it. I peeked outside, making a note that it was still midnight. The moon shone bright and full, which ironically would help me find my way.

Giving a frustrated growl, I realized the window was locked. My fingers shook as I worked on the very-rusty window latch. It took a little too much time to undo, and I almost cried in relief when the thing finally gave way. I threw the window open and took a leap, only to stop as all but my legs had made it out of the window. A voice hit my ears. "Looks like I was the one to make the *right* turn."

I looked back to see Ash's hand wrapped around my shoe. He grinned as he began pulling me back through the window.

Chapter 16

I snapped my head around and fixed my glare on Ash. Baring my sharp teeth, I twisted my body around, cracking my leg in the process. I didn't care about the pain. My body now fully bent over my leg, and I had sunk my teeth into the vampire's wrist. Ash let out a surprised yelp of pain. I jerked my head back and forth, sort of like how a dog whips around when tearing into meat or a toy. Literally chunking a bit of the vampire's flesh, I growled like a rapid animal during my attack.

Ash refused to let go. If anything, his grip tightened. Now, I kicked and twisted my foot, feeling it become looser and looser. I turned to Ash's face and spat the wad of bloody flesh toward him. He was so surprised his grip did loosen, just enough for me to twist free of my boot. I shot forward, falling a few feet from the window. Knowing the vampire would be on me in an instant, I got to my feet and bolted forward. There was no time to look back, no time to check and see if I was being followed.

I saw a dark figure leap in front of me, but I was on such an adrenaline rush that I merely leaped aside and bypassed this new threat. His voice hit my ears.

"Keep running, love. I'll catch you eventually," Goliath yelled. His smooth demeanor had turned sinister rather quickly. I should have figured I couldn't put any trust into him. Now, I was in vampire territory. I was fresh meat to anyone who happened to be hunting. And well, I had no venom on me. My snakes were caged up, and I hadn't had time to gather venom from them for my own use. But wait, something within me told me that it was not a problem. I felt liquid flowing through my gums, a natural venom my body produced.

Knowing that I needed to investigate, I looked ahead to see a looming dark forest. The sound of a babbling brook reached my ears, much to my relief. The swift footsteps of my hunters were still very closely behind me, but I had an idea on getting away.

Shadows whizzed past me as I ran. I knew that if I got away now, I would still need to get out of this kingdom and back to the human world. I knew what the vampires were planning, knew about the scandal of the hunters, and how they really hadn't been protecting the people they promised at all.

Most important, though, I needed to rescue Boomey and Copper. They came first, they were my family. I cared not if others disregarded other animals as lesser—to me, they were everything. I wasn't stupid enough to go back without a plan, not yet. I knew Goliath, as despicable as he was, would not harm them. He seemed to have a connection with the snakes like myself.

After what seemed like forever, I plunged into the shadows of the woods, running directly toward the sound of churning water. I guessed the vampire caught on when I heard a loud yell of alarm from Goliath. "No Sam! Do not go that way! The river means certain death, please, I will not harm you, come back!" he begged. Then, for the first time in a while, his voice spoke within my mind.

"The Blackwater Rapids are never chanced by even my kind. I will not lock you away, Sam. Please don't do this..."

I scoffed, running forward faster than I ever had before. "I'd rather drown than run back to you, leech!" I screamed. The brook, which now I clearly saw was a roaring river, was just ahead. I sped up one last time and took a leap.

The plunge into the river was a huge shock; my muscles locked in the deep freeze of the water. The currents ripped at me from all sides, so when I finally convinced myself to start swimming, I had a hard time. Already I was underwater, and the ice-cold river seemed to fill my lungs past capacity. I managed to hold my breath after gulping in a lot of water, now noting that my chest burned from the effort.

After what seemed a lifetime, but could only be seconds, I broke the surface. I wildly moved my arms and legs, swimming with all of my might to wherever I could go.

My strength was fading fast, and I could barely see above the rapids. When I did spot something, my heart dropped. As I knew I soon would as well. The river just stopped. It was like the edge of the world, and I was approaching it fast. No, it wasn't the shredding tide that Goliath warned me about. I would be able to handle it, had there not been a huge waterfall ahead, one that I was sure had a long, terrible fall.

I knew it was futile to swim against the river. Rather, I desperately tried getting to one of the banks as I was pushed toward the edge of death. Fear seized me as I felt the pupils of my eyes once again deform to slits. I let out an inhuman roar and swam best I could, finally able to sight land.

The edge of the falls was coming fast, but if I tried just a little harder... no, I would not make it. I'd fall just a foot short. I could tell within the split second I had that no matter what I did, death would strike me like I had wanted. Now, I wasn't so sure I'd rather die than face Goliath. At least alive I'd be able to try to save the innocents within the city, along with my family.

No, I wasn't about to give up, though. My hand grasped for anything that I could possibly grab on the edge. To my utter surprise, my fingers closed on something—or someone.

I looked up into Goliath's eyes, noting how they were worried and afraid. For me? I bared my teeth at the vampire, but didn't let go. He began pulling me toward him, when suddenly a huge branch slammed into our arms. We both had been too focused to see it coming. I was forced to let go, thereby sentencing me to a certain death.

I screamed as I went over the edge, wincing as I heard a splash above me as I began to fall. Goliath would die too. Why was he doing this? He had jumped in, for what?

Time seemed to stop as I turned my head to look down at the bottom. The perilous drop was much too far to have any chance of survival. This free-fall forced my life to flash before my eyes, primarily my huntings up to the point where I met Goliath. I had a mission to complete. I could not do that while dead.

I felt my arm being grabbed, felt myself being pulled toward the vampire. Even he couldn't survive a drop like this. With insane reflexes, he shoved me above him and wrapped his arms around my chest. That way he'd take the fall for me, and there'd be an extremely small chance that *I* would survive. The impact would be mostly taken by him, anything sharp at the bottom would hit him first. Goliath would die because of my recklessness, and I felt absolutely horrid for it.

Why I cared, I had no idea. He was a traitor. I tilted my head, wondering why he was doing this. He cared that much, huh. Well. The time to act was now.

I always knew that I wasn't truly human. The way strength coursed through me, my way with snakes, it wasn't natural. Everyone avoided me, I was so different, and now I knew why. As I threw my head back to let out another deafening roar, I knew my aura was completely off kilter for a human.

I knew why I was immune to venom.

From my back sprouted wings, bat-like wings that spanned a huge distance. Now, it wasn't Goliath who was holding onto my arm. I grabbed his, flapping once, then twice. I was sent spiraling into the air, spraying river water as I went. Lucky I had done so right in time. We'd just barely avoided hitting the sharp rocks below. I flew to the bank and landed with a thud, panting. My sharp teeth dripped with water... and something else. It was much easier to walk on four legs, rather than two, I found, but at the moment collapsing onto my side was the easiest. Goliath appeared much smaller in my eyes as well. He was sitting there in shock, staring at me like I was a monster.

"What?" I asked, but found the words only came out in a guttural growl. I sat up, narrowing my eyes from the effort. Goliath backed away, now awestruck by me. I paused and looked down at my arm. Or, what I thought was my arm.

It was covered in crimson red scales that looked razor sharp to my eyes. I growled in confusion and opened my hand. I had five fingers, yes, but on a paw-like hand. Long claws came out the end of them rather than nails. I shook my head, whipping my tail back and forth as I tried to figure out more. Wait... what the hell? Tail? I looked behind me to see a scaled, spiked tail wagging behind me. I could twist easily, and now I had a full view of my back. It had red spikes running down it, going between my wings. What was going on?

"Your dragon form. Sambuca, you've discovered how to use it?!" the vampire gasped in disbelief. I snorted, as surprised as he was. I flopped back to my side, letting my mouth hang open in exhaustion. Goliath circled around me, rubbing his eyes as if I was some illusion. Apparently he seemed to know more about this than I did.

Slowly, I felt myself shrink . My scales vanished, and I was left lying there in tattered, black clothing. Apparently my clothes morphed with me, but got ripped apart by my recent adventures. I coughed, spitting up quite a bit of water before groaning.

"My what?" I whispered, confused. I mean, I knew what a dragon was, but never really guessed that I *was* one. How was this possible?

"That's why you've grown in power so quickly. Your true powers are starting to come through. Oh gods, Sam, you saved both of our lives. You could have let me fall," the vampire added, stuttering now. He couldn't stay on one subject. I didn't bother sitting up.

"Leave me alone, leech. I might have saved you, but won't hesitate to destroy you if you capture me again," I warned in a low growl. I was exhausted, yes, but felt the power coursing through my blood. If he made a move, I would end him here and now.

"I'm not planning on harming you, Sam. For now, let's just sit here while you gather your strength. I thought your form would be dormant for a while," the vampire added.

A voice came from behind us. "Dragons died off a while ago. We made sure of that, for good reasons, but you were supposed to get rid of this last one, brother. Good thing she's just a halfling. I'll need to take it upon myself to lock her away, and hey, dragon's blood is very empowering since you refuse to kill her. More power for us!" Ash cackled.

One question formed in my mind as panic seized me. Why did vampires 'wipe out' dragons a while ago? And how long did these two know of what I was? It seemed very similar to what they were trying to do to humans.

Chapter 17

I heard Goliath let out a hiss of warning. "Ash, give it up. Clearly we've won here, we don't need to destroy her," he muttered. So he thought he won, eh? I opened my eyes wide, blinking as my pupils went to slits once again. I let out an inhuman growl of warning, knowing that once I got my strength back, all hell would break loose. The vampires knew it well enough too. Little did I know, they weren't concerned about it one bit.

Ash gave a yawn and took a step toward us.

"There's a reason we killed off her kind, Goliath," Ash growled, his voice serious. "Dragons remained a threat to our race up until recently. There's no way we could have seized control of the world with dragons guarding those petty blood bags."

Goliath shrugged, seeming to know fully what his brother meant. I blinked, confused. So what did *Ash* mean? I knew nothing of my kind, in fact, knew nothing of myself. I only knew that Ash wanted to destroy innocent lives for his greed of power, as things always went. As for Goliath, well, I didn't know much anymore. He was always leaning one way or the other, and at the moment I distrusted him as much as I did before.

Goliath's eyes darkened in thought. They glimmered mischievously as he looked toward me once more. His voice said two words in my head, two simple words that I unfortunately understood.

"Play pretend."

"Fine Ash, you win. I'll go along with your plans, on one condition—we keep the dragon alive. You do know that we can *use* her to take over the city, correct?" he asked softly. Ash rolled his eyes, crossing his arms.

"She wouldn't listen to us if her life was in danger!" spat the vampire.

Goliath shook his head, an evil grin spreading across his face. "No, she wouldn't if it was her," he began, his eyes meeting my own green. "But she would if it meant saving the lives of her precious snakes," he laughed.

I let out a weak gasp. "You wouldn't," I hissed.

"Oh, but I would, my precious little serpent. Ash has unblinded me from your prior hold on my mind. I'm aware of the tricks of your kind, trying to bend me to your will and save the weaklings of the city. Well. Now that your brood is threatened, I trust you'll betray the city to save them," Goliath whispered, loud enough for both me and Ash to hear.

I gave a frustrated roar, but could make no move to get up. Another one of Goliath's plans, and apparently he was acting. He and I both knew I had no idea I was a dragon prior to the recent events. We also knew that I didn't have control of his mind at any point in time. But Ash had no idea. Why, after he knew he betrayed me, did Goliath think I was going to work with him now?

Well. Quite honestly, it was all I had. Playing in this little game of fake-out would delay me long enough to gain strength, and eventually turn on them both.

"I'm going to keep watch on the snakes then, brother," Ash growled, untrusting. A flash of alarm could be seen in Goliath's eyes, but only for a second. The vampire nodded, accepting his brother's words.

"That's fine brother. Meanwhile, I'll train our little dragonling for the attack on the city. She'll comply if she ever wants to see her snakes alive," he chuckled. He bent down and lifted me in his arms. I was too tired from the river struggle to even move.

Yet again I was to be confined. *Please...not the blackcell...please not that...* I pleaded in my mind. To my surprise, I got a response.

"No, love. I'm not keeping you in there. My original plan to 'keep you safe' is down the drain, thanks to your escape tactic. Ash is out for your blood if you don't listen—now we'll need to both work together to prevent the bloodshed."

I rolled my eyes, letting out another weak hiss.

"We coulda worked together before, rather than you locking me away, leech!" I replied to him, knowing he'd hear. The vampire tensed, but did not slow in his step. He let out a sigh.

"Sam, please don't call me that. You might think I betrayed you, but again I was trying to protect you. I was blinded by...er... nevermind. Anyways, I'm fully aware that you're strong enough to fight for yourself. Before I was questioning it. Now I have no doubt in my mind. But you need to trust me, love, I know it's hard. Really, though, I'm the only one you got."

It was my turn to sigh lightly. What he was saying was completely true. I closed my eyes, finally giving a slight nod. I knew that Ash was walking up too far ahead to see my or his little actions.

"Fine, Goliath. I'll trust you once again, but I swear to gods if you betray it, I'm going to kill you, and every other vampire I see. Regardless of innocence, Goliath, do not mess this up again."

The vampire looked down at me, I could feel his stare. I opened my eyes up and stared dead on, daring him to say something against my word. Rather, he did something that surprised me so much, I was silenced for the rest of the walk, in mind, words and action. Stunned, rather, because the vampire leaned down toward my face, touching his lips to mine. I tensed like a snake, my eyes widening then closing. I felt something like fire brewing within me at the kiss, a feeling I never had quite felt before. And it scared me quite a bit. My mind faded out, going blank as finally I gave into the darkness of exhaustion.

BLINK... BLINK...

Again. My eyes flew open, and I was beginning to think that they'd never look like a normal human's again. I looked human, I could feel it, all but my eyes. I hadn't taken much notice of it before, but the green orbs with the tiny strip of darkness within them shoulda indicated that I was not even close to human. They used to only do this when I was upset, but now they remained this way, and would forevermore. I don't know how, I just knew it inherently. I'd discovered my true self, which of course left many unanswered questions.

I looked around the room, noting the stone walls and the chains surrounding me. I myself wasn't bound, and in fact was in a rather comfortable bed. I sat up, rubbing my eyes, feeling the extra film go over the surface and back under my eyelids as I blinked. Jeez, I was so reptilian I had an extra eyelid. That bit creeped me out just a little.

I stood up and walked to the door, which was made of wood and had bars over the windows. Figures, I was trapped again. Well, I got out every other time before, this time would be no different. Except, my captor was about to enter. The doorknob turned slowly, prompting me to take a few steps back and bare my teeth.

Red eyes met mine, and I found myself relaxing just a little. "Goliath... you've shut me away again," I commented, not really putting any weight in my words. Rather than retaliate, the vampire passed me by and just sat on the bed, staring up at me. He motioned for me to sit next to him, which I was hesitant to do so.

I observed the fact that he was again in his fancy suit and top hat. Looked like he hadn't lost it in the first place. Either that or he had another one. Anyway, myself compared to him, I felt a little...awkward. No idea why, it's just with him in that fancy clothing and me in my tattered, ripped shirt and jeans, I felt out of place.

I shook my head, annoyed with my thoughts. Narrowing my eyes, I briskly went to take a seat next to him, holding in an aggressive hiss.

"Not permanently, love. I'm doing this to lead on Ash. He thinks you're contained well enough. He doesn't know of your power," the vampire chuckled. I crossed my arms, raising my eyebrows.

"Hm, he doesn't? Nor do I; please explain," I snapped.

Goliath seemed surprised, he furrowed his brow and tilted his head just slightly. "You do not? So that show of power back there, truly, really, that's the first time you found out what you were? None of that was you just pretending not to?" he asked. At my nod, he paused for a moment. I gave a slight growl.

"I was sold as a blood slave at ten years of age, Goliath. Dragons obviously don't care for their young!" I spat, an inner hatred burning within.

Goliath's eyes filled with sympathy, something that I hated to be given. I didn't like being pitied, not when so many others had it worse than myself.

"Oh... I never knew, love. But what you say isn't true. No. Your true parents did not give you away. Dragons treasure their hatchlings, even if they are hybrids. To have a human form like yourself, and not having found out for this long that you're a dragon, you're most clearly a human-dragon hybrid. In order for that to happen, your parents loved each other dearly, and therefore loved you. You were probably their *everything*...but well, dragons didn't last very long when..." Goliath stopped mid sentence.

I nudged him, urging him to continue. He was pale, paler than normal. It was as if the story haunted him, and he was very afraid to tell me. After a deep breath, though, the vampire continued.

"When my kind decided to wipe them out. It was my father's idea, really... you see, dragons guard the humans. Human-dragon relationships are forbidden, but clearly your parents ignored those rules. That wasn't the issue, anyway. My father originally targeted humans, the wretched fool wants to wipe them out and take over the world, as you know. Well, like I mentioned, dragons guarded humans for their own reasons. I did my research—it wasn't to protect them like you want to, for your ever-so-good deeds. No, most dragons are greedy. Humans provided them immense wealth, be it after wars or raids of themselves or other beings(in some cases, even vampires).

They paid the dragons in gold and treasure, and in turn the dragons guarded the humans with their lives. Even when long forgotten, dragons aided from the shadows and were paid by the few humans that still knew of them. Well, my father knew he needed to get to humans, so he cleverly planned out how to destroy all dragons. He used deadly poison, fey iron. Fey iron to dragons kills with just a tiny dose. It does not affect humans." Goliath muttered.

His eyes fell on me, clearly he was deep in thought. "The dragons were wiped out, or so we thought. Actually, there's rumor of a city someplace that...well, that's not important right now. Gods love, your human hybrid side probably saved your life. I'm assuming you were fed a bit of fey iron at one point and survived. When your human parent caught on, they probably took you away and tried saving you by passing you onto another couple. Obviously, it backfired," he added with a slight smile.

"Yeah, that's an understatement, Goliath. How the hell do you know so much about my past when I have no idea myself?" I questioned. Goliath avoided my gaze, now I *knew* he was hiding something more.

"I guess I should say, Sam. I read in a letter, back when I was younger, that my father was on the hunt for a, to put it in 'nicer' terms, freak. A dragon mix. I had heard the dragon parent was killed, and the human was on the run with the child. I, at the time, was curious, because I never had heard of such a thing. Sambuca, that child was you. You were never caught by my father, yet he's still hunting you to this day," Goliath finished, his dark red gaze almost staring into my soul.

"And now, Ash knows," I whispered, causing Goliath to tense.

"And even though I am to inherit the throne, Ash wants it a hell of a lot more," he added in a whisper.

Chapter 18

Right at that moment, at the *best* of times, Goliath's brother made his entrance. Still clad in black with his usual spikes and such, he grinned to display his sharp fangs. I glared at him, keeping in my reptilian hiss for a later time. The vampire slowly walked up to us and leaned to my face, his red eyes crazed. "It seems Goliath has been talking to our little hatchling, hmm? It would be a shame if father found out about her, eh Goliath?" he hummed.

Goliath tensed, for the first time in a while, I saw fear flash across his features. He gave a cough. "Ash, didn't we agree we would take care of her ourselves? That bastard is too old and sick to do a thing about our master plan," he growled, his expression twisting into one of anger.

Ash merely leaned closer to me, causing my lip to curl ever so slightly to reveal my sharp teeth. "Maybe so, but he could still order her death, hm? We have thousands of guards on our side, after all. All are thirsty for just a little drop of dragon's blood," he whispered softly. He turned to Goliath.

"Like yourself, dear brother. You dined on a hell of a lot of dragons while we were killing them off, eh? That's how you're so immune to venom. If you don't want me to let the king know about her, then you must prove she is yours, Goliath. You've bitten her before. But prove it again, here and now, to me. Then we can begin training our little slave," Ash hissed. I widened my eyes at this new knowledge and hastily shuffled across the bed, away from Goliath.

The vampire in the top hat sat still, his red eyes cold and calculating. I heard his voice in my head, no words of reassurance at all. "*It must be done, love. Once more. Then, we can get him off our backs and plan out what to do from there."*

He then turned to me, his lips curving into a grin. "Why doubt me, Ash? You know I crave dragon's blood. That's why I've been hunting her!" he laughed. He then did something unbelievable; the vampire lunged right at me, pinning me down without me able to have any reaction. I let out a roar of alarm, noting how Ash stood by and watched with a cold smile.

Well. I wasn't gonna sit here and be bitten again. My roaring grew louder, and from within my stomach I felt pure heat. As Goliath leaned to my neck, I tilted my head up and opened my mouth wide. Flames billowed from within, burning off the ends of Goliath's black hair. I had not been able to aim correctly, as I sorta was being held down, but I got the message across.

Goliath loosened his grip out of surprise, enough so that I was able to cross my arms, push up against him, and flip him off of my while propelling myself away, off the bed and toward the ground. Wings sprouted from my back as scales covered my body. Within seconds I was fully transformed into the crimson dragon I'd been back at the river. I was probably around sixty feet in length, including my tail. Though I had length, I didn't have bulk. My venom-green eyes fell on Ash—he was the cause of this.

The vampire widened his eyes in surprise as he turned, obviously attempting to run. I leaped at him, gouging his back with my black claws and bringing him down in one blow. Now trapped under my claws, the vampire thrashed and hissed to no avail. I lowered my head, aiming to bite his off. Yes, I was indeed *planning* to do that, but when my maw reached where his head should have been, Ash was gone. I saw a stain of blood from where I'd wounded his back, but that was all. Giving a confused growl, I tensed as I remembered Goliath behind me.

"He's gone, love. In seconds, there will be hundreds of guards out to destroy you. We need to get away fast," he said. I twisted to see him, my nostrils flared and smoking.

His red eyes met my green as I bared my teeth in his face. "*We?!*" I snarled. Goliath looked down, letting out a sigh.

"You can feel free to try and run. I, however, know the way out of the city, and the way to your family," he added softly. Immediately I gave a frustrated cry, batting my wings in distress. The snakes! Boomey and Copper needed to be saved, and they needed it right away.

I felt myself shrink down to my human form and clenched my teeth at the effort. I used a lot of energy transforming one way or another, it was something that I'd need to get used to.

"Don't let my trust down like you almost did *again,* vampire," I replied. Goliath accepted my compliance with a grim nod. OK, perhaps I could have avoided all of this by letting myself be bitten again, but an angry dragon wasn't the most reasonable of creatures. Anyway, he lunged at me, literally sweeping me off of my feet. When I snarled in surprise, the vampire merely chuckled.

"What, it's a proper way to carry a damsel in distress, dear," the vampire joked. I snorted; this was no time for kidding around.

"Dragons are not damsels," I snapped.

"To the vampire prince they are, love. Quite fiery damsels, yes, but quite beautiful as well," he added. I rolled my eyes, because this was not the time for flirting either. How dare he even try it with me, he knew it wouldn't work. I was not going to admit that I liked his kiss, either, cause I didn't. Trust me, it was horrid. Absolutely horrid, I'd never want another one.

...Well. Maybe one, or two. Gah!

Anyway, he ran down the halls, making turns this way and that. The vampire prince knew exactly where to find the snakes. They were being kept in a cage near a bed that I presumed was Ash's. He gently put me down, causing me to shove him away as aggressively as possible(though he took it playfully and just laughed) as I snatched my snakes away from the glass tank.

I turned away only to see the door blocked by a ton of vampires. Ash's voice came from behind them. "I figured you'd come for them, dragon. Shame that my brother is working with you, he's going to die as slowly and painfully as you," he hissed. I saw him come from in between two vampires. "Don't kill her. She's mine," he told the others.

As you can imagine, all chaos broke loose right then. I shifted to dragon form more rapidly this time, giving an angry roar as I blew flames onto the oncoming vampires. The snakes stayed wrapped around my wrists, or in this case, front ankles. *"Make no move to attack-this is my battle! And when I say run, RUN!"* I hissed to them.

"But Sam—" came Boomey's voice in my head, but I cut him off with a hiss. It was important that they listened to me, it did not matter how I felt.

"Do you want me to endanger myself again by needing to save you a second time? When I say run, do it!" I scream-hissed. The snakes shut up after that, knowing that I was not a force to be trifled with.

The vampires had me backed against a wall, they pointed swords in my face to prevent me from lunging forward.

I took a deep breath and opened my jaws to let another round of flames bathe them. The problem was, their shields blocked my fire. Ah—I hadn't taken that into account. Of course they had fought dragons before.

Now, I raised my arm and struck at them with my elongated claws. Several fell, but several more sliced up my arm. I roared in pain and leaned up against the wall even more, moaning as swords sliced at me from all sides. No matter how many I took down, more took their place. Red blood flowed from my wounds like a river. Soon the previously white carpet was stained pure red from my blood mixed with those I had taken down.

I finally fell to my side, sobbing with pain as blood flowed from in between my scales.

"Freak! Kill the freak!" I heard them scream.

"NO! Mine to claim!" yelled Ash. The other vampires calmed down and parted to reveal Ash. He strolled up to my face, holding a glowing golden dagger.

"Goliath! HELP!" I cried, for the first time in my life begging for his aid. But no help came, because the vampire was gone. I couldn't even sense him in the room. I felt myself shrink down to human form, using my arms to cover my face now.

All the clamor silenced, and I could hear footsteps slowly approaching me. I felt Boomey and Copper lunge up at my pursuer, then heard their hisses of terror as they were ripped from my arm. I uncovered my face and grabbed for them, only to be held down by two very strong vampires. Tears ran down my face as Ash held the snakes by their heads in one hand to prevent biting. With his other hand, he withdrew one knife. He slammed the snakes against the wall and literally stabbed them through the tails, letting them hang there and writhe in agony.

I screamed in horror, now making a move to strike at Ash. The insane vampire just slapped me with such force that I was forced to lay on the ground for a few seconds.

He grabbed the collar of my shirt and leaned to my ear. "Well, aren't you in an awkward position, hmm? I'll take a little dragon's blood before I torment you by first slicing open your dear snakes while making you watch. Hm... I'll cut off your eyelids before I do so to prevent you from closing them, how does that sound?"

Before this point, I never thought someone could be so evil. This vampire was more corrupt than Robert Smoke. He wanted to do this to me?! I could only imagine the torment he wanted on all the innocent humans he sought to destroy. I was so wounded, and there were so many vampires, that there was nothing I could do. They all just stood there, staring lifelessly. Ash was the commander of a puppet army, and I knew he would do horrible things with it.

He leaned down toward my neck as once again there was nothing I could do as fangs sank into my flesh. I gasped in pain as the vampire greedily drank quite a bit of blood. The light began to fade to shadows. Wait, no, it wasn't only me seeing this?

"Sir...? The shadows are growing unnaturally," one of the guards said. Ash paused in his drinking, letting go and wiping his mouth of my blood before looking around. All too quickly the darkness thickened so that I couldn't even see Ash. As I heard hisses of panic, I definitely knew it wasn't just me now. Then his voice, I'm not sure I would ever be so relieved to hear it, came into my head.

"*You killed about twelve of them, that's impressive, love. I know even you can't take down the mass of them, though. Sorry I took so long, but I got a few of my close followers as well. Not the entire kingdom is against me. Luckily I knew where to find my allies*," Goliath whispered in my mind.

Now, I heard screams echoing all through the room, and knew that he really *was* coming to get me out of this mess. Not before my current captor did something about it, of course. I was tossed aside and frozen in horror for a moment as I heard Ash's words.

"You think you can save your dragon? I'm sure you can, for now, but you certainly can't save her precious serpents!"

The hisses of pain that came from above me could only be from the snakes I'd known and loved for years.

Chapter 19

"NOOOOO!" I screamed, just as the shadows parted to reveal both Boomey and Copper *split in half* by the knife of Ash. The vampire cackled in delight of my horrified expression. Their blood dripped down the walls as their eyes, forever clouded, seemed to stare into my soul. There was no light within them. They both were simply dead.

Memories flashed before my eyes.

I was a young teen again, just running through the woods, having the time of my life. I had no worries for just that one day, and my snakes slithered right alongside me. I giggled and laughed as they crawled up my legs and settled on my shoulder, tickling my ears. "Careful to pay attention to the ground, remember last time? You stepped in a hole and sprained your ankle!" chuckled Boomey in my mind.

"I know, I know! I'll be careful, I promise!" I giggled. Copper laughed along with me as suddenly I tripped over a vine and fell flat on my face. I sat, dazed for a moment as Boomey came right up into my face. His tongue flickered on my nose as he gave me a stern hiss.

"I told you so!" he laughed.

Another one right after the first.

I had killed the first one—that leech hadn't even seen it coming. Like the other times, the snakes were with me; but this time I'd done the killing all by myself. The evil vampire had been killing children walking out past midnight, which is why it'd been so easy to lure him out. I held up my fist in victory, when Copper's voice came to my head. "You gotta make a mark, to warn other vampires of your presence. They'll learn to fear you!" she cheered in my head.

"What should it be?" I asked curiously.

"Whatever you want it to!" laughed Boomey in my head.

"I know! Snakes! I'll draw one for you two!" I giggled.

"You love us that much, huh?" chuckled Copper.

"Of course! Always and forever!" I replied in a happy hiss.

Tears brimmed in my eyes and flowed like a river down my cheeks as they kept coming. The time where I got a scrape and Copper wrapped around my arm to give the proper pressure to stop the bleeding. The time where Copper got sick, and for two days Boomey and I had to tend to her every need, and boy was she was a picky snake! The first time I started training, how the snakes had to save me from several vampires before I got the hang of my own venom. The time I'd first loved a hunter, yes, there was even a time like that. I thought I'd love him before he broke my heart and went with another. The snakes had been there to wipe away my tears, to reassure me and hug my arms as I had cried.

They weren't here to wipe away my tears now.

Rage grew within me, and mixed with sadness, it was an explosive brew. I felt the transformation again, along with the adrenaline fueled by wrath of which flowed through my veins. My roar was deafening, and my fire cut through the shadows and struck down whatever it touched. The fire was a bright blue, one of the hottest fires in existence. It indeed melted whatever flesh it touched. Everything was burned; the stone of the walls melted to molten, bones melted to ash. Blood boiled away, soon all that was left was me, sitting in the corner of carnage and tears. I shrunk down to human form, more numb than I ever had been before.

My fire had not burned away the snakes' remains. I gently pulled the knife from the end of their skulls and took their bodies in my arms, cradling them like they were my parents. And in reality, they were the only parents I ever had. My tears fell on them, evaporating upon impact. My sobs echoed quietly off the seemingly abandoned walls. I had not noticed someone else in the room until his hand fell on my shoulder.

I jumped, initially turning to bite whatever was grabbing me. My eyes met Goliath's. His were equally as sad, with tears dripping down his cheeks as he spoke. "In the short time I knew them, they were more intelligent and caring than most people I associated with," the vampire whispered. I sniffed, my eyes red with anguish.

"How did you not fall to my flames?" I asked in a low voice, trying to change the subject for just one second. Goliath sat next to me, oddly enough with a suit unstained and unchanged. He wore his top hat and still looked as if he'd just come from a fancy dinner or whatever.

"You saw those shifting darkness, correct? I can melt into the shadows, it's been a power of my family for decades. Also, dragon's blood can give vampires certain powers, you see. That's probably how I'm immune to your venom, too. That's also one of the reasons they were wiped out. The weakened dragons were preyed upon by my kind. Anyway, I summon shadows that dull senses and slow movement as well," he explained. "They cloak me in a temporary immunity to fire, even flames as hot as yours," he added.

"And Ash..." I whispered, my tears still falling upon the carcasses of the snakes.

"He has the same powers. He was fully aware that I was blocking him from you at that moment. Sambuca. I had no idea he would go for the snakes. He destroyed them so quickly, I..." the vampire caught his voice, now avoiding my gaze.

I just shook my head, bringing the snakes close to my heart and crying softly a little more.

"We need to leave now, though, love. We can have a proper burial for them when we get out of here. Ash will alert more guards. You wiped out a good lot of them, and those allies I mentioned before held off quite a bit, but it cannot last forever. They are coming for us, Sam, and we need to get out now," he told me.

I didn't move at first.

However, I knew that he was right, and that I needed to listen, therefore I struggled to get to my feet. I groaned, just falling to the ground again right after. Ash had taken a lot of blood, and on top of my bodily wounds, I couldn't get very far.

Goliath immediately whisked me into his arms and darted out of the room. Down the halls, a turn here, a turn there, a broken window, and we were out. I clutched the bodies of Copper and Boomey, not wanting to let them go until I was ready to. It was strange not having their voices in my head, cheering me on or warning me, as we ran onward. I felt more tears spill from my eyes, and it'd been a while since I'd cried this much. No pain could be greater than this, not a broken heart, not any bodily wounds either.

Goliath said nothing more, and left me to peace as we ran. I thought I heard pursuers, but my soft sobs drowned out most background noise I heard.

Soon, we were at the edge of a forest. Goliath was panting, clearly out of breath. "We are almost out of the kingdom, love. Stay strong," he whispered. I was beginning to grow dizzy from exhaustion and blood loss.

After what was probably five minutes, but felt like days, we arrived at what I'd called home for years. Goliath gently put me down and began digging with his hands, moving quickly. I watched, wanting to help, but not having enough strength to do so.

When he finished, the vampire gently guided me to the hole. I was hesitant, but knew it had to be done. Slowly, gently, I placed the bodies of Copper and Boomey within the hole. Tears fell and rolled down their scales as I stared down at them. Both seemed to still stare at me, as if wondering why.

Why? Why hadn't I saved them?

I felt a cold breeze on my shoulder and lifted my head just enough to see two robins land on a branch and stare into the hole. They then both shifted their heads to gaze at me, both giving low, melodious chirps at the same time before turning and flying off into the night.

Robins had been the snakes' favorite meals, when I was able to catch them. But it was more than that. Copper and Boomey always expressed their desires to fly, high in the sky like they knew birds could. The snakes always had wanted wings, and had never been given the chance to soar.

"Rest in peace, my family. I hope you have those wings you've always wanted," I whispered, now covering the hole. I felt more at peace now, those birds had given me not a look of blame, but a look of understanding. I think the snakes knew I did everything I could and only wished the best for me.

Whether that was a real sign or not, I'd never know; I just knew that they could not die in vain.

"Goliath..." I whispered, gaining his attention. "I need to finish what I started. The snakes died for me, and I can't let that sacrifice fade away. I need to accomplish what I set out to do," I sighed.

"And what is that, love?" he asked quietly.

"I need to save the innocent people I had tried to in the first place. Be it vampire, human, snake, whatever. Not out of greed, but from my heart. I'm not a hunter anymore; I need to be a fighter for peace. Will you help me with that, Goliath?" I asked.

The vampire chuckled, taking me in his arms and staring into my eyes.

"I'd help you with anything, Sam. Especially that. I promise, your family will not die in vain. I will personally rip out my brother's heart and give it to you, if that's what you'd like," he muttered.

My eyes darkened. "No," I hissed in a low voice. "Ash is mine to kill. You hear me, Goliath? I want to personally see the light fade from his eyes, and I want to learn before his death why he's targeting me," I growled.

Goliath seemed surprised, but after a pause gave a nod. "I can grant you that. Right now, you need rest. I will make sure no one harms you while you sleep. Tomorrow night, we can see what the status is in the town, alright?" he suggested. His eyes darkened. "Ash knows it was you that killed our oldest brother and his fiance a while back, when you made your escape. When he found you, he told me you were the one, and that you had to suffer. He got back at you just now, but won't rest until you're dead. Understand?"

I gave a nod, closing my eyes. The vampire quietly carried me to my makeshift bed. It took a while to fall asleep, as my mind was clouded with memories. For the first time, the snakes were not sleeping next to me or keeping me comfortable. That in itself caused my sleep to be troubled. I was sure the vampire could hear my soft sobs as I tried to fall asleep, but honestly I didn't care.

Chapter 20

For the first time in a while, I awoke with no pain and was mostly comfortable. I sat up, noting how the sun seemed to be setting. I was becoming so nocturnal now. I mean, before I had always hunted at night, but I didn't sleep the day away. I supposed the first step to beat an enemy would be to become it in some possible way. Speaking of vampires, I tilted my head, hearing some sort of sizzling noise coming from the other room. Right as it hit my nose, my stomach growled. Good gods, I was as hungry as a dragon!

I got out of bed, shaky at first. That run-in with Ash had left me physically weak along with emotionally weak. I let out a yawn, slowly walking to the kitchen and spotting a frying pan on the stove. I moved closer, feeling saliva begin to pour over my teeth and gums. My eyes flashed hungrily, I knew they changed to be very snake-like as well. I moved closer as the smell of bacon filled my nose. I had no idea how long it'd been since I'd eaten, but apparently it had been a while.

"Hungry?" came a voice from behind me. I almost jumped a mile, and whirled to see Goliath right behind me. He had an amused smile, though there was a sad tinge to his eyes that probably matched mine to a smaller degree. I narrowed my eyes and gave a slow nod.

"Thanks for scaring me like that," I growled.

"Your fault for not being prepared, dear. We've a lot to train for, it seems!" Goliath chuckled. I rolled my eyes and snatched a few pieces of bacon from the pan, not bothering to get a plate. I eagerly ripped into it, choking it down like I hadn't eaten my entire life. Goliath watched with eyebrows raised.

"My, you're very lady-like. Who taught you to eat, a snake?" he questioned with a light smile.

Despite my sadness, the memory of the snakes was a happy one. So, I just smirked and gave a nod in response. "Actually, yes!" I giggled. I wiped my mouth with my sleeve, taking a seat. Goliath sat across from me, and my eyes turned serious.

"Now. You've been working with Ash, I know. But I also know that you are no longer. Still, you probably have a lot of information on what he is planning," I muttered, waiting for him to explain pretty much everything.

Goliath let out a sigh and avoided my gaze. "My family had been planning this for a while. A take-over of the city, to finally gain control of the world for ourselves. I had been into it, in fact more-so than my brother. The secret is out, Sambuca. I used to be even worse than my brother," he growled regretfully.

I hissed slightly, knowing what he was going to say would be horrible. "Go on," I said flatly. Goliath cleared his throat and continued.

"The first part of the plan was to wipe out the dragons. Once we did so, we moved on to executing many human officials. From there, we befriended the most greedy of the hunters... which happened to be your leaders. That was about when we found out about the flaw in the first part of the plan. That flaw was you. When my oldest brother had been slain, they took a venom sample. It had been a Boomslang snake that had killed them both. But Sam, a trace of dragon's venom was there too. Your claws must have touched the fang in some way or another. Somehow, your venom was transferred as well. I don't know how that is possible. But that was your flaw—that's how you were found.

Originally, the plan had been to kill you straight off. But my father decided to wait. He assigned me to watch you grow and become more powerful. The older, he said, the more potent the blood. He had plans for me to end you once and for all on your last birthday. In other words, the night we first met. Sambuca, I could have ended you there. I chose to act out my dying for a specific reason.

What I saw in you changed my motive. Humans, with the help of dragons, had murdered my mother. That's why my hate ran so deep. But I saw *you*, how you were not a true hunter, how you actually spared innocent vampires and even saved those in true need. You denied it to the hunters plenty of times, but I saw you. That is why I did not kill you, and that's what awoke me from my hate," he finished.

I blinked, surprised. I had no idea that by doing what I always did, I saved myself from death. I knew fully well that Goliath had the power to kill me. His immunity to venom made my advantage completely useless. And I knew Ash had the same resistance.

"Ash wants to avenge your mother and brother, doesn't he," I whispered. Goliath nodded. His eyes darkened.

"He also thinks that father is going too slow. He wants to take the city *now.* I had struck a deal with my only remaining sister to spare the innocents of the city, to conquer with peace rather than slaughter. As you saw, she tricked and ambushed me. The city will not understand we are helping them until we do just that. The first step is to free them from the vilest of vampires. Then, we need to train them. You'll be perfect for that," the vampire finished.

I blinked. This was a lot to take in. It was a lot simpler said than done, that was for damn sure. "When do we start?" I questioned. The back of my mind also told me to be wary of the hunters. Robert Smoke was still out there and probably working with Ash. But I needed to worry about the issue at hand, and that was to save as many people as I could.

"I think we need to recover for a while and then head out," Goliath responded. I sighed, wanting to leave right away, but knowing I needed a lot of rest after that incident.

AFTER A FEW WEEKS OF rest, watching, and waiting, I was ready.

"Let's go then!" I growled impatiently. My mind needed to be occupied. I had enough time to mourn, and things needed to get done now.

The wind whistled through my scales as I, for the first time, flew through the sky. Goliath kept a firm hold to the spines on my neck; he seemed tense, obviously never having flown before. Being in the same boat but the one flying, I was rather nervous as well. "Fly slowly, don't go too fast since it is your first time!" he yelled, the worry clear in his voice.

I gave a roar of acknowledgement and glided onward, flapping my wings every once in a while to keep to the same height. The city came into view, and an excited smile grew on my face. I circled nice and slowly, intending on touching down gently. That didn't happen, unfortunately. I began my descent when a burst of wind hit my wings. I gave a cry as I was thrown off and tossed closer to the ground. Out of control, I spiraled down, clashing into a few buildings and losing a few scales before finally coming to a landing.

I landed flat on my stomach, not having time to prepare my legs for the ground. I gave a groan, seeing white spots for a moment. I felt Goliath leap off as I shifted to human form. Holding my head, I shook it hard before focusing on him. He looked both concerned and amused.

"You alright, love?" he asked, clearly trying to hold in a laugh. I gave a snort of anger and shook my head, baring my still-sharp teeth.

"Not my fault! The wind hit my wings!" I growled. Goliath smirked.

"Whatever you say. That was quite a smooth landing," he said sarcastically. I was about to give a snide reply when a scream came from behind me.

I turned to see a group of humans huddled in an alleyway, shaking upon spotting me. Obviously they had seen me land and shift. Goliath joined me to walk over and see. We stayed some distance away, because clearly they were traumatized. I raised my voice to get their attention.

"Hey! We are not here to harm you!" I called. One of them, a shorter man with blonde hair, shakily took a step forward. His mouth was open in a scream, as if he was too afraid to utter it. I could see bite marks all over the group's body, and couldn't help but feel horrible. He pointed at me, shaking his head as if I were the cause of this. "No I promise! I'm here to save you!"

He shook his head again, his eyes not quite focused on me, but staring behind me. I narrowed my eyes and slowly turned to see... Goliath. He looked confused as well, but then I realized it wasn't even Goliath the man was pointing at. My eyes widened as I screamed, "LOOK OUT!" to the vampire.

Goliath dove out of the way just in time. His lips peeled back in a snarl as he whirled to face none other than Robert Smoke.

"Well well. Looks like our little prince accepted his prize and let her free. Tsk tsk, I always knew you were the rotten one," the hunter chuckled. Something was *off* about him. His skin was more pale, perhaps he'd been fed on too? I moved closer, bravely just a few feet from him. I bared my sharp teeth at him, daring him to make a move at me.

"Robert Smoke. Traitor to the bone. What are you doing here, scoundrel?" I growled. "These people are miserable enough from your betrayal!" I snapped. This only made the hunter chuckle. He moved closer to me, suddenly grabbing me under the chin. Right away, I felt a hand on my shoulder. I knew it was Goliath's, and I knew he was giving a warning glare to Smoke. But the hunter didn't make an attack move. Rather, his smile just widened, and I realized something that made my heart clench.

Robert Smoke had fangs. The leader of the hunter association was a *vampire.* And newly turned, too. "My betrayal?" he asked softly. He just gave a low laugh. "No, no my dear dragon. I've achieved immortality for my people, all but you. You're the true traitor to us. We were given an offer we could not refuse. Why hunt the beasts when you can join them, and eternally *hunt*?" he questioned.

I gritted my teeth. "You're sick!" I yelled. Robert Smoke just laughed yet again and let go of my chin, his back to me now.

"No, Red Viper. I'm merely ruthless and a very greedy person. I take what I can get. My objective is to hunt. Be it vampires... or humans. Now I can do so without surrendering to death anytime soon!" he sneered. I had it. Despite Goliath's warning yell, I lunged for the bastard. My claws came down on nothing, though; just air.

"Have you forgotten?" came Smoke's voice by my ear. "I'm not the only one who got the gift of a longer life." That was when more laughs rose to hit my ears. This was a trap. Shit! I turned to see Goliath blocking me defensively.

"Well, we'll get what's coming to us," he hissed. He drew his previously hidden silver stake and grinned. "I always knew this would come in handy!"

Chapter 21

I swiftly dodged a silver dagger that came my way. Silver was specific for vampires, I had no idea the effect it had on dragons. Still, a dagger was a dagger, and it could hurt me. Robert Smoke seemed to vanish as the fog thickened. Goliath and I stood back to back. I bared my fangs, ready to bite or scratch whatever came my way. Goliath, I knew, was prepared to stake any vampire that came near us.

Then, there was another strike by Smoke. Or maybe it wasn't him; I just knew that suddenly I was being pulled by a very strong arm away from Goliath. I heard the vampire hiss, and knew he was being pulled in the opposite direction. Just as I lunged to sink my fangs into whatever was holding me, I was let go. I stumbled, giving a wary growl before regaining my footing. I darted forward, trying to find my companion but failing. Laughter surrounded me, causing me to turn this way and that. It was getting on my nerves when a voice spoke in my head. This time, it was not Goliath's.

Focus, Sambuca. You did this before, you can do it again. Don't use your eyes and ears. Use the entire surface of yourself as a guide. You know what to do...

The voice was of a female, and familiar, but sounded also a little different. I could not figure out exactly who it belonged to; perhaps it was my own. Regardless, right now I needed to listen to whatever advice I got. I closed my eyes, breathing in deeply. I knew a second's hesitation would leave me open, but I wouldn't take more than half a second.

Left... no right... he's behind me? No... right in front of me! My arm lunged forward right as my eyes shot open. I grabbed a hold of one of the former hunters by the neck. My hand held strongly and steadily; if I had hesitated a millisecond more, they would have knocked me off of my feet and I would have been done for. I bared my fangs into the now fearful vampire's eyes.

"You're dragon food now," I growled lowly. The vampire, who was a male with red hair that matched his red eyes, struggled in my grasp. He started to beg, but I wasn't one to have much mercy. Especially not now. I raised my other hand and extended my claws. From there, I took one swipe and left five grueling claw marks across his face. The vampire stumbled and fell flat on his back. I stared as he writhed on the ground, shrieking in pure pain.

"I *do* have venom in my nails, I guess," I chuckled, impressed with myself. The victory didn't last long, as *his* laugh sounded right behind me again. I whirled to see—you guessed it—Robert Smoke. The newly turned vampire stared at me, looking oh-so amused. He tilted his head up and flared his nostrils, seeming to take in my scent.

"Dragon's blood. I can almost taste it," he whispered, his hungry eyes trained on my neck. I reacted so quickly that he had no time to move away. A neat little red mark in the form of my hand appeared on his cheek. Yep, I had slapped him pretty hard. Smoke didn't take a liking to that, as his lips peeled back into a snarl.

"You're a creeper and a traitor. I would never give you my blood. Disgusting," I snapped. Smoke's eyes went from angry to surprised. He slowly smiled, rubbing the mark where I had just slapped him.

"Ah... but you allowed the *dragon killer* to have a bite. Come on Sam. Just a taste? I'll allow you to live, along with that little lover of yours, if you do," he purred, coming closer to my ear. His eyes were supposed to be hypnotizing, but I wasn't buying it. I did, however, play along, as a plan formed in my mind. I knew how to play pretend. Let's see how it'd work.

"You *promise* to leave us alone?" I asked innocently, my eyes widening. I tilted my head, trying to look as convincing as possible. Like the last time, Smoke bought it and leaned in closer. "Of course I let Goliath feed on me, Smoke. I just *love* the feeling of being bitten, it's addicting," I added. The sarcasm in my voice was so thick I was sure for a second he'd see my little ploy. He still bought it with a laugh, however, and grabbed my arm. He leaned toward my neck, flashing his fangs.

When suddenly, *I* lunged for *his* neck. Smoke had been going slow, he'd seriously thought I had given myself to him. It was all too fast when I was the one who had bitten the vampire. Smoke was stunned, not only by my venom, but by my trickery. He had been too hungered for dragon's blood to even consider my words as lies. That would be his downfall. Or at least, what saved me for now, for as soon as I finished with my bite, I was shoved aside by several hands.

"Master!" came the cries of several turned hunters. They bared their fangs at me and lunged, trying to rip at my flesh and get to Smoke. I, however, decided I had enough. I shifted to dragon form, my pure red scales glowing as my body twisted like a snake's to my every movement. My wings spread menacingly as I threw back my head and let out a roar. My huge claws came down to trap the limp body of Smoke. I knew he was conscious for now, and I also knew that the hunters probably had an antidote for my venom. I had to let it spread and weaken him as much as possible before they got to him.

I swiped with my free claws at the hunters, who darted aside like mice being clawed at by a cat. Several sliced at me with silver knives and weapons, but it did no good against my scales. I lowered my head and opened wide. Billows of flame covered several vampires, but many knew how to dodge out of the way. I looked down to see my claws being pried loose by the lot of them. I was too late to make a move at them, but I did manage to lower my head and snatch one up in my jaws. There were just too many vampires, but here and now, I could make my point.

I threw back my head, taking the screaming vampire with me. The body of my victim was thrown into the air, and as they came down, my jaws clamped together to snap them cleanly in half. I twisted my head to devour both parts of the vampire before turning to roar after those fleeing.

"Monster! She is more of a monster than us!" yelled the 'hunters' as they ran even faster. I didn't bother going after them. Rather, I shifted to human form and waved after them, having a very wide smirk.

"And don't come back!" I snarled, spitting out a bit of vampire's blood as I said it. No, I have no idea what happened to the vampire bits I ate. Perhaps something to consider at a later time. I turned to the humans cowering in the alleyway, only to discover they weren't there. "Eh? Where is everyone?" I muttered. I felt a hand fall on my shoulder and whirled, immediately putting my fangs against the neck of...Goliath.

The vampire's eyebrows were raised in surprise. "Woah there, Sam. I come in peace. I managed to escort the humans to a safer haven. Luckily they trusted me enough after I slaughtered a few vampires who had decided to feast on them," he muttered. Goliath was covered in blood, as was I. A smirk spread across my face.

"Looks like we both enjoyed our first day of training," I chuckled. Goliath smiled and put his hand on my other shoulder, pulling me close protectively.

"How did you get so much blood on you?" he asked, his red eyes fixing on my neck to check for bite marks. Well, bite marks other than his. Upon seeing none, he sighed in relief.

"Not mine, Goliath. I took care of some attackers. Smoke got a rather dangerous wound, so he and his minions fled," I replied. I licked my lips, giving another smile. "I had a bite to eat in dragon form as well," I commented.

Goliath didn't seem phased at my words. In fact, he just shook his head with a slight smile. "Terrifying beast you are, love. That meal probably gave you some decent raw power enough to shift back easily. Just be careful. They are freshly turned. Someone like Ash will not be so easy to defeat," he pointed out. This I knew, but I gave a sarcastic nod anyways.

"Yeah yeah, I know. Let's go make sure those people are alright," I replied. We walked along in silence before coming upon a halfway-decent building. It seemed to not be damaged too much, though a few of the bricks looked run down and rotted. We entered through an old looking door that had bits of paint peeling off of it in sloughs. The air was cold and tense as we made our way through what was like an abandoned theater.

We entered a room of which looked quite like an assembly area. There was a huge group of people, all sitting in seats and looking very horrified and raggedy. There were bite marks lining their arms and necks, clearly from the hunters that had held them captive. They looked at both Goliath and me fearfully. I stepped up on the stage, feeling like I was on the spot now. Goliath followed behind me, staring out at the crowd with sympathy.

"Hey everyone. I got rid of the leader of those who hurt you, and they have since fled. Now we can work on a real enemy, one who wants to see you all enslaved," I started. The silence stretched for a second before one of the humans stood up. He was a middle-aged man with a rough looking beard and glasses smeared with blood.

"How do we know you won't turn and kill us too! You look just like them!" he yelled. Half the group stood up with him and roared in agreement, holding up things like shovels, hammers, and normal tools that could somewhat serve as weapons. The other half, though, protested.

"No! They saved us from them, they are our only hope!" yelled a young woman with dark hair and trendy clothing. It seemed like the younger generation was more accepting of us, while the older wanted to be rid of us. Chaos broke among the crowd, which angered me significantly.

"Hey! CUT IT OUT! WE'RE HERE TO HELP, IF YOU DON'T LIKE THAT, THEN GET OUT OF HERE AND DIE TO THE NEWLY HUNGRY VAMPIRES!" I roared in a voice way louder than a human's could be. That quieted them down enough, and soon everyone was sitting and tense again.

"Now are you ready to listen?!" I snapped. A voice came from the back of the crowd.

"As a matter of fact, yes. I am," it cackled, causing my heart to drop. The entire crowd's heads turned to face a single person. Goliath bared his teeth and tensed, getting ready to launch himself at the intruder.

"*Ash...*" I hissed in hatred so pure that the seats behind Ash literally lit on fire.

Chapter 22

Unfortunately, Ash managed to dodge right in time from the flames that spread rather rapidly. He smirked and took a few steps backward, vanishing into the shadows of the theater. I knew that wasn't the last of him. My wings ripped from my back, oddly still not destroying my dark clothing, rather just ripping through the holes already made from last time. My venom green eyes searched the shadows as I flew across the room. I landed in one corner, sensing him around but unable to pinpoint his location. The fire had gone out in the seats, and I knew if I lit my flames again, there was a risk of burning down the theater.

My narrowed eyes widened as a hand fell on my shoulder. I immediately tensed and whirled, my claws out and ready to strike whoever it was. I sighted the woman that had spoken up before and restrained myself from striking her down. "Whoa whoa whoa.. I'm on your side, remember?" she gasped. Her dark hair hid one of her deep brown eyes as she stared me down. Her skin, a medium ebon, had aided in hiding her well in the shadows. There seemed to be a darkness within her eyes that I could not really put a finger on. Despite this, she handed me a flashlight and gave a smile. "Will this help?" she asked. I gave a quick nod and accepted the flashlight with a mutter of thanks. At the time, I was in too much of a rush to notice that her nails weren't simply just long, rather, they were really claws.

Wasting no time, I flicked it on and pointed it in the back of the theater, searching anywhere and everywhere for the vampire. Excruciatingly, his laughter echoed through the huge room, causing the people within to gasp. The situation grew all the more terrible when suddenly red liquid began raining through the ceiling. It was the blood of who the hell knows what. Then his voice, like an announcer, rang through the area.

"This is the amount of blood your saviors have shed! Trust them not, because yours will join them!" yelled Ash's voice. The man that had challenged Goliath and I to begin with stood up and pointed again, his face red now.

"We can't trust these freaks! THEY ONLY MEAN HARM! They are just like the rest of them! They are causing this madness!" he screamed. Now, the entire crowd but the woman that had given me the flashlight stood up with accusing glares. It seemed like Ash wanted this to happen. Now, the group of humans we tried to rescue turned on us. Suddenly I was being charged at by the entire crowd. The dark-haired woman stood in front of me, spreading her arms to block me.

"Are you insane?! She is the one who brought us to safety!" she yelled. The man shook his head.

"She brought us into this bloodbath!" he retaliated. The crowd advanced, and I felt myself being lifted from behind.

"These people refuse to listen, Sam. We have to go!" came Goliath's voice in my ear. I let out a roar of protest.

"No! They will die if we leave them!" I yelled. The crowd was not stopping. They shoved the woman aside and began to claw at me and Goliath, trying to damage us in any way possible. I did not lash out against them, for they were innocent in this. Goliath listened to me no more. He lifted me and darted away from the people, leaping over them and from seat to seat. Ash's laugh just grew louder now.

"I would flee before you're all locked in!" he added, his red eyes flashing from the rafters. I widened my eyes.

"There!" I yelled, but my voice was drowned by the screams of the crowd. They rushed to the outside, a few running over the others to get out faster. The rain of blood thickened as suddenly their screams turned to bloodcurdling ones.

They were cut off, unable to flee whatever it was causing them distress.

I jumped out of Goliath's arms and rushed outside, though was blocked for a bit by the crowd. I flapped my wings(they remained the entire time despite me only being in human form) and snarled in frustration. In a few more instances I was outside, almost upchucking my guts at the horrors I saw.

The entire crowd laid in a heap. All of them were dead, with the man that had protested on the top. Their mouths were twisted into frozen in screams that they could not silence. Fang marks, fresh and still bleeding, were all over their necks. They had run from safety only to be slaughtered by an ambush. The vampire, or vampires, that had caused this were now gone. I was frozen in shock as I heard a cough from within the pile.

I saw a blur rush by me and spotted Goliath pulling a body from the pile. He held the woman that had tried to speak for us, looking rather worried. "This one is still alive. You take care of her. I'm going after Ash," he said darkly. I rushed over, taking her in my arms. She was still breathing, slowly but steadily.

"That won't be necessary, brother," came his voice from behind me. Goliath lunged and I turned only to see Ash just out of range, "Tsk tsk... you can't even save the fodder. You're gonna run out of food at this rate, brother," he chuckled. If I had not been kneeling with the woman in my lap, I would have made an attack. Goliath beat me to it, snarling as he went.

"They were not meant for food, Ash. I'm no longer bloodthirsty like you!" he yelled. Ash swiftly dodged and gave a yawn, his spiky hair seeming to now be tipped with blood. He gave a shrug, staring at his brother with an amused smile.

"Nevertheless, you are our father's spawn. And he, along with all of his fathers before him, was a bloodthirsty monster. Like you are, and like I am," Ash giggled madly. Goliath was shaking with rage but managed to control himself. Now was not the time to initiate battle, not with this young woman dying in my arms. And he knew it. But he did ask one more question.

"What do you mean *was,*" the vampire snarled in a low voice. Ash's eyes lit up like someone had told him a present he was getting for a birthday. He grinned widely, his fangs flashing in the dim light.

"Oh yeah! About that! I got rid of him, now I took your place as ruler of the kingdom. All is going well, but a few still are loyal to you and think you should be on the throne. Fortunately I will present to them your bloody head on a pike, along with your lover's," he taunted. I blinked, rage building within my eyes.

"We are not lovers, idiot, and I will enjoy ripping you limb from limb while you beg for mercy and I give you none!" I snarled. Goliath's eyes were unreadable at my words. He just glanced at me and refocused on his brother.

"I will strike you down later, Ash. That is a promise I make. You will die like the thousands you have slain," he promised. Suddenly, I was being carried at a rapid rate. I gasped, glancing over to see the unconscious woman also being carried by the rushing vampire. Ash's laugh faded in the distance the farther we got. Goliath ran in silence, with us in his arms, until we arrived at my house. I wasted no time as Goliath placed the woman on my bed. She looked limp and rather drained... she had been bitten as well.

I rushed to get a cold washcloth to place on her forehead and neck. The bleeding from the bite wounds had stopped, at least. The dried blood coated her skin, making it look worse than it was, hopefully. I could only sit there, wait, and hope. Her breaths quickened, and I knew she would awaken soon. I glanced over to Goliath, who was sitting patiently, watching me carefully.

"What's wrong?" I asked; he normally wasn't this quiet. Goliath blinked, looking embarrassed for half a second.

"Sorry, love. I just stare at you sometimes because, well, you still baffle me. Anyway, I am unsure why Ash calls us lovers. I apologize for that," he muttered. I tilted my head, thinking for a moment.

"Don't apologize. I mean, he probably thinks that because we are always together and such," I said plainly. I turned back to the woman, not realizing what he was implying for a minute. Then, my eyes widened. I turned to face him again, but he had gone, probably to the guest bedroom or kitchen. I let out a sigh, now blushing slightly.

Lovers? Did I like Goliath? Well, I had no time to worry about that now. I wasn't sure how I felt, honestly. My mix of emotions was a cocktail of insanity, and indeed memories were brought up of when he kissed me. I shook them off, there were more important things to attend to. The woman's eyes slowly began to open, and I anxiously stared into them.

"Are you OK?" I asked in a very quiet voice. The woman blinked once, then twice. She sat up, holding her head, and suddenly fear filled her eyes.

"Where am I?!" she asked, gasping. Panic filled her, and I had to hold out my hands to prevent her from springing up and making a run for it.

"Relax, we saved you. You were the only survivor, in fact," I said with a sad sigh. Realization dawned on her, and tears filled her eyes as her face twisted into an expression of guilt.

"Oh... I told them to listen, but they refused..." she whispered.

"It's ok, they were stubborn and afraid. This is not your fault," I replied. I looked down, giving another sad sigh. "What is your name?" I asked, curious now. The woman was silent for a moment before replying in barely a whisper.

"My name is Darcia Deville." Her lips quivered as the guilt remained in her eyes. The smell of roasting chicken filled the air, and my mouth watered. Her eyes widened at the smell of food, I could see them flashing hungrily.

Goliath walked in with oven mitts on, looking rather wacky for the current situation. So much so that I just burst out laughing. The vampire looked confused. "I made some food for our guest and you, Sam," he chuckled, now glancing down and realizing what he was wearing. "Oops, I ah, forgot to take these off," he coughed. He darted back into the kitchen and seconds later came out with plates that had chicken legs and wings on them. I had them in the freezer for a while, but they were still good. I was thanking the gods of the fact that I had shopped ahead a while ago.

Goliath placed the plates in front of us. I dug in right away while Darcia seemed to only pick at her food. After she ate a tad more, though, it probably would take a natural disaster to make her stop. She had finished her meal faster than me, and that was saying something. "Thank you," she said to Goliath with a smile. Goliath gave a nod back, chuckling.

"Glad I satisfied your hunger. Now tell us, exactly how did you end up where you were?" he questioned quietly.

"Well, I used to be a hunter a few towns over," she replied, causing me to tense. I choked on the piece of chicken I was devouring.

"You were? Did you know of the betrayal?" I gasped.

She gave a nod. "I did. By the time I realized, though, and said something, I had been too late. Robert Smoke knew of my protests and set after me. He knew I had been in that group of people and decided to spare me in an attempt to convince me to join him. I flat out refused, which led to my torment," Darcia explained. I frowned, disgusted all over again. Looked like Ash and Smoke were very similar. Ironic, huh?

Chapter 23

Goliath narrowed his eyes, crossing his arms as he watched us eat. "Sambuca, can I see you in the kitchen for a moment?" he asked. I blinked, curious to no end. He had not used my full name... ever. I shrugged and shot an apologetic look to Darcia. From there I stood, picking up my plate and following the vampire into the other room.

"Yes?" I asked, confused somewhat. Goliath kept on glancing toward the living room where Darcia was waiting. He let out a sigh.

"I'm just concerned about this new woman. I know she went through a lot, but she's a hunter. Isn't it sort of odd that she was spared when the rest were not?" he whispered, suspicion in his voice. I narrowed my eyes. That was absurd!

"Goliath, she would have died had we not been there. She needed our help, I don't think she would betray us for saving her. Plus, you heard her. She finds Smoke's ideas and methods insane, like I did," I replied, crossing my arms.

This was another hunter, sure. But she was like me, someone who had understood beforehand. Right now, it was rare to find someone decent in this world. I didn't want to lose a potential ally just because of Goliath's unjustified worries.

The vampire stared at me for a moment, not saying a word. I had to wonder what was going on in his mind. He finally shook his head, looking somewhat irritated. "You're not going to listen to any words I say. I know this. I can try all I want to convince you, yet you will continue to see Darcia as a friend because that's what you long to have, what you've lacked for so long. Yet I'm telling you this is going to lead to tragedy. Nothing good will come out of this. But I will follow your word anyways. Just remember my warning," he finished. Without waiting for my response, he turned away. "I'm starved. I will be back later. Just trust your instincts, Sam." A *whoosh* of air, and Goliath was gone.

I scoffed. He was acting like a know-it-all. I mean, what was the worst that could happen? Darcia was perfectly innocent, she had almost died was all. Just because she was a hunter didn't mean she was like the others. For gods' snake, I was a hunter to begin with. Yet, despite that, Goliath trusted me. So, why not Darcia? He was just being bullheaded.

I walked back into the living room, shaking my head. Darcia seemed to notice my discomfort. "What's wrong?" she asked softly, concern on her face. "Is your boyfriend giving you troubles?" she asked, widening her eyes when I gave a loud snarl.

"He is *not* my boyfriend. Goliath is, uh, my comrade. That's all he'll ever be. And no, he's just concerned. He has trust issues," I reassured. Darcia gave a nod, looking down at her lap somewhat sadly.

"I understand. He must be wondering how I survived. I have no idea myself. But all I want to do is help, Sam, I really do. It is the least I *can* do. I don't know much about Smoke's plans, he didn't actually tell me anything though. Still, I'm skilled in combat. Weapons might help, " she mentioned. I gave a nod, raising my eyebrows in interest.

"Ah, well I have no idea where to find one of those," I muttered. "My tactics were different from most others," I added. Even though I had recently picked up that claw weapon, I was somewhat shaky with using it. I loved using my venom, now natural, to defeat my enemies.

"Red Viper?" asked Darcia, not in fear but in awe. I blinked, giving a nod.

"Yeah. I had no idea I was widely known. I knew most vampires knew of me, but most hunters steered clear," I replied.

"Ah, yes, well you were talked about quite often, particularly by Smoke when he came over to our association. He never really trusted you, even though your death toll is higher than a lot of us combined," she chuckled. I winced at that. Even though I knew I just killed the black-hearted scum, and even managed to save the innocent vampires, I still couldn't help worry that I had mistakenly killed someone undeserving just out of my sheer rage or something. Back when I had first escaped being a blood slave, I was extremely vengeful.

"Yes, well, we don't need to get into that. So, obviously we need to arm ourselves against Smoke and Ash. To be honest, I have no idea who to go after first," I admitted. Darcia gave a slight smile.

"Hmm well, the worst idea would be to go in it with only the three of us. Luckily I know of several hunters who have protested Smoke, and who would be willing to work with us. I know where to find them—but it might be dangerous. I also know how to get our hands on some useful weapons," she told me. I grinned, that would be perfect.

"Awesome. I will let Goliath know, and after some rest, we can head out," I said. I directed her to the guest room and told her to make herself at home. Then, I sat in the kitchen, patient while Goliath went to somehow feed himself.

He was still rather silent when he came back. He glanced at me, not with anger, just with the same searching look he always gave me. It was like he was trying to examine something he just couldn't seem to understand. I cleared my throat, catching his attention even more. Crossing my arms, I blurted out what Darcia told me.

"We made plans to gather a force of people to help us against Ash and Smoke. Darcia knows where to find them, and where to get weapons. It will be dangerous, but I know we can do it," I muttered. Goliath blinked and shrugged, looking somewhat defeated.

"Sure, dear. Whatever you say. I just hope that we are not going into a trap," he growled in a worried voice. He was still stuck on that, huh? I just gave him a sideways frown.

"Listen, it's all we have. Even if something goes wrong, we've managed to flee from an entire castle of guards. We can handle the worst, but think of what we will gain if it isn't some trick. We will gain a lot more than if we just blow off her offer," I reasoned. Goliath gave a resigned nod.

"I will help you, Sam. I would risk my neck for you anytime. I just don't want you in that sort of danger," he mentioned.

I gave a growl. "Why is that?" I wondered. "Why do you care so much? Is it because I am the last dragon?" I asked.

Goliath smirked, staring at me with amused eyes. "I wouldn't care if you were the billionth dragon. You've done more for me than you think. Let's just say you lit up my soul when it was shrouded in shadows. If not for you, I'd be worse than Ash. A lot worse," he said darkly. He turned away and began to walk toward the other guest room. I quickly rushed to him, putting a hand on his shoulder.

"What am I to you, Goliath?" I asked. I was aware that I had asked that question, probably many times before. I couldn't remember, really, nor did I care. The vampire didn't turn to face me at first. I stood, confused, until suddenly I found myself in his arms. The prince of the shadows was hugging me tightly, as if he was afraid of losing me.

"More than you'll ever know, love," he whispered into my ear. Then, just as fast as he hugged me, he was gone. I could sense him in the other room, probably just laying on the couch. I had to remember that he was very tired from the recent events like everyone else was.

I stood in place for a while, my head tilted. After my slight delay, I gave a smile and headed toward my room. I leaped into my bed and snuggled under the blankets, looking to the ceiling. "What is he to me, then?" I whispered, my voice seeming to carry in an invisible wind as the sun began to rise in the distance.

I'm not sure yet, was all I could think to myself. A voice seemed to reply, one that might have been another inner voice. To be honest I wasn't entirely sure.

The better question would be what he is in your heart. That voice. The female voice from before, when I had been in battle. The voice was so familiar... I could not put my finger on it. I closed my eyes, my head buzzing with questions that were not replied to by that voice, sadly enough.

THE NEXT MORNING, OR rather, dusk, I awoke with a yawn. The smell of food hit my nose, and I knew yet again Goliath was cooking. This time it was eggs, and I already began to drool. I knew I needed to keep up my hygiene, though, so I took a trip to the bathroom and showered quickly before changing into fresh clothes. Yep, my usual dark, tight clothing to blend into the night and move easily.

I entered the kitchen, my eyes falling on the plate of food. Darcia was already there, casually talking to Goliath. The vampire didn't seem icy or shut-out, rather he politely answered all questions that were asked.

"So you're one of the princes, right? Are you going to try to take back the throne now?" Darcia questioned.

"Yes, indeed I am a prince. As for the throne, my motive is to end my Ash and bring peace between the kingdom and the modern town. Vampires and humans have battled enough. It is time that ends. I'm unsure what is going to happen with the throne, if worst comes to worst then I will take it," he sighed.

"You don't want to?" Darcia asked, seeming surprised. I scarfed down my food, intently listening to what Goliath had to say.

The vampire shrugged. "I never had a real desire to rule," was all he said. I raised my eyebrows, not really that surprised. He had never expressed that want, probably because with power came corruption. Though I was sure the vampire could handle it. He would be a *way* better ruler than Ash or Smoke. Which was a major understatement, I knew.

Darcia gave a nod, then looked at me. "Did you sleep well?" she asked politely, giving a smile. Her teeth were a bit unusual, I tried to focus on them, but couldn't quite get a handle on what I was seeing due to morning exhaustion before she closed her mouth. Despite that, I returned it and nodded, looking toward Goliath.

"Yeah, for the most part. We should leave as quickly as possible," I added, hoping they would agree. Goliath gave a nod, giving a slight smile.

"Just woke up and already wanting to get on the move. Typical Sam," he chuckled. I rolled my eyes and got to my feet, taking my and Darcia's plates to the sink. I would wash that later, maybe. Or maybe I could convince Goliath to do it. I smirked at the thought, but immediately became serious.

"Darcia, you know where to go, correct?" I asked. She gave a nod, and we were out of the house and on our way in no time. I had to wonder exactly where we were going, because it was obviously not the direction of my association.

"This place will be abandoned," she muttered, her eyes focused ahead. Goliath and I followed behind quietly, and I noticed the vampire watching her carefully. I knew she would prove herself soon enough. I kept telling myself she had no reason to betray us. I, of all people, should be the hardest to convince. But I just felt I could trust her, unlike Goliath. I wondered why we felt so differently from each other.

Soon enough, a building loomed in the distance. Darcia quickened her pace, forcing us to hurry behind her. I knew hunters were fast, but she was running like a child who had found the ice cream truck for the first time in years. The building was huge, with run down bricks and cracked windows. The darkness within grew rapidly as the sun went down.

"Here goes nothing," Darcia chuckled as we finally caught up to her. She stood by a window and raised her fist. After biting her lip, she plunged it through the glass and shook her fist of the shards that stuck there. Golaith glanced to the blood, oddly enough looking disgusted.

"You realize if there are vampires on the premise, they will smell your blood miles away?" Goliath whispered in an angered tone. Darcia turned to him and shrugged, her black hair hiding one of her eyes.

"This place was abandoned weeks ago," she replied seriously.

"By human hunters, yes," came a voice from behind us. I whirled to see an unknown person there, staring us down with a foreboding glare. There was something off about him. He wasn't human, and had odd-looking eyes; they were those of a bird. Goliath was in front of me in an instant, to which I gave a growl.

"I can defend myself," I whispered.

But Darcia was stunned, her eyes wide. "Xadrian?!" she gasped. It looked as if she was very familiar with him, and oddly enough, this man was alone. I had a gut feeling that wouldn't be for long.

Chapter 24

The odd-looking guy didn't look away from Darcia as she pushed past us and stared up at him. He had tawny-brown hair, pale skin, and golden eyes; they reminded me somewhat of a golden eagle. He looked to be in his twenties, older but not much more than Darcia. "Who is this," I asked in a low voice, worried for Darcia more than anything. Goliath was as tense as a snake, I could tell he distrusted this new guy already.

"Xadrian *was* my partner in hunting.... yet now it seems he's a traitor, because he left me when I needed him to work against Smoke. I know what you said, I heard you discussing plans with him," Darcia spat. Xadrian winced but slowly shook his head.

"Not like I wanted to, Darc. I was forced to hear him out, but at least you survived. I managed to escape with a few other rebels after things went wrong. I came back here for weaponry. Most of us were destroyed," he pointed out. Huh, weapons, same reason why we were here. I knew this wouldn't go over well with Goliath, he already didn't like the sound of Darcia's story.

Now, Darcia widened her eyes. "You mean our pack was caught?" she whispered. "And many just..." she trailed off, her eyes trained on the ground now. Xadrian just nodded, looking rather solemn.

"The good news is that they want to bring down Smoke more than ever now. Though he doesn't know it, and sees them as just outcasts, Smoke is gonna get what's coming to him," he promised. I frowned, because in my opinion, the main concern was Ash. Smoke controlled a bunch of new vampires—Ash had armies of very experienced ones.

"Whoa whoa whoa. Let me get this straight. So Smoke forced you all to flee for your lives, now you want to bring him down, correct? Just how do we know you're not working for him since you did before?" I questioned with suspicion.

Xadrian shrugged. "You don't. You'll just have to trust us if you want help. If not, we will continue to work against him alone. However, I suggest not getting in our way," he added darkly. I peeled back my lips in a snarl, as did Goliath.

"Was that a threat?" I asked slowly. Xadrian gave a slight smirk for a second, then shook his head.

"Nah. I just can't promise that we will be able to differentiate you from the enemy if you aren't regularly working with us. Battles are hard, you know," he sighed. That made sense, I guess. But he was being a little too aggressive in my opinion. Goliath had not said a word yet, and I could sense his anger and distrust as it emanated from him.

"I wonder how you didn't notice it about Darcia, Sambuca. Their ancient blood is as distinct as yours. Though I suppose you don't often hunt their kind," Goliath growled. His eyes switched from Darcia to Xadrian rather quickly. What was he getting at? I crossed my arms, confused all over again.

"What do you mean?" I asked, and Darcia tensed. She turned her hardened gaze to me, her eyes curious now.

"You're not human either? But you're not my kind..." she muttered. I let out an inhuman growl, one that vibrated deep from the pit of my stomach.

"I'm a half damn dragon, for gods' snake. So tell me what you are, then? What are you hiding?" I snapped, irritated that secrets seemed to be floating everywhere. I was definitely not in the mood for my trust to be betrayed yet again.

"My entire pack are shapeshifters. Smoke never really liked us, due to the fact that we weren't humans, but accepted us begrudgingly up to this point," she explained. I was unaware of that fact and let out a huff.

"I knew so little about the association. Trusting shifters. Disgusting," I muttered. That offended both Xadrian and Darcia, who glared at me with rage.

I blinked, realizing what I said, and put a hand behind my head. "Sorry. It was what I was taught. That's probably untrue, as I had learned that not all vampires were beasts, but what I learned from the little time I had spent in the academy was pretty heavy. That shifters kill and slaughter without prejudice, simple just to spread pain and chaos," I clarified. "Seeing Darcia and her relaxed nature, I can shut away that belief."

Darcia snorted. "Oh please. We learned the same about dragons. Though I know of none that can turn into a human," she added. Xadrian nodded, looking at me curiously.

"I am half dragon, a freak, I guess," I just replied, glancing toward the window and clearing my throat. "We should probably arm ourselves as quickly as possible though," I said, trying to change the subject. Darcia and Xadrian gave a nod. I could tell Darcia was still uneasy about Xadrian, as was he to the rest of us.

Goliath just kept his eyes on them, letting Darcia lead the way and me to follow behind her. He blocked me from Xadrian, glancing behind him every so often to check that the shifter would not suddenly change his mind and lunge. I knew Goliath was refraining from saying a lot, but was going along with the plan for now.

I could easily argue that we needed allies, no matter who they were. Xadrian was a shifty(hah) character that I would need to get used to. Darcia seemed to somewhat accept what he did, though. They seemed very close, I had to wonder if they really cared about each other at one point. Darcia didn't show it at the moment. She had some malice for him, probably due to his working with Smoke. Now, I wondered if she would trust me for being a dragon, since apparently she learned some nasty stuff long ago.

My thoughts shifted to my own distrust of Goliath prior to his betrayal. I knew that I had admired him before I found out what he was, then upon finding out he had fangs, I didn't want anything to do with him. I still was wary around him, in fact, more to what he did to me than anything though. I knew he couldn't help it, but still... my tiny bit of distrust was there. Perhaps the same case would hold for Darcia toward me, but time would tell now.

We walked through the darkened halls, speechless. I took everything in; this place seemed old, but it looked like there had been an effort to improve it before it was abandoned. Some places were repainted dark blues and grays, others remained untouched as the paint peeled and rotted off. The lights were off, there was no eerie flashing of any sort. This place was empty, not haunted... yet. We finally came to a safe looking room, which Darcia stepped up to and turned the dial of some code to unlock the door.

We wandered inside, and I had to admit I was impressed. Metal bows, knives, and swords hung on the walls. Various forms of body armor were neatly set on several shelves. Poisons and venom were stored in labeled vials, specialized to weaken or kill vampires. I saw a skeletal-looking glove made of metal with jagged knives coming out of each finger. I grinned and rushed over, putting it on and examining it.

There were holes, sort of like tubing within the system, obviously to store poison or venom. Convenient for my purposes; I consciously let my venom drip into the system and cover the claws. It was interesting how I could produce venom from my natural claws, like I could with my teeth.

I wondered if my teeth were actually naturally sharp, and if I really didn't need to do much to grind them sharp. I probably just never noticed beforehand because I had assumed I was a 'normal' human, of course. What a silly assumption in hindsight.

Darcia grabbed herself some claw weapons, and Goliath armed himself with knives. Xadrian got a bow and a quiver of silver arrows. He also took out a bag and shoved several other weapons within it. He turned to Darcia and raised his eyebrows. "Are you sticking with these two, or joining us again?" he questioned. Darcia looked at me in question.

"Depends on if Goliath is alright with it," I replied, now looking at the vampire. Goliath blinked and stared at Darcia for a moment. Finally he sighed.

"She can stay with us if she so wishes; if indeed this shifter's pack is what they say they are, they will no doubt be valuable allies. Darcia, will you be able to keep contact?" he asked quietly. Darcia gave a nod and shot a small smile to Xadrian.

"Meet me at the clearing at five, alright?" she told him. "We can discuss plans then. Bring the rest of the pack," she added. Goliath narrowed his eyes but kept his tongue. Xadrian just gave a nod and turned away, his back facing us.

"I'll be there," the male shifter assured. Then, like that he was gone. It was just the three of us now. We began making our way out of the building, silent at first. Then, I just had to ask a certain question.

"What shifter are you?" I asked very curiously. Darcia chuckled at the slight excitement in my voice. Obviously I had not been around many shifters.

"I am a Tasmanian Devil. Sort of like a wolf-weasel if you catch my drift... see?" she giggled. Her features changed in an instant to that of an animal after a bright flash of light. There was a little white mark across her chest, and she had beady black eyes that glimmered in the moonlight. Her back was hunched somewhat, and she had small rounded ears. She retained the mass that she had as a humanoid, therefore was the size of a large dog. That wasn't the same for me, of course, since technically I had two solid forms, and shapeshifters always had the same powers and size in either form; they just were built differently in their animal form.

I smiled and bent down to pet her, in awe. Even Goliath seemed amused. "That's cute, Sam," he commented, to which I narrowed my eyes and faced him.

"I am far from cute, Goliath!" I snarled, making his smile only widen more. Darcia shifted back to her human form, like me keeping her clothing when she shifted. I didn't understand how that happened; probably some sort of magic lost to physics or something.

We began to walk back with our new weapons when I heard the snapping of a twig nearby. All of us whirled to it; I bared my teeth, expecting the worse. Lo and behold, Smoke was standing there looking quite entertained.

"Looks like you made some new friends. Shapeshifters, huh? They were supposed to be working for me. I will have to pay them a visit then," he chuckled. He looked at Darcia, flashing her a fully-fanged grin. "I'll take care of your partner, Darcia. We'll be seeing eye-to-eye soon enough," he promised. Then, he was gone. Darcia let out a gasp and darted in the direction where he vanished off.

"We need to help them!" she gasped, worry thick in her voice.

"We can't run into something unprepared, shifter. He could just be trying to delay us even further, or even lead us into a trap," Goliath pointed out. Darcia gritted her teeth, turning to face the vampire.

"I don't care what Xadrian and my pack are to you. I have a duty to save them—if I have to go alone, I will! And you will lose an ally!" she cried. I raised my hands, letting out a sigh.

"Goliath was only pointing out his suspicion. What about we go to the clearing tomorrow; we have no idea where they are at the moment anyways. We can't just blindly run in circles. I'm sure Smoke won't attack right away, and you implied your pack was strong as hell. I bet they could take him even if he did... ok?" I muttered.

Darcia was hesitant but slowly nodded. Her eyes were dark as we began to walk back. I could only hope that she would control herself enough to wait for tomorrow. I knew that Goliath wasn't OK with this, but at this point it was our only option. I knew he would want to find those loyal to him soon as well. That could wait—every bit of force was important against these psychos.

Chapter 25

Things were still tense when we got back to the house. Darcia kept glancing behind her, as if expecting Xadrian to appear out of nowhere and reassure her. Her angered eyes slid to the vampire every so often, as if she blamed him for what was happening. Goliath kept his eyes on her, I knew he still had little trust for her. Whether it was because her entire fiasco seemed fishy or the fact that she was a shifter, I had no idea. The tension seemed to crackle like a thunderstorm until finally I let out a growl. Was I the only sane one here?

"Both of you stop shooting glares at each other, alright? How the hell are we going to face Ash and Smoke if we aren't able to stand the sight of each other?!" I suddenly snapped. We had reached the door of my house. I turned and fixed my gaze on both of them, my arms crossed and my sharp teeth bared. Both Darcia and Goliath seemed surprised and focused on me.

"What is it, Sam? We agreed to go look tomorrow, there shouldn't be any argument with that..." Goliath muttered. Darcia snorted, obviously disagreeing, but saying nothing to his words. I let out a huff.

"Yes, I'm aware. But I can see both of you shooting daggers at each other from your eyes. I'd like it if you both sat down and discussed the issue, because it's sorta obvious neither of you trust each other," I growled. Before either could protest, I pushed open the door and took my place on the couch. Goliath followed behind and sat next to me; Darcia took the chair across from us.

"Ok. Goliath, please inform me as to the issue with vampires and shifters. Your past with dragons is bloody, I can only imagine what it's like with them," I muttered, causing Goliath to wince somewhat. He looked to his lap and let out a sigh.

"Well, Sam... shifters and vampires never have really gotten along. There isn't some giant start to the conflict, no one race attacked the other first, no one falsely blamed the other. The only quarrel vampires had with shifters was land dispute. Land and prey, of which is humans. Shifters are no more noble than dragons when it comes to protecting humans. They did it to lead humans on to the fact that they are little angels, when in reality they stabbed them in the backs and devoured them when hungered," the vampire hissed.

Darcia slammed her hands onto her lap, letting out an angered chitter. "You lying asshole! My pack has done no such thing!" she shrieked. Goliath bared his fangs at her and raised a hand to shut her up. I didn't intervene quite yet.

Rather than toss an insult back, Goliath shook his head. "*Your* pack maybe. But most other packs were no more noble than the vampire clans," he replied. Darcia paused and grumbled something under her breath. His words obviously were true. Goliath's smug expression faded as he continued onward with his explanation.

"So you see, neither race really were the innocent ones nor the culprits. The land disputes just grew out of proportion, eventually leading to a horrid war. That's it. Land. It baffles me to this day, but horrible things on both sides have led both races to hate the other," Goliath finished. He glanced at Darcia, letting out a sigh.

Darcia looked away, narrowing her eyes. "What he says is true. I'm surprised he didn't try to pin the blame on us. But this war, this conflict, I even don't know why it's being continued. It's a big damn bloody mess that needs to stop," she sighed. I nodded, my eyes serious.

"Now that we got *that* out of the way, with both of you realizing just how ridiculous you are, can we please rest on it and prepare for our meeting?" I questioned, irritated. Darcia gave a solemn nod and without another word returned to the guest room. Goliath stayed, his eyes on me for a while before I shot him a glare. "Why are you staring at me?"

"You're quite the diplomat," Goliath muttered, giving me a slight smile. "Your way with words is uncanny," he added, moving closer. I didn't move away, just crossed my arms.

"And? I seem to be the only one wanting to just end the conflict. I can't have *another* one building up behind us. We can't lose potential allies, Goliath. We can't do this alone," I reasoned. The vampire sighed and moved even closer. His angle was what, exactly?

"I suppose you're right. That doesn't fully dissipate my distrust for Darcia and her gang, but it's something I will need to deal with," he hissed. He put his arm around me, causing me to tense somewhat. "What's wrong? I will leave you be if you want," he muttered, looking into my eyes.

I shrugged. "Do what you want, I guess," I replied. Goliath raised his eyebrows, leaning closer to my face. I frowned, but felt butterflies intensify within my stomach. Ever since he kissed me on the way to the castle a while ago, I was curious if another one would feel the same.

Goliath paused, then gave a relaxed smile. Suddenly I felt his lips on mine and the same fiery feeling within. I wondered if it was because I was a dragon? Probably not, it somehow felt different, natural, not relating to what I was, but rather *who*. After what seemed like hours but lasted only a few seconds, the vampire pulled away. He got up and sat across from me, giving me a crooked grin.

"What was that for?" I asked, irritated that he moved away. Goliath chuckled, his entire body relaxed as his shoulders slumped.

"I wanted to see how you'd react to me doing what I wanted, love. Obviously you didn't object," he replied in a smooth tone. I scowled and leaned on the couch armrest, closing my eyes.

"Well. I hated it so very much," I hissed. Suddenly, I felt him beside me, followed by a poke on the side. I bolted up and glared at him, surprised he was so close to my face again.

"Really now?" he wondered, tilting his head, smirking. I nodded defiantly. The vampire shook his head with a grin, this time not moving away. "I think I'll stay here this time," he told me. I rolled my eyes and shut them. Suddenly, I felt his arm go over my shoulders. I tensed, but slowly leaned into him and felt myself drift off to sleep. *This is extremely dangerous... you can't trust him,* said a voice in my head, probably my own 'evil' inner voice.

Fuck off. I do what I want, I replied to it, smirking as I slept. It was more restful of a sleep than I had in a long while.

"UH... GUYS?" QUESTIONED a voice in front of us. My eyes flew open to fall on a very amused looking Darcia. I blinked, then realized where I was. Goliath's arm was still around me, ah crap. I jumped off the couch and widened my eyes, watching as the vampire slowly came to.

"Eh?" Goliath muttered sleepily. I was blushing as I cleared my throat and turned to Darcia.

"What time is it?" I asked, trying to avoid any awkwardness. The shifter snickered, glancing down at the watch on her wrist. Her grin slowly faded.

"It's 4:30 PM. We need to leave like now," she yawned, obviously just having woken up herself. I quickly darted to the other room and changed into new clothing. When I emerged, Goliath and Darcia were standing by the door, both looking uneasy around the other. "For gods' snakes, let's go!"

We hurried out the door, letting Darcia lead as Goliath and I followed. We walked along in silence, obviously we were all a bit nervous. When we finally got to the clearing, no one was there. We were greeted by an abnormal silence. No birds, no bugs. It was eerie, and I was more tense than a snake. Darcia nervously glanced down at her watch.

"It's five after. Where is he?! I knew they needed help last night! You idiots will be the death of my pack!" she yelled. She whirled, pointing at us. I bared my teeth defensively, shaking my head.

"Wait, wait! He could just be la—" I began, but was cut off by a chuckle.

From the shadows emerged Xadrian, his golden eyes focused on us. "Relax Darc, I'm fine," he reassured. Darcia looked as though she were about to pass out from relief. The shifter let out a sigh.

"I thought Smoke had gotten you," she whispered, sadness and worry in her eyes. "Is everyone else alright?" she asked, hopeful.

"Oh they will be," Xadrian replied. I heard Goliath hiss with anger, and I myself felt something very off. Just then, we were surrounded by people with various eye colors and types. All were grinning to reveal carnivorous teeth, those of an animal, not quite human. Darcia gasped, looking from one to another.

"My...my pack! I'm glad to see you OK!" she giggled, but it was a nervous one. The shifters laughed dangerously. Despite this, Goliath and I remained passive for now. I had the deep feeling of dread, just knowing that we were in for it big time now.

"Mhmm. We want you now, you and that dragon. Get rid of the vampire. We don't need him!" Xadrian turned, saying it to his entire pack. I instantly burst into action. Lunging for the nearest shapeshifter, I withdrew my claws and sank them into his arm.

Behind me, I heard Darcia cry out. "Xadrian, what the hell?! These are my friends, they saved me!" she shrieked.

"You were never in danger, Darc. I told Smoke to leave you be, to not kill you! You led your friends right to us! Once we give the dragon to Ash, we'll get what we've wanted! Peace! Prey! Endless land!" he cheered. Goliath was defending himself against the mass of shifters, but there were just too many.

"I refuse, you traitor!" yelled Darcia. I saw her shift and lunge for him. Xadrian shook his head, grinning.

"You have no choice in the matter!" he yelled. Wings sprang from his back as he lashed out with glowing claws, slicing Darcia across the eye. He was what I suspected indeed, a golden eagle. I had no time to help her, though, because suddenly the surrounding shifters lunged at me. I was thrown down harshly, now held down by a huge brown bear.

Power surged through me as I let out a roar. I shifted as fast as I could, throwing the bear off and snapping at it. The bear was bigger and taller than myself, so I could tell in human form he was abnormally large. He towered over me at nine feet, even as I was in dragon form. I was a lot longer and bigger in terms of mass, though. I lashed out with my claws, tripping him. But I forgot to take into account every other shifter out for me.

Teeth and claws sank into me, peeling back my scales and splashing my blood everywhere. Tigers, wolves, lions, even huge snakes were sinking extremely sharp fangs into me. They were no ordinary animals at all, but enhanced creatures due to being shifters, meaning they were a lot faster *and* stronger. This was just a *walk in the park,* then.

There were too many. I fell to the ground and switched to my normal, human form, covering my face. I expected them to rip me to pieces, but that didn't happen.

"Sambuca!" I heard Goliath's yell. His voice was strained, as if he had been fighting hard too.

"Run, Goliath! Get help! I think they need me alive!" I responded. "DO NOT STOP! PLEASE! I DON'T WANT TO LOSE YOU!" I screamed. I heard the vampire cry out, but heard no more. The growls and hisses around me drowned out all sound.

Then, everything just went quiet. I peered over to see Darcia hanging from her tail in the talons of Xadrian. He flapped leisurely, and clearly the Tasmanian devil shifter was alive but in pain. "The damn bloodsucker escaped.. no matter. He wasn't a threat to begin with. Let's take them away," he growled.

I felt myself being lifted but was too weak from the blood loss to struggle. My eyes met Darcia's as she stared at me fearfully. I tried to give her a reassuring smile. We'd get out, hopefully. It didn't reach my eyes, though, as the shapeshifters carried us away.

Chapter 26

I was blindfolded and gagged roughly. I felt myself being carried some unknown distance, each *thump* of the footsteps of my unknown captor making me feel more sick. The entire time, my teeth were bared with pure hatred.

I was pretty sure Darcia *had* been unaware of Xadrian's betrayal. I was pissed, how could we be so ignorant? I should have listened to Goliath to begin with. I felt myself being shoved into a hard wooden chair. Metal cuffs were clasped over my wrists, and my legs were chained together. I felt the blindfold being untied from behind me and blinked at the bright light that hit my eyes.

I was in a stony run-down room; there was blood spattered on the walls, as if there had been centuries of murder here. The smell of dried blood and death hit my nose, making me cringe. There were no windows, and it seemed like even the dirt floor was stained with rather recent blood. I looked up to see Xadrian smiling at me, looking very excited. I didn't show my fear, but that didn't hide the fact that I was downright horrified.

"What did you do to Darcia?" I asked softly, concerned for my new friend. I knew this was not her fault, and I hoped she was somewhat safe. Xadrian smirked at my question and grabbed my chin, forcing me to look straight into his golden eyes.

"She's restrained in a room quite like this. She'll come around to join us. But you... you're like the diamond in the ruff, little dragon. My pack is going to get *big* territory and prey for your pathetic little self," he chucked. He licked his lips, displaying his animal fangs as he did so. Weird how they were like that though he was a bird shifter. I rolled my eyes.

"Ash is turning as many as possible into his little minions, isn't he?" I growled softly. This made Xadrian's eyes flash in anger.

"I am not a minion of that fool. Once he is stupid enough to grant me territory in exchange for you, my pack will rise and slaughter his armies. *We* will take over, and *we* will rule," he promised. I just laughed, spitting in his face.

"Oh please, you idiots are all the same. Smoke wants money, you want power, Ash wants chaos. All the same. For what, then? What do you hope to accomplish once you gain what you seek out so ambitiously?" I questioned, actually pretty curious.

Xadrian leaned away from me, now pacing. His eyes were dark with thought. "My pack can live in peace from both you *hunters* and the backstabbing humans we swore to protect so long ago. We can finally have freedom," he growled. My eyes widened; maybe he wasn't as psychotic as I thought to begin with.

"And you think giving more power to Ash will grant you freedom? He just wants his kind to rule, he will destroy you and your pack as soon as he is rid of all who oppose him," I tried to reason. Xadrian shot me an angered look and shook his head.

"No, he promised me my pack would prosper. In exchange for catching you, we *will* rise, we will have power," he replied in a half-hearted tone. I smiled; he was beginning to crack.

"You know what kind of person Ash is. You really think by sacrificing me, you'll prosper? It's going to backfire on you," I added, glaring at him. The shifter suddenly bared his teeth at me.

"The decision had been made long before I brought you here, dragon. Your fate is sealed, there is nothing you can do about it," he snarled. I sighed; looked like I hadn't really gone anywhere with my argument.

Ah well.

It had been worth a shot. I watched him turn to leave, and saw him pause. "It's nothing personal, dragon. You will be taken shortly," he said in a weary voice. Then, the door shut, and I was left in the flashing light of the bloody room.

I balled my fists, my venom-green eyes glowing. For some reason, I couldn't shift. I looked down at the iron, narrowing my eyes before coming to a realization. "Fey Iron. Damn it... they *are* smarter than they look," I growled. Alright, so dragon form was out of the picture. Perhaps I could make progress in human form, though. I scrunched up my hands and tried to pull them through, but the flesh of my palm kept preventing them from slipping out. An idea came to mind, though, as slowly I grinned.

"Venom can be used for more than killing..." I muttered. I tilted my five fingers upward so that my hand was now a very wide V with my arm. Concentrating hard, I let my venom flow through my fingertips to my nails. It began to drip down the back of my hand to my wrist. The flow was growing at a rapid rate, soon enough I had a stream of green liquid flowing down my hand to my wrist. Now that my entire hand was wet, perhaps I could get somewhere.

Again I tried to pull it out. Gritting my teeth, I gasped as some skin was ripped off my hand in the process but otherwise was in one piece. I flexed my fingers, wiping off the coated venom onto my shirt. My hand looked red and swelling, but at least it was freed.

Next, I needed to look at the leg chains. I peered down, crossing my arms in thought. I wiggled my legs somewhat, causing the chains to clang together. My eyes flashed as I clawed at the chains, only managing to leave deep gouges in my own legs. I let out a sigh; sometimes sheer brutality didn't work out so well.

I thought for a moment and looked at the lock on the chains. "Hmm... I wonder..." Now that my hands were not covered with fey iron any longer, perhaps I could access some of my dragonic power. I covered the lock with my hands and concentrated. It became so heated that the mechanism expanded enough so I could pull the padlock out of place, as if it were unlocked. Feeling victorious, I shoved the chains off and got to my feet, growling.

Now time for part two of five thousand. I stood by the door, waiting... waiting... I knew the heavy metals were not breakable even by me in dragon form. I slumped against the wall, feeling my mind drift off.

So much time had passed that my eyes began to blink shut when suddenly the sound of metal against metal snapped me out of it. The door slowly began to open, and I instantly made myself pay attention.

A figure stumbled in. "Sam?!" came Darcia's worried voice to my ears. I narrowed my eyes and lunged behind her, clasping my hand over her mouth. She let out a muffled scream, bucking, as I leaned to speak in her ear.

"Are you with them?! Are the others here?! Where is Ash?!" I snapped. I felt her relax at my voice. She shook her head, prompting me to let go and back off for now. She let out a gasp, catching her breath. Her eyes narrowed as she turned to me.

"The hell was that for? I'm here to get you out of here. No one knows of me," she breathlessly growled. I crossed my arms.

"Excuse me for making assumptions, Darcia. I thought you were on their side for a second, since you're free, but now obviously I know otherwise," I sighed. I held my forehead, suddenly feeling very grateful. "Thank you for saving me, though. You know the way out?" I asked, hopeful.

Darcia gave a nod as I looked at her. "Follow me," she growled urgently. We shuffled out of the door, quietly creeping down the stone halls. There were many twists and turns, leading me to believe that I had previously been in a dungeon. I shuddered.

"What happened in that room?" I whispered in question. Darcia paused and glanced back at me, her eyes grim.

"A long time ago, my race was more savage than even Xadrian is now. They used to capture, torment, and kill humans just for the fun of it. Lately Xadrian has been doing the same to vampires, but to get information. I find it horrid, but he ignores me when I tell him enough is enough. That was one thing about him that I always found...off," she muttered. Darcia seemed lost in thought as we walked onward. Soon we were faced with stairs, which we crawled up as quietly as possible.

"We are almost out. As soon as you see the forest, you need to make a run for it," she told me. I gave a nod and frowned at her.

"What about you?" I wondered.

"I need to convince the sane members of my pack to work with us. There is still hope, Sam. I'm here for you, and I will see you soon, ok? Go find that stupid vampire of yours," she growled with a joking smile. I could only smile back, but there was one thing I wondered. Why was she different from them?

"Hey Darcia, wh—" I began, but was cut off by a piercing cry from a bird. We had just opened the door, I could see the forest stretching before us. But a black shape flew down and landed in front of us, blocking the entrance.

"Xadrian... no," Darcia snarled, lengthening her claws. The huge bird shifted to human form. I narrowed my eyes to see the golden eagle shapeshifter eyeing us down.

"You both are fools. Why, Darcia? We have a chance for land, for power. Is that not what you want? To save the pack?" he snapped. Darcia shook her head.

"Not like this!" she cried. Xadrian waved his hand.

"Regardless. The vampire is here to take her. There is no way back now," he said flatly. Suddenly, a figure lunged in front of me. The smaller form of Darcia was blocking me from Xadrian.

"No. Not this time. You can kill me if you want, Xadrian. I *will not* let you take my friend!" she screamed. Xadrian snarled and began to pace, frustrated.

"Move aside, Darcia. I am not moving you, I hurt you before but I do *not* want to do so again!" he yelled. Darcia shook her head, not budging.

"It doesn't need to be this way!" was all she snapped. Xadrian had been about to reply when he was violently shoved to the ground. Red eyes met mine as a slow grin came to the face of someone I truly feared and hated. Darcia was suddenly in the air, being held by the neck by none other than Ash.

"I grow impatient, fools. You shifters are more useless than you look. No matter. The dragon is mine now," the vampire chuckled. Darcia was thrown into Xadrian, and both landed on the ground in a heap. Suddenly my hands were behind my back. Ash was so much goddamn faster than I remembered.

I felt cold iron sear my flesh, causing me to cry out. Despite being restrained, I bucked and turned my head, sinking my teeth into his shoulder. This only caused the vampire to laugh. "You think you have a chance against me, dragon?" he whispered into my ear. I cried out as his fangs sank into my neck, for he had no mercy or remorse. My energy was drained rapidly, but I was still semi-conscious enough to hear the commotion. My half-closed eyes watched as Darcia lunged for Ash.

The vampire backhanded her into a tree, causing her to shriek out in pain. Xadrian, still winded from being slammed into, was attempting to stand, however the vampire just kicked him down and put a foot on his chest. He leaned into the male shifter's face. "Make sure that rat doesn't get in my way, or your pack will face more than extermination," he spat. I then felt myself being lifted, traveling very quickly to who-knew-where.

"Your fate won't be a peaceful death, dragon," he said to me softly. His bloody eyes stared into my venom green, which formed a pit in my stomach. He leaned into my face, tilting his head as he darted along with ease.

"I know what you fear the most. A whisper of your past, hmm?" he chuckled. My pupils thinned as suddenly I knew exactly what he meant. "You'd be no use to me dead, hybrid. Keeping you alive for your blood, however, is a different story. I'll have a feast every...single...night..." he mused in a low hum.

I began to shiver, my lips forming the word, "No..." But it was too late now; we were too far for Darcia, Goliath, or anyone else who cared to find me. I saw the kingdom come into view, causing my heart to sink.

Anything but that... Anything but a blood slave...

Part 2: Duo of Beasts

Neither the Noble Devil nor the Crimson Serpent are considered prey; rather, predators in their own right.

Through the eyes of Sam and Darcia

Chapter 27: Darcia

I could only stare in shock as my friend was whisked away by the true enemy. I never felt so horrid in my life. When I was in that pile of bodies left to die, Sam had stopped to save me. Well, her and that repulsive vampire that I hated to admit was pretty cool. Regardless of whether or not Smoke had planned on killing me, I was in dire need and she had come through. Hell, she had agreed to come meet my pack in the clearing, and she'd been worried for me ever since my capture. Despite only meeting her a few days ago, I felt a responsibility as a friend. And now... she was taken by the one she feared the most. I couldn't help that I hadn't come in time, I hadn't been able to get her away. Guilt still weighed heavily in my chest despite me knowing that this wasn't my fault.

My eyes turned to the douchebag *traitor* that was laying on the ground in front of me. His golden eyes were wide open, and his teeth were bared in pure shock. I stood up, wobbly but otherwise OK, and walked over to Xadrian. Suddenly my foot lashed out and struck him on the side. The golden eagle shifter cried out, snapping out of it, and turned his eyes up to me. I took a deep breath and yelled, "YOU'RE AN IDIOT, XADRIAN! WHY THE HELL WOULD YOU DO SOMETHING SO FUCKING STUPID?! OBVIOUSLY HE WASN'T GOING TO HELP THE PACK, HE'S A FREAKIN BLOODSUCKER!" I was breathing rather hard, and my eyes were all black like they were in my Tasmanian devil form.

Xadrian made no move to strike me back. Rather, he hesitantly sat up and slowly went from a crouch to a standing position. I was tense, as if readying for an attack. He took a few steps back, knowing my temper was way worse than anyone's here. I was practically frothing at the mouth.

"Calm down, Darc... I... had no idea..." he tried, but I cut him off with a loud roar.

"YOU HAD NO IDEA?! WHAT HINTED YOU, THE FREAKIN EVIL GLINT IN THE VAMPIRE'S EYES OR THE FACT THAT HIS CRONIES ALMOST KILLED ME?!" I screamed. I was in his face now, all of my jagged sharp teeth ready to snap a chunk out of his face if he decided to say something I disliked.

Xadrian cleared his throat, and despite him being a lot taller, he was very clearly intimidated. No one liked to mess with an angry Tasmanian devil. That's why they called us *devils*. Xadrian put a hand behind his head, glancing over to where Ash had disappeared with Sambuca. "Well, now that I know Ash was lying, uh, I will help out against him?" he tried in a small voice. He winced as I snapped my teeth inches from his face. Pack member or not, he knew I could severely hurt him if I decided to right this moment. Shifters, when enraged, got a huge increase in strength and speed.

"DAMN RIGHT WE ARE! YOU ARE GOING TO THE REST OF THE PACK RIGHT NOW AND TELLING THEM HOW FUCKING BADLY YOU MESSED UP!" I roared, pointing to the door. Oddly enough, there was a significant amount of them gathering. I could see Bernard, the Bear shifter, Valiant the lady panther, even the little songbird Lilith. The rest of the pack gathered around them, drawn by my yells.

Bernard stepped forward, his eyes set on me. "Xadrian, did Ash give us what he promised?" he asked in a quiet voice. Xadrian got a sick look on his face, as if he really did not want to answer that. Slowly, he shook his head and cleared his throat.

"Ah... no. Turns out, it was all an elaborate scam. He took her and left, sort of threatening to wipe us out. He had been so convincing..." the golden eagle shifter said. He suddenly looked rather tired and sad. I didn't care, I was still seething.

"SOME LEADER YOU ARE, XADRIAN. WE COULD HAVE ENDED HIS TYRANNY BY WORKING WITH POTENTIAL ALLIES, YET YOU SOLD YOUR SOUL TO THE ONE VILLAIN WHO WANTS TO DESTROY IT!" I snarled. Xadrian suddenly was in *my* face, baring his fangs and hissing.

"I did what I thought was best for the pack. I was going with the winner! Ash will win this battle, mark my words. By working with him, I knew we could not only save ourselves, but eventually overthrow him... now..." he snarled. Obviously his plans didn't go through the way he had wanted.

Rather than flinch back, I raised my hand and slapped him cleanly across the face. A nice red mark appeared on Xadrian's face, and he had such a look of shock that I almost burst into hysterical laughter. I kept my angered glare, however, as I made no move to back away. I was almost *daring* him to strike me back. Rather than doing so, he backed off, giving me a killer glare.

I walked up to him and shoved him aside, so hard that he fell to the ground. He let out a hiss and attempted to get to his feet, but I wouldn't have it. I drop-kicked him cleanly in the stomach, winding him. He would not be able to even move for a few seconds. That was all the time I needed.

I faced the pack, ignoring the surprised glares and narrowing my eyes. "Clearly your *leader* has made a grave mistake. I knew we needed to ally with Sam and her vampire friend when I met them. They have more power than you think. If you *want* to have any chance against Ash, you need to work with *me*. OK?" I muttered, challenging anyone to oppose me.

Bernard gave a slow nod, his cold gaze falling to Xadrian. The golden eagle shifter had not bothered to get up; his guilty eyes were turned to the ground as he kept his silence. Despite my anger, I made no more attempt to attack him. The other shifters gradually nodded. My lip curled up into a smirk. "Good. Now if you excuse me, I have some rescue plans to create," I muttered.

I shoved past the other shifters, easily knocking several to the ground. The anger still burned within me, so I kept the crazy strength that I gained from it. No one attacked me, however, they knew better than anyone else that it was a horrid idea to step up against me when I was angry. The last person who had gotten me pissed like this and decided to attack regretted it. Let's just say they only have eight fingers and one eye now.

I took a seat at the table in the center of the large room. This base was my home prior to my capture by Smoke. We had one central room with a huge table that led off to several other rooms including kitchens and bathrooms. This is where we held our planning meetings and such, to talk about the pack business. This room was huge, made bigger by the fact that I was alone. I knew no one would bother me here, though, while I took out several maps and began to search for key areas, such as Ash's castle.

No one engaged me for hours, and I was almost drifting off to sleep at the table when I heard a peculiar sound. A breeze ruffled my hair, and immediately I knew something was wrong. The windows in this room had all been closed beforehand. Slowly, my eyes slid to one of the windows. To my horror, it indeed was wide open. Right as I realized this, a hand clamped over my mouth.

I let out a muffled scream, squirming and kicking as hard as I could. A hiss sounded in my ear. "Where...is...Sam?!" came a familiar voice. I relaxed, realizing it was only that crazy vampire that accompanied my friend. I didn't consider him a friend yet since I had no trust for *any* vampire, though. Goliath let go, allowing me to turn to face him.

To my surprise, he was accompanied by several other vampires. *He* looked very aggressive, what with one of his eyes hidden by his midnight black hair. He had on a suit and a top hat, oddly. I could see, though, that under his fancy jacket there was probably body armor. He had come prepared, judging by the long, silver sword in one of his hands.

The other vampires had various weapons, be it knives, bows, or even claws like I had seen Sam wearing at one point. All looked about ready to murder me. I held up my hands, cooled off now from my previous anger. "Sam is...gone. But I have convinced my pack to help," I tried.

Goliath's eyes flashed dangerously. "Gone? Gone where? I tracked your pack here, and your idiot leader had snatched her away while we didn't have enough in numbers to counter him. If you do not return her to me, I will slaughter you all with no remorse," he hissed. Woah, he was very angry and dangerous now. Quite like how I had been. Good thing I was clear-minded and could talk to him properly now.

My wary gaze looked over the vampires. They numbered my pack equally, but I didn't want any battle here. This could be a chance to not only ally against Ash, but to save my friend as well. I owed her that much. "I am not trying to go against you, vampire. I only want to save my friend. In fact, she almost escaped, had Xadrian not blocked our way. I was the one who unlocked the door to set her free," I muttered.

Goliath bared his fangs, but did not move to attack me yet. He knew it would be futile to battle with me. Deep down he knew I was not the issue here. "So Xadrian still has her then? He blocked your escape, and he took her?" he said in a flat voice. I shook my head to that, almost shaking when he slammed his fist on the table. Wow, he almost broke it. "Which means..." he gasped.

I nodded. "Ash has her now. Which is why we need to *work together* to get her back," I growled. Goliath eyed me with fury, looking as if he wanted to rip out my throat. He wasn't thinking rationally, but I knew that if he killed me now, he would have no chance of getting her back. So I stood up straighter and darted to him, now getting in his face.

"And if you do not believe me, then you can kill me here and now. But then Sam will be doomed because of *your* poor decision!" I snarled. Goliath was taken aback, he physically backed away. The fury in my eyes was not matched by anyone. I didn't care. I would *not* have anyone come in the way of me saving someone who was a friend.

The vampire took a deep breath, calming himself. He put a hand on his forehead, I could see the grief forming on his face. My voice softened as I put my hand on his shoulder. He made no attempt to move away. "We will get her back, vampire. Trust me," I muttered. Goliath's eyes met mine as we formed an understanding. Without an alliance, not only would Sam be tormented for eternity, but the entire city would be doomed as well. Goliath slowly nodded.

"I understand, Darcia. But betray me like your leader did, and I will not hesitate to destroy you," he promised. I gave a nod, smirking.

"Same goes for you, sir," I chuckled. I heard several growls behind me and saw the vampires tense. I turned to see my pack glaring at the vampires with distrust. I put my hands up, as if to block them from potentially lunging.

"Whoa, whoa. They are here to work with us, not fight. They had come for Sam—but now we need to work together to bring down Ash while saving her. *This* is better for the pack. An alliance, for once in our lives. We do *not* need to hate vampires, hell, we're both so similar as a species anyway. You're either with me or against me," I snarled.

Bernard took a step forward, dipping his head. "Do not fail us like Xadrian did, Darcia. I trust your judgement and will work with these new allies, so long as we will eventually be free," he growled. I gave a nod and smiled as the rest of the pack joined him to dip their heads in respect.

I turned to Goliath and his group of vampires, giving a thumbs up. I held out my hand, smirking as the vampire wrinkled his eyebrows in confusion. "For Sam," I whispered. Goliath heard and understood. His eyes hardened in determination as he accepted my hand, shaking it.

"And now, we plan. We have a *hell* of a lot ahead of us... and hey, vampire? How did you stumble upon these allies?" I questioned.

To my surprise, he did not step up. Instead, a vampire woman with red hair like Sambuca's took a step forward. Her hazel eyes were soft as she gave a smile. "He stands for the peace we desire in the city, back before Ash decided to destroy it. Sambuca saved me from an evil vampire during the city battle. She does not know it, but I would have lost my life had she not stepped in. I, along with the rest of my group, wish to end the cycle of evil reign and start a new era of peace. My name is Irene. Goliath found us in the city trying to fight off the tyrants," she explained.

Goliath gave a nod, and slowly I smiled. "Welcome to our home, then. There is plenty of room for you guests. But for now, let's take a seat and discuss our ideas moving forward," I began.

Chapter 28: Darcia

Progress was slow—planning and training took time, which was stressing all of us out while Sam was no doubt suffering. After a few weeks, however, we were ready to get shit done. So I thought.

I raised my eyebrows at Irene's words. We had been discussing ideas and plans for hours that night, but this one was by far the most ridiculous I'd heard yet. "Ally with Smoke? Are you serious? You do know he's Ash's main crony?" I pointed out. Goliath nodded in agreement, looking at the vampire woman like she had grown another head.

"I am aware. However, making enemies should not be our goal," she explained. I rolled my eyes, letting out a sigh. Damn peacemakers, sometimes battle was needed to resolve a conflict, especially now. I did not feel like trusting someone who'd almost killed me and left me for dead on the streets. I shivered, remembering the many times he had bitten me. And unlike Sambuca, I was not immune to the venom. He had paralyzed me with it.

"Making enemies? He is already our enemy. Smoke is dangerous, despite being under Ash's command he has his own agenda and will adhere to his greedy needs," I growled.

Irene cracked a smile. "Exactly. If we play to his desires, we could get him on our side. The one with the more power will prevail," she muttered. I shook my head, crossing my arms. What was she getting at?

"Uh, but Ash is now the king. He has more power than all of us combined," I hissed. Irene shook her head, her eyes focused on my face.

"Why did Smoke keep you alive when he slaughtered the others?" she asked quietly. I just laughed, now figuring she was crazy.

"Uh, cause Xadrian struck a deal with Ash, who in turn ordered Smoke to keep me alive? Something like that," I replied, my eyes getting dark.

"Smoke plays by his own rules, remember? He was ordered to keep many humans alive as a food source for Ash's army, but he did not listen. I know this because I'd been listening in the shadows to Ash's orders. Robert disobeyed all but *one* order. And that was to keep you alive. Do you have something he wants, Darcia?" she questioned.

I shrugged, irritated. Confused and a bit afraid now, I needed to know what the hell was going on. "No? I don't know? Why didn't he kill me then?" I snapped. Irene smirked.

"He saw that you were the most stubborn, and probably the most powerful, of the shifters. He could *benefit* profusely from keeping you alive, if he had you on his side. He could use you to raid for money, because who would want to challenge an enraged Tasmanian devil? Smoke is always on the lookout for what will benefit him the most. He knew Sambuca was Ash's target and that he could not have her. But you and your pack, well, he wants you next, " she finished.

"He is working with Ash, gods damn it. If he disobeys Ash, the vampire king will kill him," I sighed, not liking where she was going with this.

"Mhmm. And I'm sure Smoke has no idea we're against Ash, yet anyway. Keep in mind, he wasn't here when Sam was taken, and could still think we are working with both him and Ash. Perhaps if we play to his greed, give him empty promises, we can gain an ally," Irene suggested.

Goliath blinked, a slow smile forming on his face. Was I the only one not getting it? He chuckled. "I see. Promise *him* the throne, tell him that *he* is the deserving one. And when we get rid of Ash, we turn on him. But we need to convince him that we are fully supporting him," the vampire realized. Irene gave a nod, but I continued my scowling.

"So what does this have to do with how he didn't kill me?" I growled, not liking the smirk Irene was giving me now.

"You're the key player here, Darcia. He wants *you* for the power you have, that is why he didn't kill you. You also lead the pack now, so you need to be the one to approach him. He knows you will be the one to dislike him the most. You need to convince him otherwise. If you can do that, he will work with us. Think of it this way; why would you of all people go to him non-aggressively if you didn't plan on making an alliance? Goliath will talk to him as well, after you play to his desire for power. He has the city. Ash entrusted him with keeping it under siege," Irene finished. Her now amber eyes met my currently brown ones.

I snorted. "Fine, fine. I will go to him and explain 'what my pack wants' and how Ash is not providing it for us. How we seek a real king, and how if he grants us our desires, we will grant his. We can drop him once we overthrow Ash. OK?" I snarled. Irene gave a satisfied nod. I couldn't believe I agreed to this, but the plan did seem rather solid.

Well, not the trusting of Smoke part. But the more we snatched away Ash's allies, the more of a chance we had to defeat him. And Smoke was, at the moment, one of his most powerful allies. I stood up, grabbing one of my silver knives and glancing behind me. "Do I need to go alone?" I asked in a dry voice, already knowing the answer.

"Unfortunately, yes. You cannot appear aggressive to Smoke," Irene replied. I gave a nod, and after a second more of hesitation, exited. I knew my way to the city from here, and the sun was already starting to set. Night was when vampires and shifters were more active. Neither of us were affected at all by sunlight, like most of the stupid humans believed. I really, really did not want to face Smoke. How was I supposed to convince him my pack was on his side?

After about an hour of walking, it was pitch black outside. The city loomed ahead, a shadow against the pale moonlight. There was no light, none at all, aside from the moon. The vampires who controlled it had no need for such dazzling electricity. My feet met the pavement as I slowly walked the city, feeling eyes on me but seeing no one. I felt a *whoosh* behind me and whirled to see... no one yet still.

I let out a sigh, baring my teeth. "Come on out. I know you're there," I whispered. Suddenly, my hands were being held behind my back, and all I could see were tons of red eyes staring me down. I was surrounded faster than I had thought possible. My heart nearly stopped when I saw Smoke approach, his snow white hair slicked back as usual. I had surprised him, it seemed, by coming here. He was glancing around warily, as if expecting the rest of my pack to surround us. When nothing else happened, he leaned into my face.

"Hello there, Darcia. Come to provide us with a snack?" he whispered, his fangs gleaming as he spoke. That got a laugh out of the surrounding vampires, but a scowl from me. I shook my head slowly, choosing my words carefully.

"No, Smoke. I have come because of a broken deal. Ash didn't give us what we promised, and I'm sure he won't give you what you want as well. I came to warn you," I coughed. Robert Smoke only burst out in laughter at that. His finger drew across my cheek, and it took my everything to not bite it off.

"Oh really? You care that much that you'd come warn me of my demise? How touching," he mused, giving a low chuckle. His eyes narrowed. "But I am not stupid, Darcia. I know your hatred for me, and I know you don't give a damn whether or not Ash betrays me. So, why are you really here, other than to die to my fangs?" he asked in a low voice.

I gritted my teeth, squirming to no avail. The vampire that had my arms behind my back had a firm grip. "I came for the betterment of my pack, Smoke. I know you're not stupid enough to betray allies like Ash does. I know what you really want, and it's pointless to fight if our wants don't conflict. If our wants intertwine, my pack wants territory and peace. You want the throne. Working together... we can make that happen," I said in a very serious voice.

I could see Smoke pause and think for a moment. His red eyes flashed as he looked back at my face. "It's true I want more than just this city. But I also want more than this throne, Darcia. I want power, undying loyalty, and...blood. Not just any blood. Dragon's blood gives magical properties, it grants the drinker with power. Just look at how dangerous Ash is," he chuckled. I tensed, knowing exactly what he was getting at. If I promised him Sambuca's blood, Goliath would be in an uproar. But, well, I could make a false promise like the rest. Time to weave my lies.

"You want the half-dragon? Ash has her now, as I am sure you are aware. We have no need of her. You can dine on her as long as you grant my pack peace. You will need to lie to Goliath, who we tricked into working with us as well. He thinks you only want the throne, and he is willing to give it to you so long as he gets Sambuca. Of course, you can take her from him once you are king," I tried.

Smoke frowned at the mention of Goliath, but he waved it off. "Your pack will be free. I know you shifters have undying loyalty to one another, enough to betray another ally. Pity, really, it leads to your individual downfall. Yes—the ones you care about will be free. But *you...* I want you as my enforcer. You must sell your soul to me, Darcia. Why? Because I can sense your power. Not only does it flow through your blood, but you're a true leader. I cannot have another leader that could possibly have a chance to oppose me," he muttered. "Are you willing to sacrifice yourself for your pack?"

I was. I knew what he was getting at, too. The blood bond. New vampires were either born or made. To make one, there needed to be a blood exchange. The blood bond was the same concept but to a lesser degree. If he took some of my blood, and I took some of his, we could be bonded. No shifter had ever survived turning into a vampire anyway. He would know where I was at all times, thereby being able to find me anywhere. Vampire venom would decrease in toxicity for me, in turn my anger would also empower him. How badly did I want him as an ally?

If I did this, it would mean freeing the humans, my pack, and Sambuca despite my lies. Ash would lose a good amount of his army if I gained Smoke. So, I gave a slow nod, a tear trickling down my cheek. It had to be done, it was the only way we could move forward. If we had control of the city and the forest, Ash would be at a huge disadvantage. Smoke gave a wide smile, his fangs flashing.

"Perfect. Hold still then, Darcia. This will only hurt *a lot,"* he laughed. I tensed, feeling fangs sink into my neck. My blood flowed into his mouth, and I could feel the paralyzing venom lock my muscles. I made no sound, and soon enough he was done. He used a very small amount of the venom, so my muscles weren't unusable for long. Smoke wiped his mouth of my blood, and then used a nail to cut into his palm. He held it out, and after wincing, I drank the spilling blood, just enough to create the bond.

Once done, Smoke gave a satisfied smile. "Perfect. Now run along to your friends, Darcia. I will be seeing you soon," he chuckled. As fast as he and his cronies appeared, they were gone. I put a hand on my still-bleeding neck and started back, my eyes cast solemnly to the ground.

FROM THE SHADOWS...

Red eyes gleamed in the fog of the city. They watched as Smoke darted away, and the vampire seemed rather satisfied with his cunning deal. Pity...

Anyways, *he* was like a shadow to everyone else, a power similar to that of his brother's. "Tsk tsk... but you will be a mere pest, I suppose. Funny how the shifter sold her soul so quickly, thinking that it would actually benefit her to snatch away such a worthless ally. I look forward to seeing this play out..."

Ash took out the tape-recorder, smirking.

"*Fine, fine. I will go to him and explain 'what my pack wants' and how Ash is not providing it for us. How we seek a real king, and how if he grants us our desires, we will grant his. We can drop him once we overthrow Ash. OK?*"—Darcia, 9:30 PM

He shook his head, delighting in the irony. "I'll simply wait until the group decides to pay a visit. My little minion Smoke will be rather upset to hear this..." he smirked. He put the recording in his pocket and licked a few specks of blood from his lips. Sam had given up her screaming a while ago, yet she still managed to try and attack him every time he fed. She was too weak from the fey iron chains to inflict actual damage, but he had to admit he was impressed. He set off, his eyes flashing in hunger and anticipation of another meal.

Chapter 29: Darcia

My eyes were solemn when I reentered the base. Goliath and Irene were in discussion, and Xadrian was back talking to the pack. I glared at Xadrian warily, receiving a frown in return. When the Golden Eagle shifter's eyes fell on my neck, though, his eyes widened in alarm. Suddenly the shifter was in front of me, staring me down like I was dying. "Darcia, what the hell happened?!" he gasped, sounding genuinely concerned.

I shoved him away from me, baring my teeth angrily. "None of your fucking business, traitor. Why would you care?!" I snapped. Xadrian blinked, a look of hurt flashing across his eyes. It was gone just as soon as it appeared as he narrowed his eyes and showed his teeth aggressively.

"I actually care about my pack, Darcia. As much as the mistake I made was a setback, I would do it again if it meant my pack was safe. I only want the best for us. *All* of us. And for you to put yourself in danger like that, Darcia..." he hissed, not finishing his last sentence. I scoffed and shook my head.

"You had your chance to listen to me. You chose to ignore my words. Shows how you care," I replied with venom in my tone. I took my seat, ignoring how everyone was eyeing my neck like I had some sort of disease. I cleared my throat, my eyes growing very serious.

"We now have allies in the city. I did what I had to in order to secure it," I muttered. Irene gave a slight nod, her wary eyes resting on my bite marks.

"What did you need to do in order to get it?" she asked in a quiet voice. I shuddered, remembering the bite, and the pain that went with it.

"I made a deal with Smoke. I promised him the blood of the dragon, as well as our undying loyalty to be king," I began. I saw Goliath let out a hiss and suddenly tense. Irene put a hand on his shoulder, holding him back from probably lunging. I met his gaze, a deep frown on my face. "Both lies that can be broken with ease," I assured him. The vampire relaxed somewhat, but still looked rather angry. "It had to be done, otherwise Smoke would not have agreed. I told him I would lie to you in order to keep you as an ally. As far as he knows, you only think he wants to be king. Let's keep it that way," I continued.

Goliath's eyes flashed darkly. "Go on, then. I can sense it, Darcia. There is a key part to the story you don't want to tell us," the vampire muttered. I let out a sigh and rubbed my neck, wincing at the dried blood that caked it.

"Fine, fine. Smoke didn't want an opposing leader. He knows I am a powerful shifter, and being one of the few pureblooded shifters, he didn't want such a strong potential opponent. In order to remove that threat, he needed to have some control. So... I allowed him to form a blood bond," I finished, the last few words lower in volume than the others.

The pack immediately erupted into outrage as roars and hisses filled the air. Irene and Goliath looked flat out surprised, while Xadrian wore a horrified expression. I crossed my arms, waiting for the initial reaction to die down before adding, "It was the only way."

"To hell with the only way! DARCIA! Why the hell would you make such a foolish decision!" yelled Xadrian. My head turned to him as I bared my teeth angrily.

"Like I said, I had to! Now Ash has lost control of the city, and we can surround the kingdom. It was a sacrifice I was willing to make! If we want to save Sambuca before she is *more traumatized*, we need to be as effective as possible," I replied. Goliath blinked, giving a smile of respect. It seemed he was finally getting the picture that I really did want to save my friend. Irene stood from her seat, her eyes trained on my neck. She let out a sigh.

"We need to get her cleaned up. She's been through a lot, stressing her more will only hurt her further," she said reasonably. Truthfully, I was exhausted. Resting would be fine. I stood up, rather shaky as the events of what happened were catching up to me. My head hung in exhaustion from blood loss.

A girl with dark brown hair and eyes of the same color stepped forward. "I'll take care of you, Darcia," she muttered. I gave a smile. This woman was Valiant, Xadrian's sister, and while she was as stubborn as him, she was skilled in healing. The panther shifter offered me her hand. I took it, allowing her to bring me toward the medicine room of our building.

I laid down on bed that looked rather comfy, sighing. Valiant cleaned my neck off and gave me a warm glass of tea to relax me. She gave me a sad glance. "You know, Xadrian really cares about us. I know you hate him right now, but he just doesn't want to see you hurt," she began. I rolled my eyes and took a sip of my tea.

"He shouldn't have put his trust into those who almost killed me, then," I growled. Valiant shrugged, her panther fangs flashing as she let out a sigh.

"You were the only one that was spared the horrible 'deal', Darcia. The rest of us were caught and forced to work with those fiends. Xadrian didn't foresee it coming, and it happened while you were out exploring the city. He managed to make a deal with Smoke not to kill you after killing off many of us. Had he not discussed it with Smoke, you'd be dead," she said darkly.

I shook my head. "Regardless. Sam risked her neck to save me, she had no idea I was safe. She saved me purely from the bottom of her heart, as did she try to save the rest of those people. We're friends, and when I tried to argue that point, I fell on deaf ears," I growled.

Valiant gave a soft smile. "We'll get your friend back, Darcia. Just try not to be too mad at Xadrian. He only is trying to help." With that, she left the room, leaving me annoyed. So what, Xadrian had doomed Sam by making that deal. I was still extremely angry with him.

I was drifting into sleep when I began to shiver. There were no blankets in here, probably because this room had not been used in a while. Shifters tended to be too prideful to come to this room, and when brought here, were treated before returning to their normal spots. I bared through it, gritting my teeth as the temperature dropped, when suddenly I heard the door slowly open.

I kept my eyes closed as I felt someone approach. Before I could leap out and lunge at whoever it was, I felt something being draped over me. A blanket? I opened my eyes slowly to see my intruder taking his exit. My eyes caught sight of tawny brown hair... Xadrian? I tilted my head, watching as he reached the entrance of my room and paused. My heart almost stopped as he turned and faced me, his eyes locking on mine.

I raised my eyebrows in question, but he just gave me a scowl. There was concern in his gaze, however, as slowly I gave a smile of appreciation. His frown faded into a sad smile as he dipped his head. "I'll try to right my wrongs, Darcia," he whispered in promise. I snorted.

"You'd better." I turned away, snuggling in the blanket, as slowly I drifted into a deep slumber.

THE FOLLOWING MORNING, no time was wasted. We gathered around the table quickly, all of us holding very serious expressions. My eyes rested on all that were seated, including Xadrian. He was emotionless, seeming to just be ready for some action. I wanted as little dilly-dally as possible. "After we all get a quick meal, I want us to regather. We are heading out in five minutes maximum to the city. I will meet with Smoke, then the attack needs to happen *tonight*. Ash will not expect us to strike so soon," I ordered. Irene, Goliath, and Xadrian seemed to agree.

The pack and group of vampires went off to get breakfast. I sat at the table, staring at a map and tracing my finger over the marked areas where we wanted to ambush. This battle would be hard, as we still were outnumbered. Now, rather than ten-to-one, it was about five-to-one. I knew each one of us would fight like ten warriors, though. We fought for freedom while the enemy fought for power. Well... about half of us fought for a noble reason. That was what counted.

I almost jumped when a hand fell on my shoulder. "I'll get you some breakfast if you'd like, Darc," Xadrian offered. I shrugged his hand off and shook my head.

"I'm not hungry," was my only reply. Despite his kindness last night, I still felt like giving him the cold shoulder.

"You'll be very fatigued if you don't," he pointed out. He had a point, and finally I gave in and waved my hand.

"Fine, fine," I growled. A plate of bacon and eggs was placed in front of me. I dug in, eating like a rabid animal. Xadrian seemed not to mind, he just glanced at the vampires with a bit of distrust. His eyes kept flicking to my neck. "Problem?" I growled, irritated.

Xadrian sighed. "You didn't have to theoretically sell your soul, Darcia..." he muttered.

I rolled my eyes. "Yes I did, and it's too late now. Come on. We're ready to head out," I growled. With that, we set off, making haste as we darted through the forest. I led the pursuit, with Goliath and Irene flanking me. Xadrian was ways behind, having a discussion with his sisters Valiant and Lilith. Good, at least he'd leave me alone for a while.

The dark city loomed ahead as the sun set behind it. This night would be a bloody one. This was especially safe to say considering the moon would soon obtain a red tinge. We slowed as we approached, finally reaching the border between the forest and city.

Red eyes met mine as suddenly Smoke was right in front of me. He smiled, as usual revealing his very sharp looking fangs. I scowled and took a step back, to which he took a step forward.

Robert Smoke let out a laugh. "Well well. My little minion has come to pay us a visit , along with her pesky friends. I knew you were coming, Darcia. Welcome," he chuckled dangerously. I saw him eye my neck and lick his lips. Getting real peeved by that, I did not hesitate to shove him away from me.

"You know why we are here, Smoke. The time to strike down Ash is now. You want the throne? We need to take it. We have come to overthrow Ash," I snarled. Smoke sighed, glancing behind me now to Goliath and Irene. Both eyed him with hatred.

"These peasants will accept me as king?" Smoke asked warily. I gave a nod, as did the others.

"We only want peace, Smoke," I said softly.

"And once I am king? You are required to be mine," he whispered. Xadrian heard him, I could tell by how he tensed behind me. I just gave a nod in response. He cackled and continued. "Perfect! Let us move out then, not a moment to waste!" Smoke said cheerfully. He turned to face his vampiric army, in other words, the traitorous hunters. This was going to be a *long* night.

FROM THE SHADOWS...

"How cute. Your friend has given herself to the traitor in order to save you and defeat me," Ash's voice chuckled. The half-dragon struggled in her bounds. Chains restrained her, the kind made entirely of fey iron. They burned her somewhat, but were not as toxic since she was half human. Her mouth was gagged, she was unable to utter a sound.

Still she struggled.

No... Goliath was *right there*, he was coming into a trap! She could do nothing to warn him.

Still she struggled.

Sambuca was not one to give up. The new vampire king's eyes watched, amused at her attempts to get away and warn her friends and loved ones. She didn't give up at all, did she? She was so close, so close to being saved, yet so far. The irony amused him. Ash tugged the chains, turning away.

"Enough, dragon. I'm starved," he chuckled. Sambuca whimpered slightly, it was all she could do. She thrashed and shook, however being too weak from the fey iron and loss of blood, it was impossible to do much else or make more noise. Not enough attention could be brought to this little patch of shadows that Ash hid them in.

Her muscles went limp as she dizzily walked along. Ash gently picked her up and sighed. "You don't ever give up, do you. Dragons... so tough, yet it gets them nowhere. I do admire your tenacity," he chuckled as they vanished into the shadows, heading back to the castle.

Chapter 30: Darcia

We marched through the foggy shadows, hurrying along as the kingdom came into view. Smoke and his men were behind ours, which was unnerving, but I knew he wouldn't betray us. Not when he was so close to his goal, that is.

I slowed a little, wanting to put out a bit of a curiosity I was having for a while. Soon my pace was equal to Goliath, and I turned my head to talk to the vampire.

"What is Sambuca to you, Goliath?" I asked suddenly, catching him off-guard. "You seem so protective of her."

Goliath looked ahead, a sad glint to his eyes. "Sam woke me from the madness I was holding before. I had been worse than Ash, believe it or not. The blood on my hands is much thicker than what is on his. I saw what Sambuca did, how even a hunter, the type of person whom I hated the most, could show empathy. She was very picky with who she killed. I watched her for a while since she was my target. She spared vampires who were truly good. She attacked when threatened, of course, which is why she tried to kill me. But no, she even saved a child, a vampire child, who she could very well have killed. What is she to me? Not necessarily some light that came on. No, she is sort of like a fire that burned even when everything threatened to put it out. She burned the evils, and warmed the good. She is worth saving, worth protecting," he explained. Wow, this was some serious stuff.

"You're right, I guess. She did save me, and wanted to save the city too. You're a lucky guy," I sighed. Goliath shook his head, his eyes darkening.

"It is torment to see her living her own nightmare," he replied, his expression pained. I put my hand on his shoulder, surprising him. My eyes were determined.

"We *will* save her, Goliath. No matter what. We will save her *and* free the city. No longer do shifters, vampires, and humans need to battle. It is time to end such a bloody past," I growled. Goliath gave a smile and nodded in agreement.

"I hope you are right," he sighed.

We soon reached the kingdom. It, oddly enough, was not guarded by any walls. The place was like another city, but entering it was sort of like traveling back in time. Vampires seemed to like the medieval feel; perhaps it was because that was when they were the dominant species. Shifters had their times in the stone ages, when vampires fell prey to my kind right along with humans. The vampires took control all through the middle ages, but were hunted heavily and killed off in huge numbers during the Renaissance. The royal family always had wanted to revert back to those times, the *Dark Ages* of humans.

Anyway, most of the buildings were run down and made of rotting stone. The castle itself was glorious, it loomed over the entire kingdom with the typical dark look. Gargoyles sat on sharp looking pikes, there were tons of spiraling stairs, and the fixture was massive. Not much to explain, it was a usual thing to see from a typical tyrannical leader. Though, Ash seemed a lot more sinister. Like he was always one step ahead. This time I knew we were going to surprise him. Such an ambush so quickly couldn't be prepared for, right?

My pack moved quickly, shifting into their animal forms. I took a deep breath and leaped into the air, feeling the fur cover my body after a bright flash. My pupils grew to cover my entire eye, and they were an eerie pitch black. "No mercy!" I yelled, ready to throw myself into the fray.

We charged ahead, bolting up the stairs and stopping at the closed wooden door. Bernard took lead now, using his huge form to slam against the door. The abnormally large man made for an epic bear shifter. He easily crashed the door in with his paranormal strength. We were in, and immediately were met with several guards.

The battle ignited, and I bit into whoever I could see that was an enemy. I faced a male vampire with lighter brown hair and dark red clothing. In fact, all the guards seemed to wear the same garb: a red overcoat and red pants with dark boots. Each was equipped with a dagger or sword, but I knew that my army had similar weapons to counter that. The shifters didn't even need weaponry, for we had our fangs and claws.

I sliced into my opponent's chest, narrowing my eyes as blood sprayed at me. The knife whizzed by my ear, narrowly missing my face. I let out a very angry snarl, lashing out with my claws again. I winced as the knife clanged against them, because the sound vibrated my eardrums painfully.

Giving a groan, I threw myself at his face, biting onto his cheeks and aiming to slice his eyes. The vampire let out a scream as my claws met the soft flesh of his sclera, and by the blood that seeped through my paws, I knew I had hit my target. I withdrew my claws, throwing off the pieces of his shredded eye as I leaped away. The vampire ran at nothing, just let out pained moans as he clawed his now eyeless sockets.

I didn't intend on letting my enemy suffer, however. This time I bunched up my muscles and jumped onto his chest, the impact knocking him to the ground. I buried my muzzle into his chest, tearing off bits of his ribs before coming to his heart. I forcibly sank my teeth into the still beating organ, wincing as the blood sprayed to the back of my throat. Rather than getting myself too hungry, I leaped off to compose myself.

Not a second after was I scruffed by a strong hand. This time, I faced a female vampire, and she looked furious. "You'll pay for killing one of the royal guards, vermin!" she shrieked. A knife twisted into my stomach, causing me to cry out. She withdrew the knife and, faster than I thought possible, sunk it into my ear, literally splitting it in half. I gave another jarred cry but wasted no time. My claws came up in a series of slashes as I aimed for the arm that held me. Finally, I struck flesh, and that caused her to drop me.

My chest heaved from my heavy breathing, but still I would fight on. My rage empowered me, and as I fought, I became angrier. I let out a battle-cry, which sounded much like the scratching of nails on a chalkboard mixed with the cries of a dying rat. The vampire took a step back, spooked for half a second. That was all I needed.

I launched at her face, this time aiming for her neck. My back claws latched into her shirt and dug a hole, which helped me keep my footing as I plunged my jaws into her neck. I furiously shook my head back and forth like a dog would with a chew-toy. The vampire thrashed and struggled to no avail. I pulled my head back, and with it came her jugular. My teeth had gone deep enough to dislodge the vein. She fell pretty quickly after that, and soon I was standing on yet another dead body.

My fur was standing up on end, all of it soaked with a combination of my blood and the blood of the vampires I had killed. I was seeing red now, and one after another the enemy fell to my teeth and claws. My split ear bled, as did the scar on my stomach. Luckily the knife had not penetrated deep into my belly, so I was able to fight on without too much concern.

I could see that Goliath, Irene, and my pack were struggling somewhat. There were so many guards, so many vampires that it seemed like once one fell, two would take their place. Soon enough I was faced with a female holding a sword, and was ready to take her down like the rest.

She charged, slicing down at me and managing to land a blow to my back. I chittered in pain but lunged forward, gouging out chunks of flesh on her leg and falling back. I was about ready to strike again when a hand clamped onto my scruff. At the same time, the girl lunged forward, her sword pointed right at my chest.

My mouth hung open in pure fear, for there was no way to dodge this. The vampire holding me had too tight of a grip, and the vampire was running too fast for me to even attempt to get away. I closed my eyes, preparing for the searing pain of death...

...that did not come.

My eyes flew open to see a huge bird fly in front of the weapon and take the blow. The tip of the sword was touching my nose as a realization came to me.

My savior fell forward, writhing in pain. Suddenly, it dawned on me. I knew who had taken the blade.

"Xadrian?! WHY?!" I shrieked.

All was red now; I tore through the grasp of the vampire behind me, and faster than I thought possible, circled his legs, shredding his flesh as I rose up his body. Quite like the Tasmanian Devil in Looney Toons, I was a blur as I downed him quickly. Soon he was so mutilated he fell, dead and unrecognizable.

The female vampire was trying to pull her sword from Xadrian, but I gave her no chance. I let out my piercing scream and lunged right at her, sinking my jaws into her hand and thrashing back and forth. I ripped flesh and bone with ease, making my way up her arm until it too was shredded to the bone. The vampire had no time to scream as I reached her face. My claws dug into her tongue, ripping it out before I moved to puncture her eyes. This time, I let her suffer, and I did not stay to watch.

I leaped off of the dying vampire and faced Xadrian. He was now in human form, and I could see the light fading from his eyes. Still, though, I held the wound in his chest with my paws, putting pressure on it to stop the bleeding. I did not remove the sword, it would only make the wound worse. "Why, Why, Why?!" I kept on repeating.

Xadrian coughed and gave a sad smile, reaching up to cup my face. "I... did it for...the pack... I know you will be a better leader, Darcia, I made...a mistake that... cannot be taken back... You can create the peace you want to see... without idiots like me in the way..." he whispered.

I cried out, shaking my head. I shifted to human form now, desperately trying to stop the bleeding that seemed to never end. My hands did no better than my paws, unfortunately. "Don't say that! I was so angry but you didn't need to throw your life away!" I shrieked. Tears streamed down my face, but my pack member just chuckled.

"I didn't.... I died for someone I truly cared about, from the bottom... of my heart. I tried, Darc, I really did. I'm sorry I failed you...," he coughed. The light faded from his eyes, but I shook my head.

"You didn't fail me!" I screamed, but my grief was short lived. I was grabbed from behind, and felt myself being dragged off. I struggled but no one came to my aid, and suddenly I was thrown into... a room? A dark room, with what appeared to be a tinted window. I could not see out to the other side.

Blood ran down my arms and legs as Xadrian's sacrifice shocked me beyond words. It took me a moment to realize I was not alone.

"The hell is the meaning of this?! Where am I?!" Smoke's voice hit my ears. I turned to see him on the other side of the room, looking as beaten up and confused as I.

Suddenly, something played from a hidden speaker. It sounded like a recording.

"Fine, fine. I will go to him and explain 'what my pack wants' and how Ash is not providing it for us. How we seek a real king, and how if he grants us our desires, we will grant his. We can drop him once we overthrow Ash. OK?"—Darcia, 9:30 PM

Smoke's eyes fell on me, slowly turning angrier and angrier. I pressed against the wall, my own eyes as wide as saucers. I had been led into a trap...

"So, shifter... it seems like your plans had been a little different that you told me, hm?"

Chapter 31: Sam

The concept of time was a mystery to me at this point. I had no idea whether it was day or night, but I only could guess when my tormentor was going to visit me in order to feed next. My eyes were set in a permanent glow, one that was more menacing than it ever had been before. I could feel pin pricks in my fingers and toes, as if I'd lost circulation in them long ago. Truthfully I was very low on my own blood since I'd been here so long. I had been in human form and knew I would remain so until the fey iron was removed. When that would be, I had no idea.

It was true, sadly. My screams had died down so long ago that I wasn't sure if I remembered the sound of my own voice. My growling, uncontrollable at this point, had hummed and buzzed in my ears so much that I questioned if it even was my own growling anymore. Even if I 'looked' it, I didn't feel human. I just felt like a caged beast. Honestly, that's exactly what I was. And at every creak of the door, even if it was not him, I flinched, allowing my growls to grow louder and louder.

My arms were bruised and cut from my struggles against these chains. I was not depending on Goliath, Darcia, or anyone else to come to my aid. Sure, they probably would try. But I was not one to have much hope. I wanted to do this myself, I wanted to be able to go to their aid, because I sure as hell knew the extent of Ash's armies. I only could hope they didn't decide to attack.

I didn't scurry into the corner or hide when I heard the door come screaming open. *His* red eyes met mine, my stomach dropped as I saw the fiery hunger within them. I displayed my wide array of teeth as he casually strolled in, shutting the huge metal door behind him with a loud *clang!*

While I didn't run off and hide, I did try to distance myself as much as possible from the vampire. It was to no avail because soon he was in my face once again, holding my arm with his iron grip and staring at my neck like it was a treasure he couldn't believe he obtained. This time, though, he didn't lunge or taunt me, which was odd. The silence stretched for a second before I broke it with a snarl.

I snapped at his limb, surprisingly managing to sink my teeth into the pale flesh of Ash's arm. Despite being in human form, my teeth would always be very sharp. I was not surprised at all when the vampire made no move to either shove me off or attack me. He just let out a soft chuckle. "You never cease to amuse me. I wonder, how valuable is your freedom, dragon?" he whispered.

I froze, it was as if someone was offering a child the golden ticket. Slowly, my eyes moved to meet his, and hesitantly I let go of his arm. My response was a series of growls that I was sure he could not comprehend, yet at the moment, that was all I could speak.

"*What are you offering me, Ash?*" I snarled. The vampire *did* seem to understand, indicated by his widening smile.

He leaned toward my ear, as if he were sharing some big secret. "My dear brother has come to visit. He brought along one of your friends, the Tasmanian Devil shifter. Both are contained, and the shifter is in grave danger. You could get yourself and her freedom if you do me one favor," he said dangerously. I blinked, suddenly hopeful.

Goliath, Darcia... here? They *had* come for me, but immediately my hopes were shot down as I remembered the turmoil from the city. Ash's words set in, causing me to bite my lip. *Contained? What the hell does that mean?* I wondered to myself. Ash waited patiently for my response, and after a long pause I sighed.

"*What favor is that?*" I growled, my glowing eyes suddenly very tired. Ash's smile just widened, as if he was about to tell me an early birthday present. That sort of expression worried me to no end. I knew the conditions of this 'favor' would be anything but good.

"Simple, really. I do hope that you do not care for my brother as much as you believe yourself to, otherwise both you and your friend will be doomed to eternal torment. You will not be granted the blessing of freedom or death, nor will she. Unless, of course, you are willing to destroy him. That would change everything, now wouldn't it?" he asked softly.

Immediately I let out a roar and shook my head, thrashing in my chains. Ash did not step back, he merely waited for my tantrum to end. His eyes glinted evilly, it was as if this horrid war was a game to him. At this point it probably was, and he almost had a checkmate. But there would be no way in hell I would sacrifice Goliath to save myself, hell, not even would I sacrifice him to save Darcia. We were partners, we decided to work together and I refused to destroy that. Quite honestly, I knew we were something more, but at the moment, I didn't want to think about that. I knew with a sickening feeling that his 'containment' was anything but pleasant.

"Ah, I had a feeling you would say something like that, dragon. Which is why I will increase the offer, of course. With the right amount of magic, anything is possible," he replied. He took a step back, causing me to narrow my eyes. What the hell did he mean?

Soon enough, I got my answer. From his palms emitted glowing green smoke. He moved his hands to form it in the shape of what appeared to be snakes. I blinked, focusing closer before letting out a gasp.

"*Sambuca... you can save us, please, so much pain...*" came the voice of Copper. The snakes writhed together, deforming and reforming at a rapid rate. Boomey lifted his head to fix me in a smokey glare.

"*You can save usss Sssam... pleassse, if you ever loved usss....*" he begged. Tears formed in my eyes. What sort of magic was this?! I looked to Ash, whose grin was wider than usual.

"I can bring them back for you, Sambuca. Your only task would be to kill Goliath, if you do that, then you, Darcia, and your snakes can be alive and free. I will bring him to you," he muttered.

"How do I know you will keep your word?" I asked in a whisper.

Ash was suddenly leaning into my face, which caused me to gasp and bare my teeth in an attempt to get him away. My efforts, as usual, were futile.

"I'll make a promise in the blood. If I break it, my own blood will dissolve my bones and flesh. Deal?" he asked, giving a grin.

"I kill Goliath and free myself, Darcia, and my family," I quietly assured myself. My eyes flashed somewhat as I came to a decision. Slowly, I began to nod. "Deal."

Goliath

I could do nothing as Darcia was dragged off. Strangely enough, I saw Smoke being carried in the same direction. Nothing good would come of that. I was being restrained by at least four vampires. We had, it seemed, been led into a trap. I had no idea the sheer number of guards under Ash's order. Bodies were strewn this way and that, and with a sickening gasp, I spotted Bernard the bear shifter as still as stone on the bloodied floor, but much to my relief, his chest was rising and falling slowly when I gave a closer glance.

Those that had survived included Irene, Valiant, and Lilith. At least they had a chance. I met their gazes as I was carried off into an unknown place. Roughly I was dragged into a room that had a television, oddly enough, mounted on the wall. The room was locked behind me, probably enforced by silver. Such a metal slowed vampiric healing as well as dulled our strength. It was a frustrating weakness we had, and while we could be killed by other means, we were especially susceptible to it.

I should have ended Ash when I had the chance. As soon as he threatened Sambuca, whom I cared deeply about, I should have silenced him for good. I knew what this was about. Ash was never favored, while I had always been the one to inherit the throne. Then, when I decided to veer from my path, it enraged him even more. Since I was going to throw away what he always wanted but never could have, he took away the only thing I truly cared about. The one who had stolen my heart, currently being tormented by him, of course.

What a mess; but screaming at myself over it would not help. I was always one to plan things out, be it acting out for any sort of trickery or a plan for battle. I had no idea as to how to get out of this room; perhaps if I attacked whoever entered next, then stealthily disguised myself as that guard, I could successfully find and free my allies and proceed to rescue Sam.

But gods, what was with this TV? Soon enough, I got my answer. It flickered on, filled with static at first but slowly coming to focus. The sound was all the way up, and as soon as I heard the clanging of chains, I knew what was playing on the screen. "No... anything but this... please.." I whispered, the words hanging on my lips as the scenes flashed before me.

Sambuca was cowering in the corner, looking pale but not too weak from any sort of blood loss... yet. This must have been taken when he'd just captured her. I saw my brother circle her, saying nothing and just staring her down. His gaze frequently looked upon her neck, and often when that happened he licked his lips.

Sam did not beg, however. She cowered and tried hard not to shake, and I knew she was terrified by all means. But still she uttered no sound, not until Ash decided to lunge. I heard her cries as he sank his fangs into her flesh, and I myself found that I could not contain my own wail of horror. The scene played over and over, even if I covered my eyes I could hear her scream echoing through my mind again and again.

Tears spilled down my cheeks as it was coming into perspective as to how much I truly cared for her. To see her put through this, why, it ripped through my entire being and caused me to go completely insane. The worst part was my inability to save her. No matter how hard I slammed my fists into the windowless walls, sending vibrations through the structure and causing my own blood to course down my arms, I could not make any difference to break through.

I almost didn't hear the door behind me, my sobs of rage and horror were too loud. I heard someone clear his throat, though, and whirled to face one of Ash's cronies.

I darted for him, stopping mid-lunge when he held up a picture of Sambuca. "Now now... you want her back, don't you? I will take you to her, if you'll allow me to, that is," he chuckled. I gave a nod, my dark eyes set on his. I was too intent on seeing her that I did not consider how strange this was. That was probably what they had in mind, too, of which I would not weigh the oddness of this. Why would they take me to see her when they wanted to keep me away, to keep me from freeing her?

Alas, my mind was only set on getting to Sam. I needed to be there to comfort her, I knew how afraid she was of being bitten. Every time I lost control or had to act was torment for me. I felt her terror, and I knew she was still wary of me. I needed to change that, I needed to be able to prove to her that I was there no matter what. Even if it meant making stupid decisions in the mean time.

Chapter 32: Sam

I had a single goal in mind that I was determined to go through with. My eyes fell on the large metal door as it opened ever so slowly. I saw my partner in this mess, Goliath, as he entered and almost collapsed in relief upon seeing me. Little did he know, he was about to go through a world of pain from the one he cared about. Ash snapped off my chains and gave me a nod. I was still in human form and casually watched as Goliath darted towards me and took me up in a hug.

"Are you alright?!" he whispered in my ear, but I gave no response. My eyes rested on Ash as he closed and locked the metal door. Slowly, my grin turned into a smirk.

"You made a mistake by coming here, Goliath. You will be the key to getting my family back," I hissed. Goliath tensed and slowly backed away, eyeing me with worry.

"Sam...? What do you mean, love?" he asked, his voice still barely a whisper. His red eyes looked confused and shocked.

I just gave a wide smile and shifted to dragon form. Finally I was no longer held back by the fey iron. Now, I could do some real damage. A roar came from the bottom of my stomach as I slammed him to the ground and bent my muzzle to his face.

My eyes met his as he made no move to fight back, just simply stared. "Why?" he muttered. I just shook my head, my smile widening.

"My decision was easy. Kill you, bring back the snakes, save myself and Darcia. Ash provided me with a task that was so much easier than I thought. You don't know how long I've been wanting to end you, leech," I roared. Then, I bent my muzzle down, as if to attack him. Goliath just laid there, still unable to move from such a horrid surprise.

My next words probably surprised him much more. I hoped he snapped to action when I said them this time. "*Play pretend, my love...*" I whispered for only him to hear. So suddenly did I take his arm into my jaws that the vampire was unprepared. Trying to hurt him as little as possible, I flung him over toward Ash, scurrying after him on my four legs as my scales glowed a bright red.

Ash was an idiot(understatement, really). He thought my loyalty was so flawed that I'd betray someone who saved my life so many times at this point. Someone I cared about as much as he cared for me. *Someone that I loved.* Even if the snakes could be brought back, I would never hurt Goliath. No doubt they would never seek me to do so anyway.

Just like Goliath, though, I was as slippery as a snake. And I knew Ash had no idea of my real intentions. By attacking Goliath, I solidified in his mind the fact that I didn't really care about him. Now the tables had turned on Goliath, but I would try not to hurt him *too* badly. Sometimes revenge was sweet, especially when I knew our salvation was on the line and I needed to be as convincing as possible.

My laughter filled the air. "You really thought you had a chance with me, leech? I hunt your kind, I enjoy *slaughtering* vampires! It's like a sport to me, as it is for all hunters!" I screeched. Goliath gasped as I took him in my jaws again and threw him up in the air, turning rapidly and whacking him with my tail to send him spiraling to the ground. The vampire groaned in pain but managed to sit up and shield his face.

"I...should have killed you when I had the chance... I should have spread the bloody carnage....that I was meant to... I regret... keeping you alive..." Goliath gasped, looking into my eyes. I saw him wink, though, and gave a huge smile. Not bothering to give a pause, I lunged again and took his torso in my mouth one more time. This time, my eyes set on Ash as suddenly I charged at him.

The vampire had been so focused on the battle that he did not manage to dodge in time. Suddenly I was pinning him down with one claw, my tail lashing and slamming into the walls. The entire castle shook, but I paid no attention to that. I dropped Goliath right on top of his brother. I had not weakened him too much, so he was able to twist in the air and hold him by the shoulders.

I bent my muzzle into Ash's face, breathing smoke into his eyes. "Checkmate." My jaws opened wide as the structure continued to quiver and shake. Now I knew I wasn't the only one causing it.

"Sam! We need to get out of here!" came the voice of Goliath right by my dragonic ears. I was way too intent on ending Ash here and now. My jaws closed on him, I was so ready to rip him limb from limb, but my teeth only clamped onto smokey air.

"Clever trick, little dragon. We will meet again, I can promise you that. You may have gotten away this time, but I am always watching. Next time I'll destroy my brother myself, it seems you are not worthy enough for the task. Tah!" Ash's whisper sounded.

I roared in frustration and whirled, looking for where I had just heard him. The dark shadows clouded my eyes as I twisted and turned in the smoke that allowed no vision. It was not fiery smoke, more like a black, thick shadow that inhibited all of the senses.

My roars of frustration filled the rumbling castle, but the creaking and groaning structure grew louder. I shifted to human form but retained my wings, horns, and tail, desperately trying to fly after Ash. "Where are you?! COWARD!" I roared in a voice just as loud as my previous shouts. I felt someone tugging at my tail, trying to get me away from the rising darkness, but I just resisted. My tail jerked out of his grasp, and I looked down to snarl at Goliath. "Let me go! I NEED TO DESTROY HIM!" I shrieked.

Goliath weakly shook his head. "No! You cannot now, you will only get hurt!" he yelled. I shook my head, too stubborn to listen. I flew after the fading shadows only to be struck by...something.

Red marks, those of vampire bites, formed on my arm. I screamed as suddenly the shadows converged. Shapes of bats formed and dissipated from the shadows, engulfing me into a hellish darkness that began to frighten me dearly.

Bits and pieces of that horrid laughter hit my ear; Ash's laugh now sounded like it was being played backwards on a broken, scratched up record. My wings began to tear on the bottom, causing me to scream. Pain shot up all of my limbs as bite marks appeared all over my arms and legs, opening fresh wounds that bled out more and more. The shadows swirled around me, preventing me from landing, it was like I was caught in a tornado of torment.

"Sambuca!" Goliath's voice screamed. I was paralyzed here as I became more and more dizzy. That tug came on my tail again, and suddenly I felt myself forcibly being pulled out of the air. With a final jerk, I was free from the shadows that had me locked there mid-air. I went limp, unable to focus at all. My eyes were wide in shock as I shook uncontrollably.

I could see enough to distinguish the shadows imploding and forming the shape of a humanoid. The bats came together and became Ash himself. The vampire had dark bat wings jutting from his back as he casually hovered in the air, flapping leisurely from time to time. I saw him lick away a bit of blood from the side of his mouth as he smirked at us. "Well played. I will see you both soon!" he chuckled. With a bow, he dissolved into the shadow bats and like that was gone.

"Sam? Sam! Love, can you hear me?" Goliath said in a quiet but urgent voice. I managed to just nod and cough out a bit of blood.

"I...wasn't going to ever...hurt you... we needed to be convincing... I am sorry..." I tried to voice what my plans had been. Goliath's eyes softened as he brought me closer to his chest in a gentle hug.

"I knew what you were doing when you told me to *play pretend,* love. You're almost as good at acting as I am," he chuckled. I felt the castle shake and heard the structure groan once again. Goliath took a few steps forward, limping but otherwise stable. I knew I would not be able to walk. I still had my wings, horns, and tail, though my wings and tail were missing quite a few scales and were bleeding profusely.

"We need...to get out of...here..." I gasped. Goliath nodded and darted around the collapsing pillars. I had no idea where we were going; I just focused on the whimpers of Goliath as he ran along. Obviously his leg was sprained if not worse. "Stop, I don't want you more hurt..." I whispered.

"Only... a...little...farther..." he gasped. The structure suddenly crashed behind us, propelling us forward and causing us to slam into the lawn as we emerged. My head swam with confusion as both Goliath and I laid there, trying to recover enough to just think.

I heard snarls and curses somewhere near and turned my eyes weakly up to see a peculiar sight. A vampire woman was holding Robert Smoke back from attacking... Darcia? Who herself was being held back by a brunette, probably one of the pack members. They had gotten out in time, but how? I could see Darcia's eyes glowing red, a color very unusual for a pureblood shifter. Smoke's eyes glowed the same color, it was almost like both emitted a bloody smoke as they swore and stared.

"You fucking liar! I am going to rip your throat out! Unhand me, bitch, so I can destroy her!" yelled Smoke.

A redhead vampire woman hissed. "Calm down, Smoke, it was what we all had to do to convince you to work with us. Your army is dead, as is most of ours! You're lucky I intervened before you and Darcia ripped each other to shreds!"

"Valiant, I can handle this scum. I should have killed him when I first laid eyes on him, he's a greedy fool! LET ME AT HIM!" Darcia screamed. Ah, so that was the name of the female shifter holding her.

The female shifter sighed and shook her head, looking at Irene. "Darcia's anger is strengthening both her and Smoke, thanks to the blood bond. Good thing both weakened each other so much that we can now handle them", she observed. The vampire gave a nod and smacked Smoke behind the ear, surprising him so much that he was stunned for half a second.

When he snapped out of it, he turned his head to try and fail to glare her in the eyes. "THE HELL WAS THAT FOR?!" he yelled. The vampire woman just smirked, as if she was enjoying this.

"If we all fight each other, we will all be slaughtered by Ash. You *both* need to calm down before we knock you out!" she muttered.

"Speaking of being knocked out... look who else made it," said one of the shifters. Her eyes were trained on Goliath and I.

Darcia immediately squealed, her anger draining. "Sambuca! You're OK!" she shouted. Smoke's eyes focused on us. He narrowed them, crossing his arms, still trying to shrug away from Irene's iron grip.

"How...did...you...get out?" I managed to whisper. Goliath had laid me across his lap and was carefully examining my arms and neck. At this point, I knew that his leg likely was almost completely healed due to his vampiric powers.

"Those bites are deep, love..." he muttered with worry. "You need rest." I shook my head, wanting to hear the story first. Darcia put her hand behind her head. Valiant let her go, knowing she was too intent on talking to me rather than attack Smoke.

"After we led an attack on the castle and were outnumbered by far, somehow I was locked into a room with Smoke. Ash had gotten a recording he played over a speaker, the one discussing my planned betrayal of Smoke. We... went through some hoops to get him on our side. But there was no way I was gonna help him get the throne, you know? I had to say something to lie," she explained. Smoke let out a snarl and thrashed in the redhead's grasp to no avail.

"Calm down, you are the only survivor of your army. Do not make me kill you..." the vampire woman warned. That caused Smoke to relax just slightly, he knew he was too weak to put up a real fight.

Darcia continued. "The blood bond empowered both me and him as my anger grew. And man, did it grow. He lunged for me, attacking well enough before I retaliated. His venom did not affect me, which was a disadvantage to him. Looks like the blood bond backfired in that respect for his shitty little plan. Anyway, thanks to the blood bond, both of us grew in power as the fight went on. Soon we had torn each other up pretty well before the vampire, Irene, came stumbling in. She had found a way into the door, along with a few pack mates and other vampires. Immediately they disabled both me and him by throwing us against the walls. Irene yelled at us to get a hold of ourselves. That was when the castle began to shake. We forgot everything in the panic of the moment. Everyone, friend, foe, was trying to get away from the castle. It collapsed onto most of the fighters, but the room had a hidden exit that Irene knew the location of. I didn't question it, we took that as our salvation and were free. Smoke and I were gonna finish what we started but just *had* to be restrained..." she growled in an annoyed voice.

"As long as...you got out safely..." I whispered. Goliath's voice hit my ears.

"Rest, love. You lost a lot of blood in that battle. We are safe from Ash, for now," he assured me. I gave a nod and let myself be taken by the tides of sleep when a whisper hit my ears.

"No matter where you hide.. I will find you, Dragonfruit. But I am not your concern now, little one. My brother has a taste for dragon's blood. No matter how much he feels for you, the temptation will always be there. He will see from my eyes soon enough, and you will have no power to stop his frenzy when it comes..." Ash's voice hissed. My eyes flew open, seeing not anyone but the eyes of Goliath... and they were hungered.

"Just rest, love. You need it, as do I," he tried. His hand came up to his head, and I had to wonder how long ago he had eaten. My hand slowly came up to the side of his face and rested on his cheek.

Despite Ash's words, I wasn't afraid to say it. "I trust you," I whispered. With that, sleep finally closed its jaws on me without giving any other moment to think.

Chapter 33: Darcia

After Sam passed out, I looked to Goliath with narrowed eyes. "You'd better take care of her, vampire, or I will rip out your jugular and eat it like spaghetti," I threatened. Goliath blinked, surprised by my very violent outburst. I only grinned to reveal my very sharp teeth. The vampire gave a smirk and took his hat off, placing it on his chest. Somehow he had kept it through all of that.

"No worries, dear. She is safe with me," he assured me. My deranged eyes turned to Smoke, who was glaring at me like he wanted to rip me to bits right now. I bared my teeth and was suddenly in his face, letting out various, scratchy snarls.

"And *you*. Now you *need* to work with us, no deals or plans, or you'll die. I wanna kill you anyway, but your damn vampire savior refuses to let me do so," I muttered. Irene was holding Smoke back yet still, even as he strained against her now. She let out a sigh.

"Calm down, Darcia. I can handle him, alright?" she muttered. I just gave a small nod, now turning back to Goliath... who was eyeing Sam with that odd, hungry look vampires got, when....

"Hey. *Hey*... HEY! WHAT ARE YOU DOING?!" I shouted as he leaned down. That seemed to snap him out of it as his eyes turned to me. A cloud of worry festered within them. He stood up with Sam in his arms, his eyes wide with horror. The vampire shook his head, looking toward the edges of the forest.

"I... I'm not sure. Sorry. Thank you for stopping me. I will be fine. Anyway, we need to get out of here as quickly as possible. I will explain what happened with Ash on the way," he finished. I narrowed my eyes suspiciously and followed with the rest of the survivors as Goliath moved rather quickly to get out of this horrid place.

At the moment, my concern was not Smoke. Yeah, I know it was surprising, but I had a friend to protect. She looked sorta odd but really cool. If I could go into half form like her, it would be awesome. Sam still had what looked like dragonic wings, horns, and a tail. She almost looked like a demon, but anyone who knew her would know better. Her blood was not of that underworld magics, rather was far more superior when it came to elemental properties. I knew how damaging a dragon could be from my research.

Goliath looked fevered, and I instinctively knew that he was starving. A bloodlusting vampire was about as dangerous as a raging shifter. He would turn on friends to satisfy his thirst, and at the moment I knew he would go for Sam. He was trying hard not to, I knew, but something more than hunger was driving him as well. That dark glint in his eyes put me on edge, but it had not been there before. What had happened in that castle with Ash?

Finally, it looked as if he was ready to explain. His voice was weak as he spoke, and I nodded along as I listened. "You thought she was gonna kill you at first...? How harsh and ironic," I muttered. I heard a snicker and glanced over to Smoke, blinking. "What's so funny?"

"Ah, the irony..." the vampire mused to himself, looking thoroughly entertained. I crossed my arms and looked back to Goliath. The *true* vampire prince was my concern right now. He had the potential to be the salvation of my pack, maybe my entire species.

If shifters and vampires got along, they could work together to ally with humans and keep the peace alive in this area. Gods knew we needed it with the rest of the world going haywire. Perhaps I was thinking too far ahead; I would propose my idea at a later time.

After Goliath shot a glare to Smoke, he turned his head back to speak with me. "Yes. Until she hinted me into her plan with our little code word," he chuckled. He continued on the story, and I had to admit I was impressed. They had managed to surprise Ash, something that I had thought was not possible. It didn't last for long, though. My expression turned to a frown upon hearing the rest.

"I shouldn't be surprised that he got away. How he managed to collapse his entire castle is beyond me. It looks like Sam lost a lot of blood; she cannot lose anymore," I hinted. Goliath gave a wary nod, his eyes turning back to her.

"I do not want to hurt her. Something is wrong, after that fight with Ash I feel like I have less control. Perhaps once I hunt I will be fine," he sighed. The sun began to break over the horizon, which was a rather pretty sight. The shimmering glimmer was in front of us, therefore it was fun to think we were walking toward the light as creatures of the dark. Despite being nocturnal, I loved feeling the sun on my face on a fresh morning. It had to be the most refreshing feeling I had ever enjoyed.

The loss of life from last night really hit me now. My heart clenched thinking of Xadrian and how he had really come through in the end. And all I did was yell at him when he'd been trying to help us all along. I'd make sure his death would not be in vain.

I knew that Lilith was carrying the body. We'd had to do a proper burial. I was not stupid enough to think that his death was *my* fault. But I would give him the honor he deserved for his sacrifice. Him, along with the rest of the pack members that had perished.

Speaking of which... my eyes fell on Irene. "Hey, how many of yours died back there?" I asked softly. Irene frowned, her lip quivering somewhat. I could see the pain on her face, it looked as though she had lost as many as me if not more.

"About two thirds of my army are gone. All of Smoke's is dead as well. However, upon the collapse of the castle, a lot of Ash's minions perished. I'm not sure the exact amount, but if we can gather up more forces and strike when he is weak, we will be able to kill him," she muttered. "But we need intel, and I know of no qualified spies," she sighed.

My eyes lightened up at an idea. "Well, I could help with that," I suggested. After all, I was great at being quiet when I needed to be. No really, I was! Irene thought about it for a moment and slowly gave a nod.

"Alright, I will let you know what you can do when we get to that point. I know of a few vigilantes that could help our cause if we propose our problems as big enough. I don't, however, trust mercenaries," she growled, her red gaze fixing on Smoke. The former hunter just bared his teeth, not saying much. He had not spoken much at all, in fact, except to make that snide comment from before.

"What are you planning, Smoke?" I growled. In my opinion, it would be a lot easier to end him here and now. One less problem to deal with; sure, his cronies had helped us against Ash, but *he* was a despicable backstabber that I didn't trust one bit.

The vampire just glared at me and was about to speak when Irene cut in with an irritated growl. "Will you both calm down?! The battle is over, we are the only survivors. I suggest you both make allies right now or stopping Ash will be impossible. And you know Ash needs to be stopped, Smoke. Despite how greedy you are, you know that Ash is a danger not only to you, but to everyone else as well," she snapped.

Smoke just laughed. "To hell with everyone else! I know that damned 'vampire king' wants my head now. I was nothing to him to begin with; I was just on the winning side. I will work with you idiots as long as you seem to be winning. However, I will not hesitate to turn on you if the battle appears to be lost," he growled. I snorted; typical, greedy ass fool.

"You know that Ash will not take you back, Smoke. You're an idiot to assume he will," I pointed out. Smoke just rolled his eyes; I could see that he was not being entirely rational at this point. Irene crossed her arms.

"Killing with kindness is the most effective way, Darcia. That's how I formed my alliances, how we as a team will rise to power. Feeding the conflict will only brew more of it," Irene said softly. I shook my head, gritting my teeth because I knew she was right. Despite all that Smoke had done, he was a survivor in this as well. And I sorta was stuck with him as long as he lived, considering we were attached by a freakin blood bond.

So, I did something that surprised both of us. As we walked, I held out my hand to Smoke. He did not need to be restrained by Irene anymore, in fact he just looked downright tired. He stared at my hand with suspicion, as if I was going to trick him or something. Smart guy. I just smirked and moved it closer, raising my eyebrows expectantly.

"Truce, for now, Smoke? We will get nowhere being at each other's throats. You and I both know that the bond will make us stronger if we use it correctly," I sighed. Smoke, after debating for a moment, shook it. He gave a genuine smile, but it faded as soon as it crossed his face. It was gone so fast, in fact, that I wondered if he even had smiled at all.

"Fine, Darcia. No more of your tricks, though. No more lies on either of us. I told you what I would do, I need to know that you won't go back on me again. I already have been back-stabbed numerous times, all prior to this big mess," he muttered. A sad glint appeared in his eyes, but like the smile was gone as fast as it came. I gave a smile that stayed.

"I will no longer lie if you are a true ally, Smoke. I know you will betray us, you said so yourself, but in the meantime we can work against Ash. We have a common enemy that needs to be taken down, then we can go our separate ways," I muttered. I had to wonder what he meant by being back-stabbed before all of this chaos ensued, but I did not bother to ask.

Smoke took my hand and shook it. His flesh felt warmer than most vampires, probably because we were bonded. I regretted my decision to bond with him somewhat, but I knew that it had greatly helped us in the initial battle. Without his troops, we would have been slaughtered before the collapse of the castle.

We finally arrived at my pack's home, though sadly with not nearly as many as we had left it with. Lilith laid Xadrian's body down at a safe location, and I knew we would need to host a proper ceremony for him when the sun set. I saw Goliath enter with Sam still in his arms, and decided to follow a little ways behind. A hand on my shoulder stopped me, and I turned to see none other than Smoke. I bared my teeth, but his eyes looked rather serious.

"He has tasted her blood, like I have yours, Darcia. We need to be careful with him, he could attack the dragon unwillingly," he muttered. I crossed my arms, narrowing my eyes.

"And why would you care?" I muttered. Smoke just smirked and shrugged.

"I'm on your side, for now. Just felt that you needed a warning," he chuckled. With that, he turned and walked away, leaving me worried.

Wait a sec, he said 'like I have yours'. Was he implying that *he* would attack me at one point too? I snorted; fat chance. I knew I could defend myself against him, I had done so in that room. We had literally been neck to neck, that is, my biting him and him biting me. Neither of us had the advantage, neither of us lost. That could be a great battle tool... or a horrid weakness.

Chapter 34: Sam

Blink...blink... Finally, I was starting to wake up. Only the gods knew how long I'd been out, so I told myself. That battle with Ash had drained me. I already was low on blood from that damn king's feeding. I shuddered upon the memory of his fangs sinking into my neck. The feeling never changed with *him*. My green eyes began to focus, and the sun, as usual, was setting now. I could tell by the dwindling daylight, it was fading rather fast.

I sat up, rubbing my eyes and sensing no one in the room. I had no idea where I was, I only knew it was not my house. I stepped out of bed, oddly enough not very shaky or tired. How long had I been out? I placed my hand on the doorknob, now hesitant. Yes, I knew that I'd been rescued, but that didn't mean I wasn't wary of someplace I had never been.

Finally, I let out a sigh and let myself slowly open the door. The long hallway stretched in front of me, and the heavy silence made me very uneasy. As I began to walk down the shady area, though, I began to hear voices. Darcia, Goliath, and someone else, a familiar sounding woman, were talking in the room just up ahead. I let out a sigh of relief, at least nothing bad had happened to them quite yet. I opened the door and entered the room, staying silent as everyone's eyes fell on me.

There were a few people in here, most of whom I knew, some of whom I did not know. My eyes fell on Goliath, who was staring at me with nothing but concern. I raised my eyebrows and let out a yawn. "What did I miss while I was out?" I muttered in question. Goliath stood up, seeming to be examining my neck. That unnerved me somewhat, until he took out a dripping cloth.

"I was about to come in and clean your wounds, love. Put this on your neck, even though the bites are just scars, the aching will be eased," he told me. I did so, wincing at the initial sharp sting. I took an empty seat, my eyes dead serious.

"Why did you all come to the castle? Surely you knew Ash's army was too massive to face, especially with Smoke on his side," I muttered. Pausing for a second, I remembered how I had seen Smoke before I passed out. He couldn't have been working with Goliath and allies, could he?

I got my answer when the traitorous vampire himself entered the room. He took the seat opposite of me, seeming to be surprised that I was awake. "Already she's up? It's only been one day," he muttered. I crossed my arms, baring my teeth angrily at him. I trusted him no more than I did Ash. Why the hell was he here?!

Darcia gave me my answer. "Might have said this before, but to reiterate, I made a deal with him, at the time it was a lie. At this point, Smoke is working with us only because we now have a common enemy that is Ash. The vampire king was only using him to begin with. I got him to switch sides with a blood bond and a false promise. Now that all is known, though, he will work with us until we bring down Ash. To be honest, his army was wiped out in the battle, so he has no choice," she explained. A smirk formed on the shifter's face that was met with a scowl by Smoke.

"Unfortunately, I must work with you lying scum," spat Smoke. I burst out laughing at that, making just about everyone in the room jump due to roar-like growls that came with my laugh now.

"Us?! Lying scum?! You wanna say that to my face, bastard?!" I snarled. Suddenly I was a few feet away from Smoke, my eyes glowing like dying coals and my teeth bared dangerously. "Because I'd love to rip out your throat here and now. From what I am getting at, you're alone, and fully dispensable!" I roared.

"Whoa, whoa... Sam, calm down," Darcia tried. She put a hand on my shoulder, to which I whirled and snapped at with my teeth. Oddly, I felt my fangs sink into flesh and looked up to meet the eyes of Goliath. He had lunged to block Darcia from my bite, and now was being bitten in the arm by me. His eyes looked very worried now as he made no reaction to my bite. Coming to my senses, I gasped and let go.

I stumbled back, holding my head and breathing heavily. "I... I don't know what came over me, I'm sorry..." I muttered, blinking. My eyes were still glowing very brightly, which disturbed me somewhat. I could almost see the light emitted from my own eyes bounce off of my scarred skin.

Darcia stepped forward, giving Goliath a reassuring smile. "It's fine, I got this," she told him. I watched as Goliath backed up and just spectated. His glare slid to Smoke every so often, who had kept his tongue since making me snap. Hah... smart.

I flinched back as Darcia came closer, not knowing what her intentions were. Was she going to attack me back since I had lunged? No, rather, she grabbed my hand and held it, looking into my eyes. "Sam, we are friends now. You saved my life, I know it is not like you to just attack like that. You feel extremely angry and afraid, don't you? Perhaps it's time we did some research on your kind," she muttered. I tilted my head like a confused animal, not fully able to think clearly right now.

"Dragons are like shifters in a lot of ways, but are also unique. You're being pushed more and more into instability, we need to figure out how to manage your power before you do something you regret," she sighed. I narrowed my eyes and gave a nod.

"How... how do I learn more of myself, then?" I questioned. Darcia gave a smile and held up a finger, signaling to wait.

I shifted from one foot to another while waiting, refusing to meet anyone's eyes. I saw one of the people that looked familiar, a female vampire with deep red hair, glance to Smoke. She had a scowl.

"Control what you say around the dragon. You don't know how to behave around one of them, you're a youngling and you're gonna get yourself killed," she muttered.

Smoke just shook his head, gritting his teeth. "And you do? You older vampires pretend to know everything," he muttered. The red-haired vampire smirked, as did Goliath.

"We know a lot more than you," she only said, making me wonder what she meant. Goliath's eyes flashed guiltily, but I already knew why. He'd killed tons of dragons before meeting me. I was fully aware of how much he knew my kind worked.

Darcia returned with a book in hand, her expression curious. She handed me the book and opened to a particular page, one labeled, *Origin.* "Dragons have been around since the dinosaurs; they have evolved since with growing magical power. They evolved alongside humans, shifters, and vampires; but their common ancestor branched off ways before the common ancestor of vampires and humans. They are most closely related to shapeshifters, though their magic is very different, as it is most connected to earth metals and 'elements'. Certain magics enable them to be able to mate with other species or temporarily have a humanoid form.

Oh, but listen to this; here is where it becomes important. Dragons are extremely smart, but after long periods of stress, desperation consumes their mind. They snap at anyone they can, no matter who it is. Unlike shifters, dragons are not empowered by anger; it just confuses and scares them more, causing them to waste power and lash out when unneeded. Hard training can control such fear and desperation to keep a clear head while in battle for either territory or prey." She closed the book, her eyes falling upon me.

"Sounds a lot like what happened just now. I have read this book through and through, dragons have always fascinated me. I got your back, Sam," she assured me. I gave a smile, relieved that my aggression could at least be controlled eventually.

"I've got some training to do, it seems," I muttered. My eyes fell on the rest of the group. "What do we do from here?" I asked, fully aware that Ash was more of a threat than ever. The red-haired vampire stepped forward, fixing her red gaze on my glowing, venom-green eyes.

"We need to gather more allies, in the meantime training the best we can. You are the key soldier in this, Sambuca," she told me. I raised my eyebrows, somewhat doubting that.

"And who are you?" I asked, embarrassed that I still had no idea. The vampire blinked and chuckled at the redness on my cheeks.

"Ah, forgive me. I am Irene, we met in the city when you prevented a battle between me and another male vampire," she explained. Ah, that's right! I knew now why she was so familiar. I gave a nod and a smile.

"Nice to see you again! Now, how do I begin training?" I wondered. I suddenly felt someone beside me and turned to look up at Goliath. He held out his hand, and after glancing at the others, I took it with some hesitation.

"I will help you train, love. My powers are the most similar to Ash's. Be aware that I will show no mercy while we fight, you need to know just how brutal my brother can be. I promise I will not harm you too much. And I will go easy since you just awoke," he said with a slight smile. He was still wearing his suit and hat, did he really expect to be able to fight in that?

I narrowed my eyes, a sly smile forming on my face. "Go easy on me? Don't expect me to do the same, then. I fight rough," I promised him. Goliath blinked and just chuckled; to be honest, I did not know what to expect. He'd 'fought' me before, I'd seen a glimpse of his true powers. They frightened me, but he hadn't been actually trying to harm me. Now, though, it was a fight basically until the other person was unable to fight back. I'd been wanting such training, I knew it would be beneficial.

Still, though, I hoped Goliath would not be *too* challenging, cause that would only mean hell from Ash. I knew both brothers were equal matches, but Ash would go for me and probably have an entire army on Goliath.

I gave the others a wave of my hand and followed Goliath outside, anticipating a real battle. I was rested up, I felt it, and ready to go. My heartbeat was fast, though, and I was nervous. I really hoped what Darcia read would not come into play here, as being confused and afraid was never that fun.

We walked deep into the forest until suddenly... I was alone. I whirled, looking for Goliath, confused now. "Hey, where did you go? I thought we were training?" I called, my voice a slight growl. A chilling laugh hit my ears, causing me to freeze for a moment.

"Training? You mean my hunting session?" came Goliath's voice next to my ears. I turned toward it to see absolutely nothing. Irritated, I let out a loud hiss, which only made the laughter increase in volume. My pupils thinned into slits as now I began to see red. I felt a cold wind by me and clenched my fists, waiting.

Suddenly I was on the ground, being pinned down by the vampire. He was staring at me with hungry eyes.

"Your move, love..." he whispered as he bent to my neck.

Chapter 35: Sam

No, I did *not* want to be bitten again. I felt fear clench my heart and immediately thrashed in Goliath's hold, shifting and growing into my dragon form before he could lean in any closer. My massive claws shot out where he was supposed to be, but unsurprisingly met air. I got to my feet, rearing up and blowing a cone of billowing flames at the gathering shadows. The darkness spread apart and reformed, moving like fluid through the air right at me. I hissed and spread my wings, flapping them to send a gust of air in an attempt to knock him off balance(wherever he was).

His voice hit my ears again. "You really think my kind is merciful, dragon? Your blood hungers me so... we're too far from the house, you have no time to run off like the coward you are," he taunted. I let out a piercing roar, my jaws glowing as fire brewed in the back of my throat.

"Coward?! COME FACE ME, FOOL! I'LL SHOW YOU WHO IS THE TRUE COWARD!" I shrieked. I was seeing red again, I was so furious that I couldn't even breathe. How dare he say such lies! How dare he trick me like this! His voice was so serious... but I'd thought he cared for me?! Had that been a lie?

The thought of that pissed me off even more, and as I whirled and tried to follow the shadows, I crashed into several trees. As I did so, I braced myself and propelled off of the trunks, which left extremely deep gouge marks in the wood. My jaws were bared in a permanent scowl as I relentlessly followed the shadow that seemed to be just barely faster than me.

A voice in the back of my head told me that this was a trap; however, I cared little for common sense. My fury was unmet, I *needed* to destroy! My roars and hisses were matched by none. As I came to a clearing, I threw back my head and let out a billow of swirling flames, as if trying to burn down the night sky itself. "WELL! WHERE ARE YOU, LEECH?!" I snarled. My wings spread as I followed the shadows in the air, now they were forming in the shape of a bat.

"I'm right here, love. You, however, will *not* be, soon enough..." came Goliath's chilling voice. The shadow-bat seemed to have something on its head... a top hat? Wait really? My confusion grew as the bat took it in the tip of his claw and tilted it, as if trying to make a formal greeting... or a dangerous goodbye.

"The hell?" I breathed, right as the bat lunged for me. Huge wings, bigger than even me(and since I was a ten foot dragon, that was pretty huge) encircled my entire being. I let out another roar and writhed as suddenly I became very numb. Dark shadows swirled all around me, causing me to turn my head and try to follow them. I slammed my jaws several times and sent several fireballs toward any sort of movement to no avail. That in itself was making me lose energy. Letting out another desperate cry, I now hurled myself to the ground. Perhaps aerial combat wasn't my forte, maybe I could take him here.

I landed, but still the shadows did not disperse. Goliath's laughter filled my head, causing me to shake it and hiss. To my surprise, the vampire solidified right in front of my jaws. I took this as a chance to open them wide and let out some—wait a second. No fire came, I was out? How? Had he made me use it when I was confused in the air? My eyes flashed angrily as I lunged forward and clamped my jaws onto... nothing.

Goliath had dodged my bite, and now his arms were wrapped around my muzzle. He grinned, his fangs flashing, as I realized the position I was in. Aha, I could just lift my head and slam him around! I tried to do so, only to send rattles down my spine as Goliath held very firm. He was too strong, and he held his ground too well. Now, confused and desperate, my entire body thrashed around, my claws scrambled on the dirt, which sent up a huge cloud of dust, and smoke blew from my nostrils despite my inability to breathe fire right now.

All the while, my serpentine body crashed into the trees around me, which bent a few scales and left deep scratch marks in my flesh where some scales had been ripped off. Now, I was exhausted and getting nowhere. I wrenched my head from Goliath's grasp, which is what he probably wanted me to do, because it sent me crashing backwards into a tree.

I shifted to human form and held my head, groaning as I bled from several wounds on my arms and legs. The vampire approached, which made me tense and bare my teeth. He leaned in close to my face, his red eyes rather intimidating now that I was out of energy. Goliath tsked and let out a sigh.

"We have a lot of work to do, love," he muttered. I blinked, confused.

"Wait, you weren't planning on biting me?" I whispered.

Goliath shook his head and sat next to me, his gaze stern now. "No, clearly it frightened you enough to make poor decisions. Sam, I remember when we were locked in that glass room. You had sensed where I had been despite not being able to see me. You surprised me with that ability, I assume you can trace via vibrations. But love, you need to not let your fears and instincts drive you. My words horrified you, and last time you had the snakes to snap you out of your fears. Now you only have yourself. I know Ash has a plan to fight you and you alone. He can make that happen, and there will be nothing any of us can do about it... not even me. I know his plans, he wants to defeat and shame you so that you will never feel worthy enough to flee again. So that you will not ever return to me, out of pure fear of him," he explained.

My eyes flashed warily. "How do you know this?" I asked quietly.

Goliath sighed. "Because I have similar powers and used to have a similar mindset. Our shadow magic can select one other being for a limited amount of time that only we can see, and vice versa. There is nothing you can do about it, and honestly it is how we bested so many dragons. We isolated them with that particular power then defeated them. If dragons had been able to group up, if they had known before it was too late, perhaps you wouldn't be the only apparent dragon known in this area.

But that does not weaken you, Sam. You'll be able to fight, you'll be able to use every power you use now. But you need to know how we fight, and be prepared for surprises. I have my own powers, as does Ash. You only have me to train with, but that should be enough. Today, I hope you learned to think more than just flames and claws. Use *all* of your senses, love," he told me.

I blinked, thinking things through. I guess he was right; if I had not been randomly lunging and breathing fire at spots I had *thought* he was in, I could have concentrated enough to find his real location. Just like in that room, when I had sensed him before he had come out of the shadows, I knew I could do the same in this sort of combat. I just needed to calm down and concentrate.

"That's enough training for today, love. We will continue tomorrow after you rest up. I'm sure the rest of us will want to meet up and discuss more of our plans," he muttered. I gave a nod and let him support me as we walked back. The vampire's red eyes were glowing a deeper red as we walked, and I could not help be concerned. After a bit of walking, I cleared my throat.

"Are you alright?" I asked in a quiet voice. Goliath blinked and glanced down at me, the shadows of his hat hiding the top half of his face. It was just a little eerie...

"Yes love, I am fine, just hungry," he muttered. His eyes fell on the last bleeding cut on my arm, and after a moment's hesitation, he pressed his finger to it. "Applying pressure will stop the bleeding," he explained as my confused gaze met his.

Goliath's eyes looked rather tired, as if he was strained against something unknown to me. I felt him withdraw his finger and watched carefully. The bleeding had stopped thanks to him, which was great. But then he did something unnerving. He brought his finger to his mouth and quietly licked it clean, then returned his hand to his side. Realizing I was watching him, Goliath widened his eyes.

"I uh... sorry, love I..." he stammered. "I have no idea what came over me," he said truthfully. "I know what you've been through, it was a horrid thing for me—" he tried, but I cut him off with a sigh.

"I'll be fine, Goliath. I know you're not out to hunt me like Ash. Though I don't exactly know what just happened, I trust you," I assured him. The vampire gave me a sad smile, and we walked in silence for the rest of the way back.

"What is this place?" I asked, breaking the silence as we approached the large structure. It was like a huge wooden cottage that was bigger than any house I had ever seen. Goliath eyed it curiously and gave a shrug, apparently he wasn't entirely certain as well.

"The shifter pack's home, I guess. I've never seen a shifter house so large," he admitted. I gave a nod, because neither had I. I didn't associate with shifters that much, of course, but from the few I had seen, most lived in tiny houses or cities near the woods.

We came to the front door, expecting to just enter to everyone doing their own business. I almost jumped as Darcia was on the other side, her hand prepared as if she had just been about to leave. Her gaze turned from surprise to relief. "Where were you? I was getting worried," she muttered. She eyed me up and down and shot a glare to Goliath.

"You couldn't have been a little less aggressive since she had just gotten back from the clutches of Ash?" the shifter criticized. Goliath grinned, his sharp fangs flashing.

"You know how Ash is, Darcia. There is no mercy, not ever," he replied. I crossed my arms and pushed past her, muttering angrily about having lost. Darcia just chuckled behind me.

"You'll learn, Sam. No worries, and I'll bet I gotta train similarly as well," she told me. I turned my head and looked at her with my eyebrows raised.

"Hah, good luck. They'll make you feel like an idiot, after all the years of our training," I muttered. That, for some reason, made Goliath laugh.

My eyes fell on his amused expression. He just chuckled, "You never fought powerful vampires, love. None of you have, not even your leaders. Hunters aren't truly trained in combat versus royal vampires who know what they are doing."

I scoffed. "Oh please, I killed plenty of your kind. I think I know what I am doing *sometimes,*" I muttered.

Goliath eyed me up and down and shook his head. "Whatever you'd like to believe, love. Let's get you cleaned up," he said, the amused smirk not fading.

We came to a living-room-like area and sat. Darcia brought me some stuff to clean my cuts and ease the aches in my bruises. I narrowed my eyes. "There's not gonna be a day when I'm not all cut up," I scowled.

"Ain't no rest for the wicked," Darcia replied. I glanced up to see Irene enter the room with a rather disturbed look.

"What is it?" I asked in a concerned voice. The vampire sat across from me, glancing toward the window.

"Lilith was patrolling when she spotted two vampires on the border. She explained to me that they were Ash's spies, apparently they had the kingdom markings. She managed to attack one and deliver a fatal blow. However, the other got away—and now Ash could very well know where we are hiding," she growled.

I let out a groan. Sarcastically, I hissed, "Awesome. What's the good news?"

Chapter 36: Darcia

"How did you manage to kill off one of them?" I asked Lilith. We had gathered in the living room, and I was very curious to hear about exactly what had gone down with Ash's guards. The shifter lifted her face to look at me, I could clearly see that her cheeks were tear-stained.

"I was on my way back from visiting my brother's grave. I decided to patrol the borders like usual, when I spotted something unusual in the air. I was in my songbird form, and below me I saw a couple of bats circling the area, as if looking for something. Bats gather in large numbers, and these obviously were not just normal animals. For starters, they had the red royal markings on their back, probably painted in the blood of their victims.

I flew lower and watched them land, transform, and begin to walk. They blended into the shadows well, but I did not lose sight of them for an instant. They were on the verge of finding the path to our home, so I knew I had to intervene. I invoked my magic and managed to stun them. From there, I swooped in and clawed out one of their eyes, but the other seemed to snap out of it just in time. He grabbed for my wing and pulled me down, however when I sunk my beak into his arm he was forced to let go. I managed to take to the skies, but the unblinded one grabbed my wing a second time and managed to snatch me down again.

The ground battle lasted for about five minutes, claws locked and beak to fang. I ultimately managed to rip into his chest and end it. Sadly, I fear the blinded vampire escaped. Even vampires without sight can find their way around, and he was long gone.

Ash clearly sent them as a warning. We best be very careful," she finished.

A sickened frown planted itself on my face. I knew how horrid it had been since Xadrian's loss, and its effects on his siblings, Lilith and Valiant. How terrible that *another* sibling had also almost been lost. "Irene, do we have allies anywhere else? He somehow recorded my words before, too. I have a feeling he knew where we were long before this incident," I muttered in a quiet voice. The vampire gave a nod, but her face held a solemn glow.

"Indeed. However, the rest of my forces will not arrive for a while. If Ash was smart, he'd attack as soon as possible, which I predict would be within the next few weeks," she sighed.

Goliath stepped forward. "Some of my followers still reside within the kingdom, unknown to Ash. He might be 'everywhere', but I am as well. We will know if an attack is planned out as soon as it is spoken of," the vampire prince promised. I gave a grin. Evidently there was hope!

"In the meantime, we need to train as hard as possible. Even with allies, we will be severely outnumbered. We need to fight like ten deranged vampires," I growled. My eyes fell on Smoke as I walked up to him.

"Are you willing to train with me? The blood bond will empower us both if we use it right..." I muttered, not happy about the situation. I could tell he wasn't either. The ex-vampire hunter gave a shrug.

"I guess so, if you really think it'll help, then *why not,*" he hissed. I ignored his miffed tone and turned to Goliath, my eyebrows raised in question.

"How should we train for this?" I asked, wanting his advice. The vampire prince gestured to Irene, giving a slight smile.

"She knows quite a bit about how vampiric armies work, believe it or not. I would inquire her; meanwhile I will allow Sam to get rest. When you think you are ready, you can challenge me. But my job right now is to turn Sambuca into more of a deadly killer than she was before," he told me. I gave a nod, smirking as Sambuca rolled her eyes.

"Oh please, I almost killed you that one time..." she tried to point out, which only made Goliath let out a chuckle.

"Trust me, love. The only time where I thought my throat was due to be ripped out was in the castle just recently. Other than that, you posed no threat," he replied. I left them to their arguing and turned to Irene, dipping my head in respect.

"So, you're like a general or something?" I questioned, my eyebrows raised in curiosity.

Irene gave a slight smile. "Back when the city was attacked by the royals, I was one of the lead commanders. I was told a lie, however. It was that we would take over the city by diplomacy. When that turned to dust, I commanded my forces to fight against the princess. We had won, believe it or not, until we became outnumbered by Smoke's forces and had to retreat. A battle of twenty to one is just not realistic. I sat in wait until I was approached by the prince himself. I knew of his pure intentions, so I joined him in the pursuit of the dragon and the downfall goal of Ash. I've been training and commanding forces for the royal army my entire life," she finished. I nodded, impressed.

"And how do a few people beat an entire army?" I asked, doubting that it was even possible. To my surprise, Irene's smile widened.

"Simple. If you have the will to defeat thousands, you will. Our goal is peace, his is destruction. We want freedom and safety. Those most desperate will fight harder than armies. I've seen it happen before, and I will see it again. Hard training helps as well, and I can turn you into something that can take down twenty vampires at a time. Using your powers and blood bond, you are a potent weapon. I'm sure you're not aware of your power right now, pack leader," she chuckled. "I still have a bulk of my forces; if you can defeat a number of them, you'll be able to beat a number of Ash's army-men as well."

She turned and motioned for me to follow. I did so, watching as she mimicked the action to Smoke. He finally got to his feet and begrudgingly hurried along. We were led outside and into the forest, quite like Goliath had led Sambuca, I was sure. I crossed my arms, wondering where exactly we were going, when there suddenly was no one in front of me.

"First lesson: the element of surprise!" came an excited voice in my ear. Hisses filled the air as the hair on the back of my neck stood up straight. I looked around and spotted Smoke, who was just as confused as I.

"Hey! We gotta work together!" I called, but the vampire ignored me. I was fuming as he lunged toward a few hisses and tuned me out. "Are you insane?!" I snapped, running up behind him and shoving him from behind.

"Idiot! You'll only get in my way!" he snarled at me, fixing me in a crimson gaze. Right as I was about to retaliate, the vampire gasped and was thrown forward, practically on top of me. I gave a muffled snarl and shifted into my Tasmanian Devil form, slashing at him with my claws lightly before freeing myself from under him.

"If you're not gonna help, stay out of my way!" I yelled. I didn't wait for a response, as several vampires suddenly surrounded me. Swords and knives flashed in the moonlight as they were brought down on my flesh, shedding blood as they cut me.

I let out cries of agony, because even if this was just training, it was extremely painful. My ears were drawn back as my eyes obtained that eerie red tint they did now due to the blood bond. They obtained a similar color to Smoke's rather than my previous beady black. I paid no concern to it, however. I probably just looked more eerie with it. My lips peeled back in a snarl as I lunged and snapped my jaws on a knife that aimed to slice at my flank.

I ripped the weapon from the hands of my attacker and leaped at him, only to be knocked from the air by another vampire. I got to my paws again but was kicked down, much to my dismay and pain. My strained cries were met with only louder hisses. My claws blocked my face as blood stained my fur; well, clearly I couldn't take a ton of vampires all at once. At least... not alone.

However, something peculiar happened as I was just about to give up. The knife wounds stopped right as a shadow fell over me. Someone was blocking me from the blows now, was it... Smoke?! "What, why?" I whispered. Smoke just snarled and knocked away some vampires that surrounded us, he himself was looking pretty beaten up.

"We can't do this alone," he replied simply. I gave a nod and got to my paws, shaking a bit of blood off of me. We stood side-to-side, at least, best we could. Being on four legs, I didn't exactly match his height. We let out a screaming roar at the same time, his sounded very animal-like while mine sounded very supernatural. We lunged forward, slamming several vampires away from us.

I used the back of my paw to knock out several attackers(since this was just training, I didn't want to seriously wound anyone). As the group of vampires advanced, Smoke and I attacked simultaneously to ward them off.

We chased down any stragglers, 'leaving no survivors'. It was almost odd how we both could predict the attack of the other to match it and make it twice as lethal. I told myself that I would need to research this blood bond more extensively to find out just how potent it was. Especially now, when I was cursed to be bonded to someone I couldn't stand.

Soon enough, there were a ton of vampires laying flat on their backs, all of them completely out of it. I was panting very hard as Smoke approached again. He collapsed beside me in a sitting position, wiping away his own blood from his cuts and wounds. "Nice job," I commented, twitching my ear. I shifted to human form and gave a nod of respect to Smoke. "Glad you finally came to your senses, you idiot," I muttered.

Smoke rolled his eyes. "As much as I hate needing to work with you, we work well together. This stupid blood bond.... curse me for giving you some of my power," he snarled.

"If you'd have been able to kill me in that room, you'd die to Ash, so you'd better thank your lucky stars," I muttered. Smoke shrugged, knowing I was right but still wanting something to argue over.

We lifted our heads as Irene approached, clapping her hands slowly. "Nice work, you both. Of course, I had my forces go as easy as possible on you. Do not argue in the beginning of such battles, though. You need to work together from the start. The amount you got wounded initially would greatly inhibit the rest of the battle," she warned.

I muttered,"That was *so* not my fault..."

Smoke didn't have time to snap in response, for chuckles, not of any of our own, filled the air. I let out a sigh; the hell was it now?!

"We have more training?!" I asked in a growl. "I'm exhausted, can we have like ten minutes to rest up?" I tried. Irene's eyes didn't look amused. In fact, they looked a bit horrified.

"Those weren't my forces, Darcia..." she replied. Suddenly, all hell broke loose, the only thing I could see was dark shadows.

Chapter 37: Darcia

Everything was a blur from there. I tried to find Smoke, perhaps he could help me ward off these new attackers. Knives and fangs faced me as I darted onward, my eyes emitting an odd red mist that seemed just a bit unnatural. This time, the vampires were out for blood. I dodged several fatal blows before managing to shove my claws into one's chest and rip through the flesh. Yes, I was still able to do that in human form. I wanted to conserve energy before I shifted in case I *really* needed it for this battle. My goal was survival, not victory.

I felt a hand on my shoulder and whirled, fixing Smoke in my gaze and baring my teeth. "I've got your back," was all he said. I gave a nod, and we stood back to back, facing a hell of a lot more vampires than we had during training. All was frozen for a moment as no one made a move to attack.

I threw back my head and yelled, "NOW!" That caused us both to burst to action. We lunged in unison, now in opposite directions. Metal *clang!*s rang out as my claws sliced through the air and slammed against knives of silver. Blood ran down my arms and legs, but nevertheless I still fought on. I had no weapon, as shifters never really had a need for them. If I made it out of this, however, I would be sure to make a point and get one. I heard Smoke struggling behind me, but had no time to turn. My frustrated snarls and growls were met with murderous hisses and laughs.

I managed to lunge and sink my claws into the shoulder of a vampire that had gotten just a little too close. Right as I did so, about five vampires leaped on me at once. I was knocked to the ground and pinned, probably about to have my throat ripped out had the vampire not mysteriously flown off of me. My eyes met Smoke's as relief flowed through me. Yet again, he had saved me from a rather nasty wound. Actually, this time he saved me from certain death.

I got to my feet, confused now as to why the vampires had suddenly stopped attacking. I felt my arms being restrained by my back, much to my dismay. I turned my head to spot a blackened shadow, darker than the rest of the vampires descend right at Smoke. It was in the form of a huge bat, and right away I knew it was Ash. I yelled in warning, but it was too late. Smoke was slammed against a tree, a knife against his throat. The vampires that had been battling me now were fully focused on Ash. I was not a threat at the moment, not even when I tried to rip free. No, everyone was waiting in anticipation of Smoke's death.

"Hm, my little pawn thought he could try and betray me? How cute. Unfortunately, your efforts will be in vain... that is, of course, unless you'd like to take back what you've done and serve the true king," Ash's smooth voice rang through the air. Smoke was pinned by the shoulders and able to do nothing. He bared his teeth and let out a hiss, and for the first time ever I saw real fear fill his eyes.

Smoke did something then that surprised me to no end. He spat in Ash's face and snarled, "I might be a traitor, but I will never be a pawn. I refuse to join you again, Ash. My allies have spared me even when I promised to make war after this battle. I know little of dignity, nothing of peace—but at least I have more honor than you!"

My jaw dropped, but my surprise immediately turned to pure worry. Ash would kill him now, unless I did something. The vampires restraining me would be no match for my strength now.

Fury built within me as I ripped from the vampires' grasp and made straight for Ash right as he lunged for Smoke with a silver knife. I guess the vampire king had not been expecting me, for I leaped into the air and shifted as I soared right at him. The knife sank into my side as I not only blocked the blow, but shoved myself between them and managed to get Ash off of Smoke. The vampire king fell to the ground as my huge form held him there.

"KEEP YOUR HANDS OFF OF MY ALLY, YOU SORRY EXCUSE FOR A KING!" I shrieked. My piercing scream made everyone in the area wince, everyone but me. Ash looked confused, as if he'd not been expecting me to get away from his cronies. My glowing eyes met his as I shoved my muzzle toward his throat. No surprise, though, my jaws met purely air.

A bat-like shadow materialized above me as I turned my head up to look at it. The surrounding vampires began to flee as more of Irene's army arrived. I heard a furious roar behind me and assumed Sambuca had found out who was here now.

Ash materialized and frowned, his gaze not leaving mine. He was hovering in air with bat wings flapping every so often. He pointed at me, his mouth twisting into a scowl. "You might have saved my little pawn this time, shifter, but he will back-stab you like he did your entire organization!" he snapped. The vampire king looked toward Sambuca, who had just arrived. She looked seriously pissed off, and without hesitation shifted to dragon form.

Before she could make an attack, though, Ash just grinned and waved. "Until next time, my dear. No worries, we will meet again soon," he promised. I watched as he purposely dropped something and morphed into those horrid shadows. As soon as he had arrived, he was gone, and so were his army-men.

Sambuca threw back her head and let out a horrid roar, saying, "GET BACK HERE AND FACE ME, COWARD!" I watched as Goliath darted to her in an attempt to calm her down. My focus was on what Ash had dropped. It was a piece of paper with writing, the words of it were something I was very hesitant to read.

I bent down and took it, eyeing it before letting out a gasp. "Calm down! I HAVE HORRIBLE NEWS, EVERYONE!" I yelled, my eyes dismayed. Had I really just read what I think I did? There were two parts to the note; one which horrified me greatly, one of which I had no idea the meaning.

Everyone seemed to freeze and focus on me. Sambuca had shifted back to human form as her angered eyes still glowed a venom green. Goliath had a hand on her shoulder and was still trying to calm her down, allowing her angry hyperventilating to cease. I cleared my throat, not so excited to read this thing aloud.

"Ash left a rather disturbing note. It says: *Your efforts amuse me greatly, however are pointless. If you surrender now, I might give you a swift death. You might be alarmed to hear that I now have a key general in my grasp—one of yours, that is. Commander Irene didn't see my force coming, and you didn't hear her silenced screams. She is alive still, for now. Oh, and brother...*" I looked toward Goliath, not knowing exactly what this next part meant.

Goliath's dark eyes narrowed as he stared me down. I continued hesitantly. "*Nice try with your sorry excuses for spies. No worries, though. I have taken care of them. I do hope you don't drain the dragon too much, I am anticipating her as a blood slave for a while yet. It would be a shame if your bloodlust took you over like it did so many times before with your other pets...*" I finished.

Goliath seemed to wince, and I saw Sambuca's eyes flash warily as she made to move away from him. "The hell does he mean, Goliath?" she muttered in a low voice. I was curious too, but my main concern was Irene.

"Irene has been captured, we need to rescue her before it is too late," I sighed.

One of the vampires of her army took a step forward. She had short-cut blonde blonde hair, pale skin, and an expression that looked very authoritative, as if she was second in command. "Irene would not want us to throw our necks at Ash to save her. She considers herself only a casualty, a someone who can be replaced. She would want us to plan out a proper attack, even if she is in grave danger," the vampire said. I knew she was right, but loyalty to my friends always clouded my reasoning. I decided to argue more.

"We can't just let him have her! She knows a lot more than us on how to mount an attack," I gasped. The blonde just shrugged, sad but firm.

"While that may be the case, I have less combat training than her but that is good enough. She told me to take over commands if something like this were to happen. She also strictly warned me against allowing an impulsive rescue," she replied. I hung my head sadly, knowing it was pointless to argue any longer.

"What is your name, then? And what do you propose we do?" I asked in a tired voice.

"We train and spy. You remember what Irene said before? More than ever, now that some of Goliath's allies have been taken down, do we need you as a spy. We need to know exactly what Ash is planning. You volunteered, are you still up for it? My name, by the way, is Oriana," she muttered. I was surprised at her call for immediate action, but I was ready.

"Of course. When should I leave for the kingdom, then?" I asked, knowing it would be very soon.

"Rest up now. We need to be more prepared. You can leave in a week," Oriana told me. I gave a nod and turned to the others.

"Let's head back," I yawned. Sambuca seemed to be walking a distance from Goliath, as if wary of him. The male vampire just looked rather guilty; what had that note meant? I shook my head and tried not to worry too much about it. I knew they would work it out somehow. It was not my business to snoop.

I felt someone walk beside me and turned to see Smoke. "What do you want?" I growled in an irritated voice.

"You realize spying could get you killed?" the vampire asked, a scowl on his face. I shrugged, rolling my eyes.

"So? Why the hell do you care? If I die, the bond is broken, and you are free," I replied. Smoke seemed to wince at that, as if the idea disgusted him. How odd.

"We need you, and this bond, if we want to win the battle," was his only reply. His voice had a hint of worry, but I brushed it off.

"I'm aware. You'll know where I am due to the bond, won't you? You'll know if I die, and you can let the others know that and make other plans. I know I am an important part but I am not the only one. And without someone to do this, we will be blind," I snarled.

"I don't want to sense you die!" he snapped in anger. I blinked and crossed my arms, shoving him away from me.

"Stop lying through your teeth. You only want to save your own sorry skin by having me live and do what I can to stop Ash's army. You'll turn on me when I do that, I guarantee it, and kill me yourself. Why does it matter who I die to?" I muttered.

Smoke looked shocked and almost... hurt. "Do you regret saving me back there?" he asked in a low voice.

I shook my head and bared my teeth in a snarl. "No, because unlike you I care about my allies. Yes, even you. You're my partner due to the bond, as much as it disgusts me," I replied. Smoke narrowed his eyes and sighed, soon enough the house came into view.

"I care too, Darcia. I don't want to see you dead, and no, not because I want to kill you myself," was all he said as he pushed past me and stormed into the house.

I scoffed, what the hell did he mean by that?

Chapter 38: Sam

I heard what Oriana told Darcia, and I had to say, I wasn't happy about it. We already lost Irene, I wasn't about to lose her as well. Though another concern I had was exactly what Ash meant by the letter. I trusted Goliath, we'd been through a lot together. Despite that, I needed to know any sort of dark secrets he could be keeping. As much as it frightened me, I knew I would need to confront him.

As we walked, I moved closer to the horrified looking vampire, my dragonic eyes very serious. "Whatever it is, we can work it out together. Tell me what Ash meant," I ordered in a low voice. Goliath's red eyes fixed one me. For a second, they looked fevered, but they went right back to normal so fast that I wondered if they had changed in the first place. The vampire let out a sigh.

"He's referencing a time when I was a small child. Back before I was a murderous killer, I took great interest in dragons. I even kept a young one as a pet... until one day, Ash decided to spill its blood with a kitchen knife. He wanted to see how I would react, and it didn't end well. The dragonling didn't survive, to put it into perspective. Then, as the dragon killings rose and rose due to my father's orders, I turned to something else to keep whatever piece of sanity I had left. I tried to save humans, I showed them places to hide from my kind.

Ash found out about that too. He fought and tricked me into being locked into the very room I promised was the humans' salvation. The area was cursed with silver runes. I could do nothing to escape. After a while, my hunger took me over. I devoured every human I had wanted to save, like the true monster I am. Ash taught me that I was not meant to spare others, that our kind will always be mindless killers," Goliath muttered, his voice laced with sadness. I could tell those memories really wounded him.

I crossed my arms, rolling my eyes. "You really think I'm worried about that?" I growled, irritated. I'd said I trusted him, had I not? He seemed surprised by my response.

"Love, do you not understand? I might lash out and hurt you," he told me, concern in his eyes. I scoffed, my arms crossed now.

"And? I could do the same thing, you heard what my kind is capable of doing out of fear and desperation. This isn't some stupid romance novel. We're in a war, for fuck's sake. I can handle it. So spill it, what else is there to this?" I questioned, noting the doubt in his eyes.

"Ah, sometimes, when a vampire tastes someone's blood, he or she becomes enticed, per say. Sort of like an addiction. I have refrained from attacking you again, but the urge is becoming stronger as time passes. I think Smoke will have that same issue with Darcia eventually," he replied. I tensed slightly, that was something I had no idea about.

"And you won't stop until I'm dead?" I breathed in question.

Goliath shook his head, his eyes cast to the sky. "Killing a victim by draining *all* of their blood is pretty satisfying. That is why some of us slip and kill our prey. However, leaving them alive to drink from again is the most ideal, especially if their blood is rare and has magical properties. It gives me more power and energy if I do it. But I will severely weaken you if I attack you, however I will not kill you; I do have control over that much, at least. I just know how you are and I don't want to hurt you in that way," he growled, prompting me to roll my eyes.

I then shrugged, turning my gaze to the sky. "Ash's bite was horrid, and each time he did it, the pain was worse. I hate him so much. But when you bit the first time, yeah it hurt, yet it wasn't *as* horrible. If I can help you then I guess it won't be so bad," I replied.

Goliath took me by the shoulders, looking deeply into my eyes with his bloody red. "Don't throw your neck to a monster, Sambuca. It is unwise," he hissed, though rather than aggressive, he was just scared. For me, I assumed.

I just gave him a sharp-toothed grin. "In case you have not noticed, I am a monster as well. I'll be fine, just try not to catch me off guard," I snorted. I shrugged away from him and walked onward, relieved as the house finally came into view. The shifters and the rest of Irene's forces dispersed in the house, calling it for then night.

I spotted Darcia from the corner of my eye and walked toward her, my dragonic eyes glowing brightly.

"You don't have to do this, Darc," I tried. The shifter woman only gave a chuckle and rolled her eyes.

"Of course I do, the only way to defeat the enemy is to always be one step ahead!" she snarled with vigor. I shook my head, giving a long sigh.

"I swear to the gods, if anything happens to you," I muttered warily. Darcia only gave me a half smile.

"I'll be fine, dragon lady. Chill your fire," she joked. For some reason, I didn't find that all too funny. I just gave up and laid on the couch, holding my hand to my head. I felt someone sit next to me, and glanced up to see Goliath staring down at me.

"Are you alright?" he asked softly. I shook my head, somewhat upset. I knew one of Goliath's main concerns was his instability for my blood. That honestly was in the back of my mind now. I wasn't off-put by his stories, for they didn't disturb me that much. He thought he was a monster, but I knew we all were. For the gods' snakes, I was a dragon, Darcia was a Tasmanian devil, and we were working with shapeshifters and bloodsucking beings. And yet, we were monsters intent on saving our world.

No, my real concern was Darcia. Ash seemed to know everything about everyone, there was no way Darcia could spy safely. "I wish there was some other way to gather intel," was all I said. I heard someone scoff and proceeded to sit up, fixing my eyes on Smoke.

"What's so funny?" I growled in an irritated voice. The male vampire just shrugged, looking to where Darcia had gone off to. I couldn't tell what he was thinking, and I was unamused by the fact that he found this all funny.

"Nothing. I just never thought I'd agree with the likes of you any time soon," he whispered, barely loud enough for me to hear. My head tilted at his words, what was he playing at?

"You're actually concerned?" I wondered. "Probably due to the blood bond. If Darcia dies, you get weakened for quite some time," I observed.

Smoke bared his fangs at me. "I don't care about that. I don't want Darcia dead.... uh, the bond is important for a faster victory. We are both empowered by it, and in order to utilize it we both need to be alive," he muttered. I smirked, because surely there was more to the story than that. I had no idea what he was feeling right now, but I didn't press.

"I think we need to look into the exact nature of the blood bond," came Darcia's voice from around the corner. She entered the room with a book in hand, giving a small smile. Jeez, did these shifters have a book on everything? "I've been reading up more and more on it, and here's what I have found out so far."

She turned the book to a saved page and began to read. "The blood bond empowers both the vampire and their partner. As it progresses, both parties will be able to communicate telepathically, if the vampire already cannot do that on their own. Both will know at all times where the other is, as at times the partner can invoke a particular power that enables them to see through the other's eyes. In battle, wounds are partially shared once the bond progresses. A normal fatal blow will only be a severe wound that is passed on to the partner as well. The vampire's partner gets a less potent power of healing, as well as becoming immune to vampiric venom. In turn, the vampire will gain some of the powers of the one bonded. If one is slain, the other will not die, just be extremely wounded and weakened. The wound sharing is not to the extent of death, however the one left alive will never be the same in mind," she finished. Her eyes fixed on Smoke.

"I'll be careful," she promised the ex-hunter. The vampire sighed, a look of concern crossing his face. That in itself surprised me, and I could tell Darcia was caught off guard as well.

"Please do. Because if you do..." he paused, his face hardening as if he was hiding something. "I will get hurt too. And I don't want that to happen," he snarled. Darcia's face twisted into one of rage.

"I'll have your wounds, and you'll have mine... you can learn to DEAL WITH IT!" she snapped, suddenly slicing at his arm with her claws. Marks formed on her arm in the same area, though the cuts were less deep. Her eyebrows raised, but she shook her head and stormed off into her room. Indeed, their bond was clearly progressing. Smoke watched her go, making no retaliation to her attack.

"You're smooth," I growled sarcastically. Smoke just shot me a withering glare and got up, leaving the room without a word. I assumed he was going off to bed now.

I laid back down, tensing as Goliath ran his fingers through my bright red hair. My green eyes met his hungry red. My fists clenched in hesitation to say the next words. "Hey, if you need to drink, I'll not mind," I told him. Goliath's eyes flashed in fear for a second as he furiously shook his head.

"No, I don't want to, love," he growled, standing now. He turned to walk to his room when I stopped him with a hand on his shoulder.

"Yeah, but you need to now. I can tell you haven't fed in a while," I sighed. Goliath didn't try to pull away from me, rather just hung his head.

"I told you not to feed a monster, Sambuca..." he whispered.

"I already fed Ash, he's the real monster. At least my blood will nourish someone I actually care about," I reasoned. I let go and sat on the couch, letting out a yawn. "Whatever, make a decision, I told you I was fine with whatever you did," I finished. I let my eyes close, not waiting to see what he did.

I was not surprised when I felt him sit beside me and lean toward my neck. "Are... are you sure?" came his voice in my ear. I gave a slight nod, still not opening my eyes. My breathing quickened when he leaned in closer, and I had to brace myself for the feeling of fangs sinking into my flesh.

Yes, it indeed hurt, but this time it would be worth it. Plus, the worst part of vampire bites to me was the weakness that came with it. However, I wouldn't be vulnerable at risk of death from a bite now via him. Listening to my blood being drunk by Goliath was different than Ash; it was more peaceful, while Ash had hungered growls, Goliath's hiss sounded almost like a purr.

I was already tired from training, so my eyes closed as I gave in to sleep. Like I said, getting weaker usually was painful for me, but not this time. I knew the vampire would stop when satisfied. For the first time in a while, nightmares didn't wreak havoc on me. I actually felt comfortable, but I knew it would not last.

IN THE MORNING, I AWOKE to Goliath sleeping beside me on the couch. There was a bit of dried blood on the side of his mouth that I carefully wiped away, not waking him. His tophat was on the ground, probably having fallen off when he gave in to sleep the previous night as well. We'd been rather close lately. I moved away from him, being careful to remain quiet, and picked up the hat. I put it on the nightstand by him and looked up to see Darcia moving toward the door.

She gave me a nod, and unfortunately I knew where she was off to. I approached her and put my hand on her shoulder, looking into her dark eyes with a serious frown. "Be careful, alright?" I whispered. The shifter gave a smile and glanced at my neck. Her expression turned grim as she looked at Goliath.

"You too, Sam," she replied. I just gave a reassuring smile and watched as she turned away and headed out the door. I watched as she walked off toward the city as the sun dimmed behind her. It was as if she was walking away from salvation, walking from safety to death. I could only hope that it would not end up that way.

"*See you soon, friend...*" I whispered, promising to aid her when we all were ready.

Chapter 39: Darcia

Perhaps I shouldn't be a hypocrite, but gods, I wasn't sure if Sam was making the right decision. Offering your neck to a vampire, offering your flesh to a shifter, offering your soul to a demon... see the trend there? It's just not the best idea.

Yet I had done so with Smoke, for he'd tasted my blood and wanted more. I could tell how he looked at me sometimes, hell, I could sense his emotions when he was close. Well, not all of them, not yet. Most of them toward me were negative. Most. The others, well, I wasn't quite sure.

Now was not the time to focus upon that. I padded along in my Tasmanian Devil form, keeping my head to the ground. I would need to go through the human city, then the vampire's woods before I could get to the kingdom. From there, well, I would need to hope I could get some decent information on the going-ons that I could report to the others through Smoke.

That's where this bond was helpful, I could communicate through him no matter how far away I was. No need to take out a pesky cellphone or what have you, which could take too much time if I was in danger.

My claws scraped on the dirt, and there was no caked blood between them for once. That would change soon enough, I was sure. I had a bag slung over my back, which was sort of silly looking in this form. It held my canteen of water, a knife, and some dried meat. There was enough supplied there to last me about three days.

That was all I needed, I hoped. If not... Well, I could always hunt. Shifters normally didn't dine on vampire flesh, but if there was some available, why not? We didn't see *anything* as cannibalism. Everything was prey, including those of our own kind. Warring packs would eat each other from time to time to prove a point. I knew of one particular grisly story when a pack leader was tricked into eating bits of his daughter. Yeah... that war didn't end well. History was rather brutal.

My nose poked out of the underbrush, and thus far this walk had been uneventful. Now that was about to change, since I made my way into this wasteland of a human city. I walked from shadow to shadow, taking in everything and everyone. My nose twitched as I scented for anything that would potentially give me an advantage here. What I smelled was the opposite of that.

Fire... smoke... there was a gray fog hanging over the city. My red eyes turned toward the towering buildings, once proud products of the humans were now being blackened by some sort of ash. Ah, now I could see it; several fires were burning down various structures, by whom I had no idea. As I walked along, I heard screams and wails coming from within the buildings. I ran up to one of them, my red eyes flashing in alarm. The old bricks were almost bleeding soot, why the hell was everything on fire?!

"Without your petty little buildings, you'll have nowhere to hide!" came the insane voice of some man. I entered the building to see a man in all red, with royal symbols lining some thick looking clothing. He was crazy to the bone, I could tell by his aura. And to top it all off, he was a vampire probably about to kill this lot of humans. Looked like this place needed a superhero.

I shifted to human form, grabbing my silver knife and holding it behind my back. Clearing my throat, I entered the building; it appeared we were in the rundown lobby of an office. A crowd of about ten humans were staring at the vampire in pure fear. They didn't notice as I walked up to him and tapped him on the shoulder.

He turned, staring at me with a look of shock. "A shifter? Here? The king told me you were wiped out," he snapped through bared fangs. I tilted my head, giving an amused chuckle.

"I bow to no such king, so no wonder he'd tell you that," I replied. I drew back my fist and gave him an uppercut so fast that he had no time to react. Then, I pulled out my knife and shoved it into the center of his chest, making sure to bury it deep within his heart. "You nobles are horrible at combat!" I commented as he fell.

"B-but... this plot of land was given to me by the king himself..." he coughed as blood poured out of his chest. I smirked.

"You're relieved of your contract, sir!" I replied sarcastically. My eyes turned to the terrified humans. Ah great, now I had people to take care of. The first time I'd tried to rescue a group of people, it'd not gone well. Smoke wasn't nice, and Ash was worse.

"Hey, so I'm not here to kill you," I tried, not really one with words when it came to people who were afraid for their lives. I blinked as someone stepped forward.

A little girl, she looked about four, slowly walked toward me. Her eyes were a deep brown, and her skin tone was that of a light tan. She had curled, dark brown hair and tattered rags for clothing like the rest of these people.

"You're like a hero... thanks for saving us, kind lady!" she whispered. She was really close and looking up at me while giving a wide smile. I returned her smile and gently bent down, lifting her into my arms. A gasp came from within the crowd, and a woman with strong resemblance to the child rushed forward.

"Rose! I told you not to run up to strangers!" she shrieked. I blinked and handed the child to her mother, looking down for a second.

"Sorry ma'am.... your child is very sweet," I muttered. The woman paused for a moment and gave me a smile.

"That's quite alright. It seems Rose has taken a liking to you, I mean, you did save us, after all. You're our hero. My name is Gwenn. That vampire said you were a shifter... is that true?" she asked quietly. Hesitantly, I gave a nod. I put my knife in my bag and waited to be attacked or something; I was fully aware that humans hated my kind.

Surprisingly, the lady's smile just widened. I noticed she had a slight accent, and her voice was really pretty. "Yes... it is," was all I managed to say. Despite her smile, I was rather wary.

Gwenn sighed in relief. "Well, I can speak for all of us when I say I am grateful. That vampire murdered my husband," she said in a low voice. Rose shifted in her grasp and looked into my eyes.

"He ripped daddy's neck apart," she muttered, tears forming in her eyes. Gwenn paled and immediately took her child in a tight hug.

"Thank you for avenging him," was all she managed to say. I gave a bow, letting out a sigh.

"My pleasure. I am working with the true king, one that will *not* harm your people, one that only wants peace between vampires, shifters, and humans. He can help you—and I can tell you how to find him, if you'll listen," I tried.

Gwenn paused for a moment, her face twisting in thought. She turned to the other humans and approached them.

"This woman saved us from the clutches of that evil being. He has slaughtered our neighbors... friends... wives...husbands..." she whispered, wiping away a tear on the last word. But she toughened up pretty quickly and stood tall.

"We owe her our lives, and she continues to try and aid us. You heard what she said—I say we accept her offer of salvation!" she yelled. Wow, these humans were not ones to ever give up. I admired them. I mean, they had been destroyed by vampires, so my offer to help them under the promise of *another* vampire ruler probably sounded crazy. But to those clinging to any sort of hope, I guess anything was a relief to what was tormenting them.

"She coulda killed us if she wanted us dead. We've been through enough not to resist an offer of help. And we are not dumb enough to assume *all* vampires are evil due to one king. Hell, then our entire species would be damned," came the voice of one man, he looked like he worked out often, it might have been due to the stresses of recent circumstances though.

Gwenn gave a nod. "We will go to wherever you direct us to, savior," she muttered. I glanced toward the door.

"Once I get you to the forest, you will have a safe walk to the base. I can tell you how to get there. You'll be welcomed by open arms," I promised. I took a deep breath and knew it was time to activate the powers of the bond. My eyes rolled to the back of my head as I tilted it toward the sky.

I was rushing faster than the speed of light, what seemed like years yet less than a millionth of a second at the same time, my eyes opened to a dark room. He'd been sleeping and was now awake, probably due to my activation of the bond. "Eh?" came Smoke's voice in my head. He blinked, as did I; this was odd, I was seeing through his eyes.

"I have sent people I saved from the clutches of Ash's cronies to you. I am telling you now so you can let the others know and expect them. Tell them that they will find the group if they patrol, I will send them that way," I said, knowing he would hear me. I could sense his confusion and...relief?

"You saved a bunch of humans already? Don't get yourself killed. I will let them know," he said. I blinked, now back in my own eyes. Gwenn stared at me with her eyebrows raised in surprise.

"Her eyes were white!" Rose giggled. It seemed like not much disturbed her. Perhaps she would grow to be a brave warrior. Gwenn scooped her up again, nuzzling her.

"Pay no attention to that dear," she tried to assure her child, as if Rose had been afraid in the first place. Ah parents, always the protective ones.

"I let my allies know that you're on your way. I will send anyone else I can save along with you on my journey to the kingdom," I muttered, motioning for the group to follow me. Luckily the forest was right there, and my explanation to get to my home was pretty straightforward.

"You follow this path, and will eventually cross into my territory. One of my packmates will find and direct you from there. The place itself is well hidden, so you'd never be able to find it on your own," I told her. The path was very far from my home and only crossed the very edge, which is why the idea of royal vampires coming a lot deeper into the woods at 'random' was horrifying. Again, I shivered at the realization that he had to know all about where we were due to that recording.

I turned away, letting Gwenn lead the group off to their safety. Rose waved at me from over her mother's shoulder, and with a final smile I waved back. I turned away and began walking back to the city, listening for any other screams that I could hear. There would be a lot of humans I needed to save, and therefore a lot of soldiers that could fight.

If these humans were willing to stand with us, we would have a huge advantage. Our kind, along with vampires, underestimated the power of our *Homo sapien* cousins. But even *Homo sanguinem* and *Homo transfiguro* could fall to humans if they had the right magic and weapons. I also knew that they were not the kind to ever give up, which could very well mean the difference between life and death.

I walked along, drawing my bag close to me when I heard a chuckle in my ear. I whirled to see a group of about five vampires bearing down on me, a hungry glare in their eyes.

"That was a noble thing you did, but too bad it will be in vain. Once we snatch you up, we get some free blood not too far into the forest..." growled the one of whom looked to be the leader.

He was taller than myself and had bloodied black hair going to one side of his head, while the other side was shaved. He was in heavy leathers and chains, had many piercings, and wore a very crooked smirk displaying dangerous, shark-like teeth. There was something off about his eyes... They were a pure onyx, brought out clearly by the ivory of his skin. Disgustingly, I also noticed drool pouring down his face. I saw desperation, confusion, and hunger, as if he was some tiger pacing in a cage. *He was starving.*

He, and the rest of his gang, looked extremely skinny, as if deprived of food. They were looking at me like I was a sheep going into the maw of a wolf. Too bad these 'wolves' weren't smart enough to smell a Devil in sheep's clothing.

Chapter 40: Sam

The blazing heat hit my face and felt rather grand. This room was glowing red hot, and the walls were purely made of metal. Good thing too, otherwise my fire would burn down the entire building. My eyes glowed a green that looked like poisoned fire. I opened up my maw and let loose a flurry of flames, burning all of the training dummies that were in front of me to ash. Why the shifters had a training room like this, I had no idea. Perhaps it was because raw power was needed at a greater extent to destroy pure metal. I mean, they didn't have flamethrowers lying around to practice with, did they?

I'd been in my dragon form for quite some time now. My twisting coils were impressive, I felt more alive than I ever had. In human form, it was different. I had so many worries, so many things to cry or laugh about. In this form it was all about fire. Burn everything, and rip apart anything that couldn't burn. The feeling was amazing, I felt like a fiery serpent from the underworld released only to wreak havoc on the surface world. I knew such a mindset was dangerous but for gods' snake, it was amazing!

I didn't hear the door slowly open behind me, however a vibration alerted me to someone's presence. My head immediately turned as I looked for the intruder. My glowing claws dragged against the floor as I fixed my eyes on... nothing? Smog billowed from my nostrils as I gave a frustrated roar and looked around. "Come out come out," I snarled, my voice gritty and more like a growl than words. I finally was able to form words that could be understood in this form, though it took some close listening to decipher my growls.

The blotches of shadow told me one thing—Goliath was here. I snorted and sat in place, my eyes narrowed in anger. "Goliath, I know it's you. Stop playing around, are we training now?" I growled. No response. Two can play that game. I had learned a little bit, at least. Good thing I was calm enough to sense the vibrations of my enemy.

Behind me... SWIPE!

Nope, I missed. Damn it, I turned again as the waves of movement were felt next to me. Now, maybe?

SWIPE!

No dice. I let out a furious roar and backed into the corner of the room, waiting. Now he could only reform in one spot.

I reared up and let out a billow of flames, trying to burn away anyone that happened to be in front of me. He'd be fine, I was sure. Vampires survived a hell of a lot more than fire, and I knew Goliath had killed so many dragons that my fires were a minimal threat. Hell, a recent day of training had proved he could *walk through* my fire while only gaining some minor burns. Still, enough fire could burn through skin, and as soon as I saw him, I would stop.

Ah, there he was! I closed my maw and let my eyes fall on the person in front of me... that smile... that *laugh...*

"Ash...?!" I gasped.

My growls turned into terrified hisses. The vampire was here, right in front of me, standing leisurely like he'd been there the entire time. His fangs gleamed as he looked into my eyes, the blood-red more starved than ever.

"Tsk tsk, little dragon. I never said you could go free, did I?" the vampire asked in a quiet voice, so quiet that I could barely hear him over my own horrified growls. My claws shot forward and hit... nothing, again. Just shadows where the vampire had just been. I felt something on the back of my neck, a sharp tinge. My roars turned into screams. My skin was on fire, and my bones seemed to melt into magma within me. I writhed on the floor as if I was in a seizure. My eyes were wide open, my pupils dilated completely. The venom, it *hurt!* How was this possible?!

I shrunk down to human form, covering my face and convulsing in extreme pain. My pupils were growing and shrinking now as my screams died down. I relaxed, too tired now to move. My half open eyes stared up at Ash.

"Time to come back to the castle, my little snack..." Ash whispered in my ear. *No... No...*

SCREAMING... WAS IT mine? I felt someone holding me down as I writhed, my voice cracking as my yells died down to whimpers. "Let me go! Please..." I begged, tears streaming down my face. My eyes were shut tighter than they ever had before.

Back in Ash's castle, I had held back my screams after a while. I had kept calm even through the torment. He sometimes unlocked my chains to let me free, to see how far I could run, to give me the illusion of freedom. That was the biggest torment in itself, paired with the constant blood draining. The idea that I would return to *that* was too much—I could no longer hold in my fear.

"Love, calm down! It's only me!" came Goliath's voice. I felt a cold sweat covering me as I slowly opened my eyes. I was on my part of the couch, still in the shifter pack's home base. *Goliath... here? But I thought...* "You awoke and began to scream, Sam. It's alright, I'm here," he assured me in an extremely calm tone. He held me close as the pack members emerged from the other rooms.

"What happened?!" came Oriana's voice. Her red eyes fixed on Goliath, as if she expected him to have caused my screams.

"I... I had a horrible dream. Sorry for waking you all," I muttered, embarrassed. Now that I had calmed down a little, I realized how ridiculous I probably sounded.

Valiant walked up to me and placed a hand on my forehead. "She has no fever," she assured the group. Lilith, Bernard, and Oriana gathered around me to see what had happened. The others in the armies had gone back to bed once they realized it was just a dream.

Lilith stepped forward, her wise eyes resting on mine. "What did you see in your dream?" she asked in a wary tone.

"Ash. I was training and he appeared. I was backed into a corner, I thought it was Goliath at first but then realized it was the corrupted king himself. I felt a sting on the back of my neck and suddenly was in a world of pain," I murmured. The thought made me shiver once again, it was as if he had bitten me and his venom had an actual effect. But that wasn't possible, vampiric venom did not work on me, right?

I saw Lilith cringe and knew something was up. "There's something I don't know of, isn't there," I sighed in an exasperated tone. The shifter gave a sad nod, her eyes trained to the ground. I felt Goliath tense and knew I was about to get some not-so-great news.

"The royals have probably drunk enough dragon's blood for a unique venom effective against you to adapt. All vampires can control their venom, and sometimes they produce that of a rare quality, so powerful that it affects even your kind," she sighed.

My eyes turned to Goliath, and his eyes were wide in horror. "Does that mean you...?" I questioned.

Goliath shrugged, slowly looking down at me. I was still in his lap, and luckily he was here to comfort me or I wouda went on a rampage. "I never tried to paralyze you or put your through pain, love. Now that I think about it, I probably could," he muttered, wincing.

"Please don't," I growled in a resigned tone. My eyes fell on Lilith once again.

"Is there any way to become immune to *that* venom?" I asked in a worried voice. Her solemn expression gave me the answer I was dreading.

"Not quite, but you can learn to withstand it in battle. There *are* complications that come with it," she mentioned. I raised my eyebrows, willing her to continue.

"Go on," I told her, not all that excited to hear the rest.

"We have a vampire here who happens to have that venom," she said, glancing at Goliath. "One that you happen to be training with."

Ah, now it dawned on me. I tensed, my fists clenching at the thought. I felt Goliath shake his head above me.

"I refuse to put her through that," he said firmly. Lilith gave another shrug, her eyes very serious.

"If you want her to have more of a chance when she battles Ash, she will need to know how to fight even with that venom coursing through her veins," she finished. Slowly, I gave a nod in agreement with her and turned my eyes up to Goliath.

"It's fine, Goliath. I will be alright, it's something we need to do," I muttered. "I will be a more powerful dragon if I can continue battle even under that condition," I added.

Goliath blinked once, then twice. He finally let out a defeated sigh. "Fine, love. We can train with the venom. I suppose I only need to use the normal venom I use on prey. I only paralyze, though," he promised. "Even when I was a murderer," he added in a much quieter voice.

"She will need to know how to handle both pain and paralysis," Lilith mentioned. I gave a nod, my eyes worried but determined at the same time.

"I will need to be able to face him no matter what. Anything we can do to prepare me will be helpful," I muttered. "I appreciate it, Goliath," I added, looking up at him.

The vampire chuckled. "Don't thank me for agreeing to harm you, love," he sighed.

"We should start right away!" I growled. Yeah, I woke up in screams, but now I knew why my worries were there. I wanted to reduce my fear as soon as possible!

"Shouldn't you rest first, love?" Goliath asked, surprised. I shook my head.

"I was just sleeping," I replied, getting to my feet. I glanced over as Bernard took a step forward.

"One more thing, dragon. You do know that your kind can consume metals? Maybe not in your current form, but it will be melded into your scales and claws if you eat enough. If your kind had known of the impending genocide, they perhaps would have dined on more silver," he mentioned. I gave him a confused look.

"So you're saying if I eat silver, my scales and claws will *turn* silver?" I asked. Bernard shook his head.

"Not fully, no. Just very slightly, like the tips and edges. But such a change will give you a *huge* advantage against vampires. Powerful ones can still fight on with ease, though will be harmed more somewhat by your attacks. I know of one dragon from long ago with a silver-only diet that had vanquished an entire army of fresh vampires. Everything you can do to prepare is important," he growled. He obviously was very educated in combat. Darcia was aware of a lot of history, Lilith of venom and remedies, and Bernard of battle. It seemed like shifters were very educated people, which was helpful here.

"Awesome. Serve my dinner on a silver platter then," I chuckled. That got a smirk on virtually everyone around me. I began to move toward the door that led outside; I was ready to begin training!

"There's a group of humans on their way," came a voice from behind us. I turned to see Smoke standing from the door of his room, his eyebrows raised.

"Eh?" I asked him, confused.

"Darcia rescued a group of humans that are on their way. We need to meet them on the path," he muttered. I turned to Goliath, a glint in my eyes.

"Race you there," I chuckled. "If you catch me, training starts. You know what I mean," I growled. I needed to be prepped for this sorta thing. Goliath winced but slowly nodded.

"Run faster than light, love. I won't be going easy on you," he muttered in a promise.

"I'll probably make it there before you idiots," Smoke muttered as he darted out of the door. I raced after the ex-hunter, growling.

"Is that a challenge?!" I darted ahead, and judging by the hisses behind me, Goliath wasn't falling behind at all. Time for another, more painful training session to begin.

Chapter 41: Sam

F*lap...Flap...* My own wingbeats echoed in my ears as I flew along, and my eyes locked on Robert Smoke. This was a race, I could tell by his constant glances up to my direction and the twisted scowl that remained on his face for a second too long after he looked back to the path. "He wants to play that game, does he," I growled to myself.

As I had said, vampires were indeed fast—but I was faster. I flew lower, low enough to touch the ground with my dragonic hands(or paws? I wasn't sure what to call them). I whisked past the vampire, twisting as I almost seemed to slither through the air. "You're gonna freak them out, idiot!" yelled Smoke, but I'd left him in the dust.

I turned my head as my venom-green eyes flashed malevolently. "Try to stop me, dragonbait!" I snarled, smog coming from my nostrils as I swung my head back to pay attention to where I was flying. That one mistake of taking my eyes off of where I was going, however, would be my downfall. I suddenly simply couldn't see. I wasn't blinded, but rather was surrounded by shadows now. I let out a dragonic roar that echoed off of the trees in this massive forest.

I landed rather quickly, not wanting a repeat of what had happened last training session. Now, I was ready. My mission was to delay his bite as long as possible, or even stop it completely. It would be a long-shot, but perhaps I could pin him down and trap him.

A quiver at the corner at my eye alerted me to his presence. More smog gently billowed from my nostrils as I brewed the fire in my belly. My throat felt warm, not burned, but as if I had drank a cup of hot chocolate that was just barely cool enough not to scald my flesh. I closed my eyes, telling myself to trust my intuition. *He's dangerous... .be careful...* came that voice again. I just snorted. "You think I'm not dangerous too? I'm a freakin fire-breathing giant lizard," I growled aloud. I heard a chuckle from the shadows and immediately turned my head toward it, willing myself to keep my eyes closed in order to zero-in on the vibrations.

"Talking to yourself again, love? That's not gonna help you," Goliath warned in a sinister voice. His mind games again. His tone was still a bit freaky, but I could handle it without losing my cool thus far. Though I had fallen for it *every* other time, I would not bow now.

"I have better conversation with my own voices in my head than I do with you, leech," I shot back in a hiss. I heard the faint beat of his heart behind me, slightly to the right. I didn't waste any time to turn. My back-claws jabbed out and actually struck someone. I heard a gasp of pain and chuckled in triumph. Finally, I had hit him! Vampires could only fade into the shadows so much. I knew that if I could distinguish his true location, I could actually wound him.

Goliath's angered hiss hit my ears, and suddenly he was not where he'd just been. "I told you not to call me that, my snack," he snarled in my ear. That term made me freeze in my tracks. My stunned silence gave him the perfect moment to strike, for fangs sank into the top of my neck, just between my jagged scales. My roar-scream rang out as I fell to the ground. Just like in the dream, I writhed, feeling such bitter pain that tears began to pour from my eyes.

I shifted to human form, once again covering my eyes and convulsing. Goliath wasted no time; he leaped onto me and pinned me down as I cried out. My shaking faded after a minute or so, and I found myself staring into his eyes. The vampire raised his eyebrows and shook his head. "It worked," he growled flatly, his eyes distant. My green eyes flashed angrily as I struggled to no avail.

"Yeah, now let me go please. I failed, OK, I get it," I spat. Goliath blinked and looked down at me. He still had on his gods-damn hat! How the hell?! Ugh, now was not the time to dwell on that.

"I'm sorry, love. I was really hoping it wouldn't be true," he sighed, a grimace on his face. "Ash is going to use this to his full advantage," he warned me. "And you definitely cannot handle it yet."

"I know, I know! I'm weak, whatever! NOW LET ME GO!" I roared, my voice very loud.

The vampire shook his head firmly, unsurprisingly refusing to move an inch. "No, love, you're actually one of the strongest dragons I've encountered. The venom should have caused you to writhe in pain for hours longer, supposedly. You stopped after just a minute. But that minute could cost you dearly, which is why we need to do something rather unpleasant. We need to get you used to the venom," he growled.

I winced but knew exactly what he meant. "OK, so when I am?" I growled, irritated that I was still here. Damn vampire trying to prove a point. I bet I could shift right now and throw him off. In fact, I did just that. Suddenly Goliath was slammed to the ground and trapped under my claws. My eyes glared into his since I had shifted so fast that there was no way he could have prepared.

"Broken tail method. Take notes, Goliath," I snarled, breathing smog into his face. The vampire looked at me with such surprise that his jaw almost dropped.

"How the hell," he gasped. "Did you shift so quickly? I had no idea," he muttered. His red eyes flashed as if a light-bulb went off in his head.

"Sam, that strategy could work greatly in your advantage. Your surprise attacks are uncanny, I have to say," he complimented. He glanced down to his chest, where I noticed very deep claw marks that had ripped his suit(yes he was still in that too.) Hah, I had knocked him down so hard his hat fell off! THAT WAS VICTORY IN ITSELF!

"Good, but couldn't he fade into the shadows?" I asked seriously.

"Not if you tire and delay him enough first. If he thinks he's won, and you catch him by surprise, you could really wound him before he does that. He'll need to waste his powers to save himself—and at that point you can be VERY aggressive and go for the kill," he said in an excited voice.

I was about to reply when there was a gasp behind me. My head swung as I locked my gaze on...

What the hell. I became very dizzy, no, was this really...? I turned my body completely around, and ignored the newly-arrived Smoke and other humans. He had brought the group from the path to where Goliath and I happened to be. I ignored Goliath as he got to his feet, now free from my claws. No way in hell did I shift to human form now.

"You..." I snarled, more smog billowing from my nostrils. That woman. I could tell by her striking eyes straight away. The woman recognized me as well, her face twisting into an expression of pure horror.

"T-that voice...Sambuca... is that you?" she gasped. She took a step forward, but was stopped by the little girl. The woman looked down at the small child, blinking for a second.

"Don't go, mommy. That monster looks like she wants to eat you!" she cried tearfully. The woman just gave her a soft smile and picked her up. I was silent as she approached and slowly held out a hand, attempting to place it on my muzzle.

I snapped at her, just inches away from removing that hand right from her wrist. "Don't touch me!" I yelled, my tail lashing back and forth as my hisses of anger seemed to fill up the night. The woman's eyes were deeply saddened.

"Oh Sambuca... It's been so long, I am so sorry..." she muttered.

"Don't apologize for your wrongdoings, '*mother*'. Or should I call you *Gwenn the abandoner?!"* I snapped.

"Sam, the important thing is that you're OK... I thought we lost you," she sighed. My eyes locked on her now as I opened my jaws wide and gave a roar. I cared not that the little child screamed and covered her ears. Gwenn looked over, concerned, but I would not have it.

"YOU GAVE ME AWAY! YOU LEFT ME TO DIE, YOU GAVE ME TO THE ROYALS TO BE TORMENTED! YOU HAVE NO IDEA WHAT I WENT THROUGH AS A SLAVE, WHAT I HAD TO SEE! HOW I WAS HUNTED WHEN I FINALLY ESCAPED!" I screamed.

Ah, now all was revealed. Gwenn and her(I assume) late husband, Timothy, had been the ones to sell my damn soul to the leeches. My voice grew into a soft whisper as steamy tears glided down the scales on my cheeks.

"Is it because you *knew* I was a monster? A freak? Something that shouldn't exist?" I whispered. I slowly shifted to human form, feeling defeated. Seeing them, here and now, remembering what they did, remembering just how much of an outcast I really was... as an understatement, I was rather sad.

"No, Sambuca," Gwenn said firmly. I felt Goliath stand beside me, placing a hand on my shoulder to comfort me. It didn't help all that much, but it was still something. The lady approached me, provoking a hiss from the vampire. Goliath was staring her down with pure hatred, for now he understood exactly why I reacted that way.

"No?! To hell with that, I remember you giving me away," I whispered.

Gwenn put a hand on my shoulder, ignoring Goliath's growing hisses of protest and my tensing. "I would never have done it unless I had no other choice to make. My birth child, Serenity... you remember her, don't you? I couldn't let him take her. Gods Sambuca, it was you or her, I am so sorry. I couldn't let her go, I *had* to let them take you. They would have killed her," the woman whispered. Tears flowed down her cheeks now as well, as thick as my own. "I loved you like my own, but, I just..." she tried, her voice fading into choked sobs. "But you're OK..."

I shrugged away from her, the pain in my eyes not fading. "If you loved me, you wouldn't have given me to those bloodthirsty monsters. I know the real reason. You think I'm a disgrace, disgusting, a human-dragon hybrid," I snapped. Gwenn shook her head.

"No, Sam. I didn't care. I *loved* you, I wish you'd understand. But Serenity," she gasped. I clenched my fists, gritting my teeth. I felt a tug on my shirt and slowly turned my eyes to a small child. She was Gwenn's.

"Um.... dragon-lady? Please don't hurt mommy. I love her, and I know you don't, but I do, please with a cherry on top?" the little girl asked sweetly. I glanced from her to Gwenn. My eyes clouded over and became emotionless.

"No," I responded softly. "I would never hurt her like she hurt me. You and your posse are here for refuge? I won't refuse you that. But I will *never* love you or forgive you, *Gwenn,*" I hissed, spitting the name. I suddenly whirled and began walking back to the house, ignoring my neck wound and bruises from the battle.

I paused but didn't turn my head to ask my last question. "What happened to Serenity anyway, then, *Gwenn*?" I asked softly. I heard the woman stiffen behind me.

"Dead," she replied in a broken voice. "Slaughtered by the king soon after you were taken away."

Chapter 42: Darcia

I bared my teeth, refraining from shifting just yet. Perhaps I could get these egotistical fools to give me some information on the going-ons. The vampire whom I assumed was the leader of this gods forsaken place took a step forward, eyeing me hungrily. I responded by taking a step back, only to feel myself walk into the vampire behind me. Being trapped wasn't a situation I enjoyed, that was for sure.

"Whatcha gonna do now, rip my throat out?" I asked in a sarcastic, fearless voice. The vampire laughed at my question and gave a slight nod.

"Not an ignorant one, are you. Nah, we ain't the type to spare even pretty ones like you, not when this hungry. Wish it didn' have to be that way, buuuut," he laughed in a city accent. I gave a shrug and rolled my eyes when the vampire eyed me like I was a steak.

"Trust me, if the situation was reversed, I wouldn't spare any of you bloodsuckers, even if you *do* look absolutely stunning," I replied, my tone actually not sarcastic on purpose. The vampire blinked, seeming surprised at my response. He'd expected an insult, I knew it. I could only grin with the satisfaction of his confusion.

"So, why are you all starving? Shouldn't King Ash be feeding you?" I asked softly. That caused all five vampires to burst out laughing.

"King Ash? KING ASH?! Yer an interesting chick, that's for sure. Look awful tasty... but nah. Guys like us, the beggars of the kingdom, we always have been mistreated. We are street urchins, and all of us want to be. Normally we pick off humans that are trash on the streets. Y'know, rapists, murders, scumbags. But we've run out of food *completely.* It became worse when Ash was king. ALL humans ran off, left us skin and bone, and there's no blood to go around. That group of humans you saved, along with a few very sneaky ones, are rare pickings. The nobles, they get their own humans to drink from, livin' the luxury life and crap," he drawled, his eyes distant for a moment. Then, the vampire refocused.

"Unwilling ones. Not even human filth, the prisoners... nope, mostly families. Innocent fucking blood slaves. They see widdle humans as livestock! It's interesting how much of a hypocrite that damned 'king' is," he added. His red eyes stared me down with an odd wisdom that I hadn't noticed before. Perhaps I could talk to them and gain their trust.

That thought was shot down pretty quickly, though, when one of the gang members yelled, "We're wasting time, I'm starving!" That caused the leader to snap out of it and glare at me. He was holding my arm so suddenly that I had no time to move away.

"Sorry sweet cheeks. Nothing personal, but that's enough small talk," he snarled.

I took a deep breath, telling myself that it was a bad idea to attack first. "Wait. I know of someone who could help you, who will bring equality for all, including you and your group," I tried. The leader's eyes flashed for just a second. That idea sounded promising to him, I could see him contemplating it. The vampire shook his head, refusing to believe me.

"Nothing will change. I will not lose this chance to feed myself, my brothers, and my sisters. I'm sorry." he snarled, and I knew his apology was genuine, too. But he was blinded by hunger. I'd lost them right then. My reaction was to shift immediately and set my jaws to his arm. The vampire let out a yell as I ripped a chunk of flesh away and lunged again, planning on doing some decent damage. I was thrown to the ground as the other four vampires lunged to protect their leader.

Knives sank into my flesh as my jaws flashed to bite any hand that came too close. From the screams I heard, I might have taken a finger or two. There were too many surrounding me, however. Desperate vampires were the most powerful ones, and on top of that, they were direly hungry. Their bloodlust empowered them like my anger empowered me. I was not angry, unfortunately. Scared out of my mind, yeah, hopeless, yeah, but not angry. This was not their fault.

I saw a break between one vampire's legs and did not hesitate. I bunched up my muscles and jumped, sliding between the legs and hurling myself into the twisting smoke of the burning city. The vampires were right behind me as I bolted ahead, leaving bloody paw prints in my wake. Taunts came from behind me that only made me run faster.

"Now we're coming after you... run, run run... run Devil run!" sang the gang leader, and soon the others chimed in to sing along with him. Ah great, they might be street urchins but they knew modern music. This was not fun. I turned left and came face to face with a vampire. Changed course, turned right, left, right again—nope, another one was there. They were going to corner me eventually. One wrong move and I was done for. My legs were burning now too, so I would need to stop soon. Lovely.

I shifted to human form and managed to grab a hold of a rotting ladder. The vampires were right behind me, laughing and continuing to taunt me the entire time. "What's the matter sweetheart? We don't bite...hard!" he laughed. Another vampire chimed in after him.

"Man, lying is so fun!"

My day was getting better and better. My new friends were *so* supportive, they were cheering me on to win this race! I almost burst out in hysterical laughter at the thought. Yeah, I was desperate and going insane. I reached the top of the building and burst forward, shifting again into my Tasmanian devil form. The footsteps were dangerously close, damn vampires and their agility.

I began leaping from one building to the next, which any human would be capable of doing too, so it'd be a cakewalk for these assholes. I sensed one running up beside me and swiftly dodged a grab. I coughed and panted, spitting in his face when he came too close. It was that gang leader, again, and he only gave a laugh.

"Perhaps we got off on the wrong foot; hey miss, my name is Ares! Mind if we have you for dinner?" he joked. I just let out a snarl and willed myself to run faster. My legs were about to give. I needed to at least get off of the roof.

I suddenly darted into a rotting door, one of those that led from the ceiling and into the building. The clanging of my claws hitting metal would not help me hide. The bangs of the steps rang in my head, making me somewhat nauseous. I darted into a room that was full of office desks and cubicles, perhaps a blessing disguised as a mess. I didn't have much time. I darted under the low walls, knowing I would lose my pursuer. I heard Ares let out a frustrated sigh as he lost sight of me in this office graveyard.

I settled myself under a dark desk, a broken one with a hole in the side in case I needed to make a run for it. I was surrounded by the walls of a black cubicle, with a rolling office chair doing a wonderful job of 'hiding' me. Because being behind a dark pole definitely made me invisible. I shifted to human form and hid my face into my arms, curling up into a ball and willing myself not to shake.

The gang members all split up to search for me. "You. Look over that way, I will over here. Guard the door, do NOT let her escape!" I heard Ares command. I heard the sound of desks being turned over and papers being scattered to the ground. I didn't have much time. My eyes flew to the hole in this desk. Maybe I had a chance. My heart sunk as I remembered the door was blocked, however; it was pointless to expose my hiding spot.

Help, help, please... anyone... I screamed in my mind, knowing no one would answer. My heartbeat quickened as a scratchy laugh sounded right in front of the cubicle I was hiding in. I saw two legs standing there, and I knew I had been discovered. "Hey boss... found the odd-looking dog girl," he chuckled. I saw him bend down and peer into my frightened but annoyed glare.

"It's Tasmanian Devil, idiot," I muttered. I bit my tongue as Ares rounded the corner and stared me down, a small smile on his face.

"Oh? Sorry lady, we didn't always take learnin' seriously. What would a *vampire* do with zoology?... Anyways, the gig's up. You're caught. I'll make you deal. We will keep you alive, unless we can't find some other source of food. But keeping you alive will benefit us more than if you were dead, you know?" he muttered. "When we find more food, we'll let ya go. I promise. It shouldn't have to be like this. But we are *so fucking hungry...*"

I growled nervously. Now I might face what Sam had gone through with Ash, but for *five* vampires. Five! So much biting. I let out a yelp as his hand locked on my ankle and dragged me from my hiding place. Both my wrists were grabbed as I was slammed to the ground, pinned against my will.

"Leader always gets the first bite, sweet cheeks," he mused. His red eyes were intimidating, but now I saw confusion within them. "Hey wait a sec, how is a shifter's eyes tinted red?" he questioned.

I had no chance to answer, for behind the vampires came a cold voice. A voice belonging to someone I couldn't stand but right now sounded like it was owned by an angel. "Let her go. She's with me," snarled none other Robert Smoke himself. How had the ex-hunter managed to find me?! Oh... right, the bond. Yeah, that'd do it.

All five vampires turned to face Smoke. I felt myself being lifted and held firm by Ares as he sized Smoke up and cracked a smile. The gang leader's hand held my jaw still, his claws pressing into my flesh as a warning.

"You and what army?" he asked softly. Smoke smirked and stepped aside to reveal Sambuca and Goliath, right on cue. There were a few other members of my pack with them, as well; I almost collapsed in relief.

"I followed the signals of the bond, Darcia. I knew you were distressed, and as soon as I let Sambuca and Goliath know, we were on our way. Sorry we took so long," he growled. His eyes locked to Ares. "I said let her go, or would you like to meet our dragon?" he questioned.

Sam gave a wide smile and grinned, allowing smog to rise from her mouth and nostrils. Her reptilian eyes glowed dangerously even though she was not in dragon form, but in that cool halfway-form she chose every now and then. "I'll rip you all to shreds without a second thought," my friend promised.

I felt cold metal against the flesh of my neck and knew I was in for it. I gasped as a knife pressed slightly into my skin, drawing just a tiny bit of blood. Smoke's eyes flashed a dangerous red as he locked onto the droplets forming. "The knife cuts through her jugular if you come any closer..." Ares snarled. It was a bluff, for he needed me alive if he wanted blood. But, bluff or not, yikes.

Goliath bared his teeth and took a step forward. "What is it that you want, sir? I can assure you we can provide food for you and your gang," he growled.

"You think I trust you?! I can smell the stench of your royal blood from here! I don't trust you any more than I trust that rotten king of yours!" Ares yelled.

Goliath hissed angrily. "My brother is no king of ours. We are fighting against him, brother. Let us help you!" he tried. But Ares would not listen.

"No! Fuckin' royals and their blood slaves, all a buncha LIARS! I WILL get a meal tonight, even if it has to be the death of me!" he screamed. I felt him fling away the knife, and so suddenly did fangs meet my flesh that I had no chance to react. Everything seemed to freeze. As Ares drank my blood, I felt anger, not my own, rising within me.

Smoke... *he was pissed.*

Why, I wondered? I had no time to dwell, for any anger, even if it was not mine, empowered me. My pupils grew until they vanished completely, and now my eyes were completely black. My hands balled into fists as I wound up my left fist and suddenly let out a punch so hard that Ares was sent staggering back, taking a chunk of the cubicle with him. My throat was bleeding profusely, but I didn't care. The anger within me clouded all reason.

"Boss, no! GAH! Please, we submit!" yelled one of the gang members. I shifted so quickly and darted after the fallen Ares, feeling all the fury of the world well up within me. *This anger is not my own... I need to control myself.*

But I could not. My muzzle became bloodied as I ripped into *his* neck, thirsty for vengeance. I felt myself being scruffed and ripped away, I saw the members of the gang swarm their leader. Three of them had tears streaming down their face.

"Ares! Boss! Are you alright?! Please! We are brothers!" one of the members yelled. As my anger cooled and allowed me to shift to human form, I held my head and turned to look at Smoke.

His eyes were completely black, including the sclera. His fangs were bared, and I could see my pack members holding him back from lunging. He let out an animal-like growl as he muttered, "Finish the job, Darcia, BEFORE I DO!"

"No. We've wounded him enough already. They surrender, it's best to bring them back alive. They're too weak to actually be a threat. We can help them, and we can get them on our side," Goliath snapped, twisting his glare to Smoke. "Battle is not always the answer!"

Sambuca gave a nod, crossing her arms. "The more we have to fight Ash's forces, the better. Let's go back before those *humans* loot the house or something," she growled in a worried voice. What? She had quite a distrust for Gwenn and family. I wondered why, I mean, Gwenn was such a sweet lady.

Now was not the time to dwell on that. Ares was still alive but unconscious. I saw the gang members gently lift him and grimly bow their heads. "We will comply now, for the life of our leader. Please, we've been through enough," one gang female member with dark skin and a half-mohawk like Ares muttered. Oddly, she was wearing a pair of dice on a chain as a necklace. I felt a slight bit of sympathy, but right now I myself was too weak to even comprehend what was happening.

I did notice their ribs jutting out, indicating starvation. To mend that, Goliath quickly passed out blood bags he had on his person in a bag I'd previously not seen. They wolfed them down like starved dogs.

I sat on the ground, holding my head, when I felt myself being lifted again. I looked up into Smoke's eyes and narrowed my own. "I can walk," I snapped. Smoke just shook his head and ignored me. He followed as Goliath led us out of the building and toward the forest where my home was.

An awkward silence seemed to pass before I coughed and muttered, "Thanks. For saving me. I coulda handled it."

Smoke just rolled his eyes. "Clearly. I only did it for myself," he growled, though there was no weight to those words. I raised my eyebrows and shrugged.

"Still, thank you."

"You're welcome, Darcia," he whispered, his scowl fading into a neutral expression as we walked along.

"Why were you so angry, though? I know that wasn't just me being fucking pissed," I muttered.

Smoke didn't answer, only walked along. "Because *I'm* the only one that can taste your blood," he finally said, and I scoffed.

"*No one* can when I'm able to defend myself, idiot," I growled, offended. Smoke just ignored me now, but I could tell there was more to it. As usual, though, I did not press. His selfish demeanor put me off, but I could sense something under it. One feeling was fear, but what was he afraid of? Real emotion, or me finding out about something?

Nah. Smoke was a jerk, a selfish spineless ex-hunter. So why did I feel sorta honored that he got so angry back there?

Chapter 43: Sam

My eyes gleamed their venom green as I gracefully followed behind the group, contemplating what had just happened. The city gangs had been a common target of mine. Now we had them hostage, yet I had no desire to slaughter them. I knew in my heart it wasn't right to just kill off any enemy we saw. The *real* enemy was Ash, *he* was the enemy to *all* of us. Hell, if I was able to work with scum like Robert Smoke, I might as well get along with my *prey* as well.

My mind raced as I thought of the final battle. Lately I was craving one thing—training. I was able to best Goliath, pin and surprise him, last session.

Well.. until that bitch of a woman decided to come into the picture.

But before she had ruined things, I *had* been able to take the prince down. I looked to the sky, knowing that when the time came, I *would* be able to face my nightmare with a light of my own. My fire would burn through the sky and all of its clouds. My claws would puncture Ash's chest, and I was looking forward to presenting his still-beating heart to the heavens where I knew my family would be smiling.

In order to do that, I need to get along with even the one who hurt me the most, I thought to myself with a frown. No, that did not, under any circumstance, mean that I wouldn't do all in my power to avoid her. Hell, it just meant I would refrain from burning *her* to ashes for the sake of this peace. After Ash was dead, though... meh.

I gave a slight sigh, knowing that my hatred would get me nowhere. No matter how much of a grudge I had for that woman, I would not ever be able to physically harm her. Let's just say my feelings on it are rather complicated.

I saw a few members of the gang turn their heads and eye me warily. I returned their glare with a sharp-toothed grin, which only provoked more curiosity from them. One slowed down and matched my pace, making me cross my arms. He had shaggy brown hair that fell into the pale of his face, and a distant crimson gaze. "Are you a former hunter?" he asked in a quiet voice. I gave a slight nod, wondering how he guessed so quickly.

"Rumors had it that others in rival gangs were being mysteriously slaughtered by a girl with very sharp teeth. She had red hair, a color similar that of dying ashes. Her face was never revealed, but I think I remember her name. Red Viper? Is that you?" he asked me. I blinked, my eyes narrowing dangerously.

"Yeah that's me. What's it to you?" I asked in a worried voice. The vampire took a step away from me, looking at me with eyes wider than I thought possible.

I felt Goliath's eyes on me, and I could sense his worry. He was leading the group, keeping watch on the still passed-out gang leader known as Ares. "Is everything alright back there?" he questioned, the upper half of his eyes hidden in the shadows of his hat rather eerily.

I gave a confused nod. "I think so? No worries Goliath, I can handle it. Just continue to make sure these vampires behave, you know how dangerous those living on the streets can be," I reminded him.

I could handle this one guy, hell, I knew I could destroy anyone that went out of line here. The other gang members seemed controlled, though, and were just glancing back every so often to make sure the vampire talking to me was alright. Something odd was going on, and I wanted to figure out why this vampire was looking at me in such awe.

"What? I'm not one of those fancy hunters, I killed when I needed to, when I saw reports of slaughter on the streets. I know you're probably not a huge fan, but—" I stopped. He was shaking his head rapidly, as if I had said something preposterous.

"Y-you think I want to harm you, want to attack you?! I—miss, Red Viper, whatever your name is, I...do you remember," he gasped. I crossed my arms, now knowing he could barely speak. I was rather confident that he would make no move to attack me now out of a random spout of anger, at least. This vampire didn't look all that angry, just surprised beyond words.

"Speak, friend, or erm. Yeah, friend I guess, we are allies for now. Anyway, what? Spit it out!" I growled, irritated. The vampire coughed and composed himself, looking like he was about to burst into tears.

He looked to be in his late twenties, and like the others was bone-thin and wearing tattered clothing. I did not recognize him at all, honestly. The only vampire I remembered sparing was that one orphan girl, whom I promptly returned to the home down the street. One of the reasons why Goliath *didn't* end up killing me, as I remembered. So there was no connection here, right?

"Let me start from the beginning, miss. I was taken by the old king, charged for murder of a noble. He had done my lady wrong, you see, I'm not going to go into detail but she didn't survive the ordeal, either. So I killed him and was discovered. I was on the run with my little girl, and they came too fast. I hid her in that alleyway, but I myself was snatched away as they pointed to a huntress on her way to that exact spot. My mouth was bound and I could only watch as Red Viper... as *you* approached her. I thought she was going to be killed by you for being what she was. You raised your fingers, your deadly claws, and you stopped. I remember hearing your sigh as you gently picked her up, she was only six or so, and took her away. You headed toward the orphanage. My captors scowled and dragged me off, throwing me into a prison and spitting in my face. 'Your child should have been killed if that hunter woulda done her job right. We might not be able to destroy that orphanage in pursuit of her, but we *can* punish you.' That was all I remember before a world of pain, before Ares saved my sorry skin from those rotting prisons.

Red Viper, you could have slain my daughter, and you did not," he finished, tears now streaming down his face. He fell to his knees now, his head bent as he let out heaving sobs. I was caught so off guard my jaw was dropped practically to the ground. "How can I ever repay you, miss?" I didn't respond, just stared and blinked rapidly.

"You take them back, Smoke. Keep an eye on him," I heard Goliath say, probably to the pack of shapeshifters carrying Ares and watching the gang members.

"Will do, your majesty," I heard Lilith say. Their footsteps faded as I stood there and looked over this vampire that I'd never thought I'd meet. Goliath stood beside me, looking from me to him.

"I heard the story, it's quite an interesting one," he muttered in a low voice, his eyes locked on this vampire. "We can go check on your daughter if you'd like," he added. I gave a nod, still taken aback. Small world, I guessed. I had no idea that I'd see that girl's parent alive, honestly. She spoke in such a frightened voice. I don't remember much of what happened, just that I, at the time, was utterly confused and worried.

"I-I'd like that. Would your brother have killed them off?" the vampire asked in a very scared tone. Goliath shook his head, a serious look on his face.

"Ash would not have a chance to. I knew the owners of the orphanage, it housed both humans and vampires, actually. They lived in harmony, for the most part. But the staff was *very* serious about their children, they would have gone into hiding as soon as they caught any whiff of trouble," he assured.

The vampire sighed in relief, his head turning up to look at me. I held out my hand. "Here, let's continue walking. We'll make sure your leader is taken care of, then we can talk more about it, alright? What is your name?" I asked, curiously.

The vampire paused for a moment and stared at me again. It was off-putting, somewhat, but I think he was so grateful he had no idea how to handle himself. He cleared his throat and finally accepted my hand, allowing himself to be helped to his feet. He was about the height of Goliath, so again a lot taller than me. Yet, he seemed so frail right now it was almost ironic.

"My name is Clyde. I am sure they all don't call you Red Viper here, miss," he muttered, raising his eyebrows now. He was starting to calm down, which was good. Goliath smirked and muttered something under his breath. Clyde blinked and laughed in response, now both of their eyes fell on me.

"Excuse me?" I growled, my eyes lighting up like coals. "What was that, Goliath?"

"Ah nothing, love," he coughed, now avoiding my gaze but keeping a rather amused smile.

Clyde held a light smile and said, "You're known as 'little Sam' then?" he questioned. Ah, now I could assume what he commented.

"The short jokes are NOT FUNNY! I'm a fire breathing dragon Goliath and I am *not* afraid to throw you across the woods," I snarled. Clyde watched, intrigued.

"Now now, love, we both know that I still beat you in training," he snickered, then added, "I'd better be checking on the others, bye!" Oh, he was *asking* for it. Before I ran after him, though, I stamped my foot and turned to Clyde.

"We will go check on your child, Clyde, no worries. I couldn't kill her, even though I'm a hunter and she's a vampire. Your kind is dangerous to me, so I thought, a menace that should have been wiped out. But I couldn't. I will save her *again* if I need," I promised. Man, I had a lot of promises to keep, and I would give my life to fulfill every single one.

Clyde looked at me with deep respect. "You are a hero to me, miss. I will help you fight off the false king, and I am sure Ares will too when he wakes up," the gang member put his hand behind his head, looking down.

"That vampire's been through a hell of a lot. Luckily you haven't killed any of us yet, you *did* kill one vampire in a gang of our allies, but Ares doesn't look much into that. 'Course now we are your prisoners, he doesn't have any choice but to work with you," Clyde said awkwardly. I just snorted, looking into the woods and thinking deeply.

"Nah, you don't have to stay, although for hurting Darcia I'll need to have a *long* talk with him. The only one we are forcing to stay is Smoke, and I don't think he even wants to leave us at this point. But the thing is, there are two sides to this fight. Us, and *Ash*. He is your enemy, and he is ours. *We* used to be enemies, that is, me and other hunters against gangs like yours, but that is now changed. You can leave whenever you want, but it would not be wise," I growled.

Clyde shook his head, his own red eyes glancing behind us.

"No. I follow Ares, I know he'll make the right choice—and that's to stay here. And miss, I will find some way to pay you back for your deed. It's the least I can do," he told me. I gave a shrug and tensed, now focused on the wilderness ahead.

"My goal is to help you rescue her and whatever others there are, perhaps find more allies, and train to be my best right now. You have no debt to pay, the only thing you can do now is stay with us to help," I replied. I could wait no longer—"Come along, I have a vampire to catch!" I roared, leaping and shifting mid-air.

"I'm coming for you Goliath, this time I will win from the get-go!" I roared. I knew Clyde would follow, the group was not that far ahead. We would meet them back at base—for now, spontaneously, another training session had begun. This time I would definitely make no mistake!

Chapter 44: Darcia

Yaaaaaawnnnn...

I rubbed my eyes as I got out of my bed, scratching the ache in my neck. I walked into my personal bathroom, examining the bite marks on my flesh. One, the fading one, was from Smoke; the recent one was from Ares, that damned gang leader.

I turned and walked out of my room, making my way to the kitchen and groaning from the sleepy dizziness that always greeted me when I woke up. I grabbed myself a bowl and spoon, pouring myself some cereal and milk and taking my place at the table.

I brought the spoon to my mouth, relishing the sweet taste of frosted flakes and milk. I just so happened to glance up to see Ares sitting at the table, staring me down. I jumped, blinking rapidly because I honestly had not seen him when entering the room. He hadn't made a sound and must've been sitting there the entire time.

I shot him an annoyed glare, wondering what the hell he was doing here. Yeah, I know we had taken him and his group in, but that didn't mean I trusted him any more than when I first laid eyes on him.

"The hell do you want?" I asked, and you can imagine how polite and courteous the tone in my voice was. The gang leader gave a light shrug, watching me suspiciously.

"Why are your friends helping us?" he asked finally, crossing his arms. I rolled my eyes at his question, ditching my spoon and literally sticking my head into the bowl and eating like a dog would. I sat up and shook off any excess milk, wiping my face with my hands and turning my attention to the vampire. He blinked, looking taken aback by my wonderful table manners. I continued as if that were perfectly normal—and to me, it was.

"Because *we* need all the help we can get. You might have almost killed me, but whatever. I'm not the one you royally pissed off," I growled, catching a few drops of milk that dribbled down my chin with a fast sweep of my tongue. Ares cleared his throat, now looking as if he was trying not to laugh. "What?" I asked, irritated.

"I've never seen anyone eat like that," he chuckled, from there bursting out into laughter. I narrowed my eyes.

"Uh, shapeshifters generally eat like that when we aren't ripping into flesh," I pointed out, but Ares only continued to laugh. "And anyway how is it that you're not attacking us? I thought you were dead starving?"

The vampire sobered rather fast and glanced toward the door, deep in thought. "Your damned diplomat gave us a store of his blood bags. Odd, ya know. Never stored enough of the stuff myself. From the vein is much better, hehehehe..."

I shuddered and gave a shrug, stretching and standing. I was ready to go into the living room, where I assumed everyone else was. "I guess. I don't know, before I was a vampire hunter my kind ate anyone, including other shifters, that happened to stumble upon our territory. Some would say we are savages—I call it the circle of life," I replied. I pushed my chair in and headed toward the other room, only stopping when I heard Ares speak behind me.

"Yer an odd one... other people I bit that survived tend to try to avoid me at all costs. You seem unafraid. My venom normally is rather potent," he muttered, confused. I just laughed.

"I'm immune to venom now," was all I said. It wasn't a lie and it made me sound more tough. Without another word, I took a seat, observing everyone else in the room.

Smoke was sitting there looking bored, leaning on a hand and nonchalantly shooting me a glance. Sambuca was there eating something odd, as she chewed I could hear metallic clanging. Looked like she indeed took Bernard's advice. Goliath was nowhere to be found. He probably was with the other gang members, letting them know exactly where our group stood.

I remembered him saying he'd need to get everyone on the same page before I had passed out.

Sambuca continued to chomp on whatever she was eating and turned her stare to me. "Howsh awer yoo?" she asked, her mouth full. Between her words the *clang* of metal could be heard as the bits crashed together against her sharp teeth.

"I'm doing fine now. Though, I'm sorta annoyed that I never got to the kingdom itself. I'm back here all over again, and I wanna be of some help," I sighed. Sam knit her eyebrows together and shook her head, swallowing.

"You've been a wonderful help Darcia, what with the research and gathering of your pack! Don't say that you're not doing much, silly," she growled. Her hand reached to her bowl as she withdrew some more metallic bits, probably little crumbs of silver.

"I guess so. Is the gang gonna stay with us?" I asked, curious. I heard a sigh behind me and turned my head to Ares.

"Yeh, you bunch are the only ones we can stay with. Ya gave us a meal and place to stay, and I guess we wanna see Ash stopped too. We'll work with ya... for now," he replied.

I felt the tension in the room increase, and oddly I felt myself getting angry as well. *My* anger was not directed toward anyone, in fact it wasn't even my own. But still I felt it. My head swiveled to Smoke, and I had the answer as to why I was pissed.

"Calm down, Smoke. He was desperate, I've accepted the fact that he bit me, now will you please get over it?" I growled. "Your emotions are making my head hurt!" Gods, this damn blood bond was sometimes a curse. Yeah, in combat it would be very beneficial, but right now it was just obnoxious.

I felt amusement emanating from Ares behind me. Oh gods, he was gonna provoke the ex hunter, I could feel it. "Aw, does someone fancy the badger-like shifter girl? She was yummy, I'll give you that!" Ares chuckled. I facepalmed, feeling an explosion of anger. I didn't act on it, but Smoke did. I felt a *whoosh* of air as he darted past me. I heard him slam Ares against the wall, but didn't turn to even bother and watch the fight. I just heard a series of animal-like hisses and growls and crossed my arms.

Sam could see, though, and winced every so often as one managed to strike at the other. Finally, she said, "I'd break them up if I were you."

I let out a sigh and muttered, "Why is it *my* responsibility?" But I got up anyway, very simply shifting to my Tasmanian Devil form, bunching my muscles up and leaping. I wedged myself between the fist-fighting vampires, dodging a few hits myself and forcefully knocking Smoke one way, Ares the other.

I shifted to human form, my eyes narrowed. Both were on their backs, breathing heavily; Smoke had several wounds on his arms, while Ares had marks on his cheek and chest. "If you both are quite done, I'd like some quiet for a sec. Also, Mister Ares, I'm not a freakin badger, I'm a Tasmanian Devil. Get it right, or I'll do *this* again," I snapped. Without any hesitation I raised my hand and slapped him clean across the face, shocking him so much that he froze. "And that's *also* for biting me, you douche."

Instantly I was sitting back where I was, getting myself comfortable as if nothing just happened. My eyes fell on Sam, who now looked extremely angry. Like, angrier than Smoke angry. I followed her gaze and saw Gwenn's uneasy frown... ah.

Something bad had happened between them, I could tell now. Without a word, Sambuca stood up and left the room. Even Ares and Smoke were quiet as they took a seat and watched her walk out. No one messed with an angry dragon, not even two angry male vampires.

I heard Gwenn sigh and noticed Rose scamper over and leap onto her lap. "Why does the dragon lady hate us?" the child asked, her eyes glimmering with curiosity.

"Mommy did a bad thing to her, sweetie," the woman replied softly. I raised my eyebrows, but decided not to press.

Goliath strode in just then, looking rather tired. I could see several rips in his suit, probably from the last training session he'd done with Sambuca. His eyes fell on Gwenn warily. "What happened to Sambuca?" he asked in a strained voice, though I figured he knew already.

"She went into the other room," I replied, glancing from Gwenn to him. The vampire sighed and stepped aside. The man that had stayed back to talk with Sam, think his name was Clyde, came from behind him and took a seat as well.

Goliath sighed. "I'll try to talk to her later. For now, It's been brought to my attention that there are several in danger from the city. Gwenn let me know that there were other groups of humans in a similar situation to what she found herself in, and I spoke with Clyde about gang connections. I wanted to discuss ways to gather them up and possibly recruit them," he finished. His eyes fell on Ares. "We spoke about this a little while ago. I was thinking we could go to specified areas since you know the city the best and explain to them the situation," the vampire prince said softly. Ares thought for a moment and slowly nodded.

"Ya I know my way around. No one is gonna trust you, though, I still don't," he growled. Goliath shrugged.

"That's why I'll have *you*. If you agree, that is," the vampire replied, his voice laced with a hint of threat. Ares shrugged it off and rolled his eyes.

"Yeah, whatever. What is the worst that can happen?" he said sarcastically. Goliath moved onto the next part of the plan.

"This place can be a safe haven for those we rescue, if you permit it Darcia," he muttered, a question in his voice. This time there were no threats or anything, just a tint of hope. Of course I would use my enormous home to help in this cause, we had more than enough room. I waved my hand and gave a nod.

"Yeah, but we'll need people to watch over those that don't want to fight or are too weak to battle," I pointed out. I saw Gwenn sit up straighter.

"I can help. I am qualified a bit in nursing, if there are medical tools available I can help mend wounds," she chimed in a very soft voice. I gave a nod, smiling.

"That would benefit us a lot. And who is gonna go around getting the humans?" I asked.

Goliath motioned toward the door with his head. "Sam said she would help with that," he replied. Good, that left one thing.

"Well, now we have a few more on our side, but still no eyes on the enemy. I want to continue my journey to the kingdom after a bit more training," I growled in a serious voice. Goliath let out a sigh.

"If you're well enough, Darcia, that would help a hell of a lot," he replied. Smoke stood up and bared his fangs.

"This time I am going with her," he growled, and I shook my head.

"No, then we won't have someone on the other end," I snapped, finding his sudden show of aiding me ridiculous.

He crossed his arms. "With both of us there, we can easily meet any conflict and get away. Alone we are more vulnerable. We can communicate by cell or some electronic device, we don't *need* to have someone on the other end of the bond here," he said to overrule my argument. I was about to protest when Goliath nodded his head.

"That's not a bad idea, actually. Your pack mates will be here, we can give them the other end of the communications," he suggested. I was quiet for a moment when I gave in with a wave of my hand.

"Fine, fine. I'll bring Smoke along. You'd better not mess this up, vampire!" I spat. Smoke just fixed me in a glare.

"At least you won't get yourself bitten by another again," he snapped, now glaring at Ares. The gang leader just gave a wink and licked his lips, which just made Smoke even more angry. I grit my teeth and slammed my fist on the armrest.

"That's enough!" I yelled, catching the attention of everyone in the room. Embarrassed, I sat back in my chair and muttered, "Er, sorry..." Ugh. At least I'd be leaving soon. I'd be with a deadbeat, but I couldn't care less at this point. I had a job to do and I would see it done no matter what.

Chapter 45: Sam

I grumpily paced in my room; the commotion out there on a regular basis was annoying, but I didn't bother to go and shut anyone up. *She* was in there most of the time, that cursed woman.

I mean, I guess saving her blood child was important, but to give me away like that so easily, it just broke my heart and all my trust. I couldn't forgive her for what she did. I never did tell anyone exactly what I saw when I was kept as a blood slave.

Anyone who I became close to was slaughtered before my eyes as punishment for any tiny mess-up I did. I saw prisoners being tortured, heard them begging to be freed, begging for my help. Every time I helped, someone would die. So I stopped helping, and they would die anyway. Gwenn would never understand what she put me through by selling me to that vampire prince.

A few weeks of training had passed, and I couldn't get away from *her*. My heart clenched in fury every time I saw her, and it was difficult trying to retain focus. Goliath had been preparing with that gang leader to gather forces and was leaving tonight, which also had me on edge. Meanwhile, I was leaving with Clyde to go meet Maddy very soon.

I wallowed in my misery for a while before the door slowly creaked open. I didn't even look behind me, I knew who it was. "What do you want?" I growled in an irritated voice. He knew I wanted to be alone.

"Want to go take a walk real fast, love? I just wanted to chat before I left," Goliath said in a low, careful voice. My eyes glowed a furious venom green as I turned to the vampire, baring my sharp teeth.

"As long as I don't need to be near that woman, I will do whatever is needed of me. As for a walk? Not in the mood," I snapped.

"Just to reiterate the plan, I'll be going to the cities with Ares to gather some allies, and you'll be visiting the city to try and find the child," he summed up. I could tell he was being very careful to not mention Gwenn.

I crossed my arms, sighing. "Correct. I'm ready to leave now, then. Where's Clyde?" I asked.

"He is resting and saying his goodbyes to the rest of the gang. You sure you don't want to walk and cool off a little?" he questioned softly. I narrowed my eyes and slumped my shoulders in defeat. He knew I got myself all worked up over these things.

"Fine, whatever, let's go," I growled quickly. I just wanted to get out of this damn house for the moment. I exited via the window, and of course you can assume why. Goliath was right behind me, and soon we were walking in silence along the winding path in the woods.

"You're going off with Ares. How do I know that gang leader won't backstab you?" I asked suddenly. I had seen the glint in his eyes. No, not evil, just desperate. That's why he bit Darcia, of course, but nevertheless I found it very hard to trust him. Though some time had passed, and there'd been training together, I was a stubborn beast. Goliath sighed and gave a shrug.

"Sometimes you just need to have trust, even in the most dangerous of alliances. Ares *hates* Ash. I know this because my brother doesn't take into consideration the lesser even if they are his own kind. He always wanted to be royal, to rule with an iron fist and strike fear into others. He had said those not noble deserved their fate. Ash is bad news and Ares knows it. He also knows that we, our group, is the strongest one against him. He will not fail us, Sam... desperate people are sometimes among the smartest," Goliath replied. I had to agree with him there. Though I'd worry for him, I knew he could handle Ares well enough. How he'd manage to recruit other rogue gangs, though, was beyond me. But Goliath was a good talker, clearly, so he could do it.

"So where is this place? What will I expect to find there?" I asked, changing the subject rather quickly. I was impatient—I wanted to be out there aiding those who could be endangered by the bloodthirsty king. Especially now that I had learned more about that girl I had saved by bringing her to that orphanage. Goliath knew far more about the area I was going to than me.

"The underground tunnels. I have become close to one of the caretakers, they told me that if tragedy were to strike, they would hide there. They knew of the cruel king, they also knew that my transition to kinghood would not be, under any circumstance, smooth. The entrance is, ironically, in a grate on the side of the human hospital. It's marked with green paint. Humans and vampires alike would assume it abandoned due to medical concerns. What they don't know is that's a false rumor, spread to ward attention off of it," he explained.

"Alright. And Darcia...? I'm still not a fan of sending her off with Smoke," I growled, irritated that there probably no other choice. Goliath tried to look me in the eyes, but I avoided his gaze.

"You concern for everyone else but yourself, love. You do realize that Ash is after you, he despises us both, and will gladly torment you if he captures you again? I know you concern for Darcia, but I believe Smoke will not let any harm come to her. He himself won't harm her, he's not *that* much of an idiot," he reasoned. I just shook my head, unhappy with everyone now. Goliath, Darcia, the pack, all in danger, and I had no power to fully make them safe. I had failed both Boomey and Copper, so the thought of failing any of them was too much to bear.

I hung my head and tensed as Goliath's arms circled around me. I know I cared for him, just... showing any sort of affection was hard. After all, I had never been the one to kiss or hug him. He had kissed me first, and at the moment was hugging. I had offered him my blood, which was sacred yet not really initiated by myself. I cared for him, loved him probably, but honestly loving anyone would cause me to lose them. Gwenn had abandoned me, the snakes had been killed, what if something like that happened to Goliath?

"I wish you would just relax for once, Sam. I really do," Goliath whispered into my ear. My eyes hardened and I pulled away from him. I turned to face him, my glare just cold.

"That's not possible. That woman's return has reminded me just how dangerous it is to care for someone. The only ones who truly loved me were slaughtered by Ash. I was accepting once, but I won't make that mistake again," I snarled.

Without another word, I turned away and stormed back to the house. I could feel Goliath's hurt gaze on my back as we walked, but I just dismissed it. I had other things to worry about than a horrid ache in my heart. Those words, I didn't mean them, but I had to say them. I had to try to shut him out, if I really accepted the fact I really really cared, that I *loved* him, well, I could just be stabbed through the back again.

I entered via the window and sat on my bed. Goliath was right behind me; he did not sit next to me, rather, he walked to the door. "I will get Clyde for you, love," he muttered softly. His voice was broken, but I knew it wouldn't hinder *his* feelings of love toward me. Somehow that made me feel worse.

"Thanks." My voice was emotionless, more so than before. With that, the vampire left me to drown in my own thoughts. Luckily I didn't need to wait long. I heard a knock on the door, and quickly I darted over to let them in. Clyde and Goliath entered, Clyde looking at me dead on with Goliath now the one avoiding *my* gaze. Wasn't that hard, since I was trying not to make eye contact as well.

"Let's go," I said to Clyde, gesturing to the window. I nodded to Goliath. "See you later. And good luck. Be careful," I muttered.

That last statement was one I'd said in a soft voice, perhaps too soft; damn it, letting my true emotions show was a bad idea, especially when I was reluctant to accept them. The voices within only told me, *Remember Gwenn. She abandoned you. Do you really want him to do the same?* I shook my head, frowning to myself. Without any further delay, I ran to the window and leaped out. Clyde was right behind me, and soon we were briskly walking away from the house.

"I know where the caretakers and children could be. What *else* we run into, though, I have no idea," I sighed. Clyde just dipped his head.

"I am sure you can handle it, miss," he replied, confident. He had a hell of a lot of hope for someone who might have actually lost everything. If the child *wasn't* there, she was likely dead. I could only imagine how Clyde would take it. He was composed now, but that could change in half a millisecond.

"So here's the deal. They *probably,* again, *probably,* are in the tunnels, along with who knows what like I said before. I cannot emphasize or repeat enough how dangerous this is gonna be. Hopefully our enemies will not know how to fight a dragon well," I growled. Clyde cleared his throat, his eyes focused on the dark forest path ahead. It wouldn't take that long to get to the city now, both the vampire and I traveled nice and fast.

"Well, miss, I do know various gangs gather in those places. I am pretty sure they have little to no experience with your kind. I know that I knew little of dragons before I met you. I, like most others, thought they were creatures purely of legend. No surprise that the king hid that from us. I do wonder what else he knew of, sometimes," Clyde commented. He had a good point; I could tell he was refraining from acknowledging the fact that the child, along with the others, might not be there. I decided to leave it at that.

"Who knows. Hey, perhaps centaurs or griffins exist too. Maybe we know one. Hell, I had no idea that I was half dragon until just recently, so who knows what else there could be," I sighed. That seemed to amuse Clyde, for some reason, as the vampire just began to chuckle.

"I doubt that, miss, I think we would have seen something like that," he replied, then caught himself. He glanced at me, then at the sky in thought. "Well, actually..."

"Mhmm, you'd think I'd have known what I was before just recently too, huh," I growled with some sarcasm. Clyde just shook his head and chuckled again.

"Well, if there's dragons, why not what you said before. Anyway, I don't think that's a bother," he finished. We had just arrived at the city's edge and were slowly walking along the abandoned streets. Unlike when I went to rescue Darcia, there were no fires or rapidly deteriorating buildings. Everything was just eerily quiet. I stiffened and tried to walk as quietly as possible.

"And if a gang happens to see us?" I whispered, shooting a worried glance to Clyde. The gang member just cast his gaze down the street.

"Well, let's hope we can outrun or effectively fight them," he replied; I could tell from his tone that he was only half-joking.

We neared the hospital. I led the way since I knew the city well enough. I had never been into the hospital for treatment, though, since I'd known the humans there would look at me rather oddly. Back when I 'assumed' I was human, I always avoided the medical facilities because, well, I knew deep down that I really wasn't.

The side of the building came into view, and right away I spotted the grate. I pointed to it, causing Clyde to dart to it immediately. "In here, miss?" he asked, excited now. At my nod, he gripped the grate hard and pulled. I could see the strain on his muscles, but just as I walked over to help, the grate came loose. Vampire strength—never underestimate it. Though I bet dragonic strength was a good match. Meh, I didn't feel like shifting just yet.

Clyde met my eyes and tossed the grate aside. He took a deep breath. "Ready?"

I gave a reassuring smile since both of us were nervous for what we were about to face within. I knew we could take down whatever we went up against, though. "Yep. Let's do this!"

Chapter 46: Darcia

A few hours had passed since Ares, Goliath, and Sam had left for their missions. I had been ensuring my pack was all settled in and things were going smoothly. Apparently, Oriana was training them today, which was just fine in my eyes. Something felt... off, but I ignored it. Something I'd no doubt regret later.

I hadn't had a chance to say goodbye to Sam. It bothered me, but I suppose she needed her space. Gwenn was really putting her off, and now I knew why. The human woman had explained to me what happened, and it was understandable as to Sambuca's frustration. I myself didn't hold any sort of grudge against her, but I knew Sambuca always would. For that, I was uneasy around Gwenn, but I wouldn't try to avoid her. Perhaps I could help Sam feel better about her another time; it wouldn't be easy, though.

Training had gone well, but I was ready to get things going again, finally. Even taking a few weeks to prepare was, to me, far too much time. But people needed rest after all these battles, and spelling out the game plan was also of use.

Now, though, it was time to set off and complete my mission. Without any further delay, I exited, knowing that Smoke was close behind. My eyes were narrowed as we walked along in silence.

"You didn't need to come along, idiot," I muttered, directing the insult to Smoke. We'd had this back-and-forth for more than a few days now. The ex-hunter just snorted behind me, quickening his pace to match mine. I ignored his stare and directed my eyes to just look blankly ahead.

"You get yourself caught too easily, like I said before. You'll ruin everything if you manage to get yourself killed," he growled. I rolled my eyes, speeding up again.

"Oh please. Why do you care?" I snapped in reply, as I always did. Smoke sped up to match my pace again, and promptly I just moved faster, running now.

"This is *my* fight too, Darcia! As much as you despise me, I'm actually trying to help. It would not benefit me to go against you now!" Smoke replied, his fangs bared. Now we both were running really fast. I dodged one tree, then another; Smoke was keeping pace easily. That wouldn't do. I shifted to Tasmanian Devil form and now had *four* legs to work with. No more delay; I was off!

Trees whisked by until my paws hit cold concrete. The chilling, abandoned human city was no longer intimidating. I knew that gangs could ambush again, but I was in the zone, so intent on beating Smoke that I probably was just a black shadow seen for a half a second before I was gone again. My head turned to see Smoke running right alongside me. I let out a frustrated growl and put more effort into it; luckily, he was straining as well.

Now buildings passed by so abruptly that I wondered if the city was an issue at all. I had stopped before to save Gwenn's group, but I had no such responsibility now, considering the fact that this place was completely abandoned. At the edge of the kingdom's woods, I finally stopped. My chest heaved as I gulped in breaths of air; man, racing a vampire was a hell of a lot more work than I thought. But I had won! Smoke ran from behind me, breathing just as hard.

"Well, we're here," I panted, taking in another gulp of air. I shifted back to human form, my dark eyes turned toward the looming buildings ahead. Unlike the previous forest, this one was rather small. It might take a bit to get to the kingdom now, since Smoke and I would need to walk, but at least we covered a lot of ground in a matter of minutes. I uttered not a word to Smoke as I kept to the shadows, knowing our lives were on the line. Smoke kept near me, and often our eyes met in acknowledgement.

What are we planning on doing when we get there? came his voice in my head. I shot him a frown, giving a shrug.

I'm going to try and find Irene. Maybe we can rescue her, though she's probably heavily guarded, I replied, using the bond to communicate. I felt irritation, though the emotion was not mine. I shot the vampire a glare, wondering why he felt that way. *What? It's the best thing I've got in mind!*

You decided to do this with absolutely no plan?! Typical. You shifters were always ones to ruin hunts, that is for freakin sure, Smoke hissed in my mind. Oh, that did it. I gave him a murderous glare and suddenly lunged, pinning him against a tree with a hand to his neck.

"You wanna question me, vampire? I can take you and all of your little hunter friends. Oh, wait, they're all dead because you fell for my tricks. And now you're stuck working with us. How does that make you feel?!" I spat in his face.

I could feel his fury, but I didn't stop there. "Now, because of this damned blood bond, we're connected. I hate your betrayal, and all of them *deserved* to die like they did. I wish they let me kill you, Smoke, I really do. You're a traitor and always will be. I wouldn't be surprised if you tried to attack me right now. That's why you've come along, isn't it?" I taunted. Now, I let go and backed off to see what the vampire would do. Strangely, he didn't attack.

Yet.

He fixed me in a cold glare, one that shook me to the core.

"I've never had anything at all, shifter. I was a beggar on the streets when I became a hunter. I was tied to no one, and when I learned that money could buy anything, could buy the loyalty of *people,* I did not resist. I let myself become corrupted, I probably still am. But that doesn't mean I came along to *kill* you. Get that out of your head, we need to work together if we're going to get out of this alive," he replied softly. His eyes were distant; once again, he was shutting everyone out.

I only had ever seen the ex-hunter as a greedy fool. Any glimmer of emotion was shot down and hidden in the depths of his mind, so far in it that even I could not reach them. I felt guilty for half a second, perhaps my words were a bit harsh, but I had no chance to apologize, for a female voice rang through the woods.

"Darcia, Smoke! Is that you?!"

I couldn't believe my eyes! Irene was rushing toward us, looking disheveled and afraid. She fell at my feet, gasping with effort. Smoke and I moved simultaneously to prop her against a tree. "Irene, are you alright? Breathe. What happened?"

"I barely escaped... Guards, they might be on my trail... We don't have much time, Ash has an army, he is going for the human city, or what's left of it... moving north..." she babbled. I held up my hands.

"Whoa, whoa. You need to rest, and we don't have enough strength right now to carry you off. We can do this, Irene, trust me. Start from the beginning," I tried. The vampire took a deep breath and described what she had been trying to say.

"Ash kept me prisoner, concealed in the dungeons of a new castle. He had it built rather quickly after the first one fell. Even for vampires, it was so fast. Anyway, I heard guards discussing the plans, clearly they were very confident that I wasn't gonna escape anytime soon. They talked about making base in the city after purging the remains, then moving up north to take over more cities and expand the army. Ash is going to have tons of humans turned and enslave those who he does not. He has so many guarding the kingdom, he doesn't worry about an attack from his brother," she sighed.

My eyes hardened. "Our forces are growing, Irene, no worries. We are training at my house, and Goliath is recruiting gangs along with a member known as Ares. I had come to spy, but it looks like I am no longer needed to do so. Come on Irene, let's get you out of here!" I growled. That was when an *evil* laugh rang through the woods. I froze, quivering in fear and shifting in an instant. My ears went back as Ash and probably twenty vampires emerged from the shadows.

"Ah, the little Devil and traitor wants to play with the big boys now? And little miss peacekeeper! Did you really think you'd be free for long, darling?" Ash chuckled in a dangerous voice. I let out a snarl, backing up. My entire body tensed when I felt someone behind me. It was Smoke.

This is a trap, came Smoke's voice in my head. He actually sounded worried.

"Don't worry, I can delay them long enough for you to escape," Irene growled through her bared fangs. All around her, tree roots suddenly writhed to life. Like snakes, ironically, they wrapped around the vampires' feet and kept them there. I had the satisfaction of seeing Ash's face twist in frustration.

"Wrong move, prisoner," the king yelled. He broke free and lunged for Irene, tackling her and slamming her to the ground. Her piercing cry rang out.

"Go! GO NOW!" Irene yelled.

I was about to leap into action when a strong hand clamped onto my scruff. My eerie shriek rang through the woods, but I had no chance to fight against Smoke. He dragged me off as his voice snarled in my head, *We need to leave. It's too late for Irene, she delayed them in order for us to escape. We have valuable information now, we cannot throw it away!*

Tears formed in my eyes when I realized that yet again we were abandoning Irene to a horrid fate. I shifted to human form and let Smoke carry me away, not really making much effort into fleeing. "Gods damn it again!" I screamed. Suddenly I broke from his grasp and ran. No, I wasn't stupid, I didn't run back to where we had been.

I was exhausted, yet I needed to get home. I needed to tell the pack, Goliath, and Sam what we had discovered. Realizing this, I took out my phone as I ran. It was dead. Fucking lovely, they must have used disabling magic. No doubt Smoke's wouldn't work either.

Slow down, slow down! Ash isn't stupid enough to pursue us. He knows we can get away right now, he's too focused on building his army to get us. He might not even know what Irene told us! Smoke hissed in my head. For the first time, I actually listened. Of course, I was too tired *not* to. I slowed to a walk, glancing over my shoulder every so often.

"This doesn't feel right," was all I muttered.

FROM THE SHADOWS...

The king stalked around Irene as the vines dissipated. He rolled off her and watched as she got to her feet. Her red eyes glanced to where the shifter and traitor had just ran off to; pitiful, really. False information was always the best kind. Eyes returning to the insane king, she gave a yawn. "You should have let me tag along with them. I coulda led them into a trap," she growled. Ash shook his head, just chuckling.

"In due time, my dear. The time is not now to strike, we cannot lead them to be suspicious. If we had not 'followed' you after you 'escaped', it would have been too...easy. No, now you're still the helpless victim and they will come to save their friend. Little do they know you'll be alongside me when I strike them down," the king smirked.

Irene shrugged, for his plan sounded good, but she liked hers better. Oh well. She did feel just a hint of guilt, but it did not show in her eyes. Her motives had changed when those damn humans had slaughtered her mate even when she'd called for peace, shortly after meeting Sam for the first time. Damn it all. As queen, she'd make sure they'd not hurt her kind ever again. No more mercy.

"And when he's dead, when we have the dragon, I will become queen?" she asked in an impatient voice. Ash just gave a nod.

"Of course, my dear. You deserve it after all you've done. Now tell me. Exactly what are they doing to gather forces?"

Irene grinned. "Those lovely city gangs, of course."

Ash just burst into laughter. "Weak militia. This is going to be *too* easy."

Chapter 47: Sam

We crept into the tunnels, both of us more tense than a snake. Hah. Clyde was gritting his teeth and I could see his eyes glowing a low red. Oh gods, and mine were glowing a dull green. If that gave us away, I'd feel rather stupid.

Hey, it's alright, we have Christmas colors! I thought to myself, holding myself back from laughing hysterically. When a wide smirk formed on my face, Clyde glanced over, confused. I blinked and shrugged.

"Sorry, had a funny thought," I whispered. Clyde knit his eyebrows together; obviously he didn't find any joy in being here. Anyway, we walked along, not yet finding anyone, and luckily not having anyone find us. Nonetheless I felt uneasy, like I knew something was going to happen soon. Anytime now.

"Hey, this place seems abandoned. I thought more knew about it?" I questioned Clyde. He was more informed about the city than I was. The male vampire looked frustrated, for he was having the same thoughts as I.

"Well, miss, you are right there. A ton of gangs knew about it. Ares wanted to explore this place at one point. We never made it, but we were aware of the dangerous enemies here," he whispered in reply. Just as I was about to speak, hisses rang out all around us. Ah, finally. Well, at least our fears were now being confirmed.

My nails grew into claws as I allowed my own venom to flow into them. Convenient that I had such a power, though in my opinion, the snakes' venom would be better. Perhaps that was just because I missed them so much, but I had no time to dwell on that. *They* were closing in, who exactly I had no idea.

"Show yourselves, cowards!" I yelled, my night vision not exactly up to par. Suddenly there was a bright flash in my face; a torch was lit and held just a little too close. I shielded my eyes, letting out an inhuman growl in the process. "Ah, not like that!" Yeah, I breathed fire, but that didn't mean it couldn't burn my flesh when I was in human form. I didn't want to waste the energy to shift yet either.

The person who held the torch's face lit up. I could immediately see green eyes, and with a sinking feeling I thought, *Great, something new.* This guy had rather dirty ginger hair and skin the color of mahogany. He was wearing a wicked scowl to go along with his off composure. He looked older, like mid-forties, early fifties. I could see no wrinkles, but there was rough graying stubble on his chin. I held up my hands, giving a weary sigh. "We come in peace," I tried. The dude laughed, causing Clyde to step forward.

"She speaks the truth, sir. I am part of The Crows, a gang widespread through the city. We have many allies and enemies. You are in which category?" the vampire questioned. Hm, that name sounded familiar, though I couldn't put my finger on what it meant. I was too focused on the response of the torch-wielder to care, though.

The guy's green eyes flashed for a moment as they darted from me to Clyde. He ignored Clyde's words and growled, "I ain't seen a dragon in these parts for a while, not since the king ordered them all dead."

I gave a grin to reveal my sharp teeth, not really surprised that he knew what I was. "I'm not a true dragon, dude. I am a halfling. Now, please tell us are you friend or foe?"

Again ignoring my question, he glanced at Clyde. He went on as if neither I nor Clyde had said a thing. "So I can assume yer not working fer Ash. Whatcha doin down here? Don't you know it's dangerous for little girls in these parts? And gang members without their gang... tsk tsk, that's not a smart idea," he mused. Laughter could be heard all around us, clearly this guy was not alone. I crossed my arms, unamused.

"Listen, if you refuse to hear my words then I will speak with my fire. Are YOU part of a gang or not?" I hissed. He laughed as if this was one big joke. Then, he backed away, tipping his torch as if to light another. It certainly worked since several torches went on at once, probably lit by whoever else was here. All at once our potential enemies were revealed, and by the looks of it, there were TONS of them, more than I could count.

Oddly, there was a variety of eye colors. But only one pair of *glowing* green eyes. The guy who was facing us had dark-green irises that covered most of his scelera, too much of them to be human. I didn't try to figure out what he was, though, perhaps he was an odd shifter of sorts. Everyone else was a mix of vampires, humans, and normal shifters.

Some sat, some stood, but all were eyeing us with suspicion. "A gang? Nah, I wouldn't say that. We also aren't minions to the throne. We are outcasts, and have been for a while. The stuff that's been going on up there, heh, we aren't a part of it and do not wish to be," the probable leader told me. His aura was a lot like mine, which was odd. The closest aura I had seen to mine was that of the snakes, Ash, and Goliath, but that was because the vampires had drank the blood of my kind.

Clyde relaxed slightly as he realized we weren't going to be attacked. "You all have been here for who knows how long? How did you not become discovered? I mean, my leader Ares had said there were strange people down here that he never cared to find out about. They stayed on their parts, the gangs stayed on theirs, so he claimed," he said, somewhat distant.

The odd guy shrugged. "Yeah, we come and go. We hide here when there is nowhere else to run, lucky we get rid of enemies so quickly. We are great in number, see. Call me Levi. It's short for somethin', though not many know what. Why are you lot here?" he growled in the city accent Ares had. Clyde sorta talked like the cityfolk, but he made an effort to be more formal with words.

"We came looking for some runaways, sir. From an orphanage, to be exact. I figure we'd find them here after Ash's reign began," Clyde told him. Levi gave a shrug, looking at all of the odd people that seemed to live here now. He let out a cough, holding his throat for a moment before speaking.

"They're lookin for the youngins. Are they here?" he questioned the others of his group. I raised my eyebrows as two people stood up. One was a vampire woman, the other a human male. Both were eyeing Clyde and eye rather warily.

"Indeed, they are. What is your business? Our children have seen enough," the guy said. The vampire nodded, now holding the human's hand.

That sorta couple was very rare, so I blinked in surprise. Vampire-human bonds were forbidden by the king, or at least they used to be. In fact, vampires having a mate with any other species was typically forbidden. Maybe that would change when Goliath was king. I shook the thought right out of my head. Why I had thought it, I'd no idea. Silly me.

"Well, miss, one of my own was taken from me by the old king, but this lady here rescued her and brought her along. You wouldn't happen to recognize Sambuca?" Clyde questioned. The vampire's eyes fell on me and suddenly she gasped.

"You. That hunter. You spared that child and brought her to us, and now you're back? With—" Now her eyes fell on Clyde. "I see. Her father never died in the first place. I remember her constantly reminding us that you were out there, and that you would be there to pick her up soon. Though a few weeks ago she went rather quiet when you never came. I... I had thought you died when Ash came to power. So many vampires in those gangs were slaughtered for being threats to the throne," She muttered. She turned back to me, her smile nice and wide now.

"How did you both find us?" she asked breathlessly.

"Goliath, the true king, he told me that you might be down here. I am glad to see you're alive," I added, giving a full smile.

"Goliath? He's not destroyed by that cursed idiot Ash? That's wonderful news," she sighed. I chuckled.

"Yep, we are going against him right now, building forces and such. I wonder. Would anyone here join us?" I asked, hopeful. Immediately Levi shook his head.

"No. I ain't letting any of these people fight in a war, mind you. We are content down here, as we always have been. We give sanctuary, but we don' go to the surface and battle. These people have lost too much to lose any more," he growled. I looked down, disappointed but nonetheless understanding.

"Excuse me, miss," Clyde started, looking at the vampire woman. "Where is she now?" he asked, anxious. I knew he was very, very impatient to be reunited with his child. She gestured to us to follow.

"Come on, the children are housed a lot deeper in the tunnels," she assured. We followed closely, and the groups of people I saw went on their merry ways, some starting fires with bits of dried debris, others setting up what appeared to be tents to sleep in. This place seemed miserable, but somehow was made homey by the people here. I found myself relaxing. At least these people had not fallen to the corruption of Ash.

I could feel Clyde's excitement and I had to admit, I shared his enthusiasm. The human and vampire walked along, no longer giving us wary looks. They knew who I was now. Even I recognized them, though I'd dropped the girl off very quickly and left after explaining how I had found her.

Levi tagged along behind us, and I could feel his stare and glanced back in question. "What?"

"Dragon lady, it's been so long since I've seen another," he coughed. "Ever since the fey iron poison, of course. Those damn vampires are ruthless," he added. "I'm surprised you got away."

I gave a nod. "My human half enabled me to do so, actually," I replied. He was about to respond when an alarmed voice rang out behind us.

"Sir?! There are nobles on both sides of the tunnel closing in. I think they tracked those two here," a shifter male yelled. Levi immediately turned and tensed, his fists clenching.

"You led them here?!" he shrieked, and I could hear the anger in his voice. I heard Clyde's hiss and bit my lip; we were in some deep trouble now. The people around us didn't move, rather they stared with such hostility that I was afraid they would actually attack.

"We had no idea we were being followed, sir! Perhaps they found out about your whereabouts!" Clyde yelled.

Levi just stomped his foot and began to pace. His eyes were glowing brightly now, there was something odd about them that I saw for half a second, but I wasn't too intent on finding out what. Right now, my gaze was trained on the end of the tunnel, where a huge amount of vampires was walking toward us. All looked rather at ease, amused, and relaxed. Leading them, I realized with a gasp, was the king himself.

Ash... how did he find us here? I questioned in my mind. And was that Irene...? I took a step forward, baring my teeth aggressively.

"These people come in peace. The conflict is between *us*, Ash, don't be a coward and take down those who refrain from the fight in the first place!" I yelled. His voice echoed through the tunnels in response.

"Oh, my dear dragon! It's a shame that my brother is off in the cities, wasting time while you're down here, vulnerable. Your shifter friend is on the rush right now back home to tell everyone where I am *not.* And you, here, all alone, with these 'peacekeepers'. Now now, like you said, they don't need to be involved," he laughed. Irene just smirked, and the realization dawned on me.

"You traitor!" I screamed. I felt a hand on my shoulder holding me back from what I was about to do. It was Clyde; his voice sounded in my ear.

"Not now, miss. He wants you to initiate a fight. Be smart about this," the vampire whispered. I turned my head to see his worried eyes, then scanned the crowd behind me. Everyone was weary, and I knew no one wanted to lose their friends or even family here to any sort of battle. It would be cruel of me to ask them to help. So, I did the right thing. I shrugged away from Clyde and met his eyes one last time, giving a nod of farewell.

"Please, go get your child. I will handle this. Tell Goliath that I gave it my best. Feel free to also let him know that I do love him, and that I don't want him coming for me if I blow it," I replied. Before the gang member could protest, I stepped forward.

"You and me, Ash. Once and for all, a final battle. If I lose, you will have me in your clutches once more. But leave the people here out of this—it *is* between you and me, that's all. I killed a member of your family, and you killed two of mine," I clenched my fists. "All I ask is that win or lose, you leave this place. There are innocent people here that don't deserve to perish."

Ash thought for a moment and shrugged. As always, there was an insane glint to his eye. "Alright, dragonfruit. Deal. It would be inconvenient to lose forces in case these people happened to decide to fight, so I will take you on here and now. You'll be surprised to hear I had not planned on it! However, if I can save time, so be it," he chuckled, extremely confident.

Levi's voice sounded in my ear. "Why would you give yerself to him? I don't want my people to fight, but we woulda had no choice to help," he growled. I glanced at him and shrugged.

"You said to keep you out of it. I am granting you that," I hissed. I slowly walked forward, my heartbeat increasing as I now was just a few feet from

Ash and his army. This was my worst nightmare, but I would meet it head on. I held out my hand.

"I challenge you, Ash. One on one. Winner gets the life of the loser, dead or alive," I muttered. Ash eagerly took my hand and shook it. His army, including that traitor Irene, backed away, all eyes on their leader.

"Let the game begin," Ash chuckled in a low voice, and just like that, he was gone.

Chapter 48: Darcia

We walked along in silence before Smoke cleared his throat and fixed his red stare on me. "You realize that was just a bit too convenient, Darcia?" he asked. I blinked in confusion. What was he implying? My shrug was accompanied by a slight scowl. He couldn't possibly mean what I think he did. "Irene just happened to find us at the right place and right time, and had not managed to get recaptured up until then. She might be working with the false king," he growled.

I crossed my arms, gritting my teeth and shaking my head. "No, Irene probably knew where to find us or something. I don't know. But she's been working with us for so long, was so innocent before, why the hell would she be working with him *now?* Ash has never wanted peace, but Irene does," I spat.

I was mostly angry that Smoke's words were making a lot of sense, though. Betrayal wasn't so common among shifters. Even what Xadrian did was not *technically* traitorous, since he'd done it for the pack, but it *was* idiotic. We didn't accept the fact that someone could back-stab so easily, we were stubborn and thought we knew others well enough to not be betrayed.

"Think about it," Smoke muttered slowly. "Remember when we were ripping each other to shreds? How had Irene known we were there? How had she been able to find the exit so quickly?" he added. I didn't see why *he* was talking because he himself was the biggest traitor here. I guess it takes one to know one.

"You noticed that? Well maybe she was a noble before this war," I tried, my voice more tired than angry now. "OK so what if she is not a traitor though? We might throw away valuable information," I brought up. Smoke thought for a moment and looked to the sky, narrowing his eyes.

"What we can do is send an aerial scout, one of the avid shifters to see if there is some sort of army amassing where she said. Meanwhile, I suggest just continuing to train and gather forces. Besides, if it *is* found to be true, the more time we take to finalize our army, the more of a chance we can counter Ash's forces," the ex-hunter finished.

Meh, he had a point; I had to hand it to him, he wasn't as stupid as I first thought he was. Always had some sort of plan, which disturbed me, of course. I still fully believed that Smoke would turn on us at one point.

I guess the vampire sensed my doubts, because he turned his head to smirk at me. "Why do you think Irene wants me alive, Darcia?" he asked softly, leaning to my ear. I blinked and glared at him, my teeth glistening in the streetlight as we walked under it.

"Because you're a traitor and always will be!" I growled, and to my surprise Smoke just nodded.

"Mmm, that *is* the correct reputation I have. Hence why I was spared from being slaughtered with the rest of my army. She thinks I am going to continue my hatred toward Goliath and Sambuca, and eventually get rid of you too. All of you combined have a *lot* of money, after all," he mused, looking distant. I stomped onward ahead of him now, wondering why he was admitting his planned treachery to me.

But Smoke caught up easily and cut me off, preventing me from walking any further. I voiced my distaste, but he ignored my rather strong words by just leaning into my face even more than he had before. His voice was a mere hiss now. "I could have slaughtered you all while you slept, it would have been so easy. None of you seem to take any precautions, no locks on the doors, nothing. I had full access to weapons. Irene questioned me once as to why I didn't act on it. I told her that I was waiting for the right moment. Well, that right moment passed a long, long time ago."

With that, he turned and began walking again. I blinked, once, then twice. My frustration and confusion were now peaking. "So why didn't you kill us all, then?!" I snapped. Smoke shrugged and grinned.

"Hmm... I could have joined the royalty by assassinating the brother and capturing the dragon. I could have made *so much money*. But then, what would be the point. Despite Irene's suggestion not to, you could have killed me several times and did not. This war is no child's play. There would be nothing to gain if I did what I proposed I could have," he replied. I shook my head, knowing I was arguing with the devil but unable to resist doing so. Ironically.

"You just said you'd have a hell of a lot to gain," I growled. Smoke grinned, his vampire fangs flashing.

"Maybe. But that would take the fun out of it, would it not? I am a selfish bastard, I am a traitor. But I do like to switch things up once and awhile," Smoke finished. I scratched my head; this vampire was so damn hard to read. So what, he *wasn't* selfish now? Because he *could* have killed us and did not, we should give him our trust? Nah, I didn't buy it. So I did the most simple thing. I darted forward and shoved him, causing him to gasp and barely catch himself from face-planting on the ground.

"Yeah? I still think you're an idiot most of all. I still don't doubt that you *eventually* will turn on us!" I spat, knowing fully well that taunting him wouldn't be the best idea. If we both fought now, we both would be weakened. Who knew what was on the street watching us right now.

Again, Robert surprised me by just standing and brushing himself off. "If you didn't have that doubt, it'd take the fun out of it, now wouldn't it?" he repeated softly. And then he continued walking, as if this were a casual stroll in the park.

At this point, I just followed in silence. I couldn't read him, but everyone else I could pretty much figure out. The irony was, even though we were bonded, I knew nothing of him. He probably knew a lot about me, though, I wasn't exactly subtle with my motives or beliefs.

After a short bit of walking, we began to approach the house. Immediately I knew something was wrong from the roars and growls of my pack. I rushed past Smoke, intent on finding the source of the issue. I burst into the front door to see blood spattered this way and that, causing my heart to sink.

"What happened here?!" I asked breathlessly. Soon enough, I had my answer. I saw shifter versus vampire, it was the war all over again.

No wait a second; some vampires were fighting others of their kind... ah, now I could see.

Ares's gang members were actually fighting off Oriana's forces, aka the forces left after Irene was captured. So who was the target, then? Ah! No gang members were after the shifters. I now knew the culprits, I needed to attack, subdue, and question. Unfortunately silver was the enemy's weapon of choice, and it put the gang at a severe disadvantage even if the enemy themselves were weak to it. They clearly knew how to keep the situation from reversing.

I shifted in no time, and soon enough my claws had gouged the skin of my first target who conveniently was Oriana. My jaws clashed as I barely missed biting into her hand. The vampire hissed and swung at me with a silver knife, to which I ducked and maneuvered myself to grab *that* hand in my teeth.

That did it.

She dropped her knife and shrieked as I did my classic head-shaking bit and ripped off chunks of flesh at a time. Oriana used her good hand to shove me to the ground and take a good stomp. I hit it hard with an *oof* and screamed as her foot connected with my skull. I was stunned, just barely managing to shift to normal before she restrained me. Oddly, she didn't finish me off. Rather, she held me there while cackling.

My head turned up to see several vampires holding the arms of Ares and Goliath behind their backs. They were unable to face all of them and were weakened by *silver collars and cuffs*. Fuck, they knew how to take on a royal vampire and disable their powers. We were dead.

Then, I saw something much worse. Smoke, standing there with a sly smile while winking to Oriana. I groaned; Smoke had been hinting of treachery, I should have taken him very seriously tonight. Of course I knew he would act soon, I just never figured *this* soon.

"So, you remember the agreement Smoke. A huge sum of money, all you need to do is run these three through!" Oriana practically sang. I thrashed and struggled to no avail, spitting out various but effective swears. The ex hunter was not phased, though, as he approached Ares. He now had a knife of silver in his hand, one that was bloodied... ah. The one Oriana dropped.

How freakin' helpful of me.

I heard Smoke tsk and chuckle in Ares' face. The gang leader bared his fangs, spitting at Smoke. "Ya killed my people before as a human, now you do it as the kind you used to kill. I've never encountered a more evil soul, aside from maybe the current king, my brother, and my mother. Not even rival gangs. I should have hunted you down when I had the chance!" Ares yelled. Smoke had heard it all, and said it all, before. He just shook his head and gave a grim smile.

"You don't know how long I've been waiting to do this. No one can feast upon the shifter but *me,"* he snarled. With that, he raised the knife, his hand arcing in an expert motion.

Great.

The gangs were united because of Ares. He might be a lunatic, but he sure as hell was a good leader. His 'brothers', the vampires in his gang, would die for him. At the moment they were knocked out, probably paralyzed before they could even wake up. This had all been planned out behind my back.

The knife was inches from Ares' chest when suddenly Smoke changed direction. His eyes locked on mine as the knife flew out of his hand. Like an arrow it sailed smoothly through the air and wedged right into Oriana's eye. The ex hunter winked at me and bared his fangs. He had kept himself calm up until now, which sadly subdued me since I drew power on anger and needed my own as well as his to fuel me.

Blood spattered all over me as I was let go. I felt my power growing; Smoke was getting himself riled up now just by looking at Ares. "I meant what I said!" he snapped. Ares blinked and caught on. He shook his head and lunged at me, feigning a bite. That did it—Smoke let out a yell and launched at Ares, shoving him away. But now that Smoke and I both were pissed, we could get somewhere.

Oriana's army had hopelessly been confused. Hell, I still had no idea what was going on, just that maybe Smoke possibly pulled off the most traitorous stunt I'd ever seen, but *in our favor*. From what I understood, he wounded Oriana and intentionally had Ares get him angry to empower us both. Now, rather than take his anger out *on* Ares, he turned to dismantle the remaining enemy vampires. Before I joined him, I quickly aided in the removal of the silver from both Goliath and Ares.

Then, we both launched at them, and the bloodbath ensued. Soon enough, the room darkened. Cackling belonging to Goliath filled our ears, and when the shadows cleared, the remaining vampires were dead, their throats slit cleanly. Goliath tossed a silver knife aside after wiping it clean on his suit.

"What a surprise to come home to after fighting off several unfriendly gangs," Goliath sighed. Ares nodded in agreement, locking eyes with Smoke.

"Why didn't ya kill me, ya idiot? I thought ya wanted to toss me into the grave yerself for sinking my fangs into that shifter over there," he hissed, gesturing to me. The ex-hunter shrugged, his glare not fading as a smirk formed on his face.

"That would ruin the game, would it not? I have chosen my side, though I am able to switch, it would be no fun to do so now, if ever," he replied. I snorted. He went on and on about the game thing again. My eyes turned to Goliath.

"What happened?" I questioned. Why had Oriana been so hostile, had Irene not set up precautions to make sure false information was delivered? Lilith took a step forward, obviously knowing what was going on better than the prince.

"Something about the lie failing. A vampire returned from 'hunting' and let Oriana know that Smoke had unveiled the lie. That meant he apparently agreed with the plan to get rid of Ares and Goliath himself. Honestly, we all thought he would go through with it," she sighed, her wary eyes falling on Smoke for a moment.

The ex-hunter just shrugged and started off in the direction of the room he was staying in. "Yep. My telling of Darcia was the signal, pretty much. If I had kept my silence, Oriana would have tried hard to get you both to believe a lie that was told to both Darcia and I. By my taking the more...violent route and 'setting off the signal', well, we made more progress and cleaned this house of the false allies," he chuckled. He was at the entrance when I shouted out something to him.

"All of them, Smoke?" I questioned. Smoke turned his head, his eyes meeting mine. Slowly, he shrugged.

"Probably. Oh. I'll help clean up the dead later. I need to sit for a while," he growled. With that, he was gone, and not one of us was about to bother him.

Chapter 49: Sam

I took a deep breath, shifting to dragon form and mentally preparing myself for what was about to occur. This was the final battle and everything depended on me ending Ash here and now.

Or so I thought, that is.

My focus was concentrated on the air around me. The torches slowly began to go out one by one. We all were bathed in darkness, and only the faint glow of my eyes could be seen. It was very creepy, and I couldn't detect Ash's exact whereabouts right now. My eyes shut, as there was no point to them being open in such darkness.

Concentrate. You can find him, just breathe and use all of your senses, the voice in my head told me. I obeyed, letting all of my focus lock upon the sensory signals from my dragonic paws. The vibrations rumbled over them, tingling my fingers and somehow allowing me to detect where they were coming from.

Ah!

Slowly, I was able to pinpoint where Ash was. Oh gods, he was closing in! My eyes flew open just as the red eyes of Ash met mine, right in my face. I could just barely pick out his pale face in this dark; he wore a creepy grin that made me shiver. I bared my teeth and took a mighty breath, parting my jaws to let out a flurry of flames.

A hiss came from the vampire as he flew over me. I felt a sharp sting on one of the spines of my back. This fight already was being taken to a new level. Pain wreaked havoc all over my body, it was as if someone set fire to me. I writhed on the floor, smokey tears pouring from my eyes. My paws balled into fists as I picked myself up despite the pain. I would accomplish nothing if I gave into it. I held my ground right as I felt a blade sink into my flank. Ash had a weapon, but I would soon prove to him that it would not be enough.

My head turned so quickly to where I had been stabbed that the vampire could not move away. My jaws clamped onto his arm, much to his surprise. The sound of a blade clattering upon the stone was extremely satisfying. "What?! You shouldn't be able to move, the pain is too unbearable!" Ash's angered growl rang in my ears. I whipped my head around and slammed him into the wall. He hit with a huge *bang!*

It was a struggle to talk, the pain made my jaw clench. But I could still muster up a few words. "I...will...not...give...in!" my whispered growls echoed through the tunnels. I took a deep breath and let my blood boil hotter and hotter. Suddenly, my scales glowed a dark red. My entire serpentine body lit up like a lantern, giving me more vision of my surroundings. Oddly, my scales were tipped in silver. Now I saw what Bernard meant. My eyes fell on my claws as I managed to crack a smile. They too were tipped in silver, so it looked like I was going to put up quite the fight.

Ash's frustrated hiss did not stop there. "A real challenge now, I see. But let's discover if you can manage to stand long enough to severely wound me!" he yelled. My thinning pupils sighted him; he was clouded all in shadows and had what appeared to be bat wings. With a single flap he was launched towards the upper part of the tunnels. A dark trail was left behind him, and when he vanished I could watch it just faintly. Therefore when it suddenly changed directions and rapidly hurtled toward me, I knew what I had to do.

I let out a roar and parted my jaws to dispense a huge ball of fire. From there I lunged into the center of it, meeting the shadows right as they began to pass through. My glinting talons sliced into flesh, and I knew I'd hit him. Ash's scream rang out as he solidified. He slowly glided to the ground, and with a satisfying smirk I realized I'd shredded his wing. He was now stuck on the ground, but I was not.

Now it was my turn to take to higher ground. These tunnels just barely allowed me to fly, sadly I couldn't get that far off the ground. Still, it would be effective for my plans. Fire billowed from my gut as I created a circle of flames below me. I could see the mass of shadows trapped inside, though Ash had vanished within them. His voice threatened me from below. "Gonna hide in the rocky ceiling forever, dragonfruit?" he taunted. I shook my massive head and grinned. The venom he had used on me was fading fast, for he hadn't enough time to provide more.

"You don't *want* me to land, dragonbait," I replied, then suddenly lunged right for where his voice came from. Perfect—I had waited until he revealed himself foolishly to me. Ash had no time to dodge. Suddenly he was trapped between my talons, unable to move. I bent my muzzle into his face. "Out of tricks now, aren't you!" I snapped. The vampire seemed surprised, but his eyes darkened.

"Mmm, I see. Playing the game hard now. Let's turn this up a notch," he hissed, and suddenly turned into wispy shadows. I cried out in fury as the shadows easily and fluidly moved out from between my talons. Ash reformed before me, smirking, but I saw within his eyes that he was tiring. I was forcing him to use a nasty amount of energy, though I myself was doing the same.

I wouldn't wait for him to strike, not now. So fast did I rear up and slam my jaws down on where he was that Ash barely could move in time. He was a hair's breadth away from losing a limb, and he knew it. But his retaliation was worse; suddenly my muscles locked, and I fell to the stony ground. My eyes lit up in surprise as I tried to move, but could not. That split pause of when I *should* have bitten him, but missed, gave him his chance to sink his fangs into my exposed neck. It was disturbing that vampire fangs were sharp enough to pierce the scales of a *dragon.*

I shifted to human form, my eyes wide in shock. My body began to shake as I tried to cleanse the venom to no avail. I felt the vibrations of his footsteps as he approached, I could feel his aura turn rather smug. My expression was that of pure fear, now. "Not even the mightiest of dragons can take down the true king, Sambuca. You are mine again. You have fallen to me, and I will make sure you remain too weak to retaliate," the vampire hissed.

My eyes closed as I focused on everything. Fire flowed through my veins, heating up every bit of skin and organ in my body. Strangely, my muscles could function again. I could feel it, yet I did not attempt anything quite yet. Somehow the heat within me had rendered the venom useless.

I could not shift during this process, I guessed, even when I tried. But Ash had no idea, so I kept the act up as he bent to my marred neck, his fangs protruding horrifyingly. Just as he went to bite, my hand flew up to the back of his neck—and my nails were tipped in silver now as well. I sank them into his flesh, piercing through skin and hitting the bony structures of the top of his spine.

Ash stumbled back, holding his bleeding neck. The vampire was so blatantly surprised now I almost burst out laughing. But like I said before, a snake does not wait. I twisted so that now I was on my hands and feet, then launched at him. I easily knocked him down with my weight, even in human form. I was small but strong and mighty! Now, I leaned into his face.

"My tail isn't broken, dragonbait," I whispered into his ear. I then sliced into his chest with my nails, which shattered the shadow illusion. Ash and I could now be seen by everyone else, including Irene, the vampire army, and Levi with his people. I had wounded Ash not fatally, but severely. The vampire did not beg for his life, he merely glared up at me.

"End me, then," he growled, knowing now that he didn't have the strength to get away. I would have been happy to oblige, had I not been shoved away. My mouth formed in the shape of an 'O' as my eyes met Irene's.

"GET OFF OF THE KING!" she screamed in my face. So suddenly was a knife against my neck that I could not have possibly managed to avoid it. My shock was evident, so I just blinked and cleared my throat.

"I need to finish this, traitor. This is a fight between me and him. Despite him being scum, he would have died in battle, with honor," I snarled. To my surprise, Ash's voice chimed in agreement.

"A deal is a deal, Irene. Release her. She needs to finish what we started," he muttered tiredly. My eyebrows raised, but honestly I was glad he wasn't trying to get away this time. Irene, however, did not move.

Her blade sank deeper into my neck as she replied, "No deal if the dragon is dead! She couldn't save Jason, so why should I spare her?!" I winced, in too much of an awkward position to try to fight back. Any sudden move and my throat would be slit. Besides. Who was this Jason fellow?

A voice chimed up, one belonging to a small child. It was a familiar one, something I'd heard long ago. "You let my hero go! She saved me! Now I can save her!" screamed the voice of a girl around the age of six. My eyes turned up to see the small form of a child launch at Irene. She knocked the vampire woman away from me and stood her ground, spreading her arms as if to guard me. No doubt, this child was a vampire—no one could be strong enough otherwise to knock any adult creature away.

Irene was practically frothing. I spotted Ash stand and brush himself off. His chest was bleeding, as was his arm and back(from when I had shredded his wings, probably, and he retracted them). His voice, authoritative and angry, rang out. "You were a fool to intervene, Irene. But let us go, I am able to flee." Ah great, he was getting away again, but Irene would not back down.

"No! She almost destroyed you and all we have worked for! WE WILL ENSURE THE HUMANS DO NOT HURT ANY MORE OF OUR KIND! I WANT HER DEAD!" she screamed, her red eyes brighter than I had ever seen a vampire's before. I bared my teeth, recovering still from the paralyzing venom. My blood was not clear yet, and because of this my dragon form couldn't be accessed. Apparently not *all* had been burned away . How very inconvenient.

Then, Irene said something that almost chilled all the fire within. "Even if I have to kill that *child* to get to her!"

No one could stop this raging vampire woman, and this mysterious child was not moving. My hand shot forward, in an attempt to knock her down and perhaps save her. My actions wouldn't be fast enough, but someone else's would. "NO!" came his voice, so strong that it almost made the tunnels shake.

He was a blur, someone so fast, in so much of a hurry, that time seemed to stop for him. The blade sank right into his chest as he barely blocked his child in time. In almost slow motion, Clyde fell to the ground, his hands flying to his chest. The child's scream pierced my ears. "Daddy... NO!"

My mouth was open in shock. I rushed to Clyde's side, grabbing onto the knife and pulling it out of him. Irene was being restrained by Ash, and she still was trying to get to me. Spilling from her lips were rants about that Jason fellow.

I heard Ash hiss, "I gave you an order that you disobeyed. We are leaving. There will be more battles to fight, and you should have backed down before!" The *slap* of hand against flesh could be heard, and the vampire was shoved to the ground. "The battle here is lost. We are not taking this *any* further—I order a retreat!" he finished. The vampires all began to leave, and Irene was being carried by several. Ash needed support in order to walk.

I remained by Clyde's side, but the heat in my veins was no longer from the cleansing fire it had been before. I felt something *different.* Ash was getting away, and that TRAITOR had just fatally wounded someone important to me. Clyde might have just met me, but I had promised to reunite him with his child. That was no longer going to be possible. The child, the one I had saved oh so long ago, was bent by her father's side. Tears of pure sadness crawled down her cheeks, there was nothing worse than her feverish cries right now.

The light was still fading from Clyde's eyes as he coughed. The silver knife had most definitely hit right in the heart. His hand suddenly wrapped around my arm. His eyes met mine as he managed his last words. "Make sure...she is safe...please...miss... and Madeline...I love you...thanks for giving daddy a hug...one last time..." he gasped. He went completely limp, and I knew he was gone.

My frustration had reached a breaking point. The last bit of Ash's army was vanishing from the tunnels. I needed to avenge Clyde! A roar broke from my lips as I was finally able to shift, but I wasn't driven by power, nor was I by energy. Something a lot more dangerous was guiding my movements. I flew toward the vampires to no avail. They were gone before I was in range of any attacks. Anger... so angry...

Anger in a dragon can make them turn into monsters... they attack allies and enemies alike...

I could only see red. My head turned to fix on the child, and I only saw her as an enemy. She was bent over a dead vampire. *She was someone who needed to be destroyed!* No, not someone bad, *wait, yes, someone to devour, to put an end to.*

My mind was made up. Her eyes turned up to me as suddenly I was hurtling at her. Confusion crossed her features, then pure fear. Her scream rang out, but she didn't move away from her dead father. *She was ready to die there, with him, and I would be giving the death blow*. My mind was gone, I saw nothing at all, no logic. I was a ball of pure fury. Thank the gods I was not given that opportunity.

A much deeper roar rang through the tunnels, and right as I was about to sink my claws into her, I was knocked aside by a much greater force. My green eyes, lit up like fire now, fell on... wait a second. A dragon?! One twice my size. How was that possible?!

His eyes, like mine, were a piercing venom green. All of his scales were black with the faintest tint of red. He had two spiraling horns, quite different from my double straight ones. His wings were jet black, as well, and unlike mine had savage looking claws at the end of them. I was no match, but in this enraged fury I did not care.

Fire met fire, my red met his blue. His fire was so hot that when it met the inner part of my mouth, I felt my flesh burn. No, my own fire did not do that, but it was disturbing that his did. I spread my wings, reared up, and shot at him with my claws extended. I had intended on making a wicked puncture wound on his side, but he was even faster than me.

I was struck in the chest, and it felt like a train had full on hit me. I was sent spiraling across the tunnel and landed with a loud *thud.* I saw spots before my eyes, and I was so exhausted that my rage faded to just pure sorrow. I shifted to human form, holding my head as the other dragon approached.

Now, I saw him shimmer and shift to *his* human form. Was that.. Levi? My lips parted in surprise, but the man shook his head. "Not many o' us have a human form. I am a rare pure one with it," he coughed, spitting out a bit of blood. "I thought I was the only survivor of that fey iron. It seems, though, that halflings have a higher chance. You don't have my sickness. Come now, I ain't planning on killing ya. Yer rage was too much to handle and I wasn't about to let you destroy that child," he growled.

I was so stunned, so in shock that I felt light-headed. But the soft sobs coming from nearby reminded me of tonight's events. I slowly got to my feet, accepting support by Levi. "Let's go take care of this here child, dragonling," he sighed.

Chapter 50: Darcia

My mouth hung open as long snores poured from my mouth. I was comfy, despite the recent happenings, and had just drifted off to sleep. My dreams were mediocre, nothing out of the ordinary. '*Snoooore.... Sss...sss....snoooore....*' I drawled. My hair covered my face, and I could tell you one thing. I probably looked fabulous!

Something, I don't know what, woke me up, though. My mouth slowly closed as I brushed the hair away from my face, still keeping my eyes closed. Now I knew what it was.

Someone was staring at me, I had no idea who. Well, I actually had a pretty good idea, judging by how I could sense his emotions when he was near. So, I lunged up in bed, my hand closing onto his arm. Smoke wasn't caught off guard. He knew I was going to do that, curse this damn bond.

"What do you want?!" I snapped, irritated that he was in here. I wiped away a bit of drool with my other hand, acting oh so lady-like. Smoke rolled his eyes and glared.

"You're incredibly loud with your snoring, you know that? My room is right next to yours, it's echoing in my head," he snapped. So that's what he was here for, huh? I snorted, rolling to my side so that my back faced him.

"I'm exhausted from the battles, idiot. If you don't like my snoring you can go sleep outside," I growled grumpily. I narrowed my eyes as Smoke let out a small laugh behind me. "Is that all you wanted to tell me? That I'm annoying?!" I asked, growing more and more irritated.

Smoke let out a sigh and I could feel him shake his head behind me. "No. I was just wondering, just thinking. I can't read you, even through the bond. In this final battle, would you care if I lived or died?" he asked in a low, serious voice. I turned to face him, crossing my arms.

"Yeah, we are a team now, idiot. As much as your hot-shot attitude infuriates me, I appreciate what you've done. I don't care if you'd back-stab me within a second, I wouldn't do the same," I growled. I then turned around again, just wanting to get to sleep. But by the gods he would...not...leave!

"You know, I wouldn't back-stab you, Darcia. I want to make amends," Smoke tried, his voice tired. I gritted my teeth, sat up, and faced him again. You do NOT keep a shifter from her sleep!

"Amends? Really? What's that supposed to mean, that I should put all of my trust into you now?" I muttered. Smoke gave a shrug, his eyes a dark red. I blinked, realizing how hungry he looked.

Wait a second.

"You're hungry, aren't you. Now I can see it. You want to bite again. Is that the only reason why you're here then?" I growled, bringing the blankets up to cover my neck as if it'd help. Smoke leaned closer, his frown deepening. He cleared his throat, letting out a sigh.

"Not quite, Darcia, though a bite would be nice. I really do want to tone down the bickering. We can't defeat Ash if we always fight," he muttered. Then, he held out his hand. "Truce, a real one, for now?"

Hesitantly I nodded and withdrew my hand, shaking his. He turned to leave, oddly covering his mouth as if in pain. I raised my eyebrows. "At times, once a taste, always an addiction. I'd be a hypocrite if I let you ease it, but Sam was able to for Goliath, " I grumbled, still quite irritated.

Smoke paused, not turning but remaining silent. "If you can manage to pin me down, you might as well take some. I won't allow it without a challenge, though," I finally growled. Smoke turned finally, fixing his gaze on my covered neck.

"Fine then. Challenge accepted."

I GAVE A CONTENT YAWN as my eyes blinked open upon the next sunset. We all were nocturnal. Everyone's day started when dusk came around. My eyes focused on an arm that was not my own. With a loud growl I shot out of bed, shifting immediately out of sheer surprise. Smoke was there, a little bit of blood on the side of his mouth. Ah, that's right.

I had tested him last night, I wanted to see how long, even with both of us being tired and weak, it would take for him to subdue me. It was an experiment, really. I had several bruises and cuts, as did he. Smoke had bite-marks lining his arms, and some on his neck. I had one clean bite on the center of my neck.

He *had* managed to pin me down, and I had passed out upon being drained too fast and maybe other things following. After the 'battle', he must have fallen asleep too. I flattened my ears, stumbling as I walked. *'There is no doubt neither of us can win against the other,'* I told myself. Good thing the 'final' battle wouldn't be between us two.

In reality, I had him pinned down, when he threw me off and pinned *me* down. To which I responded by doing the same, with both of us exchanging attacks. I was getting to the point of being tired, though, and wanted the fight to end. Especially after the battles and runs we had to do the prior night. So I had finally relaxed and let him take a bite, since he wouldn't stop annoying me if I didn't.

I didn't expect him to fall asleep there, though, so this was somewhat awkward. I wasn't used to waking up to anyone near me, shifters tended to like their personal space. Granted, I suppose it made sense considering... bah, whatever.

I began to walk out of the room, my head lowered and my tail to the ground. I heard the creaking of my bed and froze, my lips peeling back from my teeth. My burly head turned toward Smoke. I let my black eyes meet his. "I never said you could stay, vampire. Next time leave my room or I will personally rip out your throat in your sleep," I threatened. Smoke just smirked, got out of bed, and gave me a sarcastic bow.

"Like I did to you, Darcia?" he chuckled. That did it—I bunched up my muscles and knocked him down, baring my teeth in his face.

"Don't test me, Smoke," I snarled. I then got off and began to walk out the door, ignoring the fact that he was following me. I entered the living room to see Goliath pacing, and proceeded to shift back into human form.

I straightened up and cracked my back, combing my fingers through my hair as the vampire seemed to utter worried hisses. Man, these bloodsuckers were a lot like snakes and dragons I guess. Except they couldn't formally shift, of course. The bat-thing was common, but still not equivalent to what we did.

"What's wrong?" I asked, crossing my arms. The vampire prince glanced toward me, letting out a sigh.

"Sambuca should be back by now. We've gathered a decent amount of militia, I'm sure we can strike at Ash now, but I do not intend to leave without her. I am worried," he confessed. I walked over and placed a hand on his shoulder, giving a slight nod.

"She's a dragon, I'm sure she'll be fine! Sambuca doesn't let anything bring her down," I chuckled, trying to reassure him. Goliath gave a slight smile and looked to the door.

"I can only hope. I know how bloodthirsty Ash is," he growled. Smoke chuckled from behind me, causing the prince to eye him warily.

"Mmm, you didn't work with him. You should hear what he wants to do with the rest of the world should he get allies from other kingdoms," Smoke commented lazily. He took a seat on the couch, looking bored now. "Certainly nothing to benefit anyone but his followers and himself. He's a real dictator, that's for sure. Surprised you didn't turn out like him," the ex-hunter sneered.

Goliath looked down, his red eyes flashing for a moment. "I almost did," was all he said before taking a seat in silence as well. I looked up as people started to wake up. Gwenn and family emerged from one of the rooms, rubbing their eyes. Ares strolled in, neither taking a seat nor uttering a word for a moment. That was until he glanced at my neck and smirked.

"Ya let that vampire get the best of ya?" he asked in a taunting voice. I waved my hand.

"A mere experiment. I found out what I needed and gave him the reward," I replied. It had been the best way to find out if there was any way of defeating him. Newsflash: In my case, there was not.

"Ah. Well, if you ever need to experiment with me, I'll gladly take such a reward as well," he chuckled, licking his lips. I scowled, feeling the growing anger within me. Again, not my own. I face-palmed and turned my glare to Smoke.

"He's trying to piss you off Smoke, he's like a little kid. Ignore him and he'll stop," I snapped. Smoke rolled his eyes and looked to the ground, not making a reply. Ares raised his eyebrows, his red eyes fixing on me.

"Ahah, good one. I felt a little chuckle coming on there," he shot at me. I ignored his words and glanced at Gwenn. She had just put her child on the ground. Now Rose was heading straight toward me. I tensed in surprise as tiny arms encircled me as she climbed up my lap. My eyebrows knit together as the child's bright eyes stared into mine.

"You're a hero! Good morning!" she giggled. The vampires in the room, all but Goliath, looked amused. I was supposed to be a horrifying evil little animal, and here I was being hugged by a young child. But really, did I care what they thought? Nah, I hugged Rose back and gave a soft smile.

"I'll make sure you stay safe, alright little one?" I chuckled. Gwenn's eyes sparked in relief. She approached me, bowing her head in respect. Her eyes were sullen.

"I'm going to need you to watch over her if something should happen to me," she muttered, biting her lip. I was caught off guard but gave a slow nod.

"This place is dangerous, but I doubt Ash will target you or Rose. He's after his brother, me, Smoke, and Sam. If you stay here with some shifters while we strike at the castle, I'm sure you will be safe," I assured her. Gwenn just gave a saddened smile.

"True. What I did to Sam is unforgivable. I wish to repay her, even if it means my eyes will never open again," she sighed. How she'd do that, I had no idea. She was just human. But I gave a slight nod after a second or two.

"I'll look after her, I promise. When this all ends, if somehow we don't all make it, and I'm still here, I'll make sure your child remains safe," I promised. Gwenn looked to the ceiling.

"Both of them?" she whispered. Slowly, I shook my head.

"Sam made it clear. She isn't your child anymore. You *did* give her away. Plus, I can't be the one to watch over her. If anything, she herself and Goliath is the one who seems to have that covered," I muttered, glancing over to the vampire. The prince blinked, as if awakening from a trance. Clearly he hadn't been listening in to our conversation.

A knock came to the front door, causing everyone to look up. I gently placed Rose to the ground and rushed to it, wondering who it could be. I gasped as Lilith stumbled in, holding several bleeding cuts. Her eyes looked alarmed, and as I took her in my arms and rushed her in, she coughed.

"They...have her," she gasped. Goliath darted over, alarm in his eyes.

"Who?" he whispered, urging the wounded shifter to explain.

"Sambuca, Ash has Sambuca, his guard, he bragged about it. They told me to tell you t-that she will be kept alive if you t-turn yourself in t-to the throne," she choked. I quickly got her to the couch and rushed around to find the proper herbs. Valiant was on it right away, though, and soon she was treating Lilith with haste. Goliath's mouth was hanging open as slowly he looked to the door.

"Heya, princey? Don't make any rash decisions, we gotta think about this!" Ares tried, but the prince would not listen.

"I need to get her away from him, she has been tormented for too long. I can save her, I cannot delay!" Goliath shouted. Suddenly, the room darkened, and all I could see was a group of bats now flying out the door and away from the house. I gasped and shook my head.

"He can't do this alone, we need to help him! Lilith, Valiant. You stay here with Gwenn and Rose. Ares, can you get your followers to come with? Smoke, I need you to fight alongside me, we can take on armies together," I admitted in a slight growl. Ah, the benefits of a blood bond.

Ares narrowed his eyes. "That prince should have waited. That scoundrel false king is probably lying. Rushin' into combat is not wise!" the gang leader spat. He slowly stood up, balling his fists. "Nothin' we can do now. Hey! Anyone thirsty for a bit of blood?! Come and get yer fix, we have a kingdom to ravage!" he shouted.

Several vampires emerged from the rooms, not only of Ares's gang, but the new recruits as well. We were a small, ragtag bunch, but perhaps we could get to Goliath before he was slaughtered. One of the gang members, the woman who wore dice as a necklace, sneered and gave a thumbs-up.

Smoke stood, standing beside me now. His eyes met mine as he slowly nodded. "Let's go rescue this prince in distress, and maybe a dragon too, eh?" he chuckled. I smirked and darted out the front door.

"Not a moment to waste!" I screamed. Ares's words shook me, though. I couldn't help feeling that Ash had set *another* trap. It was too late now, though. Goliath was confused, worried, and not willing to listen to even his allies. We couldn't just let him go die. I planned on fighting, and falling, with honor and nothing else.

Chapter 51: Sam

We walked in silence as my eyes remained fixed to the ground. *I thought I was the only one left...* I told myself. My grimace did not fade as we passed by the huge groups of people. They stared me down like I was a freak. Which, I suppose, was true. Now, my expression faded into a deep frown. Madeline, Clyde's daughter, had tear-stained cheeks as she kept glancing at me. I felt guilt brewing in my heart as I let out a sigh. Levi looked over to me and growled.

"Yer fine now, dragon. You won't hurt her while I am around. But there's a lot to discuss. Ash won't leave us be now that he knows you were here," he said in a matter-of-fact tone. He sat under one of the makeshift tents, grabbing one of the bags and rummaging through it for something. He withdrew an old plastic water bottle with sloshing red liquid inside. He then handed it to Madeline, who grabbed it and chugged it down hungrily. I wasn't bothered by such behavior anymore. I merely sat her and watched her curiously.

"Well, I had promised Clyde that we could come make sure his child was safe. I'd said we would find her, bring her to safety, then be rid of Ash once and for all. The vampire king's armies are big, and he himself is a nightmare," I sighed, shuddering at the memories of my being captive. Levi looked at me for a moment, not saying a word. He leaned close to my face, causing me to sort of move away. My frown deepened, it was a little awkward.

"You look a lot like one of the other dragons I knew," he only said. I raised my eyebrows but didn't really ask about that. I had an important question on my mind.

"Are we the last ones?" I asked in a whisper. Levi slowly shook his head, coughing up a bit of blood while doing so.

"The king wishes. Hah. But no, a ton of us fled when the fey iron issue came about. So many died, though, that we are extremely rare. The dragons still alive now are still affected by the fey iron, as you can see, since it affects us for the rest of our lives," he muttered.

"Is... is there a cure for fey sickness?" I asked, coming up with my own word for it. Levi gave a shrug, his eyes turning up thoughtfully.

"No idea. One good start is to be rid of the corrupted king, then maybe we can start researching," he sighed. Madeline pat Levi on his arm, causing his head to turn and look at her.

"I want you to feel better, Levi," she whispered, her beautiful red eyes sad. A stray thought had me wondering if Goliath's eyes were venom green sometimes because he killed so many dragons. I shook the thought away, as it was sort of horrifying.

The older dragon gave a chuckle. "I will, sweetie. Yerself will be safe with this dragon, though. It is no longer a good idea for you to be here," he grumbled. I raised my eyebrows in surprise and looked at the other dragon.

"You mean she can come back with me? You trust me after what I did?" I asked in surprise. Meeting Madeline formally after saving her months ago was thrilling. Her head turned to me as she stared for a moment before giving a small smile. Levi gave a nod and a chuckle.

"Yes. Tha wasn' you. Ya didn't mean it. I gotta stay here, see. We're gonna be fighting off a mass of those vampires, I can feel it in my gut," he growled. "I will see you again sometime, though, halfling. Perhaps you can be the salvation of our kind. You can rest here, but in the morning we will not be around. Good luck," he finished, bidding me farewell. I had completed my purpose here, now it was time for me to go back. I laid on the makeshift bed and stared at him, wondering where he was going off to.

"Bye, Levi. Good luck. By the way, what *is* your name short for?" I asked in wonder. The dragon snickered and waved his hand as if he wasn't going to answer. I shrugged as he began walking away. That was when his voice rang out for a final farewell.

"My name means Leviathan, halfling. You'll learn the significance eventually, I am sure," he yelled. I glanced toward him, but he, along with his people, were nowhere to be seen. Both the vampire and I swiftly fell to sleep after that.

AFTER A GOOD, LONG sleep, my eyes turned to Madeline as I cleared my throat. She was just beginning to wake up. We got to our feet, stretched, and began to walk, both of us silent for a moment before I decided to speak.

"Hey, I'm sorry for almost really hurting you, little one," I said softly. The vampire child let out a soft giggle that reminded me of a songbird.

"It's alright. You saved me from those other scary vampires. I just wish daddy was here with us," she squeaked, tears forming on her face again. My heart wrenched, causing me to lift her in my arms and hold her in a long hug that she returned. "I'm gonna miss Levi too. He took care of me," she whispered. I gave a nod, blinking.

"I will bring you back to him when it's safe, if that's what you'd like," I promised her. I felt the little child nod and quickened my pace. "Hey, we would get back a little faster if I went to dragon form," I mentioned. The child squealed in delight, which caused me to smile widely now.

"Levi used to let me hold onto his scales as we flew through the tunnels!" she giggled. "It was so much fun!"

"Well, let's do it again then!" I suggested. I shifted to dragon form, my scales still tipped in silver. I lowered my side to her as she climbed on rather easily, keeping a firm hold on my spines. I winced as her hand brushed over the sensitive bite. "Careful sweetie, that's where Ash bit me," I warned. She gasped and promptly removed her hand, grabbing onto a different scale now.

"I'm sorry!" she said, her eyes wide. My head turned to look at her in amusement.

"It's alright. Hold on tight, I'll be flying fast!" I warned. I then spread my wings and cut through the air with ease. Smog billowed from my nostrils as I gave a dragonic grin. It was nice to feel the wind in my face again, even in these dank tunnels. Regretfully, I swooped down to pick up Clyde's body as I flew, intending on burying it near the cabin.

Then, I flew for a while before a light at the end appeared. I looped up and out of the hole, emerging from the underbelly of the city with a loud, joyous roar. The vampire child behind me attempted a roar too, but it only came out as a joyous squeak that caused me to growl-laugh. "Nice one!"

My flapping wings caused the muscles to ripple under my scales as I flew. My tail trailed behind me and whipped back and forth. Flying by buildings, by trees, and by the city itself, soon I was going to be home. Home, thank the gods. I thought I was due to perish in the underground when I saw Ash's army. That despicable vampire might be pure scum, but he at least respected honor *somewhat*. If he had ordered an attack on us all, there would be a lot dead, including, sadly, Madeline. Luckily the child was spared and here with me, much to my delight.

I spotted Darcia's abode and grinned, my teeth flashing as I circled in for a landing. Madeline climbed off and looked at the house with awe. "It's so big!" she giggled. Yeah, I forgot how huge her cabin was.

Though, without another word did I quickly land and dig into the ground for a moment as Maddy watched wordlessly. I deposited her father's body into his grave, carefully covering it up and letting out a sigh. "Let's... get inside," I muttered. The child nodded, sniffling slightly.

I led the child to the front door and knocked, patiently waiting for it to open. The battle was looming ahead, and Clyde wouldn't want us to hesitate. There was something else on my mind as well—hopefully that wretched woman wouldn't be here.

The door opened just slightly, and I saw two little brown eyes peeking at me. A gasp came from the other side of the door, now it opened completely to reveal Lilith, the bird shapeshifter. "Sambuca?! Is that you?! But how?!" she exclaimed. I wrinkled my eyebrows, looking past her. Normally everyone was awake and discussing issues in the living room. There was no one around, from what I could see, which worried me.

"Yeah? I got Clyde's child, Madeline. What happened to him is, well, a *long* story. Where the hell is everyone?!" I asked, alarmed now that I sensed no one near. Lilith hustled us in. Madeline looked worried but followed with haste.

She spotted another little child... ah. Rose. I had no qualms with her, at least that's what I told myself. It wouldn't be right to blame her for what her mother did. Nonetheless I pushed past her, not sparing so much as a glance. I was aware that one of my flaws was holding a deep, deep grudge. Yet, at the moment I was unwilling to work on it. I took a seat in the lounge-chair and fixed my eyes on Lilith.

The little shifter took a seat across from me. She had been through a lot, I knew, especially judging by the bite marks on her neck. Like the others in Darcia's pack, she had been forced to work with Xadrian for his foolish plan and was probably bitten as a result. Darcia hadn't been spared due to the incident in the city, now especially due to the blood bond. Lilith's hand wrapped around a cup of water. She took a sip, wincing somewhat. What was going on?

After letting out a drawn out sigh, Lilith finally spoke. "You see, I was told you were captured again by Ash. Some patrol beat me up and forced me to return with the news. I believed it too," she began.

She looked me up and down, as if confirming I were still there. "I see now that isn't the case. Sam, you must know, Goliath ran off. Darcia and Smoke, along with Ares and his people, followed behind to help him. The proposition was simple. You'd be free if Goliath turned himself in. He's going into a trap and will not listen," she finished. My heart almost stopped. He was turning himself in, probably going to his death, to free *me?*

I shook my head, baring my teeth. "Well then, you know what I need to do. I need to go after them, it's the only way, maybe I can make it there in time," I gasped. Lilith shook her head.

"He left a few hours ago and probably is there now. There might be a full out war going on, who knows. They left me and a few others including Bernard here to watch over Rose and—" she paused. "That other human. Come to think of it, I don't know where she went off too."

I cut her off. "Can you watch over Madeline? I need to go after him, I *need* to face off Ash again!" I gasped. Madeline shrieked and shook her head, tears streaming down her face.

"I could feel it! He wants to hurt you really bad Sam, please let me come! I want to save you like you saved me!" she gasped. I felt touched, and turned to her. I bent my head to hers and brought her to a hug.

"I promised your father that I would protect you, sweetie. It's wonderful that you want me to stay safe, but you must realize, I want you safe too.

The short time I've known you, you've been one of the most amazing vampires I have ever met. So pure of heart, so caring, you'll grow up to be just like Clyde, who sacrificed himself for the child he loved. Please, promise me you'll stay," I sighed. Madeline wiped away her tears but slowly nodded.

"OK, hero. Please come back alive... promise?" she asked. I slowly nodded, kissing her on the forehead.

"I promise," I whispered. I glanced at Lilith. "Look after her and Rose, please," I added, finally including the other child. The little human seemed to be avoiding me, but I forced her a smile. Lilith nodded, and I turned away.

"Time to go burn down a kingdom, then!"

Chapter 52: Darcia

I was in Tasmanian Devil form as I ran along, my teeth glistening in the moonlight. This prince was foolish, and I had to hope he wouldn't make rash decisions like this when he was king.

I guess he really cared about Sambuca, huh. Well, he had to understand that we all did too, and as annoying as Goliath was, he was included in our little *I care about whether or not you die* circle. Smoke was keeping pace with me easily, as was Ares on the other side. Instinctively I knew there was gonna be some sort of conflict arising from this. So I was not surprised when Ares made the first 'attack'.

He moved closer to me, smirking as the ex-hunter let out a loud growl. I rolled my eyes, feeling anger(again not my own) rise within me. "Yer lookin mighty sweet. Hows about letting me have a teeny tiny bite when you get back to human form?" he questioned. His eyes fell on Smoke, who was now hissing very *very* loudly. I growled and really wished I could facepalm while running, but one of the disadvantages of four legs was the inability to do so.

"You wanna take that back, or will I need to rip out your vocal cords?" came Smoke's threat. Oh here we go. Soon their bickering rang in my ears, and finally I had enough. I let out an ear-breaking screech. Both of them shut up *real* fast.

"This is serious, Goliath is in trouble, all of our damn necks are on the line!" I shouted. My breathing was fast as my gleaming black eyes switched from vampire to vampire. Ares had a smirk, I knew he was gonna crack one more. I tensed, waiting for it.

"So long as yer neck is not harmed too much, darling, I'll be fine!" he laughed. Smoke balled his fists but made no move to attack.

"She's mine, scum of the streets. Don't challenge that or you'll face my gun *and* fangs!" he spat. Once again here we go.

"Oh? You think yer all tough, son? I could end you before you would be able to land a blow on me, then take that pretty little shifter for myself!" Ares shot back. I myself didn't feel offended, I knew for a fact I could shred Ares's flesh quite easily if he tried anything. His attempt to 'lighten up the situation', or whatever he was doing, certainly was not working.

"Hah, you want to test that then, scum?! I could wipe the floors with your ass, you're a weak fool!" Smoke yelled. Ares tensed, his red eyes glowing in fury. Now the insults.

"Guys, you're both pretty we get it, can you please stop?!" I tried, my irritation growing each step I took. Both of them ignored me, which was a VERY BAD IDEA. I spotted Ares move with speed toward Smoke and knew that had to be the final straw.

I stopped and whirled, managing to leap between them before an actual fight brewed.

"YOU! Stop taunting me to piss off Smoke," I spat in Ares' face. Then, I turned my head to Smoke. "Are you really that thin-skinned to let him get to you? NOW BOTH OF YOU SHUT UP! WE HAVE A FREAKIN' KINGDOM TO SAVE, WE DON'T HAVE TIME FOR THIS! LET IT GO!" I roared, my voice very loud now.

Ares's people all stopped and stared at me in utter surprise. Obviously they hadn't seen an annoyed shifter before. They'd learn fast not to mess with me. I turned away and continued walking, satisfied that I had gotten my point across. Both Smoke and Ares walked along in silence now, their eyes wide and trained on me. I ignored the smartass singing *Run Devil Run* behind me, it was one of the gang members who for some reason found my words hilarious.

My rounded ears flattened as we got closer to the city. As far as I knew, this would be a smooth passage. Ares and Goliath hopefully cleared the place out. I could only hope that the prince wasn't too far ahead. Buildings flew by as we ran, all of us faster than any normal human could run. I heard

Valiant panting behind us, and frowned for a moment. Hadn't I told her to stay back...?

I turned my head to check if that indeed was her, but there were too many people in my way to truly see. I knew when certain people in my pack were here, even if there were tons of other people surrounding me. I most certainly told Valiant to stay back with Lilith.

But whatever.

I couldn't dwell on that at the moment. I lowered my head as the city-lights blurred. It took a long while, but finally we were through the city. Now, the forest, then the kingdom. I had never made it as far as the kingdom, to be honest. The last time I attempted spying, Irene had tried her nasty little trick.

I shoved that thought out of my head as we got closer. I was ready now, I could feel it. We emerged from the dark shadows of the woods; my eyes took in everything, it was quite a sight to see, to be honest. I had to say, I was impressed and disgusted at the same time. The human city was in shambles while it seemed this place flourished.

The buildings were all, yes all, painted red. You can guess the symbolism there. The streets were newly paved, and it had a new-age look now. There were plenty of hints to the medieval, like the castle-like houses made of reddish stone. But cars, fancy ones, lined the streets. There were telephone wires and electric cables running through the city, obviously empowering it. For what, I wondered? There were no lights; vampires had no need to see in the dark. Did they seriously finally accept the new technology, that being cellphones and computers?

Hopefully they hadn't adapted modern warfare. Normal guns couldn't really hurt shifters or vampires, but if the bullets were made of silver, well that was a different story. Silver was very dangerous to vampires, for it slowed their healing and poisoned them.

I figured Ash wouldn't stoop that low, for we could retaliate in the same way, and such warfare would be nontraditional, I guess. There was no fun in killing from a distance, in my opinion. Hand to hand, blade to blade, that sort of combat, it was what empowered both races. There was no honor in not giving the opponent even the slimmest of chances, at least. Though Ash wasn't one to follow the common codes, so I could only hope I was making the right assumption.

The silence stretched. I tucked my tail between my legs, waiting for the worst. Nothing came, there was no sound until Smoke's whisper came in my head. *I don't like this. It feels like he's waiting for something,* he said. I turned my head to him, giving a slight nod. Something was off.

We moved more toward the center of the kingdom. It was almost like a city square, there were traffic lights, cars on the side of the road, but no vampires. No people were inhabiting this place, it was so freakin eerie. I shifted to humanoid form and took a seat on the red bench, staring at the dark red buildings a moment before clearing my throat.

"I...uh... anyone know where the hell Goliath could be?" I asked aloud, breaking the silence. No one piped up, until *his* voice met my ears. The fun was going to begin now, it seemed.

Above us, covering the full moon with his huge bat wings, was the corrupted king himself. He had a crown made of bones, held together with what looked like tendons.

How lovely, Ash was growing more and more insane.

Who those belonged to I didn't feel like finding out. He looked down upon us with a smirk, and suddenly I was blinded by very bright lights. It was as if we were all on stage. Smoke and Ares covered their eyes, letting out hisses. I shifted back to devil form and let out a shriek/roar.

"So glad you could make the final act of the show!" he chuckled, as if he was having the time of his life. He gave a snap of his fingers, and all around us were vampires in what looked to be modern body armor. They clearly outnumbered us, probably ten to one. The mob trailed down the four parts of the intersection. To say the least, I was concerned.

Music blared from all around us, causing everyone to wince. '*Here we are now, entertain us!'* Ash withdrew a vial of blood, it looked to be some pretty potent stuff. He moved aside to show Goliath tied up in thick silver wire on the lamppost. The vampire bared his fangs, I could see the prince's eyes red with fury.

"Sorry, children, it's not *only* me who you'll be fighting with, but my lovely brother too. No, he'll be fighting right next to me!" he chuckled. His eyes fixed on me as he pointed. "And once your blood is spilled just a little, so will that ex-hunter, my dear," he yelled to me. What the hell did he mean?!

I felt a sharp pain along my flank and whirled to see one of Ash's cronies vanish into the crowds. Ow, I was bleeding again! That's what I got for not paying attention. Ash uncorked the vial, and suddenly every vampire's eyes were pure black. They had no pupils, which disturbed me.

Ash grinned, his fangs flashing in the moonlight. Goliath had the same look as the rest. Everyone turned their eyes upon me and other members of my pack. Smoke looked utterly starved; his eyes were trained on my now-bleeding wound.

My eyes widened in panic as I looked up to Ash with worry. "What the hell?! How—what did you do?!" I screamed. Ash let out a horrific laugh.

"You poor, defenseless shapeshifter. You have no idea the horrors you're about to endure, do you? Have you ever heard of demon's blood?" he asked.

My heart dropped at his words. No... so he did pull that card. How did he obtain the stuff? It was so rare, the only way to get it was to either find and subdue a demon(which was extremely hard) or travel to the underworld yourself. The qualities of such blood were so freakin dangerous. The properties could command armies if they were vampires. That was because if spread, vampires would go into bloodlust, but the situation was far worse than that. The primal, dark side of them was brought out at the scent of the stuff. They were not in full control, and any non-vampire caught in the crossfire would be due for very, very bad torment by them.

Ash was well controlled—probably had an enchantment set up, or something, to prevent his *own* insanity.

Now, though, all of my allies focused on me since I was bleeding. My pack was at risk, but to a lesser degree. I glanced to Smoke and guessed the blood bond would have been of benefit had I not been cut. He was not *as* affected by the demon's blood because I was bonded to him, and he had an inability to actually subdue me. But.. now that the smell of my blood mixed with the demon-blood-scent, though, the bond was turned against me, for he perhaps wanted my blood most of all.

A shriek came from the back of the crowd as someone, a woman, pushed her way through. The vampires were, at the moment, static. No one made a move as the girl... was that Gwenn?!... made her way toward me.

"What?! How did you get here?!" I snapped. She shook her head and looked at the vampires with horror, standing beside me as they began to move closer. I heard Goliath snarl, and heard the metallic clanging as Ash untied him.

"Mine. A-all mine. T-the shifter is *mine,* h-hands off," the vampire in the top hat snarled. I never heard him sound so threatening. A dark shadow materialized in front of me, forming into Goliath. His hat hid part of his eyes. He looked like a formal freakin demon from hell. And now I was nervous, especially when Smoke let out a hiss and walked along with the prince.

"Don't do this, Goliath. It's not you!" I snapped. I unfortunately knew that Goliath was strong enough to overpower me.

Smoke let out a snarl and spat, "She is mine!" He darted between us, facing the prince, which at the moment was somewhat of a relief.

Goliath began slowly walking toward the ex-hunter, the gleam of his eyes anything but friendly.

Just then, a voice rang out, one I was so relieved to hear that I almost passed out.

"Hey, Goliath! LEAVE MY FRIEND ALONE! Stand down my—love..." she stammered on the last word. A *whoosh* came from above until a huge dragon landed behind us. Oddly, there had been plenty of room for her to land. Her body encircled me and Gwenn, protecting us from Smoke and the prince. Her dragonic eyes met Goliath's.

"Or I *will* have to knock that hat of yours off again," she snarled.

Chapter 53: Sam

My eyes glowed a nervous green as they met Goliath's. His were insane, bloodthirsty, and horrifying. I found myself intrigued. I'd never seen him look that way. The only one I'd seen with those eyes was Ash. Now Goliath looked like the evil monster he feared.

Me, afraid? Maybe. But I was ready. My attention was captured as he spoke. "Try me, love," came his inhuman growl. Ash looked on, amused. How was he immune to the demon's blood? I didn't have time to dwell on that though.

Smoke was looking at Darcia in the same crazy way, but suddenly I felt myself grow light-headed. Everyone vanished but Goliath. No Darcia, no Ash, no Smoke. Just us two in the world of shadows. Now I remembered—Goliath had warned me of Ash's power.

Little did either of us know, it was *him* I was destined to battle. I straightened myself and arched up like a serpent, towering over the vampire prince. All of my training had come down to this moment. I would need to subdue him without killing him. This was going to be tough.

We stood there, our eyes locked for a long while. My lips slowly peeled back from my dripping fangs. Green, acid-like liquid was being excreted by my teeth. My venom—the stuff he was immune to. Yet I automatically produced it out of pure fear and exhilaration.

Metal flashed in the moonlight as my claws met sword. The prince had a weapon, then; I wondered when he had obtained it. I'd ask him later if I actually made it out alive. He parried my claws easily, giving a fully-fanged grin. This was like a twisted fairy tale. Here he was, a prince, fighting off a monstrous dragon. Yet it was *he* who needed to be stopped, and it was *I* who needed to win if the kingdom had any remote chance.

Goliath lunged forward, his sword very sharp and intimidating. My eyes locked on his sword-hand. As he landed a blow on my arm, my claws flashed out and sliced into his. However, my roar of pain filled the air, for this sword was made of fey iron. I heard it clang to the ground and fixed my eyes upon it.

Fast as a snake, I lunged for it, my green eyes desperate. My jaws locked on the weapon, but immediately I needed to toss my head and throw it away from me. The metal burned horribly, and that moment of distraction had caused Goliath to dart up and sink his fangs into the back of my neck. I screamed in agony and spread my wings, taking to the sky with haste.

I could only see red as I flew in circles, my muscles convulsing in pain. A dark blotch formed in my face. Goliath was a giant shadow-bat with that goddamn top hat sitting atop his head. The bat smirked, its horrid, emotionless eyes locked on my neck. I knew that was his target, so I would need to do all in my power to prevent him from getting to it.

I shot straight up, going higher and higher into the air. The bat followed as my tail trailed behind me, twitching from the pain of Goliath's venom. I coughed, spitting out a bit of blood. Ow, that sword had somehow cut the inside of my mouth before I got rid of it. Not only had I gotten burned, but I had a cut. Hmm.

I turned my head toward the bat, opening my jaws wide and letting out a billow of bloody fire. Dark red liquid, mixed with my green venom, was now raining down, mixed with my fire. Some of it fell onto Goliath's hat. He wavered in flight, now looking confused and starved. The blood falling in all directions messed up his tracking, I could tell.

Time to take things up a notch.

Gritting my teeth from the pain, I changed course and suddenly charged right at him. My savage claws ripped through his wing while he flew in the air, confused. More flames surrounded us as I let loose all hell on the vampire. Oh please; I knew he was strong enough to survive. The bat spiraled toward the ground, seeming to be hurt. I flew after him, landing with a *thud.* I hurriedly locked him in place with my claws, hoping to pin him and catch my breath again.

I didn't get the chance; the vampire easily pried my claw apart and lunged for me. I dodged and let out an angered snarl. He wanted to keep this up, eh? My venom green eyes turned to the sword as he spotted it. He gave a grin, suddenly rushing at it.

"No!" I roared, following. He turned so fast that I had to skid to a halt in order to avoid being impaled. My wings spread as I took to the skies again. He followed after, not a bat anymore but with bat wings like Ash's coming from his back. The sword sank into my tail, but I used that to my advantage. I thrashed in the air, using the spikes that erupted from my tail to sink into his side and shoulder. Goliath hissed and dropped the sword.

Spikes made from solidified shadows wedged between my scales, causing mass discomfort. I twisted in the air and used the full force of my body to knock into him. The vampire didn't expect that. With an already injured wing that was healing incorrectly, he was knocked from the air once more. Again I pinned him down, this time with my muzzle in his face, ready to give a harsh bite if he decided to try his escape again.

Suddenly, Goliath looked tired. "Please, spare me love," he whispered. I tilted my head, confused, blowing smog into his face regardless to try and intimidate him. My eyes were narrowed in effort; it took everything I could not to collapse in pain.

I removed my claws, watching as he got up and looked at me with relief. "Thanks, Sam. I knew I could count on you. I care about you so, so much," he sighed. His eyes looked normal, for a second, but wait. I saw too late that they faded back to that demonic glare. He grinned, his fangs flashing, and suddenly I was hurling toward a darkened building.

I hit the brick with so much impact that I left an indent. Several bricks fell and slammed into my head, causing confusion and a headache. I let out a roar of fury and shot a billow of flames toward where I thought Goliath was. I managed to alight the benches in front of me. The fire spread from bits of rubble to bits of rubble. I lifted my head and got to my feet, trying and failing to stay up. I fell flat on my stomach, groaning from the aching pain that wracked my entire body. I shifted to human form, now holding my head and curling up from the pain.

My eyes fell on the flames as a dark shadow seemed to swiftly move through them. I was in for it now.

Oh gods.

Goliath wore a grin similar to how Ash's had been when he was tormenting me. I was seeing the most evil part of his soul, and damn, it was scary. I did not move toward the wall, and did not attempt to run. No, not because I couldn't. I was now ready to face him head-on. I laid flat on my back, my head following him as he reached me and bent over my broken form. "Game's over, love. You lost," he hissed.

Then, pain, so much pain. His fangs were latched into my neck as my blood, once again, began to be drained. I screamed inhumanly, really it was more like a roar. I wasn't about to go down like this.

Despite the pain, despite the weakness, I felt power grow within me. I was a dragon, maybe a halfling, but I was a powerful monster that could face other monsters with equal viciousness. And that was what I was about to do.

My arm shot up, my nails extended, and sank into the back of the vampire's neck. He paused in his greedy drinking, his red eyes wide and glowing. With my nails in his flesh, I could do something that might kill him, which would kill me. But it would *also* kill him if I died now to his fangs. So, I had to hope he would survive *my* next attack.

I used the last of my strength to shift back to dragon form. My claws sank into his flesh even deeper as I used my other arm to wrap my dragonic paw around his neck. From there, I ripped him from my flesh, which was extremely painful. Goliath chunked my neck, taking a bit of scales, but now I had him asphyxiated. I raised him to the sky, rearing up on my hind legs and looking into his red eyes. Blood poured like a river down my body as I stared him down. My fangs glistened as I brought him close to my mouth as if to devour him. But I did not. The vampire was weakened by a lot due to the silver of my claw. His groans rang through the night, yet he held my glare.

"I lost? I'm afraid you fell for the broken tail again, Goliath," I snarled. I then threw him to the ground and trapped him under my claws again. Both of us were bleeding horribly, and he could not heal as fast due to silver poisoning. The shadows around us began to fade as the prince's powers dwindled. He was running out of energy, as was I. His eyes slowly, finally, faded to an actual normal red. I let out a sigh, my breathing irregular as I shifted to human form. I weakly laid on my stomach, in the center of the road, right next to him. I felt his hand meet mine as he choked weakly.

"You did it...love...you managed to defeat me... I knew you were strong enough," he whispered. I turned my head and nodded, using one of my hands in an attempt to put pressure on my ripped neck and stop the bleeding.

"It's not over yet, Goliath. Even if I have to die doing it, I *will* kill Ash," I promised. "We can't give up yet," I finished. My eyes scanned the crowd of hungry vampires. They were high on the smell of demon's blood.

There was a stain of the stuff on the ground—wait, that's it! I had just enough energy to do it. Goliath, out of sheer loss of blood and gain of wounds, had snapped out of the spell. Everyone else had not, and I could tell Darcia was fighting for her life by her fevered growls and continuous whimpers.

My body grew as I shifted to dragon form. I opened my jaws and blew the fire over the blood. Above me came an angered hiss—it belonged to Ash.

"No! What are you doing, dragonfruit?! Don't you dare," he warned. Ah, he caught onto my plan, but it was too late. I took another deep breath and let out a second billow of flames. Now the puddle evaporated from the dragonic fire.

Ash screamed in rage. Ares and his gang had frozen, no longer under the demon blood's spell. Smoke did as well. When I turned my head to look, Darcia was between them, being bitten in the neck by Smoke and the wrist by Ares. Both vampires let go and backed away, horrified.

Darica fell to the ground, groaning but shifting at the same time. "Glad you made it in one piece... Sam... Smoke, damn you.. you're so dead if we live through this!" she yelled. Good. She still had that fiery spirit within her. Now too dizzy to stand, I fell to the ground, my own blood covering the burned-away demon's blood.

Ash's furious growl rang in my ears. I managed to look up and see a glowing golden blade in his hand. *Fey Iron.* And he was heading right at me with it. There was nothing Goliath nor I could do, either. Both of us were too weak to even move.

Chapter 54: Darcia

O*w...ow, OW!* My own whimpers and snarls of pain filled my ears. My wrist *and* neck were being bitten, but at least I had vampiric venom immunity. The insane look faded from their eyes rather quickly, and I was let go.

Suddenly, both Smoke and Ares had three jagged claw marks going over their eyes, dragging all the way down their necks to their chests. I had even managed to rip *both* of their shirts. Both's jaws were dropped as they stared at me. I had a mark on my eye, too, due to the damn bond; but mine probably didn't hurt as bad because *I* had dealt the original wound.

"Oh you'd better hope we don't make it through this or so help me," I began. My pupils grew, covering my entire eye. My anger was empowering me, I was royally *pissed.* Smoke could feel it too; his eyes reflected mine, and suddenly we were in each other's faces, baring our fangs and snarling.

It was only when Ares leaped between us that we got a hold of ourselves. "Hey HEY! Shifter, we weren't in control, use that anger to our advantage! We have a freakin' army surrounding us!" the gang leader yelled. Sadly he did have a point. With a huff of frustration I shot a glare between him and Smoke.

"I'll *discuss* this with you later," was all I said. I turned away to see a bunch of noblemen advancing on us. Ares' people looked ragtag and run down, they had simple knives to the swords of these insane puppet vampires. But my pack, Ares' gang, Smoke, Goliath, and Sambuca all had something much greater we were fighting for. I bared my teeth, letting out a warning gekker, getting ready to attack when someone ran out in front of me. Was that... Gwenn...? I turned my head, watching as the human lunged in front of Ash to take a sword aimed for Sam.

She cried out, and since the human was already very low on blood, a wound like that was sure to kill her. I heard Sambuca let out a weak gasp. "Gwenn?! Why? I always pointed out m-my hatred for you," she stammered. The human coughed up some blood.

"Darcia! We don't have time!" yelled Smoke. I turned my eyes, locking them on his.

"I need to help Sam. Hold them off!" I replied. The ex-hunter was skeptical but slowly gave a nod.

"With the bond, I might be able to," he growled. He glanced to Ares. "Let's go, make yourself useful for once," he snapped at the gang leader. Ares grinned, his fangs flashing as his smile widened.

"I could ask the same of you!" he shot back. Both vampires dove into the fray, and I could no longer see how they were. Meanwhile I turned back and ran over to where Gwenn was covering Sambuca. Sam was in dragon form still, Gwenn had barely managed to take the blow for her. "I have little left, but my blood can feed the prince and give you strength..." the human gasped. My angered glare fell on the bleeding dragon, then back to the human.

"How did you get here?!" I snapped at Gwenn. She was about to reply when an arm swiftly knocked her away. Ash had ripped the weapon from the dying human, which was a huge problem. I lunged for his arm, managing to snatch it away and toss it a small distance. The vampire hissed at me but went after the knife. He was desperate, I could tell. I ran to Gwenn, knowing I had very little time.

"Please tell me," I begged. Gwenn weakly coughed and managed to give one last word.

"V...a..lia...nt..." she uttered before the light faded from her eyes. That was all I needed.

"VALIANT! FRONT AND CENTER!" I yelled. The panther shifter slunk toward me, dodging various vampiric soldiers. She looked as if she was caught.

"The cat's out of the bag, Darcia. She begged me to bring her here," my pack-mate gasped. I shook my head.

"No time for that. You have the gift of healing. Sambuca needs you now!" I ordered. Without further ado the shifter darted to Sambuca. I grabbed Gwenn's lifeless body and hauled it to Goliath. "Drink, prince. As repulsive as it is, you need it. We need you well for the defeat of—" I began, but was cut off.

My body flew through the air, wait, I had wings?

Nope.

I slammed to the ground with a shit ton of force, shaking my head from the pain. What the hell...? I spotted Ash, knife in hand, rushing straight at Sambuca again. This time, *I* was ready to face him. "LEAVE MY FRIEND ALONE, YOU SON OF A BITCH!" I screamed, shifting into Tasmanian devil form as my voice sounded out like claws on a chalkboard. Ash winced at the noise, which bought me a second of time. That was all I needed.

I launched at him, ignoring my headache and dizziness. My claws sank into his shoulders as I pinned him to the ground. My jaws lowered as I began to gore his chest, digging deeper and deeper with my teeth to get to the flesh. I had successfully managed to rip through his body armor before he dissolved into shadows. Ash reformed behind me, looking very, very angry.

"Your kind always seems to get in the way, hm. Good thing you will never be half the leader that golden eagle was. He had the intelligence to make an alliance with a greater power!" Ash shot at me. I gasped, feeling my entire body heat up. Oh, he was in for it now! You *never* insult a shifter's ability to lead. Ash suddenly had wounds going all the way up his arms. I had speedily used my claws to shred his flesh. The vampire was caught by surprise, for he had never seen me that fast. When I was angry, hell broke loose. He was to learn that the hard way.

His red eyes locked on mine. Before I knew it, my neck was in his grasp, and I was gagging. I struggled hard, which only made him tighten his hand. He leaned toward my ear, his fangs extended evilly. "I will enjoy ripping your throat out, in fact, I will force the dragon to devour your remains if she survives this ordeal," he whispered.

"Shifters don't go down nearly as easily as vampires, Ash!" came a roar. Sambuca! But how? We were knocked from where we stood and I was sent flying. I turned my head up to see Sam still managing to keep her dragon form despite looking exhausted.

"No! You need to rest for a bit, Sam! Let them fight, you need to recover!" came Valiant's worried growl. Sambuca proceeded to stumble and fall flat onto her back, writhing like a wounded serpent. She groaned, much to Ash's amusement.

"Pathetic. You all make me laugh. You're losing, don't you see? Several of your pack have died, several of that weakling's gang have been slaughtered. There is nothing you can do!" he yelled. His words were true, but the royal army was falling fast as well. Smoke was emitting savage growls as he took his weapon and sliced through several vampires with ease. He wasn't an ex-hunter for no reason.

Ares was fighting dirty; he went right for the eyes, and if they were male, you can guess where he aimed to kick. The vampires expected him to go for the neck or chest, but he was successful in their misunderstanding. While they writhed in pain, he decapitated them and moved on.

Blood flowed into the sewer systems and flooded the fighting area. I didn't know the toll, but it was big. Ash lunged for me this time, knowing I was a real threat. Still high on anger, I met his lunge with a growl and viciously slashed at his neck. I landed a blow on him, but he retaliated by sinking his knife into my shoulder. Fey iron wasn't special with respect to my kind, but a knife was a knife. I whimpered in pain and fell back, not hesitating to launch myself right back at him. I sank my teeth into his arm again, now chunking a bit of his flesh.

Ash dissolved into shadows and reappeared behind me, panting. I whirled, but it was too late—I took a horrible blow to the eye. The knife went right into it, the pain was so great that I crumbled to the ground. Blood poured from my eye, and I was afraid that I'd never be able to use it again. Ash loomed over me, laughing at my pain. He held the knife before me, his flesh dripping out some of his own blood. At least I had wounded him well enough.

"Sweet dreams," he began, but suddenly froze. His eyes went down to his chest as I saw something protrude from it. Venom green eyes glowed behind him as a maw with glinting teeth grinned. I held my bleeding eye with my paw, watching in awe with my other good eye as Ash shuddered.

Claws tipped in silver had gone right through his body. They closed around... something. The sound of ribs cracking filled the air as Ash fell to the ground, his eyes still wide in surprise. As he fell, I finally saw the creature behind him.

Green mist came from her nostrils as her grin grew. Within her claws was his heart, still beating.

Lubdub...lubdub...lub...dub...lub........dub.....

It stopped now, frozen forever in time. Ash had fallen. I had wounded and distracted him long enough that he hadn't paid attention. I watched as Sambuca tilted her head up and slowly devoured the heart, her teeth gnashing together as the sound of flesh squishing between jaws filled the night. Blood poured down her maw. It was as if the dragon was high on victory, on what she'd just accomplished.

Then, though, she collapsed. It had taken a lot of effort just to make it here. The wound Goliath gave her wasn't bleeding anymore, but it indeed was probably painful. She was out of strength, I could tell, and had fulfilled her goal. But the battle was far from over.

I shifted to human form to better be able to hold my eye. I laid there, knowing that I'd need to get back into it momentarily. Several pack members had fallen, and I spotted Valiant running over to help Sambuca.

I groaned as the *thud* of a footstep sounded right by my head. My good eye turned up to see Irene, and my lips peeled back in anger. She looked to be in utter shock. "My king... I was to be queen! HOW DARE YOU EVIL FIENDS TAKE THAT AWAY FROM ME! DON'T YOU UNDERSTAND?! THE HUMANS WANT US ALL DEAD!" Well. So much for her idea of peace.

She growled and before I could do a thing, withdrew a sword. Valiant had no time to move. Irene sliced off her leg without hesitation. I screamed in rage as Valiant's blood spurted out everywhere. No! She was one of my closest pack-members, and I needed to protect her for not only the memory of Xadrian, but for the welfare of the pack. Her healing abilities were unmatched by any other, had she not have been here, Sambuca would have died.

I spotted shadows spreading toward her and grinned. Goliath appeared behind Irene and backhanded her away from Valiant. My pack-mate was desperately trying to stop her leg from bleeding, and I got to my feet, keeping my hand on my eye as I rushed toward her. "Valiant. You know what you must do," I growled. I held out my arm. The shifter stared at me, teary-eyed.

"No, Darc, you've lost so much already," she whimpered.

"You'll die of blood loss if that wound doesn't close. I'll be fine. Do as I command, I am the leader!" I growled. Valiant, after a moment's hesitation, finally obliged.

Animal fangs sank into my arm, chunking bits of flesh as my fellow shifter consumed some of my muscle. This sapped my energy to quite a big degree. I became dizzier and dizzier, and finally had to lay on the ground. Valiant stopped when she had just enough to speed up her healing and close her wound. My arm had several chunks missing, but I wouldn't be losing it like Valiant lost her leg. At least this would enhance her power to close both her wounds and mine. She took me in her arms and hugged me.

"It'll be OK Darcia, we can make it through this," she whispered into my ear. "Thank you, sister," she added. We were indeed like sisters. It was an honor to ensure her survival. I could only hope that I'd make it as well. The blood-loss was too much. My eyes closed as I passed out, giving into the cold darkness. My life was in the hands of everyone still fighting. Ash had fallen, but Irene was still fighting, as was the royal army. I could only hope we weren't all doomed to die.

Chapter 55: Sam

Long live the king. Long Live the King. LONG LIVE THE KING!

Those words, like a battlecry, rang through my mind as I slowly tore the heart from Ash. I was dizzy, I felt sick, but I had done it. He had tormented me for too long, had killed too many for me to just let go. Finally, I'd accomplished my goal. I fell to the ground, hating how weak I was at the moment. I could do nothing as the shifter who'd healed me as fast as she could raced to my side, only to become gravely wounded. Had Goliath not gotten Irene away in time, there would be no time for Darcia to aid Valiant.

I watched warily as Goliath and Irene faced-off. My eyes were half closed. I could feel something like soft fingers gliding over my scales. Valiant, despite her wound, had got back to work. She was using her powers to slowly and surely close my wounds, along with promoting my red-blood cells to multiply. She had given me enough strength by doing so before. Now hopefully I would be back in battle, temporarily if nothing else, within the next few minutes. I hated being on the sidelines.

My eyes fell on Goliath and Irene as they circled each other. The prince had been battered from his fight with me. Even after he'd fed off of the little blood Gwenn had provided, he was more sluggish than Irene. The vampire woman struck first, her blade clashing with Goliath's. The prince's blade glowed a bright gold since it was made of fey iron.

Ah, that's right, I remembered now; that was the only one he had, apparently. Irene's blade was made of silver, so the prince had a disadvantage. I was pretty sure Ash had been the one to give him that feyblade, the bastard. He parried several of her strikes before making a fake one and slashing cruelly at her leg.

Irene screeched and narrowed her eyes. She snapped her fingers, causing vines to come up from below the ground. Goliath was caught off guard and stumbled as he was rooted in place. Irene took her blade and sliced at Goliath's chest, barely missing puncturing through his heart. He was left with a deep cut on top of the wounds I had dealt him already. This was brutal, watching but not able to do a thing at all. Irene furiously made to punch the prince, but amazingly Goliath grabbed her fist as it swung at him. Her eyes widened as he twisted it and jerked her forward.

From there he reached forward, gripping the silver sword. Clearly it cut into his hand, but he didn't let go. Irene tried to wrench it from his grasp, cutting him more, but he wouldn't give. Goliath shoved her forward right as he got the sword away from her. He tossed the fey iron sword aside and moved his hand to the hilt of the sword of silver. He wiped the blood away from his hand and hacked at the vines holding him in place. Irene meanwhile screeched in alarm, her eyes suddenly wide with fear. Goliath, freed now from the vines, darted toward Irene. Right before he reached her, he dissolved into the shadows, leaving the vampire royally confused, her eyes darting around feverishly.

Goliath reformed behind her and struck; the sword sank into her back, but not all the way. Irene had been able to dart forward before the blow had killed her. She panted, whirling and dodging right as the prince attempted to deal another wound. I had no time to growl in warning as three vampires of the royal army rushed at the prince from behind. He was knocked to the ground as silver knives sank into his back.

The prince dissolved into the shadows, reappearing behind the vampires and slicing right through one of them. The other two realized what he was doing—they darted out of the way as Irene again summoned the vines to hold Goliath in place once again. The prince held his chest as he paused, for he was having a really hard time now.

Suddenly, the two vampires that had attacked Goliath yelled out in pain. I spotted Ares' laid-back grin as he pulled back his knife from the back of one, and turned my head to see Smoke smirking as the second fell to his knives too. The royal army was huge, but it lacked discipline and valid purpose. The training was a failure, I could see, as most enemy vampires began to flee. A few did stay though, and man did they give us a tough time.

Irene backed up, letting out a deranged hiss. Smoke, Ares, and Goliath slowly walked toward her, it was a three on one. Until, that is, a few remaining vampires surrounded the three of them. Now, it was an eleven on three, which it had pretty much been this entire fight. Smoke and Ares bared their fangs and launched at the enemies while Goliath stayed locked on Irene. I could feel my strength returning. If he could pull through just a little while longer, I would be able to help.

The prince lunged at Irene right as she dodged to the side. Her blade sank into the back of Goliath's neck, and ouch, that looked like it hurt. Goliath fell to his knees, wincing as his hand flew to the wound. His red eyes were confused and exhausted as he knelt there. Smoke and Ares were too busy fighting off the rest of the vampires. Smoke's anger empowered him, and Ares' sheer knowledge of survival enabled him to beat the odds. Goliath, though, was so battle weary that he just could not win his duel. Irene cackled and raised her blade, preparing to end the prince's life once and for all. Now it was time for my entrance.

My roar filled the air as Irene paused. The vampire looked up to see me rushing at her. "Sambuca, please be careful!" came Valiant's plea. I dismissed it and knocked into Irene so fast that she had no time to react. The knife flew off to who knows where; Irene was locked in my claws as I lowered my head in her face.

"Game over, vampire. No one attacks *my* prince like that. He's mine, you hear? Not yours to destroy!" I shouted. I parted my jaws and let out a flurry of flames onto her. Irene's screams filled the night as her skin burned to fat... which burned to muscle... which finally burned to bone. The skeleton was blackened, and with ease I took it in my jaws and tossed it toward the remaining vampires fighting against us. Ares and Smoke leaped back at the same time they did. When our enemies spotted the charred bones, they took one more look, whirled, and ran for their dear lives. Smart move.

I limped toward Goliath, shifting to human form finally and offering him a hand. The vampire looked up at me and gave a small smile. "Well well, love. Looks like you defeated me, my brother, and my brother's second-in-command," he chuckled. He accepted my hand as I pulled him in for a hug.

"I couldn't have done it without anyone here—Darcia, Valiant, Ash, Smoke, Ares, you. We all claim victory tonight. Even Gwenn," I sighed. I let go and slowly walked toward the dead human. I knelt before her corpse and dipped my head. "I forgive you, Gwenn. Despite what you did to me, you came through in the end. Thank you," I whispered, shedding several burning tears. They glided down my cheek and onto the cold corpse. I weakly stood up, approaching Darcia and Valiant. I winced at Darcia's wounded eye and Valiant's decapitated leg.

"I told you, you need rest," Valiant scolded me softly. I grinned, my sharp teeth glistening.

"I'll be fine, alright? Thanks for your help," I sighed. I bent down and let her arm wrap around my shoulders. With effort, I supported her and helped her walk. Goliath soon was by my side, and the three of us supported each other together. I spotted Smoke and Ares approaching, surprisingly looking impressed with each other.

"Ya did good back there, but yer still an idiot youngling," Ares muttered, giving a look of respect to Smoke. The ex-hunter only rolled his eyes.

"Oh please. At least I have more than half a brain, unlike yourself," he shot back. Both of them looked at Darcia, and then at each other.

"I'll carry her back," Smoke demanded. Ares shook his head and grinned, stretching. He had several bruises and cuts, and oddly enough a grisly scar over his eye from some sort of animal. I had no doubt that was Darcia's doing.

"No can do. *I'll* be carrying her back, got it?" he snarled. Smoke and him got into each other's faces, and I had to sigh.

"HEY! You *both* can carry her back, alright?" I snapped. The fighting vampires stopped and glanced at me. Reluctantly Smoke took one of Darcia's arms and draped it over himself, while Ares took the other. The shifter was out cold. Smoke's concern was evident.

"Her eye. That bastard half-blinded her," he hissed. Ares smirked and looked off in the distance.

"Good thing she has two eyes," he commented. No one seemed to find it funny, though, but him; he chuckled to himself as we walked. Silence fell upon us as slowly and surely we made our way out of the kingdom, through the forest, through the city, and back into the shifter woods. It took more than a few hours, as we often had to stop and rest.

Finally, though, we made it home. Ares and Smoke dropped Darcia off into her bed and sat themselves on the couch. Smoke fell to sleep right away while Ares fought to stay awake. I took the other couch, careful to gently let Valiant take up the space she needed. Goliath vanished somewhere into the house, probably to rest as well.

Lilith flew in, shifting from bird form to human form and squealing in delight. "You all made it!" she cheered. Her face twisted in horror at the sight of Valiant. "Well, at least part of you did," she muttered sadly. I could hear Rose and Madeline playing in the other room and smiled to myself.

Lilith sat next to me, careful not to disturb the sleeping Valiant. "I watched over them for you. I told them you were too wounded to see them, though," she told me. I shrugged.

"It's alright. I need to tell Rose some horrible news," I sighed. Lilith winced.

"It's Gwenn, isn't it," she questioned in a depressed tone. I gave a nod, and slowly Lilith approached the room where the children played. "Rose, Maddy? Please, Sam would like to see you."

The two children hastily rushed at me, slowing down when they realized how exhausted I was. I forced a smile and focused on Rose.

"Hey sweetie. I have some horrible news. Your mommy. She died to save me. She was very brave, and I promise I forgive her. Oh Rose, I am so sorry..." I barely managed to whisper. The small child stared at me for a moment as if trying to comprehend my words. Slowly, she approached me. I leaned away, expecting rage but got none. The small child's arms wrapped around my torso as she gave me a light hug. Her eyes met mine.

"You were worth saving, dragon lady. Mommy loved you, she did, she always regretted her mistake. I think she was happy to die for you. Thank you for forgiving her, dragon-lady..." Rose replied. I felt my throat close and gently returned her hug. Tears now fell from my face as my heartbeat increased. The love of a child, one I once couldn't stand to look at, was more precious than any gemstone that could possibly exist. Madeline came and peeked over Rose.

"Can I have a hug too?" she asked in a quiet voice. I gave her a soft smile and extended my other arm.

"Come here, Maddy, of course you can," I replied. I looked up as Goliath entered the room. He gave me a smile and sat beside me. Now, the couch was full. Lilith had fallen asleep next to her sister. Goliath, the children, and I took up the other half. I felt strong arms wrap around me and looked into the prince's eyes.

"You're not a freak, Sam," he suddenly said. "You're you. Not someone that doesn't belong, not someone who was given away. You're someone who gives her all for those she loves. You're a treasure, love," he finished. I gave him a big grin and leaned into his chest as both Maddy and Rose fell asleep in my arms.

"Same to you, my prince. I couldn't have done any of this without you, love," I replied, 'mocking' him. That only made him chuckle. Granted, I did mean that word. I blinked, noticing that his top hat was gone. I wrinkled my eyebrows together.

"What happened to your top hat?" I asked. Goliath blinked.

"You knocked it off while I was battling you, love," he replied. I slowly grinned.

Taking a deep breath, I giggled, "Finally! Oh, wait. Now I've gotta go get you a new one. GODS DAMN IT!"

Chapter 56: Sam

We awoke in the morning, lying there together quite comfortably. I gave a yawn and rolled out of bed, almost face planting on the ground but catching myself before doing so. Wandering over to the door, I picked up a newspaper, scanning it a bit before sighing. Goliath was just waking up as well, hatless of course. Something I still was happy about for no apparent reason. Regardless, I'd get him a new one. Eventually. Though he probably had a stash of those things somewhere.

"What is it, love?" Goliath asked, seeing a scowl on my face.

"Well," I began, turning the newspaper toward him so he could get a good, long look. He scanned it a moment before his gaze darkened.

"I see. The hunters are at it again. Well, we got rid of one threat and now have to deal with another, love. We can move into the castle for planning, if you want," he muttered, looking about. Staying in Darcia's home was wonderful. I enjoyed mine as well, much farther into the woods, but truth be told, living in a castle would be really, really cool. I hid my excitement though with a mere nod.

"I'm entirely game for being a dragon in a castle, Goliath. Trust me," I chuckled. "But I want to check back in a few days on Darcia. She seems entirely out of it."

Right on cue did Robert Smoke emerge from his room, holding a warm washcloth on the wound over his eye. He shot a glare toward me, and muttered, "That damned shifter will be just fine. She's tougher than anything I've ever had to deal with. Now even tougher due to the bond, though that goes both ways."

My venom green eyes fell upon the ex-vampire-hunter, and I tilted my head, some strands of my deep red hair falling into my face. "Well well, aren't you just a ray of sunshine, Smoke. I still am baffled that you're still with us. I wonder... could it be because you have a crush on a devil?" Slowly, a smirk crawled upon my face.

"As much of a crush as *you* do on princey," replied Smoke. A tinge of red flushed over my face, and I decided to drop it for now. Goliath was staring at me inquisitively, and I decided that now was a perfect time to change the subject.

"Well, anyway. I'm going to go with Goliath back to the Kingdom and work on its recovery, along with planning to combat the corruption in that damn hunters' society that you, by the way, made worse. Therefore, you'll be helping us too. Won't you, Smoke?" I growled in challenge, throwing the newspaper at him. The vampire rolled his eyes and caught it before it smacked him in the face. Damn.

"Maybe. Depends on how I'm feeling," Smoke replied with a smirk. Truly, though, I knew he was on our side now. I sensed deep down that he really did care for Darcia. Perhaps he even loved her now. I would tease him about that later, though. For now, I saw an annoyed scowl wash over his face as he stared behind me. A hand fell upon my shoulder, one with vampiric claws... ah, it was Ares.

"Hey there, miss dragon. I s'ppose we're done here too and can return to the city, eh? Ya ain't gonna rip us to shreds if we do so? And... where is Clyde?" the gang leader asked in my ear. I shrugged him off, whirling to face him and baring my teeth.

"Personal space, ever hear of it?" I snapped. Sighing, I fixed him in a glare. "If you promise not to go after innocent people, I will leave you alone. Got it? We can set up a blood bank for you and your people. But *no funny business."* I avoided the second question just for a moment, realizing that Clyde had been an important part of his gang.

"Funny business? Whatcha think I look like, a clown?" he cackled, but then shrugged. "Bah. Fine. I will behave. I only went after innocent widdle humans in the end there because I was desperate as hell. I'll get goin' tonight and get organized, how's that?"

I nodded, and then bit my lip. After a moment, I motioned for him to follow me to the corner of the room. Ares's eyes narrowed with worry, and I just had to gulp. "...Clyde. He didn't make it. Irene, the red haired vampire back in the final battle... she killed him on our mission to save his daughter."

"What?" Ares whispered, taking several steps back and sinking to the ground. I stepped forward, but he shook his head. "N-no... jus'... I need to take it in, is all."

"...I understand," I muttered, watching as tears began to glide down his cheeks. Loss was a horrible thing. "I need to take care of his child, Maddy. I will do well by her. I promise."

He only nodded, covering his face with his clawed hands. After a long pause, he whispered, "Ya, take care of the kid. H-her dad was strong. She'll grow up s-strong just like him. I'll... see you around." I wasn't sure if I should leave him to his grief, but after a moment, decided it was for the best. I turned and walked back to the center of the room with a heavy heart.

Suddenly, I felt tiny arms wrap around my legs and looked down to see Madeline. A soft smile fell upon my lips, and an idea struck me. "Hey there kid. If you want, you can come to the castle with me. But I understand if you want to go back to Leviathan forever," I muttered. The child considered my words for a moment.

"I wanna move between you! I wanna go visit the castle, though!" she squealed, causing me to chuckle and nod. It was settled then! I gave a final goodbye wave to Smoke, who said he'd tell Darcia I said hi when she woke up. That would have to do for now.

With that, we were off. Red scales spread across my body as I elongated into my dragon form. I huffed, shaking off the exhaustion, for it still had only been only a day since Ash's death. I shuddered upon remembering just how close we'd been to completely fucking things up. Goliath climbed upon my back and held on tight, giving me a thumbs up when I turned my head to check on him. In his arms was Madeline, of whom was squealing with delight. "WE GET TO GO ON A COOL FLYING RIDE!" she yelled. "I LOVE DRAGONS!"

Giggling to myself, I spread my wings and took to the skies, avoiding clouds so I didn't soak either of the vampires upon my back. In the distance, the sun was just beginning to set, a stark reminder that I was at this point just as nocturnal as the vampires. Ah well, I couldn't be too upset.

I looked down upon the city, observing the damage with a frown on my dragonic features. There was no more smoke or ash (hah) coming from the burned-down buildings. Humans looked like ants from up here, but I could see some finally coming out of hiding. Thankfully not the entire city had been slaughtered in that mess. I didn't entirely trust Ares, but I really did hope he kept his word, for these people needed some stability. I would visit him later and ensure he wasn't ruining anything.

Soon enough I flew over the small forest and entered the kingdom, circling the town square where the battle had taken place. It was a *bloodbath.* Limbs were strewn everywhere, alongside several corpses. But none of that could compare to the amount of red that was splattered in every corner of that area. Quite a bit of that blood was likely mine, considering my battle with Goliath and Ash caused a lot of it to gush out.

Not wanting to dwell on that for now, we landed in front of the castle, and immediately I tensed. My lips peeled back to reveal glistening fangs as my eyes fell upon several vampires standing guard in front of the castle. Goliath warily leaped off of my back, walking in front of me and baring his fangs as well. The vampire guards did something unexpected—they took to their knees and gave a bow. What?

"The true king has returned. All hail his majesty Goliath!" one shouted, causing the others to cheer. Relief crossed Goliath's face, but I wasn't buying it.

"What if this is trickery?" I growled. Maddy hid behind me, afraid of these strangers. Smart girl.

"Nothing to worry about, love. Ash lied about many things, and it looks like this is one of them. Some of my people survived. The ones with the same ideology as me. Thank goodness," he sighed. In confirmation did the guards nod, and I had to accept it. Besides, I trusted Goliath now quite a bit. Well, more than quite a bit, really. I shifted back into human form. Sort of. I rather enjoyed looking like my true self, so I kept my horns, wings, and tail.

We entered the castle, looking around to realize that it had been kept in pretty good condition. The dark stone walls were not messed with, and much of the art pieces (things like portraits of past vampire kings, you know, that cliche) were intact. Some of the lighter carpets had blood stains upon them, causing me to shudder quite a bit. I knew both the old corrupted king's and Ash's terrible and evil reputation.

A vampire woman with glowing red eyes approached us and stared at Madeline with delight. Her voice was full of joy, and her sharp claws combed through her dark hair as she spoke. "Oh! A child! How wonderful. Your majesty, would you like me to help settle her in?" she asked. I looked to Goliath, raising a brow, and slowly he nodded.

"That's Astrid. She took care of the vampire royal children prior to this whole mess. In fact, she looked after me and my brother when we were younger," he explained. Astrid winced a bit and let out a soft sigh.

"Ah, it is a shame about Ash. He had so much potential, but ended up being such a bad apple. I am so sorry he put you through that, my king," she grumbled. Maddy hid behind me, peeking out to stare at Astrid. The woman got to her knees and motioned for her to come over. "Hi there, dear. I can read you some stories if you'd like. You look like you have many stories to tell too. What about we do that?" Slowly, the child emerged from behind me and made her way to Astrid. An excited smile crossed her face.

"I LOVE STORIES!" she squealed, instantly making a friend. Maddy really didn't know how to use her indoor voice, but Astrid didn't seem to mind. Off they went into another room, leaving me and Goliath to walk along toward his room. Come to think of it...

"Have I ever actually seen your room? Was that the one you kept me in after we found out that I was a dragon?" I asked, and he shook his head.

"No, that was a guest room. Er, would you like to sleep in your own room or with me?" he asked awkwardly. Suddenly, he coughed, realizing what his question sounded like. "Oh, let me rephrase that love," His face was flushed a deep red now, matching mine. Luckily, I laughed.

"I get what you mean, Goliath. No worries. I'll join you, that is no problem. We can stay up and discuss some plans of action for those damned hunters that will inevitably be a thorn in our side," I replied. Then, I added after nudging him with my shoulder, "Besides, I'm comfortable and feel safer around you. Considering I'm still quite weak from that whole fiasco, I think we both need some time to feel safe."

Relieved, the vampire nodded, and soon enough we arrived at his room. He slowly opened the door to reveal a room inside full of deep reds and blacks. Why was I not surprised that he used such dark colors? He had crimson sheets covering a very comfy-looking bed, and this room was gigantic. Amusingly, posters of dragons were hung up on the walls. I shot him a questioning look, and he sighed. "I never said I enjoyed having to kill those dragons. Many I tried to spare, because I admire them. Sadly my hesitation wasn't appreciated, and I was made ruthless, love."

I nodded and wandered over, taking a seat on his bed and lashing my tail. Still in half-form, I let out a yawn and stretched, closing my eyes for a moment and rubbing my temples. "I wish we could jump right into things, but we still need a plan of action. Ugh," I grumbled. I felt Goliath sit beside me and opened one eye, fixing it upon him.

"For now, it is best to rest," he replied, turning to lounge about. Some of his shaggy hair fell into his face, which was admittedly quite cute. I positioned myself to lay next to him, debating a certain action before finally giving in and moving closer, cuddling.

A silence stretched between us, and finally I sighed. "So...Goliath," I coughed. "You know how we constantly are questioning what we are to each other? Well, maybe we should define that."

His red eyes fell on me in question, and he tilted his head. "What do you mean, love?" he asked.

"Well...are we a thing now? Like, you know," I casually grumbled.

"A thing? Oh! You mean...well, if you want to be, I would honored to be your lover," the vampire replied, a soft smile on his face.

In response to him, rather than using my words, I leaned toward his face. Surprised at first, he hesitated, but caught on fast. Soon my lips met his, and we exchanged a good, long kiss. That was my answer for him, then. It looked like we were indeed together. But I'm *sure* everyone saw that coming.

After the kiss, I went into another bathroom to get ready for bed. I felt warm inside, like a fire was brewing in my stomach from who knows where. What were these feelings?! Goliath had gone off to take a shower, leaving me to those strange thoughts.

Getting into a nightgown and wandering back to the room soon after, I entered and met the deep red eyes of Goliath. I couldn't help but let my jaw drop as I examined him in just red boxers with bats on them, of course. My venom-green eyes took in all of the lithe muscles of the vampire, scoping his strength out. His black hair was still wet and fell into his face, and I watched as he stretched, causing said muscles to ripple and his fangs to flash. He then noticed me eyeing him and couldn't help but smirk.

"Something the matter, love?" he asked in a seductive tone.

I snorted, cursing as blush filled my face. "Nothing. Let's lay down. We can, uh, discuss plans and make sure all of our wounds are tended to."

"Riiiiiight," he purred, simply turning around and chuckling, heading to the bed. I fumed. Damn him for...whatever it was he was pulling.

I followed behind him and slipped in, crossing my arms as my blush only got deeper when I felt him beside me. I looked at a wall and cleared my throat, muttering, "So, plans, and wounds, we need to tend to them."

I felt his lips brush my ear and gulped, my heart pumping even harder. In a soft tone, he whispered, "Oh? Tend to them? How do you plan to do that?" I could feel his eyes hungrily taking me in as he stared me down.

I stole a glance toward him now, licking my lips nervously. He wore that usual sinister grin of his, some of his wet hair falling into his face and making matters even worse. I lashed my tail in thought, trying to figure out how to find my voice and failing.

Goliath proceeded to climb on top of me, leaning into my face and tilting his head, nuzzling down and giving a low growl. "Mmm..." I hummed, trying to figure out my best response to him now. At the moment, my mind was on how much I wanted to feel him inside of me, really, but I didn't speak up about that quite yet. "...We could, uh, I don't know," I finally stammered, tripping over my words shyly.

A dark chuckle emitted from his lips as he drew his tongue over his jagged fangs. I let out a low whimper, which caused him to purr curiously. Damn him, my entire body was red now, possibly as red as my scales. "You seem to have lost your words. Vampire got your tongue, love?" he asked, soon enough leaning in and kissing me deeply, delicately slipping his tongue into my mouth. He explored for a moment and I closed my eyes, allowing the scent of his cologne to drown out my senses. Had he put that on right after the shower? How sneaky like the snake he was.

He moved to my ear now, and once again I felt him brush against it, which made me shiver with need. My venom-green eyes were completely distant as I heard his whisper once again. "Would you like me to tend to your desires, my dear? Give you what you'd want? I can smell the lust in your blood. Your scent is so *delicious.* What will it be, little dragon? Shall I take you? Will you give into me?"

I pretended to think this over, but the answer was already clear. Finally I took a deep breath and replied, "Yes. Please make me yours, Goliath." He leaned away, grinning and giving a wink. Without pause did he dispose of my nightgown and lick his lips. He glanced down to my breasts but didn't touch, not yet.

No, first he moved downward until his face was between my thighs. I widened my eyes and gasped, realizing what he was about to do. Without pause did he sink his jagged fangs into my inner thigh, causing me to growl in surprise and gasp out in pain and pleasure. I felt him drink and squirmed, growing quite a bit wet from this action. Then he slowly changed positions after letting go, once more straddling me and leaning into my face.

He proceeded to trace along my flesh with his claw, teasing, poking, and implying he could do a very many dark things with said claws. This sent many shivers through my body as I sank down further into the bed, once more lashing my tail. His deep red gaze stared into mine, and I glared back, trying at least to hold it steady.

The sinister grin never leaving his face, he reached down to squeeze at my breast, pausing to play with my nipple a moment and causing me to give a keeling squeal of pleasure. The chemicals shot through my body as I arced my neck, breaking eye contact and prompting him to lunge for my jugular. Once more did he drink, this time in long pulls and much more deeply. His hungered growls and gulps were intentionally loud on his part so I could be assured what he was doing, of course. Not that I needed it, but such noises sent even more whimpers of pleasure through me.

With his freehand, the one not grabbing at my breast, he reached downward and played with my hips a moment before he slipped one finger inside of me, followed by another. My body jolted as he did so, sending spasms through me as I moaned in ecstasy. Right away did I release, clearly having pent up tension. Encouraged, he moved his fingers in and out rather quickly, forcing more fluid to spill out for him. A third entered me, then a forth as his thumb rubbed at my clit expertly. It was dizzying, really, and I threw back my head and let out an inhuman snarl as once again, I released.

Satisfied, he removed his hand, released my neck, and reached over to the side of the bed, grabbing a collar conveniently sitting there. Bastard, did he plan for this? Well, I absolutely loved it, here in the privacy of the bedroom. He effortlessly clicked the collar on, gently pulling at the chain with one hand which slightly applied pressure to my throat. With his other, he disposed of his boxers and my panties, and I felt my heart quicken even further as I felt him press his member against me, showing what was to happen soon enough.

My attention remained on his face as I gulped and stared up at him, my pupils thinning into slits as that dark grin spread across his face. He tilted his head, his voice deepened, seductive, and hungry. "You tremor with fear before me. Lust and *delicious* fear," he purred, his nostrils flaring as, for a moment, he closed his eyes, licked his lips, and took in my scent. Then, he opened them again, raising a brow. "Mmm... you know I can rip you to pieces in an instant, dear little dragon. You know the danger, and you *love* it. Well. I'll show you my strength. How's that? And eat you all up~"

From there, he lunged for my breast, sinking his jagged fangs into my skin and at the same time as impaling me. I arced my back and let out a whine of ecstasy again, squirming and choking as he pulled the chain even more tightly, pressing the collar more firmly against my neck and causing me to feel light-headed. The feeling was *amazing.* There was no pause as he pummeled into me, cascading me into one orgasm after another. His hungered growls and moans hit my ears, only forcing out even more pleasure.

He pulled away from my breast, panting and returning to staring me down, my blood dripping from his lips. Some of it landed upon the pale flesh of my neck, prompting him to lean down and lap it up hungrily. More shivers ran through me at this action of course as I was completely taken. The vampire leaned up and held a steady gaze, watching me closely, frequently licking his lips. I tried to remain staring at him, but soon enough the intensity was far too much. My eyes closed as I lost myself, feeling him shudder above me. Soon, he'd reach his end as well.

But not before one more dark threat. I felt him brush against my ear again and whisper, "Good girl, you're doing so well. However, I cannot promise I won't devour you up entirely now, my love. Losing control is as simple as..." He reared up, giving a particularly hard thrust and causing me to cry out in both pain and pleasure once more. "...this." The actions of the vampire grew even more rough. I writhed under him, releasing more violent orgasms as he snarled, clearly reaching his end soon. We'd both realized that his threats sent me over edge even further. I of course had no idea why, but I *loved* hearing him say that stuff, in private of course.

It didn't take long after for him to finish. He let out a very animalistic growl into my ear, clenching up and sinking his claws into my sides, spilling out even more blood. The bites from the vampire were bleeding out, sending ribbons of blood gliding down my skin. He pulled out and observed this, soon enough lapping up any remnants, closing the wounds with chemicals from his saliva as vampires did after feeding.

He nuzzled into my neck, purring loudly and running his claws through my red hair. "Mmm... you were wonderful, my love. Rest now, my sweet," he whispered into my ear. He removed the collar, placing it aside. We laid there together for a few seconds before he chuckled and said, "Let me clean up for us, alright? Then we can cuddle."

I only hummed in response, off in my own little world, my eyes closed and my cheeks red. I heard him go about the business of cleaning before returning to my side and pulling me close. My wings fluttered a bit as I was brought against his chest. I buried my face into him, careful not to catch him with my horns. Luckily they were a bit smaller in my true form, barely an issue, really.

My thoughts were only on him as I drifted off to sleep, completely relaxed. His claws ran down my back in a comforting manner, and I smiled. There was nowhere else I wanted to be.

~~To be Continued~~

About the Author

Des M. Astor is a writer in the Urban Fantasy genre. She twists things in a unique way and brings a new flavor to the mythical creatures you know and love. Des has been writing her entire life and decided to refine her craft by going professional. In her works, she tries to tell important lessons through her characters, such as the importance of working together in a romantic relationship and consent. In terms of friendships, she likes telling stories where a group of friends struggle in battle but come through in the end. She has a mixture of strong female and male protagonists. Her stories are character driven. Des graduated from the University of Connecticut with a Bachelor's degree in Biology in May of 2019. She has a deep love for reptiles and seeks to become a herpetologist. Often, she will blend in her knowledge of science to enhance her writing, which brings about sci-fi elements.

Read more at https://therealdesastr.com/.

Made in the USA
Middletown, DE
13 July 2023

34969902R00205